Catherine Cookson was born in East Jarrow and the place of her birth provides the background she so vividly creates in many of her novels. Although acclaimed as a regional writer — her novel THE ROUND TOWER won the Winifred Holtby Award for the best regional novel of 1968 — her readership spreads throughout the world. Her work has been translated into twelve languages and Corgi alone has over 20,000,000 copies of her novels in print, including those written under the name of Catherine Marchant.

Mrs Cookson was born the illegitimate daughter of a poverty-stricken woman, Kate, whom she believed to be her older sister. Catherine began work in service but eventually moved South to Hastings where she met and married a local grammar school master. At the age of forty she began writing with great success about the lives of the working class people of the North-East with whom she had grown up, including her intriguing autobiography, OUR KATE. More recently THE CINDER PATH has established her position as one of the most popular of contemporary women novelists.

Mrs Cookson now lives in Northumberland, overlooking the Tyne.

Also by Catherine Cookson

KATIE MULHOLLAND
KATE HANNIGAN
THE ROUND TOWER
FENWICK HOUSES
MAGGIE ROWAN
THE LONG CORRIDOR
THE UNBAITED TRAP
COLOUR BLIND
THE MENAGERIE
THE BLIND MILLER
FANNY MCBRIDE
THE GLASS VIRGIN
ROONEY
THE NICE BLOKE
THE INVITATION
THE DWELLING PLACE
OUR KATE
THE INVISIBLE CORD
THE GAMBLING MAN
THE TIDE OF LIFE
THE CINDER PATH
THE GIRL
PURE AS THE LILY
THE FIFTEEN STREETS
FEATHERS IN THE FIRE
THE MAN WHO CRIED
TILLY TROTTER

The 'Mary Ann' series
A GRAND MAN
THE DEVIL AND MARY ANN
THE LORD AND MARY ANN
LIFE AND MARY ANN
LOVE AND MARY ANN
MARRIAGE AND MARY ANN
MARY ANN'S ANGELS
MARY ANN AND BILL

The 'Mallen' Trilogy
THE MALLEN STREAK
THE MALLEN GIRL
THE MALLEN LITTER

By Catherine Cookson as
Catherine Marchant
HOUSE OF MEN
THE FEN TIGER
HERITAGE OF FOLLY
MISS MARTHA MARY CRAWFORD
THE IRON FACADE
THE SLOW AWAKENING

and published by Corgi Books

Tilly Trotter Wed

Catherine Cookson

CORGI BOOKS
A DIVISION OF TRANSWORLD PUBLISHERS LTD

TILLY TROTTER WED

A CORGI BOOK 0 552 11960 1

Originally published in Great Britain by
William Heinemann Ltd.

PRINTING HISTORY
William Heinemann edition published 1981
Corgi edition published 1982
Corgi edition reissued 1982

This book is set in 10/11 Plantin

Corgi Books are published by
Transworld Publishers Ltd.,
Century House, 61-63 Uxbridge Road,
Ealing, London, W5 5SA

Printed and bound in Great Britain by
Cox & Wyman Ltd, Reading

Contents

Author's Note

With regard to some of the details in the second part of this book, I feel I owe a debt of gratitude to T. R. Fehrenbach and Sue Flanagan.

Having read two histories of the USA, I was led to *Lone Star* (New York, Macmillan, 1968) and *Comanches* (London, George Allen & Unwin, 1975) and from then on became lost in admiration for Mr Fehrenbach's knowledge of the Indians in the early history of Texas. But his scholarship made me pause and caused me to ask myself how I dare attempt to write about a place I had not even visited.

When I had the urge to move for once out of my milieu, I chose Texas. Why, I don't know. And it wasn't until I was advised to read the above books that the audaciousness of my effort opened up before me and I hesitated whether to continue with my story. Only the fact that I was in no way attempting to emulate, even as a faint shadow, the scholarship in these books but was merely imbibing the flavour for a background to a novel allowed me to go ahead.

Apart from the facts I have gained from these books, my personal interest in Texas has been aroused and my education certainly furthered.

From Sue Flanagan's work I received great help too. The wonderful photographs in her book, *Sam Houston's Texas* (Austin, University of Texas Press, 1964), and the information attached, I found invaluable.

Finally, I may say I have tried within my capacity to

keep to facts, but like most authors of novels I may have resorted now and again to a little licence; so should this be noted by a Texan I beg his forbearance, for after all I am merely a teller of tales.

Catherine Cookson,
March 1980.

PART ONE

Back to the Beginning

1

'She should leave the house, and now!'

'You can't turf her out just like that, Jessie Ann, she's entitled to stay until after the funeral; and there's every possibility, naturally, she'll be mentioned in the will.'

'Naturally, you say!'

'Yes, naturally, because she's acted as a wife to Father for years.'

'She's acted as the creature who's kept us away from our birthright for years.'

'Y . . . you, you . . . talk like a penny magazine, Jessie Ann.'

Mrs Jessie Ann Cartwright, one time Jessie Ann Sopwith, rounded on her nineteen-year-old brother, crying, 'Don't talk to me like that, John! I won't be spoken to in that fashion.'

As the young man opened his mouth to stammer out a reply his elder brother sat down heavily on a chair, put his hands to his head and said, 'God! I wish this was over. And I wish you, Jessie Ann, would stop bickering and acting like a matronly bitch.'

At this the young Mrs Cartwright swelled so much inside her black taffeta that the silk rustled, and her indignation was such that she found it impossible to speak. And now John, as always aiming to smooth matters, approached his sister, saying, 'Luke didn't mean that, we . . . we are all t . . . tensed up. And . . . and you know, Jessie Ann, y . . . you . . . you used to be as fond of Tro . . . Trotter as any of us, so what's made you so b . . . bitter?'

'Don't be stupid!' Jessie Ann thrust out her hand towards him as if pushing him aside. 'You know as well as I do we'd

11

have all returned home four years ago when Mother died if it hadn't been for her.'

'Oh. Oh, be fair.' Luke was on his feet now, pointing towards her. 'We all had the chance to come back.'

'Yes, on terms that we accept her status in the household, she who had been a maid, a nursery maid, and then assumed the position of mistress.'

'Well, she was mistress, his mistress, and mistress of the house. And for my part I think she did it very well because what you seem to forget, Jessie Ann, is that after Father had the accident in the mine and lost his feet he became a different person altogether, and as the years went on a most trying individual, and if it hadn't been for Trotter, God only knows what would have happened to him.'

As their sister stared at them the two young men returned her look, but not with her hostility; then John put in softly, 'Sh . . . she had a lot to p . . . put up with, had Trotter, she was in a very difficult position and . . . and what you forget, Jessie Ann, is that sh . . . she didn't marry him and she could have. He told Luke and me here, di . . . didn't he Luke? that he had tried to per . . . persuade her, so I think that's very much in her favour.'

'She's got you two besotted, like she had Father. Well, she didn't have that effect on Matthew or me.'

'I . . . I wouldn't be too sure of that if I were you.'

She now jerked her plump chin towards Luke. 'Well, I am sure of it. Matthew went to America when he got the chance because he couldn't stand the situation.'

'No, he couldn't stand the situation, but not for the reason that you imagine.'

'What do you mean?'

'Well, partly I mean that he couldn't stand the set-up in Scarborough any longer, and Mama's whining and then Grandma's domination after her going.'

'Oh, how dare you, Luke!'

'I dare, Jessie Ann, because it's the truth. And when the invitation came from Uncle Alvero for Matthew to go and try his hand out there he jumped at it. And with Grandfather dying and leaving him pretty warm there was nothing to stop him, so there you have it.'

Jessie Ann's taffeta rustled again and John, after walking towards the blazing fire whose flames were illuminating the room on this dark January afternoon, bent forward, holding out his hands to the warmth as he said, 'Th . . . that's always puzzled me about Matthew, no . . . not Grandfather le . . . leaving him all that money but that he didn't offer to help Father. He could have reopened the mine and go . . . got things working again.'

'Flogging a dead horse.'

John turned his head and glanced at Luke. 'You . . . you think so?'

'Yes, yes, of course. In any case, I think he did offer but Father would have none of it.'

'Did he tell you?'

'No; you know Matthew, tight as a drum and off like a cannon if one probed too deeply. No, but it was something Father said.'

'I think he should have made an effort to come for the funeral.'

'What are you talking about, Jessie Ann?' There was a note of weary impatience in Luke's voice now. 'Word can't possibly have reached him yet that Father is dead.'

'He knew months ago that he was fading. I informed him myself; I told him he had better come.' And Jessie Ann nodded from one to the other now.

'Oh!' The two brothers emitted the word simultaneously.

'Yes.' She kept nodding, and her fair curls hanging beneath her black lace cap bobbed up and down as if they were wired. 'He's the heir and he should be here; I told him so.'

'Yes, I suppose you're right in one way.' Luke hunched his shoulders. 'But then, what is there here for him if he has no intention of reopening the mine? After all these years of lying under water, the thought of that task I should imagine would keep anyone in America. I know it would me.'

'But there's the estate.'

Luke now shook his head as he stared at his sister. 'Estate!

13

What is it after all? A farm, half a dozen houses, two lodges, a few cottages and seven hundred acres; that's all that's left; there's no shooting or fishing. Oh, I think he's doing the wise thing in staying. . . .'

'Well, will you tell me what's going to happen to it?'

'Yes, I will, Jessie Ann.' He bowed his head deeply towards her. 'After the will is read I'll tell you. But then, of course, there won't be any need, will there, for you will know too by then?'

'Oh!' Jessie Ann bounced from her chair, her short plump body bristling as she glared at the young army officer, the second of her three brothers and the one whom she disliked most heartily.

Returning her look and reciprocating her feelings, Luke said, 'Be funny if in some way Father has managed to leave the whole damn lot to Trotter, wouldn't it, Jessie Ann? Then, of course, you would have some reason for venting your spleen on her, whereas as things stand now Trotter, in my opinion, is deserving of our gratitude.'

The two young men both watched their sister now hold her hands palm upwards against her waist, not in the front of it but slightly to the side. It was a stance, dating from her nursery days, which she always assumed whenever she was about to deliver some piece of news which she hoped would startle them. And now the young matron succeeded in doing just that as she gave the reason for her heightened animosity towards her one-time nurse. 'Gratitude!' she said. 'Well, I hope that you are prepared to shower it on her abundantly when she presents you with a half-brother or sister, or perhaps both, in . . . in five months' time.' She now savoured the look of astonishment on the faces before her; then inclining her head first to one, then the other, she turned slowly about and went from the room, whilst Luke and John Sopwith turned and gazed at each other for a moment, and while both of them attempted to speak they changed their minds and, turning about, they walked towards the fire and, their hands on the high marble mantelshelf, they stared into it.

2

Tilly Trotter stood in the library of Highfield Manor looking
down on to the face of the man whom she had served for the
last twelve years as wife, mother, nurse and mistress. That she
had no legal claim to the word wife made no difference for she
knew she had been as a wife to this man. The thick grey hair
parted in the middle came down to the top of his cheekbones.
The face, which in the last three days had assumed a smooth-
ness of youth denying his fifty-seven years, was now shadowed
with the blue hue of decay.

She looked at the hands folded on his breast. She had loved
those hands. They had been gentle, always gentle; at the
height of his passion they had still remained gentle. She could
feel them even now combing through the thick abundance of
her hair. He had liked to do that, spreading it all over the
pillows; then, like an artist, his fingers tracing the bone formation of her face while his deep voice murmured, 'Tilly! Tilly!
my Tilly Trotter, my beautiful wonderful Tilly Trotter.'

He had disliked the name Trotter yet he had called her by
such since he had taken her into his service as a nursemaid
when she was sixteen, after the McGraths and the mad vin-
dictive villagers had burned down her granny's cottage and
brought on her death.

Immediately after the fire Simon Bentwood, the tenant
farmer on the estate, had taken her and her granny to his home,
only for her to be confronted there with the further vindictive-
ness of his new wife, and when her granny died within a few
days she herself had refused his invitation to stay on at the
farm, even while her heart, full of young love for him, wanted
only to be near him.

Destitute, she had taken up her abode in an outhouse behind the burnt-out shell of the cottage; and it was there that Mark Sopwith, the owner of the cottage, because it too was on his estate, found her and offered her the post of nursemaid to his children.

She had been both thankful and yet feared to accept the situation because she knew that her reputation as a witch had gone before her. The tragedies that she had inadvertently created had, through the village family of McGraths, stamped her as being possessed of supernatural powers; but she knew that anyone less like a witch than herself would be hard to find, for she had never wished bad on anyone in her life, except perhaps Hal McGrath who had been determined to marry her, even if it had meant raping her first, and all this because he imagined that there was stolen money hidden somewhere in the cottage in which her grandparents had lived all their married life.

That her fame had gone before her she soon found out, for the majority of the staff at the Manor both feared and hated her; and it was when the man, lying dead here now, had been indiscreet enough to have an affair with a newcomer in the vicinity, Lady Agnes Myton, that his wife had made this an excuse to leave the invalid couch where she had for so long taken refuge from the obligations of married life and return to her mother at Waterford Place near Scarborough, taking with her her four children, and that the housekeeper, in her turn, then took the greatest pleasure in turfing 'the witch' out.

Tilly often wondered what she would have done if it hadn't been for the Drews, a pit family, most of the members of which, both male and female, worked in Mark Sopwith's drift mine. Biddy Drew had taken her in when there was hardly space for the ten people already packed into two rooms.

Looking back now Tilly saw the events in her life as pieces in a jigsaw all dropping into place and leading to her sojourn in the mine — that nightmare period of her life, which reached its climax when she was caught in the flood with, of all people, the owner, Mark Sopwith himself. The result of those three and a half days in the blackness was that he lost both feet and she herself narrowly escaped death.

From the time he called her back to the household to be his nurse she had sensed what his ultimate aim was, and when he finally invited her into his bed she had refused, even while knowing that the love she bore Simon Bentwood was hopeless.

That what she imagined to be undying love could be killed at one blow she was to learn on the day she heard of the death of Simon's wife, actually weeks after the woman's passing. She had flown to him, only to find him in the barn with the very lady who had ruined her master, and she as naked as the day she was born.

Although her love died at the sight, the death throes stayed with her for some time, right until the night she voluntarily gave herself to the man she was now gazing at through misted eyes.

Her fingers gently touching the discoloured cheek, she whispered, 'Oh Mark! Mark! what am I going to do without you?' When her hand left his face she placed it on the slight mound of her stomach. He had been determined to live to see the child. The very day before he died, he had written to his solicitor to tell him that he wished him to call as soon as possible.

She didn't know what he had put in the letter, she only knew that he had written it after she had promised to marry him. But she wondered now why she hadn't given in to his repeated request before. And yet she did know why. After his wife left him his friends had shied off for a time; then the notoriety attached to his name when he took herself as mistress did not improve matters, and so, had she consented to marry him she would have been looked upon as a scheming wench, and his position in the county would have been worsened because she would not have been accepted.

This particular fact wouldn't have troubled Mark, but it would have troubled her. Isolated as he was, he needed friends. He could protest as much as he liked to her that she was all he wanted from life, but she knew he needed other company.

Not even the companionship of the children for the short periods, two or three times a year, they were allowed to visit, nor the daily companionship of Mr Burgess the one-time children's tutor, she knew, had been enough; he had needed contact with the outside world. Sometimes she thought that he'd had ideas of starting up the mine again. She guessed that when Matthew came into his grandfather's money he had been tempted to accept his son's offer to reopen it, but it was about this time that his heart began to trouble him and the doctor advised against all stress. And so the mine remained as it was, flooded, except in those roads where the water had seeped away naturally.

Over the years she wondered why she hadn't become pregnant; his loving passion had been such that she should have been surrounded by a brood. Then one morning she had woken up to realise with amazement what was causing the strange feeling that couldn't be placed under the category of illness yet was making her feel so unwell. When she broke the news to him he had laughed until his sides ached, then held her tightly as he said, 'That's what you have always wanted, isn't it? And now you'll have to marry me.' And he had added, in a strangely sombre note as if he knew his future, 'And once that is done I'll die happy for then, Tilly Trotter, I'll know that Tilly Sopwith will live in some sort of security to the end of her days.'

She bent now and placed her lips against the blue lifeless forehead. It was the last time she would touch him, the last time she would see him, for in a short while they would be screwing him down. She turned blindly away, the pain in her heart not sharp and piercing as it had been when she found him dead in his chair, but dull now and so heavy that it forced its way into her limbs and all she desired to do was to drop where she stood and sleep, preferably the everlasting sleep with him.

She went out of the library, through the hall and upstairs, conscious as she did so that the family were in hot discussion in the drawing-room.

Up to four years ago two of the boys and the girl had seemed to accept her position in the household, but not Matthew. Matthew had never countenanced her position, in fact his manner towards her had at times reverted back to that of the insolent little boy she had first encountered up in the nursery.

She hadn't been surprised at Jessie Ann's changed attitude towards her. At the time of her mother's death Jessie Ann was seventeen, and she had wished to return to this house, to act as its mistress, but her father had told her that although he would love to have her back, have them all back, the house already had a mistress, and if she returned she would have to accept the situation. It was from that time that Jessie Ann's open hate of her was born. But Luke and John had taken the situation as a natural event. John had come home, but Luke had gone into the army. Then there was Matthew. Although he had not acted towards her with the same open hostility as his sister, his manner at times had hovered between aloofness and sarcastic jesting. She was always glad when Matthew's visits ended and more than glad when, after leaving university three years ago, he had gone to America.

Slowly now she went up the stairs, across the gallery, down the broad corridor and into the bedroom, the master's bedroom, their bedroom. Everything was neat and tidy. She looked at the bed in which she would never again sleep. Then she walked into the dressing-room, and from there entered the closet. She sluiced her face in cold water, and as she stood drying herself she looked into the mirror. There was no colour in her cheeks, her eyes lay deep in their sockets and appeared black instead of their usual dark brown. Her wide full-lipped mouth looked tremulous. She was thirty years old. Did she look it? No, not really. Mark had always said she had stayed at twenty. Well, that, she knew, had been a loving exaggeration. Yet she was aware she had the kind of bone formation that would fight age, and she supposed she must look upon this as compensation for her unfashionable figure, for even with the years neither her bust nor her hips had developed. Her body, because of its slimness, had at one time worried her, imagining she was deprived of womanly grace. But Mark had viewed her lack of flesh as something beautiful.

And then there was her height. She was too tall for a woman, having grown to almost five foot ten inches.

But what did it matter now how she looked? She was carry-

19

ing a child, Mark's child; in a few months she would be a mother. In the meantime her stomach would swell and, with it, her breasts and her hips. She would at last have flesh on her. When it was too late she would have flesh on her because, whereas a few weeks ago she was delighting in her condition, now it had become a burden and the old fears were rising in her again. What would she do if they didn't let her stay here? She doubted very much if Miss Jessie Ann would countenance her presence in the house one moment longer than was necessary. She had talked her future over with Mr Burgess and he had said she must go to him. It was kind of him but what would life be like in that book-strewn little cottage?

There was another thing she now regretted, and that was since becoming Mark's mistress she had refused to take a wage, for that had appeared to her as being too much like pay-ment for her services. Moreover, she knew that it had taken him all his time to pay an allotment to his wife and keep his children at school, and still pay the expenses of running this large establishment. Of course, with regard to the latter she had some long time ago halved these expenses when she had got rid of the thieving staff and brought in the Drew family.

Biddy Drew was still down in the kitchen there, and Katie, now promoted to house-parlour-maid, could do the work of two young women. Then there was Peg, who in the last few years had been married and widowed. She had become a sort of female butler, seeing to the door and the dining-room. Young Fanny, of the same calibre, now twenty-one, was doing the work of both scullery and kitchen-maids. Sam had returned to the pit, and was followed by Alec, and both were married now. But Bill, Arthur and Jimmy still worked in the grounds and between them kept the place spruce. The men slept in the rooms above the stables, and the four women of the Drew family lived in the North Lodge, which after a two-roomed hovel of the pit row appeared like a palace to them.

Tilly had no fear that the Drews would be dismissed; they kept the place running smoothly. Of course, there was no butler now and no footman, but Fred Leyburn still saw to the coach and the horses and the yard in general. But Phyllis

Coates, who had been first housemaid and who had married Fred Leyburn ten years ago, had no more time for work inside the house for she had filled one of the cottages on the estate with eight children.

Together with herself, the entire staff only numbered nine and, as Mark had often pointed out, must be the smallest staff running a manor house such as this in the county.

Tilly now went out of the closet and along the corridor into what was still known as her room but which, until the past few days, she had only used when the family was visiting. Sitting near the window she looked out into the lowering sky, and as she did so there came a tap on the door and she turned and said, 'Come in,' and was surprised to see Biddy Drew with a tray in her hands. It was usually Katie who brought her tea up.

Having placed the tray on the table, Biddy proceeded to pour the tea out from a small silver teapot, saying as she did so, 'Sitting in the gloaming, lass, 'll do you no good, you should light your lamp. Here, drink that. And look, I've brought you some sandwiches. You've got to eat because, whether you like it or not, you've got to go on, and if you don't want to damage what's inside you through starvation you'll make yourself eat.'

'I've got no appetite, Biddy, I don't feel like eating.'

'I know that, lass; but we've all got to do things we don't want to do.' She now sat down on the edge of the window seat opposite to Tilly and asked quietly, 'Have you heard anything more?'

Tilly shook her head. 'No,' she said, 'and I don't suppose I shall until tomorrow after the funeral.'

'She's turned into a little madam, that one, hasn't she? My God! a proper little upstart if I've ever seen one, you wouldn't credit it, knowin' what a canny bairn she was. Marrying into that family I suppose has given her ideas. Dolman Cartwright, my God! what a name. She's bad enough now, but when the old fellow dies and she becomes Lady Dolman Cartwright there'll be no holdin' her.' Biddy's tone changed as she said quietly, 'She's determined to have you out, lass. Katie heard them going at it in the drawing-room. The lads are for you, but not her.'

21

'I know that, Biddy; but the house, the estate isn't hers, it will go naturally to Matthew. The only thing is, I don't know who'll be in charge until he comes home, likely Luke. But then he's got to return to his regiment. That only leaves John, and I doubt if he'll leave university to look after the place. So we are left with Miss Jessie Ann, aren't we, Biddy?'

'Well, she won't be able to stay here and see to things.'

'Oh, I don't know, she will if she has to. Anyway, she could engage a housekeeper.'

Biddy got to her feet. 'Never on your life! she wouldn't dare.'

'Oh, she would, Biddy, and she can. And she'd be within her right.'

'My God!' Biddy stamped down the room and came back again before she said, 'After all you've done: you kept the master from going barmy; you've run this house like nobody else could. The place is a credit to you.'

'I've had a little help.' Tilly gave a weak smile.

'Aye, I suppose so; but you were the instigation of the help in the first place. If it hadn't been for you gettin' us here this place would have been like a ghost house. Aye, my God! the things that happen in life. 'Tisn't fair. All your young days you had your bellyful of one an' another, then although you may have been happy with him and I'm not sayin' you weren't — he wasn't an easy man to get on with; I know you had your work cut out at times to pacify him and then for this to happen. You should have married him.' She brought out the last words on a low growl. 'I told you years ago. I said the door was open-ing for you and you should grab everything inside it. But what do you do? Leave it until it's too late. You're daft. Do you know that, Tilly? You're daft. One side of you is business-like and this makes for a good manager, but the other side, the bigger side, is soft, as soft as clarts. . . . You should have married him years ago.'

Tilly sighed and closed her eyes for a moment, then said, 'Hindsight, Biddy, hindsight; we realise, on looking back, the things we should have done. But I didn't, did I? So I've got to face up to what's coming.'

'Drink your tea.' Biddy's voice was soft now. 'And you needn't bother comin' down if you don't want to, I've got the dinner all mapped out: vermicelli soup, then rissoles 'n patties; and the main dish is what you ordered, leg of mutton and a curried rabbit 'n boiled rice; an' there's plum puddin' and apple fritters for puddin', whatever they choose. There's no Stilton left, just the Bondon cheeses. Anyway, if they get that lot down them they won't starve. Eeh my! it amazes me where they put it. You would have thought there'd been thirty around the turkey yesterday instead of three of them, and they even scoffed the whole lot of chestnuts. As for the partridges, as I said to Katie, hawks couldn't have cleaned the bones better. Mind you, I think it's Master John that gollops the most. By! that lad can stow it away, you'd think he was workin' double shift instead of lying about all day. Yet of the lot, I think I like him the best, him and his poor stammer. Aw well, I'll get down. Don't worry your head about anything, I'll see it all goes smoothly. She'll have no need to complain.'

'Thanks, Biddy. I'll be down later.'

'Aye now, that'll be wise, company is what you need now. Ta-rah, lass. Try not to fret.' She nodded twice and then went out.

The door had hardly closed when it was opened again and Katie, pushing past her mother, said in a whisper, ' 'Tis Miss Jessie . . . I mean Mrs Cartwright. She wants to see you, Tilly, down in the mornin'-room.'

Tilly rose slowly to her feet before she said, 'Very well. Thank you, Katie. I'll be down in a minute.'

After the door was closed she still remained standing. The temporary mistress of the house had sent for her, she should be scurrying to obey the order; but it was years since she had scurried and she had no intention of doing so now.

Slowly she walked to the mirror and smoothed her hair back. She no longer wore a cap, nor yet a uniform; her dress today was the darkest one she had, a plum-coloured corded velvet. It had been Mark's last Christmas present to her, together with a small brooch designed in the shape of a single spray of lily of the valley, made up of fourteen small diamonds set in gold, which had once belonged to his mother. It was the only piece he had retained from the last case of jewellery that had been brought from the bank and which he had been forced to dispose of two years ago to offset losses from his shares.

It was a full five minutes later when she opened the morning-room door without knocking, and this impertinent gesture was not overlooked by the young matron who was sitting in the leather chair to the side of the fireplace.

'You wished to see me, Mrs Cartwright?'

'Yes, Trotter, otherwise I wouldn't have sent for you.' She stared up at the tall stiff figure. 'I shall come to the point. I have no need to tell you that your position in this house is an embarrassment.'

'To whom, Mrs Cartwright?'

'Don't be impertinent, Trotter, and remember to whom you are speaking.'

'I do remember, and I wish it could be otherwise because the person who is addressing me as you are doing has no relation whatever to the young lady I once knew.'

Jessie Ann Cartwright's face became suffused with colour, but even so the redness did not indicate to the full the temper that was raging within her. This menial talking like a lady! the result of old Burgess's coaching over the years. She had the desire to stand up and slap her face; and yet at the same time she couldn't explain why she was feeling so vehement towards her one time nurse. It wasn't only that she had alienated her father away from the rest of his family, even though that was a great part of the reason. No, if they had all been able to return here after their mother died she herself would not have been in such a hurry to marry and get away from the domineering influence of her grandmother. Not that she disliked Cartwright, but marriage was such a trial in more ways than one, and living with her husband's people was almost as frustrating as life had been under the domination of both her mother and her grandmother.

She swallowed deeply before saying, 'I have no wish to bandy words with you, Trotter, I merely brought you here to tell you that from now on I shall be taking charge of the house,

24

and I shall thank you to keep to the nursery quarters until after my father's funeral.'

Tilly stared down into the round almost childish plump face, and she forced herself to keep her voice steady as she replied, 'I am sorry, Mrs Cartwright, that I won't be able to comply with your order; I intend to carry out my duties as housekeeper until your father's will is read, then I shall know his wishes. I may also inform you, Mrs Cartwright, that over the past four years your father tried to persuade me to marry him. I had my own reasons for refusing, but at this moment I am very, very sorry I made such a foolish mistake. However, even if I had been in the position of mistress of this house I should have hoped I would have had the courtesy to hide my feelings whatever they were concerning you.' Her chin jerked slightly upwards as she ended, 'If you will excuse me, Mrs Cartwright, I shall go about my duties. Dinner will be served at seven o'clock, as usual.'

Tilly had reached the door when Jessie Ann Cartwright's voice, in a most unladylike screech, cried, 'Trotter!'

'Yes, Mrs Cartwright?'

'How dare you! How dare you!'

Tilly stared across the room at the small bristling young matron before saying quietly, 'I dare, Mrs Cartwright. Having played the part of nurse, mother, wife and mistress to your father for twelve years, I dare.'

Jessie Ann Cartwright was actually thrusting her hands under the black lace cap and gripping handsful of her fair hair when the door leading from the morning-room into the dining-room opened and she turned, startled, to see John entering the room. He came in quietly smiling, saying, 'Sorry. S . . . s . . . sorry, Jessie Ann, but I just happened to be next door. W . . . well, I was on the point of c . . . coming in here when y . . . you started on her. By! I'll say she can hold her own can Tro . . . Trotter. She had you on the floor there, Jessie Ann.'

'Shut up you! Of all the fools on this earth, you're one. Shut up! you gormless idiot.'

John's countenance, from expressing slight amusement, took on a stiffness and his voice was no longer that of the fool of the family, as he was often called because of his desire to amuse and mostly through his stammer. But his stammer now very pronounced, he said, 'I s . . . say with Tro . . . Trotter, don't speak to me like that, Jessie Ann. It's y . . . you who forget yourself. If I've never witnessed the l . . . lack of breeding in an approach to a s . . . servant, then I've just heard it n . . . now. You are a li . . . little upstart, Jessie Ann. And why you don't like Tro . . . Trotter is because she's a beautiful woman with a pr . . . presence. Yes, that's what she's g . . . got, a presence. And you'll never have a pr . . . presence, Jessie Ann, not because you're too sm . . . small and p . . . plump, but because you have no dig . . . dig . . . dignity. And now there you have it. I've been wanting to say this to you for a lo . . . long time, so don't think I'll come and apologise because if you w . . . wait for that you'll wait a long time.'

And now to Jessie Ann's amazement she watched her brother who was only two years younger than herself but whom she had always treated as a stupid boy march out of the room.

To say that she was astonished was putting it mildly. John had turned on her. All her life she had used her youngest brother as a whipping block while at the same time feeling that nothing she could do or say to him would change his affection for her. But now he had turned on her, and all through that woman.

Her face crinkled, her eyes screwed up into slits and, turning to the fireplace, she beat her soft white fists against the marble mantelpiece while the tears of frustration and temper ran down her cheeks. Oh, she wished it was tomorrow. Just wait until tomorrow; she would then personally see that woman go out of the door. She would. *She would.*

It said something for the nature of John that he looked for an opportunity to get Tilly alone, but it wasn't until after dinner when his sister had cornered Luke in the drawing-room and was waging a private battle with him, over what he didn't know and at the moment didn't care, that when crossing the gallery he espied Tilly leaving her room and making her way

26

towards the nursery staircase. Hurrying after her, he caught up with her at the bottom of the stairs and as he took the lamp from her hand he said, 'L . . . let me carry it for you, Trotter.'

She offered him no resistance, nor did she speak; but he, having set the lamp down on the old nursery table, looked around the room and said, 'Hasn't altered a b . . . bit. C . . . could have been yesterday, don't you think, Tr . . . Trotter?'

His evident concern for her made it impossible for her to give him any answer, and she bowed her head and swallowed deeply.

Coming close to her, he put his hand on her shoulder as he said, 'Don't be upset Tr . . . Trotter, I know how you feel. Jessie Ann is behaving ab . . . ab . . . abominably.' His mouth had opened wide on the word, and he closed his eyes and wagged his head a number of times before managing to bring out, 'C . . . c . . . come and sit down. Is it too cold for you?' He looked towards the empty hearth. 'There used to be a blazing f . . . f . . . fire there.'

When Tilly sat down in the wooden chair near the table he too took a seat, opposite to her, and said softly, 'I remember the early days, Trotter. I . . . I can look back right to the first time I s . . . saw you. You came into the b . . . bedroom and you hung over me. Your face hasn't altered a bit since then. Was it the f . . . first night or the s . . . second night that Matthew put the fr . . . frog in your bed and you came back and p . . . pushed it down his shirt?' He now put his head back and laughed. 'I can hear him screaming yet. He was a de . . . devil, wasn't he?'

'Yes, he was a devil.' She didn't add 'Master John' and she couldn't say 'John', but aiming to stop herself from breaking down she brought the conversation on to a less emotional plane by asking, 'Are you happy at Cambridge?'

'Yes and no, Tr . . . Trotter.' He turned round and looked about him before going on to say, 'I . . . I'm not one of the booky s . . . sort, you know, Trotter, not intellectual at all. You know wh . . . what I'd like to be? I'd like to be a f . . . f . . . farmer.'

'Would you really?' She smiled gently at him.

'Yes, Trotter. I like the country. C . . . can't stand the towns. Yet you know, it's funny, when I go to London to dine with Luke. Oh' — he pulled a long face at her — 'L . . . Luke dines very well and in the most unusual places.' He winked his eye now and she was forced to smile at him. 'And he stands all the expenses. I'm mostly b . . . broke and everything is so expensive up there. Do you know what a c . . . cabby charges from the Eastern Counties Railway to Le . . . Leicester Square?'

She shook her head at him.

'Two sh . . . sh . . . shillings and fourpence.' He bowed his head deeply. 'You could almost buy a h . . . horse in Newcastle for that.' Again he had his head back and was laughing. Then looking at her once more, he said, 'No one can help liking London, Trotter; there are so m . . . m . . . many marvellous things to s . . . see. Last year Luke took me to the Exhibition of Industry. It was s . . . s . . . simply amazing. All the nations had sent their products: chemicals, machinery, cloth, and . . . art—sculpture. It was amazing. Luke is very g . . . good to me, Trotter.'

'I'm sure he is.'

'Of course he has the money to do it with because Grandfather left him a t . . . t . . . tidy sum. But he was very measly to m . . . me, was Grandfather. And you know why, Trotter?'

'No.'

'Well — ' His head went down now, his eyes closed tightly and he had to open his mouth wide before he could bring out, 'Just because he c . . . couldn't stand to hear me st . . . stammer. He imagined I must be wr . . . wr . . . wrong in the head.'

She put her hand across the table and placed it on top of his as she said, 'Your head's in the right place, John, as is your heart, and that's the main thing.'

'Thank you, Trotter. You . . . you were always so k . . . kind. That's why Father l . . . loved you I suppose. And he did love you.'

'Yes, he loved me.' Again guiding him from the painful subject, she said, 'Are you going straight back to Cambridge?'

28

'No, Trotter. Although term begins on the thirteenth I'm
. . . I'm going up to London with Luke.' He smiled now as he
said, 'And I'm afraid that Luke will not c . . . continue in
mourning because, after all, we . . . we didn't know F . . .
Father very well, did we?'

'No, you didn't.'

There followed a slight pause before he said now, 'L . . .
Luke likes the gay life. He goes to the th . . . th . . . theatre
regularly, and to exhibitions. But mostly to the theatre, the
one called the Adelphi, and another in Covent Garden. Th . . .
that's where the fruit market is. Oh, and so many more. And
all the sights you s . . . see there, Trotter, you wouldn't
believe. Newcastle? Well, Newcastle is like a vi . . . village
compared with London.'

'Oh, I can't believe that.'

' 'Tis, Trotter, 't . . . 'tis. At the theatre, oh, the ladies!
They don't go to see the pl . . . plays you know, Trotter.'

'No?'

'No, they go to outsh . . . shine each other in their dress and
jewellery. And the gentlemen are as bad. Oh, the . . . the
powder. I feel ve . . . very much the boy from the country
because, as you see, I don't p . . . powder my hair.' He now
grinned widely and ended, 'I couldn't afford to p . . . pay the
tax, one pound three shillings and sixpence tax, oh no!'

She found herself smiling. He was so likeable, even lovable,
different from all the others. Luke was all right, but so taken
up with himself and the army; and Jessie Ann, well, there was
only one word for Mrs Dolman Cartwright, and that was spiteful. She was a spiteful little vixen. Whoever would have
thought she would have turned out as she had done . . . And
Matthew, the new master of the estate? She had always felt a
little uneasy in Matthew's company. His manner towards her,
although not offensive, had held a quality to which she could
put no name. On his visits she had often caught him looking at
her with an expression on his face very like that on his father's
when he was angry; and no doubt he was angry at the position
she had come to hold in his father's life and esteem.

The nursery door opened suddenly and they both turned

their faces towards it and breathed easier when they saw that the visitor was Luke. Moving towards them, he said, 'I thought I'd find you here.' He was nodding at his brother now and he added, 'The sparks are flying downstairs and you'd better show yourself. I'm sorry, Trotter.' He brought his gaze kindly on to Tilly and she, rising to her feet, merely inclined her head towards him, then watched them both leave the room.

The door closed, she sat down again and looked about her. Perhaps this was to be the last night she would sit in this room. Unless Mark had made provision that she stay on as the housekeeper until Matthew returned from abroad Jessie Ann would have her out of the door quicker than the old housekeeper had pushed her out years ago. Strange how things repeated themselves.

How would she take to living in a little house of only four rooms, three of which were strewn with books, and sleeping in the loft under the eaves? Well — she straightened her shoulders — it was no use asking herself such questions, for it was no use planning until tomorrow. But she knew one thing, and the thought brought bitterness on to her tongue, if she was turned out the village would celebrate.

Although she hadn't been near the village for years she knew that they were aware of everything that transpired in the Manor House; they had always made it their business to find out what the witch was up to. The word no longer frightened her because Mark had used it so often, his beautiful witch he had called her. She had never felt like a witch, beautiful or otherwise, and not since Hal McGrath's death had she wished bad on anyone, yet she knew if it lay with some of the villagers their wishes would bring her so low that she would be face down in the mud and they dancing on her. There was evil in people. Some picked it up from their parents, its growth fostered by listening to their superstitious chatter, their jealous venom, while others were born with evil in them. Hal McGrath had been such a one. And the old cook, that overflowing receptacle of gluttony, had been another. And both had tainted those with whom they came in contact. As

Mr Burgess said, one advanced through education to reason and one retreated through ignorance to evil. He was so right. At least she was convinced she herself had advanced through education to reason. And yet she couldn't reason out the fact why it was some people loved her on sight, whereas others could hate her with an equal passion.

3

The breath issued like puffs of white smoke from the horses'
nostrils, seeming to mingle with the black plumes dancing on
their tossing heads before thinning in the still biting air.

Tilly stood at the bedroom window, one hand held tightly
across her throat, not to stop any flow of tears — these she had
spent during the long sleepless nights — but in order to quell
the long moan that was bent on escaping and which, she felt,
given rein, would increase into a wail similar to those vented
by the Irish women in Rosier's pit cottages at the news that yet
another of their men had been taken by the coal.

The hearse was standing opposite the front door and behind
it to the left and reaching to the end of the house and round
into the courtyard was a row of carriages, the blinds of the
windows drawn, the horses black-draped. To the right, where
the drive wound its way for almost half a mile before reaching
the main road and for as far as the eye could see, were more carriages. These were already occupied and were being arranged
along the verge in some form of precedence to follow those that
were to hold the relatives and associates of the deceased.

At the head of each pair of horses stood a groom, black
streamers hanging limply from his high hat.

The whole scene was a picture of black and white. The frost
had not lifted, and the only break in the black-garbed figures
were the faces, some very white, some pink, some florid red.
All the hands were covered in black gloves.

The coffin was being borne down the steps towards the
hearse, and as Tilly's eyes followed it her mind did not
whimper, 'Good-bye, Mark'; because she knew that in that

elaborate box there lay only his crippled body; his spirit was strong about her in this room where he had lived, where they had both lived for the last twelve years. A short while ago she had thought she would be happy if when having to leave this house she could take this room with her, but she was wise enough to know that once she was gone from the place time would erase the essence of it until it became merely a faint imprint on her mind, and with the fading the pain in her heart would ease. In this moment she longed for the power to leap years ahead into age, deep age with which would have come tranquillity, for age surely earned tranquillity.

The thought conjured up her grandmother and grandfather, who had acted like parents to her from when she was five years old. Loving, caring, tender parents, too tender, too loving, for their care hadn't prepared her for the onslaught of animosity that had attacked her from all sides since she was fifteen and was with her to this day for there, going down the steps now, was the epitome of it, Jessie Ann. She couldn't associate her with the fancified name of Mrs Dolman Cartwright. She didn't look a Mrs Dolman Cartwright. Even in her elaborate black she looked fussy, plump, a little matron who as yet had acquired no knowledge of what was expected of a real matron, a real mistress.

She was followed by Luke and John. They stood at the bottom of the steps while the hearse moved slowly forward, then they entered the first carriage. When this moved on there came a second carriage, and a third. Fourteen carriages passed by the window before the courtyard was cleared and those waiting on the drive could join the cortège. Half the county seemed to have come to pay its respects. And all the mourners were male, with the exception of Mrs Dolman Cartwright.

That Jessie Ann had insisted on attending her father's funeral was, Tilly knew, merely in order to give point to her position. There had, years previously, been a great deal of talk when their grandmother had attended her grandson's funeral. Gentlewomen did not attend funerals whether the deceased be male or female, it was unseemly.

When the last carriage passed from view Tilly turned her

face from the window and brought her eyes to rest on the big four-poster bed. She walked slowly towards it and placed her hand gently on the near side pillow, and her fingers stroked it as she murmured 'Mark. Mark.'

She had half turned away from the bed when she stopped again and looked down on the square bedside table. It was this very table he had knocked flying one night when, in the depths of his loneliness, he had used its crashing noise and the breaking of the water glass and the spilling of the carafe to bring her scurrying from her bed to him. Yet that night she had refused him, for, young and silly as she was, she had imagined her heart was still with the farmer, Simon Bentwood. She'd had a lot to learn, and Dear . . . Dear Mark . . . Dearest . . . Dearest Mark had taught her.

It would be two hours before those invited would return to the Manor to gorge themselves on hot soup, warm fresh bread and the cold victuals laid out in the dining-room: hams, pressed tongue, boiled capons, roast ducks, pasties, pies and an assortment of sweetmeats and cheeses. She had seen to the last of the preparations this morning and it was all finished before Mrs Dolman Cartwright put in an appearance and, as Tilly had expected, found something to criticise, not only something but the whole layout.

'There should have been a hot meal ready for the mourners. See to it!' she had said, and Tilly had enraged the little lady still further by answering quietly, 'This is what I have ordered and like this it will stay.' She had no need to reiterate what she had said earlier: 'I consider myself mistress here until this afternoon; then we shall see who it is who will legally take over,' because the look in her eyes was speaking plainly for her.

She went slowly from the room, along the wide corridor, across the gallery and down the shallow stairs into the hall. The whole house was dark and gloom-filled, the drawn blinds shutting out the meagre light of the sombre day. Only in the kitchen were the windows bare of heavy black drapes.

Biddy, as usual, was at the table. She was preparing the meal for the staff, a plain roast with suet pudding, but she stopped and, wiping her hands on her apron, turned to Tilly and, like a mother addressing a daughter, she said, inclining her head towards the stove, 'I've made a fresh pot of tea and if I were you I'd lace it with a drop of whisky, 'cos I fear you're going to need it, lass.'

'Yes, I think you're right, Biddy. Yes — ' Tilly nodded her head in small jerks — 'I feel I'm going to need it.'

A few minutes later, sitting on the short wooden settle placed at right angles to the corner of the great open hearth, she sipped at the whisky-laced tea and stared towards the hanging spit from which was suspended a sirloin of beef, the fat dripping slowly into the iron receptacle below. Automatically she leant forward and, gripping the iron handle, turned the spit, after which she sat back and looked at Biddy Drew, the woman who had been as a mother to her and whom she loved as a mother, and she said, 'I'm not only anxious about myself, Biddy, but I'm now worried about you all because if that little madam takes over she'll take it out on you, merely because I was a means of bringing you here.'

'Don't you worry yourself about that, lass. With the steady wage we've had all these years and nowt to do with it except buy our Sunday best we won't starve. We'll manage until the lasses get set on some place, an' the lads an' all.'

'But it's the lodge, you've made it such a comfortable home, and the girls love it.'

'Aye, I know that, and I admit it'll be a wrench if we have to go. There's no doubt about that. But God tempers the wind to the shorn lamb, and we'll find some place; as long as you've got the money in your pocket you can always rent. And as I said to the lads last night, they've had it easy for a long time now and their characters must be gettin' soft, there's nothin' like trouble and turmoil for pickin' out the men from the lads.'

'Aw, Biddy!' Tilly closed her eyes and turned her head to the side as she said, 'The lads and all of you have worked like Trojans in this place. In the ordinary way it would have taken twice their number to keep it as it is; they've put their whole heart and soul into it, they couldn't have done more if the place had belonged to them.'

'Aye, yes, I suppose they have worked. We've all worked

35

because we were grateful.' Biddy's voice sank as her hand came out and gripped Tilly's knee. 'God! lass, you'll never know how grateful we were to be taken out of that stinkin' hole and brought here, never! I'm not a prayin' woman 'cos I suppose up till you appeared there was little to thank Him for, but there's never a day gone by these past years but I've said to Him "Thank you for creating Tilly Trotter". . . . Aw, lass . . . lass, don't. I didn't mean to make you cry. . . . Aw, don't give over.'

Tilly got abruptly to her feet and, swallowing deeply and her lids blinking rapidly, she said, 'And I don't want to cry, Biddy, not now, not today . . . I'm . . . I'm going to put a coat on and walk round the grounds, blow the cobwebs away.' She smiled now, and Biddy nodded at her but said nothing; not until Tilly had gone from the room, when she looked upwards and whispered half aloud, 'Make it right for her, please. Do that, don't let her be downed again.'

4

Mr Blandford's buttocks were poised on the edge of a Louis XVI chair and as he read each name from the parchment in front of him he rocked forward bringing the back legs of the chair off the carpet. He was a nervous man, by nature retiring, that's why he always left the business of the court proceedings to the junior partners in Blandford, Coleman and Stocks. Even dealing with wills affected him, especially, as now, the reading of them to relatives, because almost never did he face a family group without encountering dissension, animosity, and even venom, causing his left eyelid to twitch and the flesh to wriggle on his bones as if bent on leaving its support.

Today, he was finding, was no exception; in fact, there was a mixed tension in the room. Such was his nervous system that it picked up the separate emotions and anxieties from those sitting to the right facing him. These were all members of the staff, while the small group of three to the left of him represented the immediate family. He had no doubt in his mind that it was from his late client's daughter that the vexatious vapour was emanating, while interest . . . keen, yet remaining merely interest, were the feelings being expressed by the sons.

In a seat by herself in front of the staff sat the young woman who had for some years held a precarious position in this house. That she could have been its legal mistress any time during the past four years he was well aware, for Mr Mark Sopwith had made no secret of this when he made his last will two years ago. That he had perhaps intended to alter it was more than a surmise, but his message had come too late. He had himself answered the letter from Mr Sopwith which had said he required his presence here at the Manor as soon as was conveniently possible. But on his arrival it was to find the master of the house dead.

He had already read the usual preliminary statements about being of sound mind and such, and had delivered the fact that the estate would go to his eldest son, Matthew George Sopwith, who was now residing in America. And here he paused, wetted his lips, rocked twice backwards and forwards on the chair before proceeding in a voice devoid of emotion or even inflexion as he read, 'I have very little money to leave any of my children but this can be of no great concern to them as I understand their grandparents have left them considerable amounts of money, that is with the exception of my youngest son, John, and to him I leave my three per cent consols due to mature in 1853.' Here Mr Blandford paused and the twitching of his eyelid increased as he looked at the plump young figure in black who was staring at him as if he were to be held personally responsible for her being omitted from sharing in any part of the estate. As for her older brother his reaction was to purse his lips. He could not see what expression was on the youngest son's face because he had his head lowered. He liked that young man, he was the nicest of the family.

He took a deep breath, rocked himself once again as if preparing himself for another effort, then continued. 'To Matilda Trotter, who has acted, not only as my nurse, but as my wife for many years and brought me great comfort, I should like to be able to say I leave all my possessions including my estate because she has earned it, and if I could have been successful in persuading her to become my wife, which attempt I have made many times, things would have been much more straightforward at this moment, but because she did not wish to embarrass my family, a matter which I may say did not trouble me, she would not consent to such an arrangement, so, therefore, to my dearest Tilly all I can leave her is two sets of shares, five hundred East Indian stock and five hundred in Palmer Brothers and Company, Jarrow shipyard, hoping that they will both rise to procure security for her in later life. . . .'

When the daughter of the house made a quick movement on

her chair, which caused her younger brother to imagine she was falling and to put out his hand to steady her, all other eyes in the room turned towards her. But Mr Blandford only allowed his glance to pass over her for her bristling indignation was causing his nerves to jangle. Clearing his throat once more and again bringing the back legs of the chair from the carpet, he went on, 'Now to my staff, an odd assortment, having been miners, both men and women, all their lives with no domestic experience until they came into my home, from which time they have worked like no others, I leave each the sum of ten pounds, and moreover because my dear Tilly wished it, I bequeath to Mrs Bridget Drew the North Lodge, together with an acre of land taking up three sides of it and excluding the drive. And I would trust that my son, Matthew, would be happy to keep them all employed, together with my dear Tilly in her capacity of housekeeper. Lastly, to Mr Herbert Vincent Burgess I bequeath fifty books of his choice from the library; and to Fred Leyburn, my coachman, the sum of £30.

Signed this 14th day of March, 1851.

Mark John Henry Sopwith.'

Tilly was the first to rise to her feet and, turning round, she put out her hand and helped Biddy up, because that woman seemed too stunned at the moment to move. The rest followed, Katie, Peg, Fanny, Bill, Arthur, and Jimmy Drew, and lastly Fred Leyburn. . . .

Luke and John were now standing in front of the table looking down at Mr Blandford who was busily and fussily arranging his papers, and it was Luke who said, 'Thank you, sir.'

Mr Blandford did not answer him but looked past the young men to where their sister was still sitting, her back straight, her hands gripped tightly on her lap, and what he said now was, 'I don't make wills, I merely take down my clients' wishes. The late Mr Sopwith, I may say, was most insistent that his should be expressed in his own words.'

'I understand, sir, and . . . and I think my father was . . . well, he was very fair. And it's true my sister and I don't really need money. Of course' — he gave a shaky laugh — 'it's questionable that one can have too much.'

' 'Tis, 'tis' — the solicitor nodded at him — 'it's question-able, but it's no good thing. Speaking from experience, 'tis no good thing.'

'No, sir, perhaps you're right. But I'm glad my father thought of John.' He turned now to his brother.

John, his face pink-hued, said, 'V . . . very good of F . . . Father. S . . . sur . . . surprised. 'Twas very thoughtful of him.'

'Yes, yes, indeed.' The solicitor was nodding at him. Then rising from his rocking seat, he took up his case and moved from behind the table and paused for a moment in front of Jessie Ann and suffered her malignant gaze on him as he said, 'Good-day, madam.'

She gave him no answer, merely stared unblinking at him; but as Luke escorted him from the room she turned her head slowly in their direction until the door had closed behind them. Only then did she get to her feet and, like an army ser-geant who had been maddened by some indiscipline, began to march up and down the room.

As she passed John for the third time he dared to com-miserate with her, although he really did not know why she should need sympathy. 'I'm s . . . sorry, Jessie A. . . .'

'Shut up will you! Shut up!'

Stung to retort, his mouth was wide open in an effort to bring out the words when the door opened and Luke entered the room again to face the brunt of his sister's fury.

'It's damnable, damnable! Not even to be mentioned. Did you know anything about these bonds? That woman! That . . . !'

'Oh, give over, Jessie Ann; anyone would think you were on the stage acting a part. Lord! you don't need the money, it's as Father said.'

'That isn't the point.'

'What is then? You tell me.' His voice was flat, cool; it was the soldier speaking now, not her brother, and for a moment she was nonplussed. Her mouth worked, her nose twitched before she brought out, 'The point is, he put that woman before us, his own flesh and blood.'

40

'And . . . and wh . . . what had we done for him? I ask you.'
John pointed his finger directly at his sister. 'Don't you dare
tell me to sh . . . shut up again because if you d . . . do I won't
be answerable for my re . . . re . . . reactions.'

There was a quiet smile on Luke's face now as he looked at
his younger brother, a smile which seemed to say, Good for
you, and it made Jessie Ann pause but did nothing to direct her
temper away from its objective, for now she cried, 'She's not
staying here!'

'Father's wishes were that Matthew keep her on as his
housekeeper.'

'But, my dear Luke, Matthew is not here, is he? And we
have to act for him in his absence. Now it should be you who
takes over, but you are returning to your regiment tomorrow,
aren't you? And John here' — she thumbed towards her
brother — 'is going up to London with you for a time, so I am
the only one free to take charge and I'm going to tell you something now. One thing I was certain of in the will was that
Father couldn't leave the estate away from Matthew, and as I
knew he couldn't get here in time I wrote to him and told him
that I'd be pleased to keep things going until he arrived to take
charge himself.'

'You little bitch!' Luke's words were brought out on a laugh
half-filled with admiration at the duplicity and foresight of his
sister; then more soberly he added, 'You do hate her, don't
you?'

'Well, if I haven't made that evident by now I've under-
estimated your intelligence, brother.'

'I . . . I d . . . don't think she'll want to stay anyway.'

'She's not going to get the chance, conniving hussy! And
anyway, she made quite sure she was going to have some place
to go to, getting Father to leave the North Lodge to the cook.
Really! it's fantastic when you think of it. That's an excellent
lodge, better than the main one.'

'Oh really!' Luke thumped his forehead now with the palm
of his hand. 'Give me a war any day in the week.' Then he
turned towards John who was looking at Jessie Ann and was
saying with hardly a stammer to his words, 'You know some-

41

thing, Jessie Ann, you'll l . . . live to regret this day. Trotter will come out on top, you'll s . . . see. I've . . . I've got a feeling about Trotter, she's different.'

'Oh!' — Jessie Ann waved her hand at him now — 'don't come the witch business, grow up.'

'Well, witch or n . . . no witch, there's something in Trotter, an attraction. I can understand Father. . . .'

It was on the point of Jessie Ann's tongue to cry again, 'Shut up!' but thinking better of it, she stared from one to the other of her brothers, her plump breasts swelling with her temper; then she turned from them both and stalked out of the room; and John, looking at Luke, said, ' 'Tis all because she's je . . . jealous, insanely jealous because Tro . . . Trotter's beautiful. She is. Don't you think so, Luke? F . . . Father thought her beautiful, and sometimes I thought Matthew did too, in spite of the way he w . . . went on.'

Luke didn't answer for a moment, and when he did his voice had a thoughtful note to it as he said, 'Yes, I think Matthew did too.'

'You will leave the house immediately. You will take nothing with you but what belongs to you personally.'

'Thank you. Is that all, Mrs Cartwright?'

'That is all.' It was as much as Jessie Ann could bring out without allowing herself to scream or stamp her feet.

Again Tilly said, 'Thank you.' Then after a slight pause, she added, 'And may I wish you, Mrs Cartwright, all that you deserve in the life ahead of you.'

For a moment Tilly had the satisfaction of seeing the little madam look startled, there was the same expression in her eyes as used to be in those of the half-witted scullery maid Ada Tennant when she'd had occasion to speak to her sharply. But whereas Ada's look would cause her to smile inwardly, the expression in Jessie Ann's eyes was too much akin to that she had seen so often on the faces of the villagers to cause her any amusement, had she felt like being amused at this moment.

She went out of the morning-room, across the hall and into the kitchen. There, they were waiting for her, and she looked from one to the other, saying in a voice from which she tried to withhold a tremor, 'It's as I expected, my marching orders, and right now.'

'Oh my God!' When Biddy sank down on to a chair, Tilly put her hand on her shoulder as she said, 'Don't worry, I'll not starve. Nor will mine.' She now patted her stomach gently. 'And for the present I'll be well housed. And I couldn't have a better companion than Mr Burgess, could I?' There was now a break in her voice and no one answered her.

'The bloody unfairness of it!'

'She's a little sod.'

'I won't want to work for her long.'

At this Tilly, looking from one to the other, said, 'Stay put all of you. When Master Matthew comes home things may be different.'

'I don't know so much,' said Jimmy. 'As I remember him, he was a bit of a hard 'un; had very little to say, snooty like.'

Nobody contradicted this, not even Tilly, but what she said now was, 'Come and help me get packed, Katie; and as I won't be allowed to use the carriage, will you see that my things go on the wagon, Arthur?'

She did not wait for Arthur to reply but hurried from them up the kitchen, through the green-baized door into the hall, and as she was crossing it, Luke and John came out of the drawing-room, and when they met at the bottom of the stairs they looked at each other. And it was John who spoke first, saying, 'I'm . . . I'm so s . . . sorry, Trotter.'

'It's all right. It's all right.'

'Me too. Me too, Trotter.'

She looked at Luke now, and he added, 'When Matthew comes home he might see things differently.'

She gave no verbal answer to this but made a small movement with her head, and when they stood aside to allow her to pass, she went up the stairs, past the bedroom, past the dressing-room, past the closet and into her own room. There, turning her face to the door, she pressed it into her hands, but she didn't cry. . . .

Half an hour later she was ready dressed but not in black.

She wore a plum-coloured melton cloth coat with a fur collar and a matching velour hat with a feather curling round the brim, and as she walked across the gallery and down the stairs again she could have been the lady of the house going out on a visit.

She did not go to the kitchen again but walked straight across the hall and through the front door and down the steps to where Arthur was waiting with the wagon. Fred Leyburn, she knew, would gladly have driven her in the carriage, as he had done during the past years, but now he had his position to think about and that depended on his new mistress.

Arthur helped her up on to the front seat of the wagon, called, 'Hie-up there!' to the horse, and they were off.

As they rumbled slowly along the drive towards the main gates there rose from the deep sadness of her heart a thread of wry humour which said, 'At least, this time of being thrown out you're not leaving by the back drive.'

Arthur had already lit the side lamps and before their journey ended, two miles along the main road and another quarter mile up a rutted lane, the winter twilight had dropped suddenly into night, and so it was dark when the wagon pulled up at the small gate which opened into the equally small garden of Mr Burgess's cottage.

Before she had alighted the old man had opened the door. A blanket around his shoulders and nodding his head at her, he cried, 'I expected you. I expected you, my dear.'

She did not answer him, merely took his outstretched hand; then with her other hand pressed him back into the room towards the fire.

After Arthur had brought in two bass hampers, a bass bag, a wooden box and a hat box, she turned to him and, her voice thick and her words hesitant, she said, 'Thanks, Arthur. I'll . . . I'll be seeing you.'

He stared at her for a moment, then said, 'We'll be waitin' for you, Tilly.'

Before turning towards the door he nodded to the old man, saying, 'Ta-rah, Mr Burgess'; at the door, he looked at Tilly again and, his voice husky now, he said, 'It isn't the end, Tilly.

You'll see your day, you will, you will that,' and, nodding confirmation to his words, he turned about and mounted the wagon.

Having closed the door, she bowed her head and paused for a moment before going towards the fire; and there she stood near the man who had taught her all she knew, with the exception of love. And yet in a way he had taught her that too because, as he often said, there were many kinds of love, and whichever one you were experiencing lessened your need for the others.

The first part of his particular philosophy she could agree with. There were, she knew, many kinds of love, but that one kind lessened the intensity of the main one wasn't true, for no other feeling she had as yet experienced had lessened the love that had grown within her for Mark Sopwith. Perhaps Mr Burgess had never known the love of a woman, the only love he had ever spoken of was his love of literature; and it was evident in this room and right through the cottage.

She had lost count of the times she had arranged his books on the stout shelves she'd had one of the boys erect for him round the walls of the main room, but every time she returned to visit him there they were, strewn on the floor, on the table, and on the couch Mark had allowed her to take down from the attic rooms and bring here for his comfort.

He had dropped the blanket from his shoulders and was now taking her coat from her, saying, 'Look, I have set the tea. Aren't I clever?' He pointed to the side of the fireplace to a round table covered with a white lace cloth and holding crockery and a teapot and milk jug. 'And I've kept the muffins in the tin; we'll have them toasted. You must be frozen, sit down, my dear.' But as he went to press her into a chair she took his hands and said quietly, 'You sit down; I'll see to things.'

'No, no.'

'Yes, please let me; it will ease my mind.'

Readily, he allowed himself to be persuaded, and sat watching her as she took off her outdoor things, then busied herself between the table and the open grate where the kettle was boiling on the hob, and not until she was seated opposite to him and had handed him his cup of tea did he say, 'Well?' and she answered, 'Her little ladyship took great delight in turning me out.'

He looked down into his cup and slowly stirred the spoon round it as he said, 'I want to say I cannot believe it of her, yet as a child I detected a slyness in her, a vanity; but because she was so small, so petite, one said to oneself, she is but a child. Yet in later years as she grew I watched her during her visits to the house, and she could not bear the fact that her father could care for any other female but the one he had created. Tell me, how did he leave you, the master?'

'As far as I can gather, provided for. He had bequeathed me two lots of shares, five hundred in each.'

'Oh, good, good, my dear. I'm so glad. What are they?'

'One lot is in Palmer's shipyard in Jarrow and the other is some kind of East Indian stock. I don't know really what that entails.'

'Oh, but that's fine, fine.' He nodded at her. 'I'm so glad. They will keep you in good stead. Was there any other stock mentioned?'

'Only some consols to John.'

'Really!' He nodded his head. 'Did you know he was in very bad straits? Did he ever mention that he was selling his bonds and such in order to keep the house going?'

Her eyes widened slightly as she answered, 'No; he . . . he never discussed money with me, nor I with him.'

'Well, I'm afraid he would soon have had to, my dear. I think he intended to write to Matthew for help.'

'Really!'

'Yes. I gathered so much when we talked about finance, as we often did you know, among other things, and very often about your dear self, because he so admired the way you ran the house, and on a mere pittance too, and the comfort you brought him just with your presence. No, no; please, don't cry, my dear.'

'No, no, I'm not.' And she mustn't cry, not yet, not until she was in the room above the rafters upstairs when she could smother her moans in the feather tick. She prayed that tonight

46

the wind would rise to such an extent that Mr Burgess wouldn't hear her crying for, once alone, she would be unable to contain her agony.

She stretched her eyes, opened her mouth wide, and then said, 'And he didn't forget you.'

'Me? What . . . what could he leave me?'

'Fifty books. Your own choice from the library.'

His two hands were raised in the air and his head went back on his shoulders as if he were witnessing manna dropping from heaven, for nothing could have pleased him more on this earth. Looking at her again, he repeated softly, 'Fifty?'

'Yes; and of your own choice.'

'Dear, dear. The thoughtful man. Oh, he was kind. In so many ways he was kind.'

He became silent for a moment while savouring the joy of adding to his enormous collection of what he thought of as gems because every book he possessed was dear to him. Then leaning forward, the white silken quiff of his hair falling between his brows, he put his hand out towards her and, his fingers touching hers, he said, 'I'm so happy to have you with me, so happy to have you with me, Tilly.'

She made no answer for a moment; then said, 'What when the baby comes?'

'Oh that!' He moved his head from side to side and, his face crinkling into a wide smile, he answered her, as he was wont to do at times, in poetical language, 'I shall be born again. Its first cry will stimulate my mind, and the touch of its hand will rejuvenate this old body, and I will see in it a new receptacle into which I'll pour a minute grain of wisdom from the crucible of my life pounded by the pestle of my seventy-odd years.'

'Oh! Mr Burgess.' She now gripped his hand between both hers as she said, 'What would I have done without you all these years?'

'Being you, you would have managed very well, my dear.'

'Oh no, no. Years ago I was thrust into a different world, into a different class, and I viewed it as a servant because I was a servant; but when Mark took me into his life it was you who took my mind in hand, as it were. From our first meeting in the nursery when you realised I could read and write and you loaned me Voltaire's *Candide* — you remember? — and I told you I couldn't understand a word of it, and I didn't until years later, you took me under your wing. And now I can almost say with Candide's old woman, "So you see, I'm a woman of experience." '

Mr Burgess smiled appreciatively. 'Yes, Trotter, my dear, you have grown into a woman of experience. But I hope I don't end up like Candide's old tutor, Doctor Pangloss.' Then leaning forward again, he said, 'The word tutor reminds me I am very greedy for my inheritance. When may I collect the books?'

'At any time I should think, but I wouldn't venture out, not until we have a fine day. I'll arrange for Arthur to come and take you and bring back your treasures.'

'Thank you, my dear . . . Well now' — he leaned back — 'shall I start preparing some supper?'

'No, no.' She made play of keeping him in his seat by flapping her hand gently at him. 'Leave that to me.' And to this he answered, 'Just as you wish, my dear. Just as you wish.' Then bending to his side, he picked up a book from the floor, put his hand down the side of the couch to recover his spectacles, placed them on the end of his nose, and lost himself in the main love of his life.

And Tilly, after unpacking the bass bag into which Biddy had put enough food to see them over the next two days, set out a meal. When it was over and she had cleared away, she humped the two hampers and the boxes upstairs to the room under the eaves, and there she unpacked her things.

An hour later she saw the old man to his room, then cleared the books from the floor, banked down the fire, and once again mounted the stairs.

The attic was freezing cold but she did not scramble out of her clothes, and when finally she crept between the sheets and sank into the feather bed it smelt musty and damp, even though Katie had been over twice during the last few days and aired the sheets, and placed the hot cinder pan on the tick, just in case the bed should be needed for the present emergency.

Her knees drawn up, and lying on her side, her hands pinned tight under her oxters, she waited for the avalanche to overtake her. But strangely it didn't. It was as if all her tears had solidified to form a mountain that was now resting on top of her stomach pressing down on the child.

'Mark.' She said his name aloud; then again, 'Mark,' louder now. And she saw it winging away across the countryside over the frozen earth and dropping down through the loose black mould until it reached the wood of the coffin; then, forcing its way through, touched his lips and he became alive again. And there he was, his head on the pillow beside her, his eyes looking into hers through the lamplight, and his voice murmuring, 'You're beautiful, Tilly Trotter. You know that? You're beautiful.'

5

January slipped out on ice-laden roads, the frost so heavy that even at midday it settled on the brows and the eyelashes of humans and brought the cattle to a premature stillness of death.

Tilly spent most of her time sawing wood to keep the fire going. It was as if she were back in her childhood and early girlhood, only now she found no joy in the exercise.

When February brought the snow up to the window-sills she was cut off from all contact with those at the Manor for over a week, and she knew that if Mr Burgess had been left on his own he would never have survived this period. Living, as he had, the scholastic life, he paid little attention to the needs of the body, and the blankets he would have heaped on himself instead of braving the elements to fetch in wood would not have been sufficient to keep out the piercing merciless cold; added to which he would not have bothered about meals, except to make porridge and drink tea. So she told herself that at least one good thing had come out of her present situation.

Her stomach seemed to be rising daily; her body was noticing her weight. Physically she was feeling well enough, that is if she didn't take into account the misery in her heart and the perpetual cold, because the little house, its surroundings being bare of trees, was open to the weather on its four sides, and although the walls were fifteen inches thick they and the stone floor did not tend to engender warmth.

After the sun had shone for two days the thaw set in and there was movement on the roads once more; but not by horse or carriage, merely by those on foot. But they had to walk through drifts still half-way up their thighs.

When Arthur eventually managed to make his way to the cottage it was with the added burden of a bulky sack across his shoulders, and after he had thumped on the door and Tilly had opened it to him, he slid his burden from his back and pushed it into her arms before kicking the snow from his high boots and shaking it from the tails of his coat.

'Why! Arthur, what made you come out in weather like this?'

'Mam thought you would be starving. I'd better take me boots off, they're sodden.'

'No, no; come inside, you'll freeze.' She reached out her hand and gripped his arm and pulled him over the threshold, where he stood stamping his feet on the matting as he looked across the room to where Mr Burgess was sitting, his chair pulled close up to the hearth; and he called to him, saying simply, 'Snifter.'

'Yes, yes, indeed, Arthur, 'tis a snifter as you say; and a long, long snifter it's been. Do you think we've seen the end of it?'

'Not by a long chalk, Mr Burgess, not by a long chalk. The sky's laden with it again.'

'Come over to the fire.' Tilly beckoned him further into the room, but he hesitated, saying, 'I'm mucky, Tilly; I'll mess up the floor.'

'Well, it won't be the first time it's been messed up. Sit yourself down, Arthur.' There was a command in her voice. 'I'll make you a drink.'

She put the sack on the table, then looked at him and said, 'How did you manage to get this out?'

'She's gone, Tilly. Madam God Almighty went just afore the heavy fall. I tried to get in to tell you afore but I had to turn back. You'll never guess what.'

'Matthew's come?'

'Oh no! no! not Master Matthew but Master John. He came back from Scarborough; he had gone on there to get away from her; he had only been gone a week or so. Apparently he had had a letter from Master Matthew, it had been sent on to him from here, saying he'd like him to look after things until he could get back, never mentioned his sister. Of course, you

51

would likely know that Master Luke couldn't do anything about it, him being in the army. Anyway, the young 'un was simply over the moon. Katie said she heard him letting the young madam havin't hot and strong with hardly a flicker to his tongue. Oh, and how she went on. An' you know what? She was goin' to have her husband down and her sister-in-law, and she wasn't going to take any notice of the letter Master John had until, so Katie said, the solicitor had been informed. Well, Master John said he had, and that he was coming out to confirm things like. Eeh! me ma did laugh. As she said, the little madam went round the house as if she had been stung in the backside by a bee. I didn't know she hadn't a proper home of her own, Tilly, but lived with her in-laws, and that was why she wanted to play the madam back at the house. . . . Did you know that, Tilly?'

'Yes, I knew she lived with her . . . her husband's people.'

'It makes things clear, doesn't it?' Arthur looked towards Mr Burgess. 'I mean, why she wanted to stay on here.'

Mr Burgess smiled widely as he nodded and said, 'Yes, it certainly makes things clear. In-laws are noted for their inability to hand over power to either their sons or their daughters. Man's ego is not entirely man's alone, woman has a share of it, and with her she used it as a weapon.'

'Aye. Aye.' Arthur nodded at the old man, his face slightly blank, being unable, as usual, to follow his way of talking and reasoning, yet at the same time aware that the old man was in entire agreement with what he himself had been saying. He turned now and, looking at Tilly, said, 'Me ma wants to know how you're feelin', Tilly.'

'Oh, tell her I'm very well. Here — ' She handed him a bowl of hot soup and a shive of bread, saying, 'Get off your feet and drink that.'

Arthur lowered his stubby form down on to the wooden stool at the other side of the hearth, and as he gulped at the soup and chewed on the crusty bread he talked, giving snippets about the goings on during the past weeks in the house. And then, as he reached forward and put the bowl down on the corner of the table, he said, 'You could be coming back now, Tilly. Me ma says there could be every chance of you coming back.'

She was standing some way behind Mr Burgess's chair and she made a quick jerking movement with her head towards Arthur as she answered, 'Oh, I don't think that will be possible, Arthur; it would only cause more dissent among the family, and there's been enough of that already.'

Arthur, holding her gaze and taking the message indicated by her shaking head rather than what she had said, nodded at her as he got to his feet, muttering, 'Aye. Aye, I suppose you're right, Tilly. I suppose you're right. Well, I'll be off. Mr Burgess.' He bent stiffly forward, and Mr Burgess, as if coming out of a doze, said, 'Oh. Oh, yes, Arthur. It's been very nice seeing you. Give my regards to your mother.'

'I . . . I will, Mr Burgess. Yes, I will.'

Tilly walked with him to the door and when, pulling his cap tight down about his ears and turning the collar of his coat up to meet it, he said, 'Sorry, Tilly. I put me foot in it somehow, didn't I?' she answered, 'It's all right. Arthur.' Her voice was low. 'I think he would worry if he thought he was going to be left on his own. He's . . . he's a sick man, and he knows it. No matter if I had the opportunity of returning, I couldn't do it at present. In any case, I don't think it would be wise for me to go back there, not under the circumstances.' Her hand went involuntarily to her stomach, and he lowered his eyes from hers as he said, 'Perhaps you're right, Tilly. Perhaps you're right. But . . . but we miss you. Me ma misses you a lot. The house isn't the same. The work's bein' done but, as me ma said yesterday, not with good grace. You know — ' His straight lips slipped into a wide smile and he added, 'I remember what me da used to say. I was only a little bairn at the time, but he created a very strange picture in me mind about God and the devil 'cos he used to say if he had the option of working for God who would say, "Well done, thou good and faithful servant," or the devil who'd slap him on the back and say, "By lad! you've done a good job there," he knew for which one he'd work.'

As he went to turn away from her on a laugh he turned as

53

quickly again towards her, his hand across his mouth, saying, 'Not that I'm likin' you to the devil, Tilly.'

She was smiling widely herself now as she said, 'Well, if you're not, Arthur, you're having a very good try.'

'Aw, Tilly!' He flapped his hand towards her. 'So long. I'll see you again soon, that's if that holds up.' He pointed away into the distance to where the sky seemed to be hovering just above the hills.

She watched him until he had gone someway down the road before going in and closing the door. Oh, it was nice to see one of them again. Each one of the Drews seemed to belong to her, like a member of her family, the only family she had.

When she turned towards the fire and Mr Burgess, he was sitting up straight in his chair. Putting his hand out towards her, he said, 'Come here, my dear.' And when she stood in front of him, he blinked up at her through his watery eyes as he said, 'Now you must not consider me. If Master John asks you to go back you must do so. I'm all right. I'm not in my dotage yet and it's about time I took a hand in looking after myself.'

'Yes, it is.' She nodded her head towards him; then leaning forward, she pulled the shawl around his shoulders before pressing him back in the chair and adding, 'So get yourself well and on to your feet and trotting round again, and then we'll talk about where I'm going to go.'

'Oh, Trotter.' His head drooped towards his chest and there was a break in his voice as he murmured, 'I don't deserve you. I don't. I'm a selfish old man. I've been selfish all my life. All I've thought about are these.' He waved his hand slackly over the books on the little table to his side. 'You can say I've given them my life, and what use are they to me now? Inanimate things. All my life I have called them my companions but do they speak to me now and bring me comfort? All the knowledge I have garnered from them is not going to help me to die in peace. All they say to me is, don't go yet, enjoy me more. In the night they talk to me, Trotter, and ask what will happen to us when you're gone? Don't go, they say; we can keep you happy for years yet. And when I tell them I cannot stay much longer, they look at me blankly and not one of them says,

"Here, take my hand for comfort." There is only you, Trotter, who has ever held out a hand to me in comfort. The master, he was good and kind to me, but his goodness was of the mind, while yours comes from the heart.'

'Oh, my dear! My dear!' They were the only words she could speak as she pressed the white head against her waist. Presently releasing her hold on him, she dropped down on to her knees by his side and, gripping his blue-veined hands, she said, 'You're not going to die for a long time. You're going to get better; you're going to be the first to hear my child cry. You're going to nurse him . . . her . . . whatever, on your knee while I get on with my work. And another thing' — she shook the hands within her grasp — 'your books have been your true friends, don't desert them now.'

'My dear, dear, Trotter.' The tears were welling from the corner of his eyes and dropping slowly down the furrows of his cheeks. 'I once prophesied that you'd come into your own, didn't I?'

When she nodded at him he said, 'Well, I shall repeat that. One day you'll be a lady in your own right, Tilly Trotter. You are indeed a lady now, and that is true; but one day you'll be a lady in your own right.'

6

There was the promise of spring, the sun was shining and the air had lost its bitterness, although the snow still lay in brown-capped moulds against the hedges and the sides of the roads and there was time yet for other falls. Tilly remembered that two years ago they had been snowed up all over the Easter, but today was bright and warm and Mr Burgess was on his feet walking about the room, picking up this book and that and looking as if the spring was also bringing renewed life into his old bones.

She turned from putting the last of the logs from the wicker basket on to the fire and saw him standing gazing out of the window. 'Good to see the sun,' she said.

'Yes, yes, isn't it, my dear, the life-giving sun. And it has brought the children out.'

'Children?' She came to his side and, looking through one of the small panes, she saw three boys coming down the road. They were jumping and pushing each other and Mr Burgess remarked, 'Like lambs, the spring has got into their legs.'

She smiled as she turned away, went back to the fireplace, picked up the wicker basket and went down the room, through the small scullery, took her cloak from behind the door and went into the yard.

There were only two small outhouses and they were placed at the bottom of the yard. One was a closet which had a modern touch in that it had a wooden seat with a hole which was placed directly above the bucket. The other was a woodshed, only large enough to hold a sawing block and with space for a single stack of logs around its walls. The walls were now two-thirds bare and they told her that before long she must get them covered again, because soon she would not be able to hump wood or saw. Arthur was kind but it was only at odd times he could get away, apart from his monthly leave.

She had half filled her skip when her body became still, and it was still bent when she turned her head and cocked her ear towards the door. And now she felt the colour draining from her face, in fact seeming to drain from her whole body as the word floated over the cottage towards her: 'Witch! Witch!'

Aw no! not again. She closed her eyes for a moment before hurrying towards the back of the house. But she hesitated at the door, then went swiftly round the side, there to see the three young boys standing on the roadway. They had their eyes riveted on the front door, and so they did not at first notice her as she stood between the corner of the cottage and the privet hedge that marked the boundary of the small piece of adjoining land, and she listened to them chanting:

'Witch, witch, witch,
Come out without a stitch;
Tis time you learned
You're going to be burned,
Witch, witch, witch.'

The two smaller boys had snowballs in their hands and they pelted them towards the door. It was the biggest of the three who, finding a large stone in the snow, threw it with perfect aim towards the window.

At the sound of the breaking glass she ran forward and the boys, expecting the front door to open, were for the moment petrified at the sight of her, for they saw an extremely tall creature flying towards them, her head hooded and the sides of her black cloak spread wide.

The biggest boy was the first to turn and run, but the other two, springing out of their fear-filled, almost petrified state, turned to each other as they made to scamper away, and so collided. As they stumbled, Tilly's hands grabbed at their collars; and it would have been no surprise if they had there and then died from fright.

Her arms were thin but still extremely strong, the result of the saw bench and the manual work she had undertaken in the mine, and so she shook them, staring as she did so from one face to the other.

It was the bigger one who found his tongue, and he spluttered, ' 'Twa . . . 'twasn't me, missis. I . . . I never broke your window. 'Twas Billy.'

'What is your name?'

'T . . . Taylor, missis.'

'Where are you from?' But need she ask, for she knew the answer before he spluttered, 'Th . . . the village.'

'And you?' She now shook the smaller boy until his head wobbled on his shoulders. 'What is your name?'

'Pear . . . Pearson, missis, Tommy Pearson.'

Pearson. There was only one Pearson in the village, at least there had been only one twelve years ago, and his name was Tom Pearson and he'd been a friend to her.

'Is your father called Tom?' she demanded.

'Yes, missis.'

'Well now' — she bent her head over him — 'you are to go back now and tell him what you have done. Do you hear me?'

'Ye . . . yes, missis.'

'I shall know whether you have or not. You understand?'

'Yes, missis.'

'Tell him he has to give you a good thrashing.'

The 'Yes, missis' did not come as promptly now but the boy gulped, then muttered on a whisper, 'Aye. Yes, missis.'

'As for you' — she now shook the other boy — 'tell me this: Who sent you along here? Who told you to come?'

'Billy McGrath, him.' He jerked his head backwards as his arm swung outwards towards the boy standing some way down the road, and Tilly lifted her head and stared over the distance. A McGrath . . . a McGrath again, the son of one of the remaining brothers. It couldn't be Steve's boy because Steve had left the district years ago, and Steve, too, had been her friend. The trouble with Steve had been he'd wanted to be more than a friend, as Hal had. That was the reason he had killed Hal; well, part of it, for he had been bullied and ill-treated by his elder brother from when he was a child. And now here was another generation of McGraths starting on her. Surely it wasn't going to begin all over again. Aw no!

As if in answer to her question, the young McGrath yelled now as he danced from one side of the road to the other, 'Witch! Witch! you're an old witch an' a murderer. You killed me Uncle Hal, you did, you did. But me granny 'll get you. She says she will an' she will. Witch! Witch!'

It was on the last 'witch' delivered by the boy at the pitch of his lungs that the rider came round the bend in the road and reined up behind him, and the boy turned and jumped into the ditch, and there stood looking up at the man on the horse.

'What's your game, boy?'

'Getting at the witch, Mr Bentwood.'

The rider lifted his eyes and looked along the road to where Tilly still stood holding the younger boys by their collars and, taking in the scene, he bent down towards the young McGrath and, his whip cracking over the lad's head, he said, 'Now get back, you young scoundrel, to where you belong, and if I catch you along this road again I'll skin you. Do you hear me? And tell that to your father, and your granny. Understand?'

The boy made no answer but he sidled along the ditch away from the rider as Simon Bentwood walked his horse towards Tilly.

Tilly did not raise her head, but she looked at the boys and she said, 'Remember what I told you!' and on this she brought their heads together with a crack that could have been much harder had she cared. Then releasing them and pushing them from her, she watched them turn and run down the road, their palms to their foreheads, before she herself looked up at the man on the horse. And what she said now was, 'I am quite capable, Mr Bentwood, of managing my own affairs. I will thank you not to take any part in this.'

'Aw, Tilly!' He put the whip into the hand that was holding the reins, then shaded his eyes for a moment with his free palm, and when he looked at her again it was some seconds before he said, 'Can't you let bygones be bygones, for after all there's neither of us turned out to be a saint?'

What he said was quite true. He had had an affair with a married woman, and she had had an affair with a married man.

It could be said that she was worse than him, for her affair had lasted for twelve years whereas his had quickly fizzled out. The man-crazy Lady Myton had tired of him, and that, she understood, hadn't been long after the day she had found them naked in the barn together.

She had often wondered why that discovery should have hit her so hard. Perhaps it was the shattering of an ideal, a dream, her first love. And he had been her first love, for she had loved Simon Bentwood from the moment she had set eyes on him when she was five years old. On the day he broke the news that he was going to be married and that he wished her to come and dance at his wedding she told herself her heart was broken. But she had been given proof on his wedding night that she still meant something to him, for on that night he left his bride and came to her rescue and saved her from being raped by Hal McGrath. When the McGraths burned down her granny's cottage and he took both her and her granny into the shelter of his home, her love for him increased, if that were possible, and this had not escaped his wife.

When he later found out that he had married the wrong woman he had wanted to set her up in a house in Shields, but she was having none of that. She had even preferred working down the mine rather than being known as his kept woman.

She was already established on the staff in the Manor when she heard of his wife's death and was amazed to know that this had happened some weeks previously. The reason for his non-appearance she had put down to his sense of decency. But no sense of decency had needed to be considered on her part when she decided to go and commiserate with him on his loss, while at the same time knowing that she was a hypocrite and was only hoping that she would be strong enough to contain her joy. But what did she find when she reached the farm? She found him in the act of love, or so called, with the very lady who had been the means of ruining the master.

It was because of Mark's affair with Lady Myton that his wife had left him and taken their four children with her, leaving him as desolate as Simon Bentwood had left her. Yet it wasn't desolate, until she had gone willingly to the master's bed that she realised, as Mr Burgess was so apt at quoting, there were so many different kinds of love.

Looking up at the figure on the horse she noted how changed he was from the man she had known. There was the suspicion of jowls to his broad face meeting the flesh of his neck pressing upwards out of his high collar; only the top button of his riding coat fastened, and the gap in his waistcoat from which his stomach protruded and seemed to rest on the saddle in front of him were all evidence of the physical change in him. Even his eyes were not the same. They lay in pouches of flesh and were slightly bloodshot.

She thought, with amazement, he was only forty years old, and then he was remarking on the change in her. Bending from the saddle and looking down into her face he said, 'You've changed, I can see that. You know, we've never been so close for over twelve years.'

'We all change with the years.' Her tone was as cold as the air.

'Oh yes, yes' — he patted his stomach — 'I'm not the man I was. Is that what you're meaning?'

'My words had no special meaning, I was merely making a statement, an obvious statement.'

'Huh!' — his chin jerked upwards — 'we do speak correctly, don't we? Of course, you've been mixing with the gentry for a long time and naturally it rubs off. And then, you have your private tutor.' He turned his head quickly in the direction of the cottage, where Mr Burgess could be seen standing.

When she did not take umbrage at his remark but returned his gaze, saying quietly, 'Yes, I have been very fortunate. It does not fall to everyone's lot to meet two such men,' he jerked at the reins and caused the horse to rear before he brought out on a growl, 'Oh for God's sake, Tilly, come off your high horse, be yourself, your memory's short.'

Her voice was now as angry as his as she glared up at him and replied, 'No, my memory isn't short, Simon Bentwood, it's very long. And looking back down it, I have nothing to thank you for.'

'No? Well, let me tell you, Tilly, that's where you're mistaken. I kept you and your grandparents alive for years with the sovereign brought them every month. The stolen money had run out long afore that. But there's more let me tell you. My marriage might have got off to a good start if it hadn't been for seeing to you, like the bloody fool I was. And anyway, what have you done that you can hold your head up while I should bow mine? That affair with her ladyship was over and done with as quick as she finished it with your fancy man. She liked variety, did her ladyship, but even so she didn't cause half the scandal in the county that you did when you went to bed with Sopwith. And you're still managing to set fire to scandal, for after twelve years what has he left you? A bellyful, and thrown out on your backside into the bargain, because the family hates your guts. And another thing I'll tell you, although I chased that little beggar of a McGrath away, it isn't the last you'll hear of them because old Ma McGrath wanted to build a bonfire the day they knew you had been shown the door. And if I know her she's not finished with you yet, and when they start on you again, the villagers as a whole, because you spell bad luck for the lot of them, who will you run to this time, eh?'

Her eyes were steady, her voice equally so, as she gazed back into his infuriated face and said quietly, 'Not you, Simon, never you.'

Again he pulled the horse into a rearing position; but then, all anger seeming to seep from him, he brought the animal once more to a standstill and, his voice now holding a deep sadness, he spoke her name.

'Tilly! aw Tilly!' he said; then leaning forward, he added, 'I'd give anything — do you hear? — anything in this wide world to put the clock back.'

A tinge of pity threaded her thinking and caused her to pause and change the tart reply that was on her tongue, and what she said now was, 'That's impossible, Simon, and you know it.'

'Could we be friends, Tilly?'

'No, Simon' — she shook her head slowly — 'not again.'

He turned his body in the saddle and, leaning towards the horse's head, he stroked its neck twice before saying, 'When the child comes, what then, who's to see to you?'

'Myself Simon. Always myself.'

'You'll find it hard; you're a lone woman and the whole place is agen you.'

'The world is wide, I won't remain here always, just as long as Mr Burgess needs me.'

Again he was bending over the horse's neck, and stroking it, and he said, 'I'd be good to you, Tilly. I would take it and bring it up as my own.'

The swift angry retort 'You bring up Mark's child as your own, never!' stopped at her lips; then she bowed her head. And her tight lips and her attitude must have given him hope, because he was leaning well out of the saddle towards her when she raised her eyes to him and said, 'Thank you, Simon, but I have no intention of marrying.'

'You might change your mind.'

'I don't think so.'

'You know something, Tilly?' His voice had lost its softness again. 'I could have been married twelve times over during these last years. But I waited, aye, I waited, hoping for this moment. I felt sure something would happen sooner or later, and it has. And you know something, Tilly? I'm going on waitin'. I was going to finish by saying you'll need me afore I need you, but that would be wrong. I've always needed you, and I always will, and I'll be here when you whistle.' He gave a wry twisted smile now as, changing the last word of the song, he said, 'Whistle an' I'll come to ye, me lass. Remember that, Tilly, you've just got to whistle. Get up there!' He brought his heels sharply into the horse's belly, and it kicked up the snow-covered stones in the road before going into a trot.

She did not stay and watch him ride away but turned swiftly and went up the path, round the corner and to the woodshed again, and there she finished filling the skip before returning to the house.

But as soon as she came into the room she dropped the skip and hurried towards the couch where Mr Burgess was sitting, his hand in a bowl of warm water.

'Aw no! you're cut.'

'Just a splinter, just a splinter. It's all right. I put some salt in the water, it's cleansed.'

She looked at the towel on the seat beside him, saying, 'It's bled a lot.'

'Just a little. It's stopped now.'

'The devil!'

'Village boys, were they?'

'Yes, one of the McGraths, a new generation.'

'And the rider was the farmer?'

'Yes.'

'Come to rescue you?' He raised his wrinkled lids and smiled up at her.

'You could say that.'

'Did he get a flea in his ear?'

'Yes, you could say that too.'

'He wants you to marry him and save you disgrace?'

She patted his shoulder and nodded, 'Right again.' She left him and went to the end of the room and picked up the skip of logs, and as she placed them near the fireside he said soberly, 'I wish you were back in the Manor, you're not safe here. I wonder why Master John hasn't called?'

Master John called the very next day. He, too, came on horseback and when Tilly heard the sound of the horse's hooves on the road she hurried to the window and stood to one side looking out from behind the lace curtains. Upon ascertaining that it wasn't Simon Bentwood, she drew in a long relieving breath and, turning to Mr Burgess who was dozing before the fire, she said, 'It's Master John; he must have heard you yesterday.'

From the open door she watched the young man tying the horse to the gate-post, and she went over the step to greet him, saying, 'How nice to see you.'

Coming swiftly forward, he held out his hands and his mouth opened wide before he could bring out, 'And . . . and you, Trotter.'

She said formally now, 'It's a lovely day, isn't it?'

' 'Tis, Trotter, 'tis . . . Ah! there you are, Mr Bur . . . Burgess.' He was crossing the room now and when he took the old man's outstretched hand he added, 'You're looking very well, ve . . . ve . . . very well.'

'I am feeling very well, thanks to my good nurse.' Mr Burgess inclined his head towards Tilly and she, looking at John, said, 'What can I get you to drink?'

'What have you? Brandy, sherry, p . . . p . . . port, liq . . . liqueur?'

She flapped her hand at him playfully. 'Bring it down to tea or soup and you can have your choice.'

'Tea then, Tro . . . Trotter. Thank you very much.'

'Do sit down. . . . Here, give me your coat.'

He handed her his coat and hat and riding crop and when he was seated opposite the old man, Mr Burgess said, 'Your visit portends good news I hope?'

'Oh well.' John turned his head first one way, then another, and his eyes came to rest on Tilly, where she was coming from the delf rack with a tea-tray in her hands, and he flushed slightly as he said, 'No . . . not really. N . . . n . . . nothing I'm afraid that can . . . can be of any help at the mo . . . moment, but I thought it b . . . b . . . better to . . . to come and explain.'

She laid the tray on the table, then stood looking at him; and he, addressing her slowly now, said, 'When Jessie Ann left I wa . . . wanted you to come back to the house, and I told her this was one of the fir . . . first things I was going to do. It was th . . . then she' — his mouth now opened wide and he closed his eyes and his head bobbed before he brought out the next words on a rush — 'informed me that she had already wr . . . written to Matthew telling him what she had do . . . done, so I was, well, sort of stum . . . stumped, Trotter. You understand?'

She inclined her head towards him and waited, and he glanced at Mr Burgess before returning his gaze to her and going on, 'I wrote immediately to Matthew and explained the situation and str . . . str . . . stressed your — ' he blinked rapidly now and, his mouth once again open wide, he said, 'Con . . . condition, and only yesterday I got a reply from him, in which he states he's c . . . c . . . coming home. He should be back about August or September because Uncle — ' Again he glanced at Mr Burgess, explaining now, 'He is not really our uncle because he is . . . is . . . was my grandmother's half-

65

brother and the youngest of the f . . . f . . . family.' He laughed now, his mouth stretching wide illuminating his pleasant features as he ended, 'I do . . . don't know what relationship that makes us to him b . . . b . . . but having n . . . no children of his own, he addresses us as nephews. Matthew seems to l . . . l . . . like him very much, he says he's a fine man. I don't really think that Matthew wants to leave Texas but anyway he is c . . . coming back.'

'Texas? Texas!' Mr Burgess nodded his head now. 'What a state for Matthew to choose to live in! It has been called the state of adventurers, and a slave state; everybody seems to want it and nobody seems to want it. After the tragedy of the Alamo and the massacres that followed you'd have thought politicians both Mexican, American and British would have allowed it to remain an independent republic. We wanted it to remain independent' — he nodded from John to Tilly now — 'oh yes, it was to our benefit those days that she should remain independent. Now Master John' — he leant towards the young man — 'I'm going to ask you something, the same question that I asked your brother not all those many years ago in the schoolroom. What was the Alamo?'

John cast a laughing glance now towards Tilly, then said, 'I . . . I think it was a mission chapel, sir, in which the American soldiers took refuge in the w . . . w . . . war against the Mex . . . Mex . . . Mexicans.'

'Yes, yes, you're right. But you know what the answer Master Luke gave me to that question when I asked him what the Alamo was, eh?'

'I have no idea, s . . . sir.'

'He said it was a river that ran into the Mississippi. Can you imagine that?'

'Yes, yes; I can w . . . well imagine that, sir. Luke was never v . . . very strong on history. When I saw him last I said I hoped he has a g . . . g . . . good sergeant when he is due to go to India and a g . . . g . . . guide book.'

They all laughed; then Tilly, stirring the tea in the teapot with a long-handled spoon, asked, 'Are you home for good, Master John?'

'It . . . it all depends, Tr . . . Trotter. I . . . I hope so but I cannot say anything def . . . definite until Matthew comes. I have a strong f . . . f . . . feeling he might want to return to America. If that is so I . . . I would be pleased to stay and se . . . see to things.' He turned his head now and looked at Mr Burgess as he ended, 'I di . . . didn't really enjoy university life, sir. I'm s . . . s . . . sorry.'

Tilly handed the two men their tea and when presently the conversation became general and Mr Burgess's head began to nod, John made a signal towards Tilly and, rising softly from the seat, he picked up his hat and coat and tip-toed towards the door, and she followed him.

Outside on the path, she asked a question that had been in her mind since John had mentioned the letter he had received from his brother. 'Did Matthew make any reference to me, John?'

The young man struck at the top of his leather gaiters with his crop before saying, 'No, Trotter. I explained things to him but he m . . . m . . . made no ref . . . reference in his reply. You see' — he looked at her shyly — 'I asked him if I c . . . could take you back in the position of housekeeper because th . . . the place needs a housekeeper, Trotter. B . . . Biddy is very good, and K . . . K . . . Katie and the rest, but there is no gui . . . guiding hand. I wish he had mentioned it.'

'Don't worry, John.' She put her hand out and touched his sleeve. 'I'm sure Biddy won't let things slide. As for me, well, I'm all right here.'

His face flushing slightly now and his stammer more pronounced, he said, 'It isn't the . . . the pl . . . pl . . . place for a ba . . . baby to be born, Trotter.'

'Many have been born in worse places than this, John.'

'Yes, undou . . . dou . . . doubtedly, but what I'm thinking is the ch . . . child will be my half brother or s . . . s . . . sister.'

'It's nice of you to look at it in that way. You are so kind, John, I wish there were more like you.'

'St . . . stammer or no?' He was laughing now.

'St . . . stammer or no.'

'I worry about the st . . . stammer, Trotter.' He again struck

67

his gaiters. 'No young l . . . l . . . lady is going to p . . . p . . . put up with me.'

'Nonsense! nonsense! You've got a fine figure and you have a face to go with it. When the right one comes along how you speak won't trouble her.'

'Not even when I have to say I . . . I lo . . . love you?'

She looked at him sadly for a moment. That was one of his most endearing points, he could make a joke of his affliction, even while it hurt him, even tore at him as now when presenting him with a bleak and loveless future. She wanted to put her arms around him and say, 'I love you,' for she did, like a mother, because she was the first one to have shown him love even while smacking his bottom.

Copying his light mood, she leant towards him now and gripping his arm tightly, said, 'They're positive in the village that I'm a witch, and your father at times said I was too, and sometimes I believe it myself. I believe that if I wish for a thing hard enough it'll come true, and so, from now on, I'm going to conjure up the image of the young lady who is going to throw her heart at your feet.'

'Oh, Tro . . . Trotter!' His mouth wide open, his head back, he gulped and said again, 'Tro . . . Trotter you're a pr . . . pr . . . priceless gem. I've always underst . . . st . . . stood why Father loved you. Good-bye, Tr . . . Trotter, I'll keep you in . . . formed. I'll p . . . p . . . pop over often from now on.'

'Good-bye, John.' She watched him mount the horse and answered his wave before turning to go back into the cottage.

Mr Burgess was fast asleep now, his head resting against the high padded arm of the couch. Softly, she made her way up the stairs and when she reached the bedroom under the eaves she sat on the side of the low bed and after taking in a deep breath she dropped her head forward into her hands and the tears spurted through her fingers. She had experienced loneliness before, but never like this. Within the last few minutes it had become intensified, the result of that kind young man bringing the essence of the house with him, the house which had become to her as home, and the feeling brought from her the plea, Mark! Mark! what am I going to do?

7

Tilly's baby was born at five minutes past midnight on the 27th of June, 1853. It was a boy, and when Biddy held him up by the feet and smacked his blood-stained buttocks he yelled, as any boy would, and when Katie stumbled up the steep stairs with a dish of water in her hands, her mother cried at her, 'It's a lad! Here, put that down and take him while I see to her.'

Peering down through the lamplight on to the sweat-streaming face of the young woman she thought of and loved as if she were of her own flesh, she said softly, 'Look lass, you've got a son, and he's a whopper. Lie still, you're all right.'

Tilly touched her son's face, then closed her eyes and only now when she let out a long weary breath did her stomach subside, its walls seeming to touch her backbone. She was tired, so very tired. It had been a long struggle, thirty-six hours in fact, but she had a son. She and Mark had a son. 'Oh, Mark! Mark! I wonder if you know.'

'What do you say, lass?'

'Do you think he knows, Biddy?'

'Who, lass?'

'Mark . . . the master.'

'He'll know all right, lass. He'll know. Now I'm just gona tidy you up, then off you go to sleep because if I know anything you need it. An' that fellow there's gona be at you afore you know where you are.'

'Thank you, Biddy. Thank you.' There was no strength in the clasp of her hand now. . . .

The daylight was coming through the small window and in the light she could see Biddy holding the child out towards her. She took it into her arms and when it nuzzled her breast

Biddy said, 'Now you know you're a mother, lass.'

She looked down on her son and was surprised to see that he had hair, and more surprised still to see that his face was an almost exact replica of his father's every feature in miniature. She gazed in wonder at the small hand kneading her breast. It was broad, the fingers square. She laughed as she looked up at Biddy, saying now, 'If he doesn't change there won't be much trouble in identifying the father.'

'No; you've said it. Even Katie remarked on it right away.'

'Will he change much?'

'Oh, he'll change, they all do, yet at the same time remain the same, if you know what I mean.'

'No, I don't' — Tilly laughed gently — 'but I follow you.'

'Master John's been along.'

'So early?'

'Well, it's on seven o'clock now.'

'How are they managing up there?'

'Oh, we've got it all arranged. He said we had to see to you, so I've fixed everything. Arthur's trotting us back and forward in the wagon. Then in a few days' time when you're feeling more like yourself Phyllis's girl, Betty, she's coming over to stay with you until you're nearly on your feet. She's a sensible lass.'

'But I thought she was over at the Redheads?'

'She left when her bond was up. Couldn't stand the cook. Sixteen hours a day was a bit too much for her, for anybody, but for a ten-year-old, well her legs were swollen as big as a porker's hock. Master John said I can take her on and start her in the kitchen. . . .'

It was later that day Tilly heard a knock on the door and when, later, Biddy came upstairs but didn't mention who had called, she asked, 'Who was that at the door?'

'Oh, just some lass. Got the wrong house I think.'

'Wrong house? Someone starting service?'

'No, no.' Biddy was busying herself at the wash-hand-stand tucked into the corner under the sloping roof. 'Gentry, I'd say; come on her horse.'

'Who was she looking for?'

'Somebody . . . oh, somebody of the name of Smith.'

Tilly's brows came together. 'Smith? There's no Smith round here, not that the gentry would visit. And they wouldn't be living in a cottage like this, would they? Now who was it, Biddy?'

Biddy turned to her. 'I've told you. As true as I'm standing here it was a young girl on a horse, but she had come to the wrong house. You don't believe me?'

'It's very strange.' Tilly shook her head.

'There's lots of strange things happen in the world and that to me isn't one of them. She's just a lass, or a lady if you must have it, who mistook a house. Likely she was visiting a dependant or some such. I hope that when I'm in my dotage you'll come and visit me at the lodge.'

'Oh, shut up.' Tilly turned her head to the side and Biddy, making use of one of her boys' jocular retorts, said, 'I would if I had a shop, a music hall, or a coal mine.'

All Tilly could reply to this was a huh! accompanied by a shake of her head with closed eyes, which she opened quickly at the sound of a heavy tread at the bottom of the stairs. They looked at each other, and Tilly said, 'Go and give him a hand, Biddy, he'll break his neck one of these times.'

'The quicker you're downstairs the better, lass.' Biddy jerked her head. 'This is the third time since last night an' I'm puffed out helping him through that hole in the floor.'

As Tilly watched Biddy lower herself gingerly on to her knees and extend a hand through the open hatchway from which the stairs descended, she marvelled at the compensations life offered one; for every two enemies she had she had a friend, and as Mr Burgess was always quoting, one ounce of good outweighed a pound of evil. If only that ounce of good would outweigh the void inside her, fill it up and take away this great sense of loneliness, for even the child as yet had not entered the void.

What if it never filled the void; what if time would offer no replacement? Time erased all pain, they said.

'There you are, my dear.' Mr Burgess was bending over her, smiling down on them both, and as he so often did he seemed to pick up her thoughts, for he said, 'You'll never be lonely again. He'll bring love into your life. You'll see.'

8

The child was three months old. He was a lusty infant, good-tempered, crying only when he was hungry, when it was more of a whine than a cry. He gurgled at every face that hung above him, particularly that of Mr Burgess whose sparse beard had an attraction for his fingers.

The old man seemed to have lost the new life that came in with the spring and he now spent most of his mornings in bed and his afternoons dozing by the fire.

Tilly had to keep the clothes basket, which served as a cradle for the baby, well out of his way, for in his sudden spurts towards his books on the shelves he was apt to stumble over anything in front of him that was not any higher than his knees.

Sometimes she could go almost a week without seeing any-one other than Mr Burgess, the child, and a quick visit from Arthur bringing some dainties from the kitchen. But on this particular day she had three visitors.

The first one came in the morning and he was Tom Pearson. When she opened the door to him she could not hide her sur-prise. She had not seen anyone from the village, except the children, for years. The Manor had protected her like a for-tress. And she had no need to go through the village ever; whenever she went into Shields, or as far away as Newcastle, she went by coach along the main road.

'Mr Pearson!'

'Aye, Tilly. It is a long time since we met.'

'Yes, yes, it is.' She did not invite him in because Mr Burgess was still asleep, but she stepped towards him, drawing the door closed behind her, and as she did so he said, 'You'll be wondering why I'm here, or why I haven't come afore.'

She was puzzled for a moment until he added, 'My young 'un . . . I only heard yesterday of what he got up to some months back. He let slip something and I whacked the rest out of him. I'm sorry, Tilly.'

'Oh, it's all right, Mr Pearson. I should say I'm used to it by now, but somehow I feel I'll never get used to it.'

' 'Tisn't likely. So unfair. I've said that all along, 'tis so unfair. But they're ignorant an' they breed ignorance. That young McGrath is a chip off the old block, and I've warned my Tommy that if I catch him runnin' round with him again I'll take the skin off him. Anyway, how are you, Tilly?'

'I'm very well, thank you, Mr Pearson.'

'An' . . . an' the bairn, can I ask after it?'

'Yes, and thank you. And he's very well too.'

'I'm glad to hear that.' He sighed now. 'Bairns . . . well, they're a blessin' and a curse, all in the same breath. My eldest, Bobby, he's heading for America next week.'

'Really!'

'Aye. All happened through gettin' into conversation with some fellow on the quay at Newcastle last year. The fellow was off to join his brother, who was working in some factory picking up money like nuggets he said. I'll believe that when I see it, but you can't stop them once they get something in their head like that.'

'Well perhaps he will make his fortune and then send for you.'

'Not me, Tilly, not me; I'm past pipe dreams, me. And I can't get his mother hardly over the doorstep, never mind America. She's even afeared of the few horses and carriages an' the like in the village.'

Tilly merely nodded now. She had heard years ago that Mrs Pearson was afraid of anything that moved on the roads, and that she wouldn't even let the children have a cat or a dog in the house in case they came to harm.

'Well, I just thought I'd come and tell you, Tilly, it was none of my doings or with my knowledge he came along pesterin' you.'

73

'No, I'm sure of that, Mr Pearson.'

'And while I'm at it I can tell you that I'm sorry for your plight.'

'There's no need, Mr Pearson, I'm quite comfortable.'

'But it can't be the same, lass, not like up there.' He jerked his head and his hand at the same time in the direction in which the Manor lay. She made no answer to this, and so, after shuffling his feet on the rough path, he said, 'I'll be off then, Tilly, an' good luck always in whatever you do.'

'Thank you, Mr Pearson. And thank you for coming.'

'Aye. Aye.' He bobbed his head at her, then went marching off down the road.

He'd always been for her, had Mr Pearson. She remembered the couple of rabbits he had left outside in the shed before the cottage was burned down. At first she had thought Steve had put them there. . . . Steve. She didn't know what had happened to Steve; she only hoped he was happy and had found a nice girl and settled down. He should have married Katie. Katie had liked him, more than liked him.

The second visitor was more surprising still. The baby had come to the end of its midday meal and was lying contentedly in her arms, its pink cheek against her warm breast, when she heard the sound of a horse being brought to a stop. Quickly she put the child in the basket, covered her breast, buttoned up her blouse, then went to the window, there to see a young lady walking towards the front door.

She let her knock before she went and opened it, and she stared at the young person who stared at her, and they both showed surprise. It was the visitor who spoke first. 'I . . . I must have made a mistake again, but . . . but they told me that this was the cottage, a . . . a Mr Burgess's cottage.'

'Yes, that's right. Do you wish to see him? He's not very well at present.'

'No! no!' The young lady shook her head so vigorously that the feather in her velour hat bobbed up and down.

When she did not go on to explain whom she wished to see, Tilly's eyes narrowed as she stared at her. She could be pretty. She had a round heart-shaped face and warm brown eyes; her lips, although wide, were well shaped, but the face missed prettiness because of its expression. She guessed that the girl was around eighteen years old but the look on her face, given off by the expression of her eyes and the drooping corners of the mouth, was that of someone deeply aggrieved, not angry, but hurt. She was speaking now, her words hesitant, 'I . . . I don't know what to say but . . . but perhaps it is your mother I am looking for.'

'My mother?' Tilly's gaze narrowed even more now. She repeated. 'My mother? My mother has been dead for many years.'

'Someone called Trotter, a Tilly Trotter.'

'Well, you have found Tilly Trotter because that is my name. Why do you want to see me?'

'You!' The girl seemed for a moment as if she was about to step backwards; then shaking her head, she said, 'I'm sorry; they must have been mistaken.'

'Who are they?'

'Oh, well, it's hard to explain.'

Tilly's voice was stiff now as she said, 'Well, try. I would like to understand why you wish to see me. And who sent you here?'

'No . . . no one sent me here, but I heard them talking. It was the maids.'

'Whose maids?'

'My grandmama's and aunt's. My grandmama is Mrs McGill of Felton Hall, and I am Anna McGill.'

'Felton Hall?' Tilly's eyes now opened wide. Felton Hall was all of eight or nine miles away, beyond Fellburn, beyond Gateshead. She had heard, as everyone in the county had, of Felton Hall because Mrs McGill's only son and his wife had been lost at sea last year. This girl must be their daughter.

She said quietly, 'And what had your grandmother's maids to say about me?'

The girl now hung her head as she said, 'There . . . there must be a mistake, I must have misunderstood them. I . . . I suppose it was because I . . . I felt so desperate, I became stupid and . . . and clutched at any straw.'

75

Tilly continued to look at the now bowed head for some seconds before she said, 'Please come in.' When the girl hesitated, she said again, 'Please.'

Once inside the room and the door closed, Tilly moved her forward with a motion of her hand to the easy chair set to the right of the fireplace. Mr Burgess was not in his usual place on the couch, not having yet risen from bed.

Seating herself on the couch opposite the girl, Tilly said, 'Why are you in need of help and why did you think that I would be able to afford you that help?'

Unblinking, the young girl stared at Tilly; then slowly her hands, going up to her neck, swung aside the white silk scarf that almost reached one ear, and as she unfolded it she exposed the deep purple stain running from the lobe of the left ear, under the chin and almost to the middle of it, then spread downwards until it disappeared into the collar of her riding jacket, and as she turned her head slightly so she showed where it covered her neck right up to the hair line. Her voice almost a whisper now, she said, 'It . . . it goes down to the top of my breast and halfway across my shoulders. I . . . I cannot wear an evening gown or . . . or go out like . . . like other young people.'

Tilly looked into the eyes before her. She seemed to draw the sorrow into herself and in this moment and for the only time in her life she wished that she was a witch and had the power to erase the hideous birthmark. It was no use offering polite platitudes to this girl whose face had aged well beyond her years.

She watched the girl winding the scarf about her neck again and listened to the murmur of her voice as she said, 'It wasn't so bad when I lived in Norfolk. I met so few people there. I had a private tutor and I rarely went out beyond the grounds. My parents did not entertain and they took their holidays alone. But now, this last year coming to live with Grandmama, there is so much going on, so much activity, coming and going, she says I should accept it. What cannot be cured must be endured is her slogan. One night she made me come downstairs in an evening gown, my shoulder bare. Everyone was embarrassed, except her. That . . . that was the night I tried to jump out of

76

the window. My Aunt Susan caught me. She understands, my aunt, but not my grandmama, and so when I heard this maid talking about — ' She shook her head now and bowed it deep on her chest.

'About me being a witch?'

The head was slowly raised and the eyes looked into hers for a moment before she said, 'Yes; but . . . but you're not, are you?'

'No, I am not.'

'I can see that; no witch could look like you.'

'What was the name of the maid who said I was a witch?'

'Short, I think, Maggie Short.'

'It would be.' She smiled at the girl now. 'You see, I was the means of getting her aunt, who was cook at the Manor, dismissed because of her thieving, and apparently she and her niece, Maggie, still follow my career, hoping for my complete downfall. . . . What did you expect me to do for you?'

'I don't know. Touch me perhaps and it would disappear.'

'I take you to be an intelligent girl; you know that couldn't happen.'

'Yes, one part of me knows but the other part, the painful part, keeps hoping for miracles, or just one miracle. They . . . they said it would fade with the years, but it seems to get deeper.'

'You know what I think?'

'No.'

'I think in part your grandmother is right. Oh please!' She lifted her hand against the look on the girl's face. 'I don't mean that you should wear evening dress and expose your shoulders, but there is no need to cover up your neck. You see, a moment ago when your head was level all I saw of the mark was the stain coming from your ear down on to your neck, I didn't see it under your chin because you've got quite a broad jaw-line. You could wear clothes, at least daytime clothes, that would almost cover up the defect, a boned lace collar, a starched frill, so many things.'

'Do you think so? I mean, you don't notice it so much if I keep my head level or slightly forward?'

'Yes, that's what I mean. And you must smile more. You're very pretty, you know.'

'Oh no! My . . . my mother said that I was un. . . .' She stopped and turned her head away, and Tilly now put in, 'I don't know what your mother said but I'm telling you you are very pretty. You also have a very good figure, and have some way to develop yet I imagine. How old are you?'

'Eighteen . . . and a half,' she added as if giving a weight to her maturity. Then as if taking her mind off herself she looked about her and said, 'I've never seen so many books except in the library at home, and then they were mostly in glass cases. These look very used.' She smiled faintly now.

'Yes, my friend Mr Burgess, who was tutor at the Manor for some years, is a great reader. At the moment he's in bed. He doesn't rise very early because he's getting old and isn't too well, but I'm sure he would have been very pleased to meet you. He's a highly intelligent and amusing man, also a very discerning one. . . . Would you care to come again?'

'Oh . . . yes . . . yes.' The words were drawn out. 'So kind of you. I . . . I've never felt so good, I mean . . . well, so happy — and no, that isn't the word — comforted perhaps is a better word . . . before, ever.'

Tilly rose to her feet now, saying, 'Well, shall we do things in the proper manner? Would you care to come for tea on Saturday, Miss McGill?'

'I . . . I should be delighted, Miss . . . Mrs Trotter.' The hesitation had come as the girl glanced down on the sleeping baby whose presence until now she had pointedly ignored.

'You were right first time, it is Miss Trotter.'

They were both walking towards the door when the young girl turned sharply towards her and asked, 'Would you do something for me? Would you touch my neck, put your fingers on it?'

The brightness went out of Tilly's face and her voice was stiff as she said, 'No, I will not touch your neck, Miss McGill, for I have no power in my hands, the only power I have is in my mind. And that's no more than the power you have in yours. What I can do you can do equally; **the only** way I can help you is to suggest that you tell yourself to face up to this affliction, adopting an attitude of confidence. Tell yourself that you are a whole woman and that some day you will meet a gentleman who will take you for what you are. Tell yourself that some day you'll meet a man who will put his lips to that stain. Believe this and it will come about.'

The girl now said simply, 'Thank you.' Beyond the door she turned and, looking at Tilly once more, she said, 'I'll never forget this day. As long as I live I'll remember it. Good-bye.'

'Good-bye,' said Tilly.

When she entered the room again she leant with her back against the door and, looking upwards, she murmured, 'Poor soul! Poor soul!' To be afflicted so in youth. Yet that stain would not be erased when that girl's youth stepped into maturity, that stain would be there until the day she died. Would she ever find a man big enough to bear with it? Men were strange creatures. Not so often afflicted with illness themselves, rarely did they bear such in women except through compassion. But that girl needed more than compassion, she needed love, because by the sound of it she had never known it. . . .

It was around teatime when John rode up, and he almost ran up the path in his excitement, opening the door even as he knocked on it.

Tilly hadn't heard the horse because she was in the back room settling Mr Burgess down to his tea in bed, for he had shown a disinclination to get up at all today.

John hurried in towards her, saying, 'M . . . M . . . Matthew is c . . . c . . . coming. He should be l . . . l . . . landing next week. I received his mail only this afternoon. Oh, I am so looking f . . . f . . . forward to s . . . s . . . seeing him. Once he's here we'll g . . . g . . . get everything fixed up and you'll come back.'

She now held out her hand, palm upwards towards him for some seconds before she said, 'I think I've told you before, John, I couldn't possibly leave Mr Burgess.' Her voice sank low. 'He's not well at all. He's fading; slowly but surely he's fading. He could last a few months or perhaps a year, but . . .

but no matter how long I must stay with him.'

Matthew w . . . w . . . would have him up at the house.'

'He wouldn't want to go, he's lived here too long. There's a thing, you know, about dying in your own bed.'

'Oh, Tr . . . Trotter, that was half the f . . . f . . . fun, half the pleasure in Matthew c . . . c . . . coming back that you would once again be over w . . . w . . . with us at the house.'

'John' — she pressed him gently down into the seat opposite her — 'you make all these plans but you know I shouldn't have to point out to you it's Matthew who is head of the house and his ideas, if I remember Matthew aright' — she now turned her head to the side and slanted her eyes at him — 'never ran along the same lines as yours, or Luke's, or, thank goodness, his sister's. No, I think we had better wait until he is home and settled before we start planning. Do you know' — she shook her head from side to side — 'this has been a day of events, you are the third visitor I've had. I wonder who'll be next?'

'Who . . . who were the others?'

'Mr Pearson, you know from the village. He's the painter and odd jobber.'

'Oh yes, yes, I remember. May I ask wh . . . wh . . . what he wanted? You don't often have v . . . v . . . visitors from the vill . . . vill . . . village.'

When she had finished telling him the reason for Tom Pearson's visit he nodded his head and said, 'He seems an honourable man.'

'Yes, he is, he is.'

'And your other v . . . v . . . visitor?'

'Oh' — she shook her head slowly at him — 'here lies a tale. It was a young lady, a beautiful young lady.'

Now why had she said that? Well, she supposed the girl could look beautiful, at least full-faced and at the right side.

As she watched him now put his head back, his mouth wide as he endeavoured to repeat her words, a beautiful young lady, there crept into her brain an idea. But once it had become an idea it no longer crept, but leapt into a scheme, and she could again hear his voice saying, 'No young lady is going to put up with me.' And she saw the girl with sadness imprinted on her face by the handicap that she must bear alone for all her days, and so, leaning forward, she said, 'Will you do something for me, John?'

'Anything, Tr . . . Tr . . . Trotter. You know that, anything.'

'Will you come to tea on Saturday?'

'Tea?'

'Yes, to tea to meet the young lady I've just mentioned.'

'Oh.' His face fell. 'No, no, Tr . . . Trotter, don't ask me. You know wh . . . what I'm like with strangers. I'm b . . . b . . . bad enough with you and you put me at my ease more than anybody else that I know of.'

She leant forward and caught hold of his hand, saying now, 'Be quiet for a moment and listen. If you saw someone in great distress and they were very lonely and you knew that by even looking at them, smiling at them, you could alleviate that loneliness, what would you do, walk away?'

'I . . . I don't f . . . f . . . follow you, Trotter.'

'Well, it's like this, John. This young lady has a handicap. She is beautiful.' And she had no doubt that when Miss McGill came to see her on Saturday she would look beautiful.

'Beautiful with a ha . . . ha . . . handicap? Is she a cripple?'

'No; her body as far as I can see is perfect. Her features are good; she has lovely eyes and lovely hair.'

'B . . . b . . . but she has a h . . . handicap?' He now lowered his head and looked at her from under his eyebrows and he said, 'Don't t . . . t . . . tell me, Tro . . . Trotter that she st . . . st . . . stammers.'

She burst out laughing at this, and shook her head; then raising her hand to his ear, to his amazement she began to trace her finger along his jawbone, then down over his throat to the top of his collar, and when her finger stopped there she said, 'She has a birthmark; it is about there where I've drawn with my finger. Apparently she has always been made aware of it until now she is a sad and lost young girl. And you know why she came here today?'

He shook his head.

'She heard one of the maids who used to be at the Manor telling another maid about a witch by the name of Trotter.'

'Aw no! Aw no! How awful for you.'

'But how much worse for her when she was so desperate she had to come in search of this witch.'

'And you ha . . . have asked her b . . . b . . . back to tea?'

'Yes; and I would like you to come and help me prove to her that people will not spurn her because of her birthmark.'

'But she'll want a fellow, a m . . . man who can talk to her, Trotter. I'm not the one to do it. T . . . t . . . talking of handicaps, I have m . . . m . . . my own and I would exchange it for hers any day in the w . . . w . . . week.'

'Well, I hope that you'll tell her that some day.'

'Oh, Trotter.'

'Please, John. I don't think I've asked anything of you before, have I?'

He stared at her blankly. Then smiling ruefully, he said, 'G . . . G . . . God help the poor girl if she's expecting a s . . . s . . . saviour in me. I'll not be able to get one w . . . w . . . word out, you'll see.'

'Yes, I'll see.'

And Tilly saw, but not until she had given up hope of seeing either of them for it had poured hard since early morning, and now at half-past three in the afternoon she'd had to light the lamp. Looking towards Mr Burgess, who was dressed in his well-worn velvet jacket that she had brushed and sponged down yet again for this occasion, she said, 'It won't surprise me if neither of them turns up.'

'Give them time, especially the young lady; as you say, she's got all of eight miles to come through this.'

It was John who arrived first, and his relief was evident when he knew he was to be the only visitor. But he had hardly taken off his wet cloak and said, 'I've taken B . . . B . . . Bobtail round the b . . . b . . . back, it's more sheltered there,' when Tilly, glancing out of the window, said, 'And you'd better put your cloak on again, John, and go and take Miss McGill's horse to keep Bobtail company. Good gracious, she looks drenched.'

'Oh! Tro . . . Trotter.' He almost grabbed the cloak from her and he put it on as he went down the path.

She watched from the open doorway as he took the reins from the young girl's hands without saying a word and then led the horse around the side of the house.

When the girl came into the room she looked quite strained and said immediately, 'The young man, who is he?'

'A friend of mine; he just happened to pop in. Here, let me have your coat and your hat, you're drenched.'

'I . . . I shouldn't have come, I mean if there had been any way to let you know. Oh dear! my hair.' As she pulled the long pin out of her velour hat the coil of her hair became unloosened and fell on to her shoulder, and she had her hands above her head pinning it back into place when John came hurriedly through the door, only to stop and stand with his hand behind his back holding the iron ring of the latch staring at the girl.

She, patting her hair into place now, looked from one to the other, saying, 'I'm . . . I'm afraid I mustn't stay long, my . . . my horse is very wet, and . . . and I have no cover.'

'I've s . . . s . . . seen to that; I took some s . . . s . . . sacks' — he was looking at Tilly now — 'from the w . . . w . . . wood-shed, Tr . . . Tr . . . Trotter, and put over them both.'

'That was sensible. Come along now, both of you.' She went to turn away, but then said, 'Oh dear me, I'm forgetting my duty. This is Mr John Sopwith. . . . Miss Anna McGill.'

'How do you do?' The girl inclined her head towards him, and he, bowing slightly from the shoulders, answered, 'a pl . . . pleasure to meet you.' Then they all turned towards the voice coming from the fireplace, saying, 'And I am Herbert Vincent Burgess and nobody cares a hoot that I'm dying for my tea, and that my horse is champing on its bit in the bed-room waiting to gallop me to London Town, there to have supper with a man called Johnson and his friend Boswell, and from where in the morning I shall set sail for France, there to have breakfast with Voltaire; and the following day I shall return to the City, although I have refused my Lord Chesterfield's invitation because, do you know, his lackeys expect to be tipped as you leave his house. . . .'

'Oh! be quiet. Be quiet.' Tilly laughingly pushed him gently. 'Behave yourself, will you? Nobody understands a word you say.'

'I do.'

Tilly turned amazed to see the girl smiling widely, and when Mr Burgess held out his hand to her, saying, 'At last, at last. Come here, my dear. A soul mate at last, at last. Would you believe it, Trotter?'

They all started to laugh, and when young William, unused to the strange noise, let out a high gurgle the laughter mounted and there was nothing for it but that Tilly should pick the baby up to be admired and cooed over. The ice was broken.

An hour later, from the window she watched John leading the horses on to the road, then helping Miss McGill to mount, before taking his place at her side and riding off, not in the direction of home but towards Gateshead.

She was still watching from the window when Mr Burgess's voice, tired-sounding now, brought her swiftly round as he said, 'They'll be married in a year or so, thanks to your witchery.'

PART TWO

The Homecoming

1

They had finished dinner, they had drunk their port and smoked their cigars and were now making their way towards the library, not the drawing-room as one would have expected, for since his return Matthew had shown an open aversion to sitting in the drawing-room in the evenings.

The library was a long room with a plaster-panelled ceiling. The circular motifs in the triangles had long since lost their colour of rose and grey, taking their tones from the smoke that every now and again billowed out from the open hearth whenever a gust of wind roared down the chimney.

Matthew coughed and blinked his eyes before pointing to the fireplace, saying, 'When was that last swept?'

'Couldn't s . . . say, Matthew, b . . . b . . . but it doesn't often smoke. It's the wind, it's a howler tonight.'

'It's a howler every night if you ask me.' Matthew now seated himself in the leather chair and, stretching out a leg, thrust the end of a burning log further on to the iron fire basket, then lay back and looked about him.

The room was as he remembered it, and as he had pictured it so many times over the past few years, yet it was different, though not smaller, not shrunken as houses and places kept alive by memory alone appeared when viewed in reality. If anything it seemed larger, but that likely was due to comparing it with the homestead.

He couldn't exactly put his finger on the change, not just in the room or the rest of the house, but even in the land outside and the people on it everything was alien to him. It was as if in leaving America he had left home, and over the past days he had asked himself many times why he had come back. It wasn't an enormous estate he had to manage, and there was no industry connected with it that would need looking into. It might have been different if the mine had been working. . . . The mine. He'd go there tomorrow; he'd have to do something, this stagnation would drive him mad.

He started slightly when John, picking up his thoughts, said, 'You're . . . you're finding everything ch . . . ch . . . changed, Matthew. You d . . . d . . . didn't w . . . ant to come back, did you?'

'No, you're right there, John, I didn't want to come back. And there's nothing to be done here, the place is dead.'

'Yes, r . . . r . . . round here, but not in the towns. You were in N . . . N . . . Newcastle today, there's plenty g . . . g . . . going on there. Now you c . . . can't say there isn't.'

'Yes, there appears to be plenty going on but' — he leant forward now and looked into the fire — 'it seems to me that all the enterprises, shipping, factories, mines, the whole lot could be put into a teacup.' He turned now and held both hands out towards John, saying, 'You see, for the last three years I've been used to space, admitted mostly empty space, thousands of miles of it, but when you did get into a township the activity . . . well, it was incredible. In Newcastle today I had the impression that everybody was marking time, whereas in a similar town over there, although there are no towns similar to Newcastle, I admit, with regard to buildings, but the difference is those in America are making time, they're using it to the full. It's a different world, John. No talking, no explaining can give you the picture of it, you've got to be there. . . . Oh, let's have a drink.' He put out his hand to pull the bell rope to the side of the fireplace, but stopped, and his square face taking on an almost pugnacious look he said, 'I hate ringing for women. If I'm to stay here there'll have to be menservants again. No house can be expected to run efficiently without a butler and a footman, the very least.'

John got to his feet, saying now and almost as irritably as Matthew had spoken, 'I'll b . . . b . . . bring the tr . . . tray; and the house has been r . . . r . . . run very well for years without menservants. Anyway, father c . . . c . . . couldn't afford them and we wouldn't have had the c . . . c . . . comfort we have had, had it not been for Tr . . . Tr . . . Trotter.'

There, he had said her name again. Well, a man should speak as he found, and Matthew was unfair to Trotter. He wasn't in the house twenty-four hours before he had said, 'Look, I don't want to hear anymore about Trotter. As for having her back, no! definitely not.'

The brothers stared at each other. Matthew, his head pressed against the high back of the leather chair, looked steadily up into the thin long sensitive face above him. The black hair lying smooth across the high dome of his brother's head was in sharp contrast to his own fair matt. He'd had his cut and trimmed quite close a week ago but already it was aiming to become a busby again, and he ran his fingers through it as he said, 'Dear, dear; I fear that if Father hadn't fallen on his face his youngest son might have; after all, what does eleven years matter when one is in love?'

'Matthew!' John's shocked indignation came over in the name that was spoken without a tremor. 'How dare you! Tr . . . Tr . . . Trotter's been like a m . . . m . . . mother to me. . . . Damn you! M . . . M . . . Matthew. D . . . D . . . Damn you!'

Matthew was on his feet now holding John by the shoulders. 'I'm sorry. Really I am. It's only that she's . . . well, she's disrupted so many lives.'

John was gulping in his throat now, the colour was seeping back into his face which a moment before had looked blanched, but his tone remained stiff as he said, 'I . . . I don't agree with y . . . you. You c . . . c . . . couldn't blame her for what F . . . F . . . Father did in the first place. And I think she was a k . . . k . . . kind of saviour to Father. He would have gone insane without her.'

'Perhaps you're right.' Matthew turned towards the chair again. 'Anyway, don't let it raise an issue between us. Look.' He turned his head towards John now. 'Tomorrow I'm going to the mine; I have an idea I might open it again.'

'Open up the m . . . m . . . mine! It would take a small fortune.'

'Well, I've got a small fortune, a couple of small fortunes.'

'Does that m . . . m . . . mean you're g . . . g . . . going to stay, I mean settle here?'

'Oh, I don't know about that; Uncle wants me back there. In the meantime, getting the old mine going again would give me something to exercise my wits, otherwise I'll become like the rest of them around here, riding, drinking, whoring. Not that I'd mind the latter.'

'Oh, Matthew!'

'Oh, Matthew!' He mimicked John, then said, 'You're too good to be true you know, brother.'

'I'm n . . .n . . . not too good to be t . . . t . . . true. You don't know anything about me really. B . . . B . . . But I think, there's a lim . . . limit; one must draw the l . . . line.'

'And where would you draw the line?' Matthew was grinning at him now.

'Oh, you! You!' John pushed out his fist towards him. 'You're im . . . po . . . po . . . possible.'

'Are you going to get that tray or have I to ring for a female?'

As John went out of the room, his head moving from side to side, Matthew settled deep into the chair. Presently, thrusting his foot out towards the end of the log from where the resin was dripping on to the iron dog, he muttered between his teeth, 'Trotter! Trotter!'

'Well, he's on his last legs I think, lass.'

'Yes, it won't be long now.'

'Now, lass, you mustn't grieve.' Biddy put her hand on Tilly's shoulder. 'He's an old man and by all accounts he's enjoyed his life. All he seemed to want was his books, an' he's had them. And he's been lucky to have you an' all to see to him.'

'I've been very lucky to have him, Biddy.'

'Aye well, six and two three's, if you look at it like that. And you've got a roof over your head for life if you want it. It was as little as he could do to leave it to you, not that I think it's a fit settin' for you but it'll do in the meantime. I get a bit mad at times.' Biddy went now and picked up the long black coat from a chair and as Tilly helped her into it she said, 'Your place is over yonder, an' your child's place an' all. Eeh!' She shook her head. 'I can't make him out. He comes back from that pit, glar up to the eyes, lookin' worse than my lot ever did. They say he goes into places where none of the others 'll venture. And yet he's so bloody high-handed. The master never acted like he does: gentlemen take it as their right to have the whip hand but at times he speaks to you as if you were dirt 'neath his feet, then the next minute he goes outside and hob-nobs with the lads, talks to them as if they were equals. One minute he's playin' the lord and master, the next it seems to me he doesn't know his place. Now Master John, he's a different kettle of fish altogether. He even tried to apologise for t'other one, said that in America they live differently. Well, I could understand it if he remained the same with everybody, but with the lasses and me he's as snotty as a polis. . . . But I say, lass' — she thrust her head towards Tilly — 'what do you think of Master John an' the miss he's hooked on to?'

'I think they're both very lucky.'

'Aye, an' I think you're right. I've only seen her once, that was from a distance, she looked bonny. She was in the yard lookin' in the stables. He didn't bring her into the house but, as Katie said, he likely didn't want her to encounter Master Matthew 'cos that bloke's got a thing against women. I'd like to bet he had an affair out there that went wrong.'

'I shouldn't wonder, Biddy.'

'Oh, what am I keepin' jabbering on about, you've got your hands full.' She pinned on her hat now, wound the long woollen scarf around her neck, pulled on a matching pair of gloves, then said, 'I'll be off then, lass. Katie or Peg 'll look in this afternoon. You know, that's funny' — she turned from the door and stabbed her finger into Tilly's chest — 'he knows I come along, he's seen our Arthur fetch me. He's even passed us on the road on his horse. An' twice or more Katie's said that he's watched her going down the drive. She was sure he followed her one time to see in which direction she went. Now, he knows we come here an' he's never said, "Stop." Aw! he's a funny fellow. Well, bye-bye, lass. You say the doctor'll be along the day?'

'Yes, Biddy; he promised to look in.'

'Well, there's nothing he can do, but it's nice to know he takes such pains. He's different to old Kemp. Bye-bye again, lass.'

'Bye-bye, Biddy. Mind how you go. If Arthur isn't at the cross-roads you wait for him; don't attempt to walk all the way.'

'Aye, aye; don't worry.'

When Biddy was lost to sight, Tilly shut the door on the icy wind and, going towards the clothes basket set near the fireplace, she bent down and took her son's face between her palms and shook it gently, and he gurgled at her and grabbed at her wrist. He was in his fifth month and thriving. He was so bonny awake or asleep, he brought a thrill to her heart. She put a small linen sugar bag into his mouth and he sucked on one end while grabbing the other in his small fists.

She now went to the hob and stirred the pan of mutton broth that was simmering there. She didn't feel like eating and it was no use putting any out for Mr Burgess, he hadn't touched food for two days now, he no longer required it. She pulled the pan to the side, dusted her hands one against the other, then went down the kitchen and into the bedroom.

The old man was lying propped up against his pillows. He did not turn his head when she came into the room but, sensing her presence, his fingers moved, and when she took his hand he murmured, 'Trotter. Dear Trotter.'

She put out her other hand and pulled up the chair close to the bed. She did not speak, and when he turned his eyes towards her and smiled at her she felt a constriction in her throat.

'Time's running out, my dear.'

She made no reply.

'Been a very fortunate man. I . . . I must tell you something, Trotter.'

She waited, saying nothing; but when he told her in words scarcely above a whisper the lump in her throat expanded until she felt she would choke, for what he said was, 'I have loved you, Trotter; like all the others I have loved you, but more like he did in so many different ways. When he died, his hands in yours, I thought, if only I could be so . . . so fortunate. There is no God, Trotter, it would be utterly childish to imagine there is, there is only thought and the power of thought, and my thought has arranged it so I get my wish.'

The last word was scarcely audible and she could no longer see the expression on his face for her eyes were so blinded with tears as soundlessly she cried, and brokenly she whispered. 'Thank you for coming into my life.'

The parson's wife had taught her to read and write, but she could never have imbued her with the knowledge that this old man had, for to her he had been the storehouse of all knowledge. There was no subject on which he couldn't talk, yet he was so humble he considered himself ignorant. Once he had said to her, 'Like Socrates, I can say I haven't any knowledge to boast of but I am a little above other men because I am quite aware of my ignorance and I do not think that I know what I do not know, but what I do not know I make it my poor business to try and find out.'

She had been fortunate, she knew, in having been the companion of a gentleman for twelve years, yet it wasn't he who had taught her to think. But he had taught her to love, and that was a different thing; he had taught her that the act of love wasn't merely a physical thing, its pleasure being halved without the assistance of the mind. But it was Mr Burgess, this old man breathing his last here now, who had taught her how to use her mind. Right from the beginning he had warned her that once your mind took you below the surface of mundane things, you would never again know real peace because the mind was an adventure, it led you into strange places and was forever asking why, and as the world outside could not give you true answers, you were forever groping and searching through your spirit for the truth.

She remembered being shocked when he had first said to her there was no such thing as a God. There were gods, all kinds of gods, and different men brought up in different spheres created these beings in accordance with the environment about them. As for Christianity, he likened it to a slave driver with a whip and this whip had many thongs called denominations and all made up of fear that had the power to thrust souls into everlasting flames, flames that would sear them for all eternity. Who, he had asked her, would not profess a belief in this particular God who, if he withheld his forgiveness of your sins, could cast you into this everlasting hell. Why! he had told her, had he not begun to think for himself he, too, would have believed in this God, for he did not relish pain, either in this world or the next. Such ideas had now ceased to shock her.

She still could not see him when she felt him lifting her hand to his cheek, and she leant forward, resting her other forearm on the bedside; and she remained like this until her arm became cramped.

It was sometime later when her tears had stopped and her vision had cleared that she gently withdrew her fingers from his hand and, bending over him, she put her lips to his brow although she knew he could no longer feel them.

Dear, dear, Mr Burgess. Dear, dear friend. The eyes that were looking straight into hers were smiling at her. Slowly she closed the lids and when she went to cross his arms on his breast she hesitated, as in death so in life. He did not believe in any cross and wherever his spirit was winging to now it would certainly not be to a hell. If there was a God, and she, too, had her doubts, oh yes, grave doubts, but should there be such a being He would at this moment be taking into account all the good that this man had done in his life. True, she had only known him for fifteen years but during that time his one aim in life had been to help people, help them to help themselves. He had certainly helped her to help herself. His going would leave a void in her life that would never be filled.

But as she drew the sheet up over his face she experienced for a fleeting moment a strange sense of joy. She imagined that they were there, both of them, talking and laughing as they had done so often, Mark and the tutor of his children.

She would cry no more for his passing.

2

It was a very small cortège that attended the funeral. Arthur, Jimmy, and Bill Drew and Fred Leyburn carried out the oak coffin, and when they had placed it in the hearse and the driver had urged his horse a few yards along the lane, Matthew and John Sopwith entered their coach; behind that, the four men got into the second coach, if it could be called such. It was merely a covered vehicle used mostly for carrying stores from the town and occasionally pigs' carcases and vegetables to it. But today it was very welcome to the men for the wind was cutting and the sky was low, its leaden colour portending snow.

Biddy, standing beside Tilly at the window, said softly, 'He'll be lucky if he's underground afore the snow comes, I can smell it in the air. Come on, lass; no use standing here any longer.'

Biddy turned from the window but Tilly remained looking out on to the narrow empty lane. The joyous feeling she had experienced at the moment of his passing had not remained with her; there was on her now a deep sadness. She felt alone again, as she had done at Mark's passing. Biddy's voice came to her from the fireplace, saying, 'I didn't expect his lordship to show up. Is that the first time you've seen him?'

For a moment Tilly didn't answer, then as if having just heard the question, she said, 'Yes, yes, the first time,' and she recalled now the surprise, even shock, she had experienced when not a half hour ago he had stood in this room facing her. There was nothing remaining of the Matthew she remembered; the boy, the youth, the young man, had always carried an air of arrogance, but this had deepened, widened, as his body had done. She had imagined him to be taller; perhaps it was his growing so broad that had taken off his height. His shoulders were thick, seeming to strain the Melton cloth of his greatcoat. His face was broad, his eyes more deep set, and his hair, the hair that had been golden and inclined to curl, now looked like a thick unruly matt. It was cut in the most odd way; she had understood Biddy's description of his hair when she had likened it to that cut under a pot pie basin, for his neck was bare of hair, and none of it she imagined was more than two inches long. She could not believe that he was only twenty-five, he could be taken for a man of thirty-five; and his voice and manner gave the impression of maturity, hard maturity.

He had stared at her unblinking for almost a minute before speaking, and then it wasn't to give her any kind of greeting, he simply said, 'We all have to die sometime, and the old fellow had a good run for his money.'

His words, so unfeeling, so out of place, brought sweeping through her that rare feeling of anger, and it was as much as she could do not to turn on him, even order him out. John, on the other hand, had been courtesy and kindness itself and his stammer, bringing with it the balm of oil, said, 'I'll m . . . m . . . miss the old man, Tr . . . Tr . . . Trotter, b . . . b . . . but not as much as y . . . y . . . you will; and he w . . . was very f . . . f . . . fond of you.'

She had not answered John, she had not opened her lips while the two men were in the room; not even when the men were carrying the coffin out did she speak, nor yet show any emotion, for tears shed in front of Master Matthew would, she felt, have certainly evoked some derisive or sarcastic remark.

She understood fully now Biddy's inability to get on with her new master; but then, of course, hadn't he always been difficult right from the beginning? And Biddy had expressed a hope that now she might return to the Manor. Never! Not under him.

She went towards the table. Biddy had covered it with a white cloth and set out the tea things.

'We'll have a cup of tea, lass,' she said, 'an' a bite. There'll be nobody coming back here. The lads will go straight to the

96

kitchen, Katie will have set a meal for them. But anyway I'll be back meself by then to see to things. Sit down and get off your feet, it's over.'

After they had been sitting at the table in silence for some minutes, Biddy asked quietly, 'What are you going to do with yourself, lass? Stay here?'

'Yes, Biddy. I can't see me doing anything else, not until he's a little older.' She turned and glanced at the child and he laughed at her and made a gurgle in his throat. Then she added, 'That's if they'll let me be.'

'Oh, they'll let you be all right. That's one thing I don't think he'd stand for. If not him, then Master John wouldn't. I can see that lad down in the village with a horse whip if you had any trouble from that quarter again.'

'As long as there's a McGrath in the village I'll always have trouble, Biddy.'

'Well, there's not many of 'em left; there's only her, and the son.'

'And his children.'

'Aye yes; and his children. Bairns are worse than grown-ups sometimes. Anyway, don't worry about that.'

There was a silence until Biddy proffered the question, and tentatively, 'What would you say if he asked you to come back?'

'He won't, and I wouldn't.' Tilly's voice was sharp. 'So don't bank on that, Biddy.'

'No, you're right, lass, he won't and you wouldn't. But anyway, this is your own house now and you've got your own income. An' if you're gettin' rid of some of these books you could make it nice.'

Tilly nodded, then said, 'I'll make it nice but I won't get rid of his books; I'll put them up at the end of the loft.'

'He never came for those fifty that he was left, Tilly.'

'No.'

'I suppose they're yours now, as he's left everything to you.'

'It could be said they are, but I'll not claim them.'

Biddy gave a huh! before she said, 'He'd likely make a court case of it if you tried, he's that kind of a young bugger. You know, it's hard to believe he's still a young fella; he looks older than my Henry and he's almost kicking forty.'

Tilly made no comment on this, but she wondered in an aside how life in America could change anyone so much, externally that is, for inwardly she sensed he was the same as he had always been, arrogant, bumptious, spoilt. He had to be top-dog, master of all he surveyed or else somebody suffered.

In the beginning it was the nursemaids, then it would have been her, but he didn't get off with it; the boarding school seemed to have tamed him for a time but only for a time, for the young man who had visited his father on rare occasions had been what her granny would have called an upstart. And yet this description would not have been accurate because he had not risen from nothing, he had been born into the class. There was a difference. A week had passed; snow had come and disappeared again leaving the roads slushy. But if this wind kept up and the temperature kept dropping as it had done since noon, there'd be a hard frost tonight and tomorrow the roads would be like glass.

Having told herself that the best antidote against loneliness was work, she had for the past days carried the maxim to the extreme, for from dawn till dusk, stopping only to feed the child and tend to a light meal for herself, she had carried the hundreds of books up the steep ladder to the room above; then crawled to where the eaves met the floor and began the stacking of what she imagined would be close on two thousand volumes.

She had decided she would still keep the end of the loft as her bedroom and clear the main room downstairs entirely of books and turn what had been Mr Burgess's bedroom into a study. With this in mind she had sorted out the books she intended to keep downstairs and which she told herself she would peruse during the coming months, for once the cottage was straight there would only be the child to see to, and she must occupy her spare time with some undertaking. And what better than reading and learning. Mr Burgess would be happy to think that she was going to further his coaching. Yet even as she planned her future she experienced a sense of dismay that such activity practised without someone to share it, to discuss her progress with, would become stale.

She hadn't seen anyone from the house for four days, which was unusual, and she wondered, too, why the child, loved as it was, should leave room in her being for the need for other people. The fact that it was so created in her a feeling of guilt.

She looked towards him. He was sleeping peacefully in his basket. The fire was bright in the open hearth. She had re-arranged the room, washed all the curtains and covers, brought in all but one of the six rugs that had been shared between her own bedroom and Mr Burgess's, and placed them at intervals over the stone floor, so that there was now an air of comfort about the room.

She had changed from her working clothes into the soft plum-coloured cord dress that Mark had liked to see her in and that Mr Burgess had always remarked on. This changing of her clothes in the middle of the day had become a habit picked up when she had first begun to dine with Mark in the upstairs room. Before her close association she had always worn a kind of uniform, but on the day that she first ate with him, he said, 'You will change each day for dinner, Tilly.' And she had liked the idea and adopted it until it had became a pattern of life.

A change in the wind brought a grumble and growl down the chimney. She went to the fireplace and, taking some logs from the skip, she went to put them on the bank of red hot ashes but paused for a moment. It was a lovely fire for the griddle pan, she could make some griddle cakes. But then, why bother? she hated cooking for herself alone. And anyway she had changed. Tomorrow morning she'd bake some bread.

She placed the logs on the fire, dusted her hands and went to pick up the child; then, her back bent, she turned her head towards the door. There was someone knocking. It must be someone on foot, she hadn't heard a horse or cart.

When she opened the door she stared at the man who was staring at her. 'May I come in?'

She stood aside and watched him walk into the room, stop and look about him for a moment, then walk on towards the fire, and there he stood between the table and the couch.

She hadn't moved but two steps from the door.

'I have come to apologise; John said I was rude to you the other day.'

She continued to stare at him, giving him no answer until, hunching his shoulders upwards, he exclaimed, 'Well! what can I say except that my stay in America hasn't improved my manners . . .?' He looked from side to side now, saying, 'May I sit down?'

She moved slowly towards him and, pointing to the chair opposite the couch, she said, 'Yes, certainly.'

He didn't immediately take the seat, but with a gesture of exaggerated courtesy he extended his hand towards the couch and when she had seated herself on it, he sat in the chair opposite, facing her now and also the child where, at the end of the couch near the fire, it was lying still asleep in the basket.

Tilly returned his unblinking stare until she became embarrassed. Turning her head to the side, she said, 'I have known you long enough, Matthew, to realise that you didn't consider your manner towards me the other day as warranting an apology. Will you come to the point and tell me the reason for your visit?'

He smiled now and the movement of his features altered his whole face, the arrogant look going, the coldness seeping from the eyes. He became attractive, even handsome, and the smile slipped into laughter as he said, 'That is the Trotter I remember, straight to the point, no beating about the bush. Now, me lad, let's get things straight. You put a frog in my bed, I put a frog down your shirt.'

Her head jerked back and he nodded at her, saying, 'Oh, yes, yes; John is always saying Trotter has done a lot of good in her time, but I say that Trotter has done one or two not so good things in her time, things that have repercussions to this day, such as nightmares.'

Her lips moved soundlessly on the word, and then she repeated aloud, 'Nightmares?'

'Yes, Miss Trotter, nightmares. I experienced the first one at boarding school. Raised the dormitory screaming my head off because I was being smothered in slime with all the frogs crawling over me.'

She shook her head, her face straight, her eyes troubled now.

'The boys nearly jumped for the windows, they thought there was a fire. But that was nothing to the bunkhouse in Texas. They were tough lads those, but when I scream, I scream, and to a man they sprang for their guns; they thought it was a raid on their horses. Imagine ten men in their linings rushing out into the night. And it was the first time they'd had their clothes off in months!'

She looked at him. His head was back, he was laughing loudly. The concern seeped from her eyes. She said stiffly, 'You're exaggerating.'

He brought his head forward and stared at her for a moment before he said soberly now, 'Yes, perhaps a little, but it's true about the nightmares. I've had nightmares, Trotter, ever since you put that frog down my shirt and always, always about frogs; big ones, little ones, gigantic ones, all crawling over me, smothering me.'

'No!' She shook her head and pressed herself back against the couch. 'Don't say I've caused you to have nightmares.'

'But it's true, you did.'

She swallowed deeply, wetted her lips. 'Then I could have had nightmares, because it was you who put the frog in my bed.'

'Yes, I give you that, but then you were a young woman, sixteen years old, and I was but a boy of ten, a sensitive boy.'

Again she jerked her head to the side while keeping her eyes on him, and she repeated, 'Sensitive?' and she knew she sounded like Biddy when she said, 'If you were a sensitive child, then pig-skin is made of silk.'

He laughed again, but quietly now while he continued to look at her; then he asked, 'Why do you think I was such a little devil?'

'I think you were born like that.'

'Nobody is born like that, Trotter. I thought you would have learned that much with all the wisdom you've imbibed from Mr Burgess. It is environment that makes us what we are. I saw my mother for five minutes a day, no longer, living in the same house day after day, year after year. Even before she took to her couch I can't remember seeing her for any length of time. I can't remember being held in her arms. I can't remember feeling loved. None of us did, but I was her first-born. I resented the others even while knowing that she gave to them no more than to me. If I'd been brought up in the home of your Biddy, who is apparently so fond of you, and you of her, I would I am sure have emerged a much happier person. I would not have had any cause to force myself on people's notice. And I did that by playing tricks on nursemaids, so that my father would come and threaten to thrash me. He never did. I longed for him to thrash me because then I would have known I meant something at least to him. I loved my father. Do you know that, Trotter?'

She paused before she said, 'My answer to that is, you had a very odd way of showing it. You left him lonely for years before he died when it was in your power to come and see him.'

'He didn't want me, Trotter, all he wanted was you, and he had you.'

'And that's why you . . . you hated me?'

'Who said I hated you?'

'You showed it in every possible way during your brief visits, and I don't find that your sojourn abroad has softened your attitude.'

He looked down towards his hands which were now placed on each knee, and he said quietly, 'I'm sorry that you should think that way. But you are right, in part that is, I did hate you. As for my attitude towards you not having altered, I'm . . . I'm afraid I would have to do a lot of explaining before I could make you understand, and it has nothing to do with my sojourn abroad. Yet again that isn't true. Oh' — he now tossed his head — 'this is not the time for delving into the whys and wherefores of one's reactions; the only thing I will say' — he looked straight at her now, one corner of his mouth lifted in an ironic smile — 'that no man, English, Irish, Scotch, Welsh, or any other for that matter, who spends three years in any state of America, or in Texas, particularly in Texas, could remain

102

unchanged or, let me add, retain his refinement. America is another world. Although the majority of the people you meet have hailed from here, one generation is enough to change them into practically different species. They tear at life to make a living, or, like a few, scheme to make it. They are different, and I suppose some of the difference has rubbed off on me. It has undoubtedly shown in my irritation, as John informs me.' He rose now and took two steps towards the fireplace as he added, 'The pace of life is so slow here, even the horses seem slower.' He laughed on the last words and looked at her over his shoulder. 'I was in the hunt the other day. There we were, lolloping over hedges and gates, pushing our way through woods, hollering and yelling; yet I had the strange fancy that we were all standing still for I could see the vast, vast plains, no sight before the horse's head for miles and miles and miles. There's no world beyond the plains. Like the sky, they go on for ever. What they call a township is merely a meteor dropped from the heavens. Oh dear, dear.' He dropped his head now and laughed. 'Shades of Mr Burgess. That's how he used to go on, isn't it?'

He turned his back to the fire now and stared at her, and as he did so the child in the basket awoke, coughed and spluttered a little, and the sound brought Tilly from her seat. Bending down, she lifted up her son and held him upright in her arms, supporting him with her hand on his back, so that his face was on a level with Matthew's.

For a moment she thought he was going to turn away; she could see the muscles of his jaw pressed tight against the skin. She waited for him to speak, to acknowledge the child, and he did so.

'My half-brother?'

'Yes.'

'You were a long time in bringing it about.'

She knew the colour was suffusing her face. She turned the child now and pressed its head against her neck, and he said on a defensive tone, 'Well, you were, weren't you? And it's a pity you didn't leave it a little longer because he won't be recognised other than as a bastard.'

Her lips were tight-pressed for a moment before she could bring herself to say, 'I chose to have him as a bastard. I could have married your father years ago. I wish I had now. Oh! how I wish I had. And then my son would have had his rightful place, and you wouldn't be standing here daring to insult me.'

'Aw, Trotter!' His voice and manner had changed so dramatically that as he swung round and reached up to the high mantelpiece above the fireplace and gripped the edge of it, she felt for a moment she was dealing with the young boy in the nursery, and there flashed across her mind a picture of him standing at the top of the nursery landing telling her he didn't want to go back to boarding school. And she remembered the reason why they were standing there. He'd had a fight with Luke as to who was to marry her when they grew up. And he had told her that a boy at school had said he had kissed a girl on the lips. She could see his face now as he had appealed to her. 'You cannot kiss anyone on the mouth until you are married. Can you, Trotter?'

She stared at his broad shoulders, his head hanging forward, the odd cut of his hair, and it came to her that the great Matthew was a very unhappy man. He had been an unhappy boy but that she suspected was nothing to his present state.

When he turned slowly to her his voice was low and his question had a plea in it. 'Will you come back? That's the reason for my visit today. You may have what rooms you like, and . . . and you can run the house as you did before.'

A lightness came into her body. There was nothing at the moment she would have welcomed more than to be back in the house. Coming down in the morning into the kitchen, talking to Biddy about the day's menus, writing down what stores she needed, going from room to room seeing that everything was in order; then some part of the day, winter or summer, walking in the garden, not solely for pleasure, yet it was a pleasure to see the work that the boys were doing, and she never stinted in telling them of her pleasure.

Why was she hesitating? She stared into the face of the man before her. There was no arrogance on his countenance now. The scowl, the ever present scowl that gave one the impression of ugliness, was no longer present. Again she saw the boy, but with more knowledge of him now that he had told her the cause of his actions when young. So why, why was she hesitating?

She seemed to surprise herself as she said, 'It's very kind of you but I'm . . . I'm afraid I can't accept.'

Her head drooped forward and stayed bent in the silence that followed her refusal, until he said, 'Why?'

'There . . . there are, I suppose, a number of reasons. First your sister, Mrs. . . .'

'Oh, Jessie Ann.' He threw the name off as if with scorn. 'She is a little bitch. She always was, she always will be. I went to Scarborough before I came on home. She acted like a fish-wife, solely because I had put John in charge.'

'Well, what do you expect her reactions to be if you engage me?'

'Hell's flames!' He flung one arm wide now and walked past her and round the table. 'The Manor is my house, I own it, I can do what I like with it, engage whom I like to run it. Jessie Ann has no say in my life. Anyway, we never got on together. And look!' The arrogance was back in both his face and his actions for, thrusting his arm out, he pointed his finger at her now, saying, 'If you don't take my offer I'll bring in male staff, a butler, a footman, the lot, and your Drew family won't like that, will they? Both inside and out they run the place as if they had been born there, owned it, as if they were. . . .'

'Concerned for its welfare.'

'Oh —' He turned his head on to his shoulder and, his voice dropping, he muttered, 'Why are we always at loggerheads? Can't we call a truce? What is past is past, I am willing to forget it.'

'That is very noble of you.'

'Don't be sarcastic with me, Trotter.' The voice and the look was that of the master speaking to the servant, and now her voice and look was that of an equal as she almost barked back at him, 'And don't you take that tone with me. You have no control over me whatsoever, I am an independent person. This is my house, small and humble as it is, it is mine. I've enough

105

money to keep me for the rest of my days and to educate my son as I think fit.'

'Don't be too sure of that; you only have shares, they've been known to flop.'

'Well, say they do; I still have my hands left and, what is more, my head. Now you've had the answer to the question you came to ask me so I'll thank you if you will leave.'

He stood, one hand gripping the front of his cravat, staring at her, glaring at her.

He looked like a man who at any moment could lash out with his fist. For an instant she had the impression he was one of the villagers, a working man, untutored, no grain of a gentleman in him.

As he snapped his gaze from her there seemed to be an audible click, so sharp was the movement, and, grabbing up his cloak and hat, he went to the door. There he turned and his lips hardly moved as he said, 'You'll need me before I need you Trotter.' On this he went out, banging the door behind him with such force that the child jumped in her arms and his face crumpled and, what was most unusual, he began to whimper, then cry loudly.

Dropping on to the chair, she rocked him backwards and forwards. Her eyes closed, her mouth open, she took in small gulps of air. A feeling of fear that she hadn't experienced for a long time was sweeping through her. It wasn't the kind of fear engendered by the villagers; she couldn't put a name to it, she only knew that she was afraid, afraid of him. And then she asked herself, Why? He could do nothing to her. Of course he could dismiss all the Drews and get in a male staff but he couldn't put Biddy out of the lodge; that was her property now. Yet the fear somehow wasn't connected with the Drews; it was an unexplainable fear. . . . Yet was it so unexplainable? The answer that thought brought to her was: madness, sheer madness.

3

Tilly had never made use of a carrier cart since she had taken
up residence in the Manor and she was loth to start now for she
would have to rub shoulders with the villagers, that's if they
allowed themselves to get near enough to touch her shoulder;
and so for her visits into the town to replenish her cupboard,
she had to rely on Arthur taking the cart into Shields. Even
that trip had become hazardous, not for herself, but for the
child, because the weather was cruelly cold.

There was only a week to Christmas and she felt she must do
some shopping, not for presents but for necessities; the only
presents she had to give were to the Drews. She had been knit-
ting scarves, mufflers and gloves for weeks past now, and she
had made a fine shawl for Biddy. She had also decided to give
herself a Christmas box. She was going to buy the material to
make a warm winter dress, as well as more flannel for petti-
coats for the child.

She had arranged yesterday with Katie for her to sneak out,
and that was the word that Katie used, in order that she could
look after the baby for two hours or so. Arthur was to bring her
on the cart, and then pick herself up and take her into Shields,
where he would leave her while he went and collected the
weekly supply of fodder for the horses. She would later meet
him at the top of the Mill Dam bank and return home.

She was ready except for putting her hat on when she heard
the stamping of the horse on the road and glanced out of the
window in passing, then took one step back and became still. It
wasn't Arthur with the cart, it was Simon Bentwood. She
nipped hard down on her lip and allowed him to knock on the

107

door before she opened it. He was smiling at her, his arm extended towards her and from his hand was dangling a medium-sized goose.

'I thought it might do for your Christmas dinner, Tilly.'

She looked at him sadly now and, shaking her head, said, 'Thank you, Simon, but I can't accept it.'

'Why can't you?'

'Because I can't take presents from you.'

' 'Tis merely a gift like from one neighbour to another.'

She turned her head away and looked down towards the step for a moment, then said, 'We both know, Simon, that it is no ordinary gift. If . . . if I accepted it you . . . you would think. . . . Oh well!' — she spread out her hands — 'it doesn't need any explaining. I appreciate your kindness, Simon, and I hold no bitterness towards you now, but . . . but I cannot take anything from you.'

His face was stiff, his lids half lowered. He looked down at the bird dangling from his hand; then he hit it almost savagely with his crop as he said, 'You can't stop me from trying to get things back as they once were, and you've no intention of going up there again.' His head jerked to the side. 'You refused to go back so what do you intend to do, spend the rest of your life in this little hole?'

How did he know that she had refused to go back to the Manor? She had, of course, told Biddy and she would, of course, have told Katie and Katie would have told . . . on and on, until it reached Fred Leyburn and then the two part-time outside men that Matthew had engaged lately.

'You can't mean to remain on your own for the rest of your life, Tilly, you're not made that way. And you won't be allowed to, men being what they are. I made one mistake, but as I said afore I'm not the only one, am I? We both could forgive and forget. I'd look after you, Tilly.'

'I'm quite capable of looking after myself, Simon. And Simon, listen to me, I want to make this final, I shall never marry you, Simon, loneliness or necessity would never drive me to marry you. I have known one man. I looked upon him as my husband, I hope he suffices me.'

108

'Suffices you, did you say? Huh!' His face was one large sneer now. 'By what I hear you're going to run through the family. One man sufficing you? They're never off your doorstep. Huh! Do you know your name's like clarts, a whore could claim more respect than you round here. I could make you into a decent woman.'

The blood had drained from her face and she felt as if it was draining from her whole body, her legs were weak. She put out her hand and supported herself against the stanchion of the door, but she kept her head up and her gaze steady on him as she answered, 'If my name is like clarts then our names are well matched; you've had to come down in the social scale since Lady Myton, for I understand you're quite at home in the Shields brothels.'

She thought for a moment he was going to strike her. It was strange but there was the same look on his face as had been on Matthew's a few weeks ago when he had stood by the table and glared at her as if he could kill her. That Simon might actually have hit her, or at least grabbed hold of her, she was sure except at that moment the cart came into view round the bend in the road and Arthur, jumping down from the high front seat, came smiling towards them, only to jump to the side as Simon flinging round from Tilly went striding past him, the goose swinging from his hand.

'Something wrong, lass?'

She had pushed the door wide open and was leaning against it.

'Here! has he done owt to you?' He had his hand on her shoulder whilst looking back to where Simon was mounting his horse; then he exclaimed on a high note, 'God! he's thrown the bird into the thicket, he's as mad as a hatter. What's happened, Tilly?'

She walked away from him and, sitting down by the fire, she said on a shaky laugh, 'He . . . he brought a proposal of marriage, Arthur.'

'Oh. Huh! Oh, I see. Well, I've heard of rejected suitors but I've never imagined one as mad as he looks. Are you sure you're all right, lass?' His face was serious now.

'No, Arthur, quite candidly I don't feel all right; encounters like that rather shake you.' She looked towards the doorway. 'Where's Katie?'

'Well' — he pulled off his cap and scratched his head — 'she couldn't get away. The master's going round like a bear with a sore skull. He had me mam in this mornin' tellin' her he was implementin', that was the word he used, implementin' the staff. He told her to send the lasses over and prepare the other rooms above the stables. We don't fancy anybody next door to us now 'cos as you know, Tilly, we've been there since Katie and Peg went down to the lodge. . . . Anyway, just afore I came out he ordered Fred to get the coach ready 'cos he's off somewhere. I laughingly said to Fred it might be to pick up the butler and such, as if he would, but as he said you'd just get the throw-outs at this time of the year. Anyway, the butlers are generally recommended men. Anyhow, Katie can't get away so there's nowt for it, lass, but you'll have to wrap the young 'un up if you want to come along of us. 'Tisn't all that cold the day, in fact it's pleasanter than it's been for weeks; and you've had it out afore in the cart.'

'Yes, yes, of course. I'll . . . I'll wrap him up well.'

'You can take the basket an' all. Put it in the back at your feet. He'd be better in there than on your knee.'

'That's a good idea, Arthur. And I can put an extra blanket over the top.' She turned to him now, saying on a weary laugh, 'I'll have to leave the basket in the cart while I go shopping, so don't forget to lift it out before you start loading up.'

'I'm not daft, Tilly. Here! give him to me and get your hat on.'

Whilst Arthur carried the basket and the child out to the cart Tilly stood pinning her hat on; then she banked down the fire and placed the iron screen in front of it. But before she went towards the door she stood with her hands on the table and, looking down at them, a familiar thought came back into her mind, for she told herself she wished she was old. Oh, how she wished she was old, so old that this thing that she possessed that drew men to her would have withered and died as if it had never been and the shell of her would at last know peace. . . .

The ride was pleasant, smooth in parts, that was until they reached Shields, and there the traffic had defied the wind to harden the surface of the mud roads. But in the main shopping centre of King Street was a pavement and there Arthur put Tilly down with the baby in her arms, together with her bass shopping bag, and as he placed the latter in her hand he said, 'Now don't pack that too full 'cos he's enough for you to hump.'

'Don't worry, Arthur. Remember what you once said? I've got arms like steel bands.'

'Aye, that was once upon a time but they've softened a lot since then. Well, I'll see you in an hour, eh?'

'Thanks, Arthur.'

Although the streets were crowded she had no difficulty in making her purchases, and she was able to rest in the drapery shop on one of the many seats provided for the customers while the assistant unrolled bale after bale very anxious to please her, knowing that here was a customer who didn't want a rough serge or a moleskin, nor yet cheap prints, but a good cord velvet — she had already purchased five yards of the finest flannel. The assistant was puzzled by her. She certainly had money to spend and she spoke well but although her speech was correct it was interspersed with ordinary words; she looked like a lady, yet her dress wasn't fine enough, and then again she was carrying her own baby and she hadn't arrived by carriage. The street was full of them passing by but there wasn't one standing outside the shop. Moreover, she carried a bass bag and no real lady would carry a common bass bag.

'Eight yards, madam? Thank you, madam. And you would wish for a good lining, madam? Certainly, madam. Certainly, madam.'

Tilly looked at her watch. It was almost twenty minutes to three; she had plenty of time to take a quick walk round the market. She liked the market, it was an exciting place. It was strange but she'd always preferred Shields to the city of Newcastle. Although Newcastle had more in the cultural line to offer, such as galleries, not to mention very fine shops with huge plate glass windows and in which you could stand and gaze for hours, she still preferred Shields. Perhaps it was because of its sea front and the wild waters of the North Sea so near. Whatever it was she preferred it, and she wished she could visit the town more often. Lately, she had been toying with the idea of a pony and trap; she had sufficient money to buy both, and the pony could graze on the common land.

The shop assistant showed her to the door where he condescended to place the handle of the bass bag over her forearm, and so she smiled at him as she thanked him even as she thought, That's what I'll do as soon as the year turns, I'll get a pony and trap. Why haven't I done it before?

As the shop assistant was bowing her out he still held the door open to allow a man to enter; but the man stopped, and Tilly stopped, and both said, 'Why! hello.' And both were surprised.

'What are you doing here, Fred?'

She did not mean why was he entering a draper's shop but why was he in Shields. She had understood from Arthur that he was taking his master into Newcastle, yet she remembered that there had been no place mentioned.

Fred Leyburn, smiling at her broadly, said, 'I don't need to ask you what you've been doing, Tilly, been buying the shop it looks like. Where are you off to?'

'I'm just going to walk round the market and then meet Arthur at the corner, he'll be there at three o'clock.'

'Well, wait a minute, I'll walk with you; I just want some thread for Phyllis.' He turned to the assistant who was still holding the door open and, handing him a piece of paper around which was tied a few brown threads, he said, 'Could you get me two bobbins of that, please?'

'Certainly, sir.'

As the assistant went back into the shop, Fred, bending towards the child, said, 'Hello there, Big Willy. How you gettin' on?' And the baby laughed at him and grabbed at his finger and Tilly said, 'Have you come in on your own? I thought you were. . . .'

'Me! on my own?' he cut her off. 'Me life's not me own

112

these days, lass. I'm here, there and everywhere, like a cat on hot bricks. No, the master's gone to see some solicitor bloke with offices just down the street. He said he'd be half an hour, so I haven't stabled the coach, I've left a runner hanging on to it at the end of the market. Of course if his nibs knew I'd done that I'd likely get the sack. Eeh! Tilly, I'm tellin' you, that fellow doesn't know where he is half his time. He's not here afore he's there, and he's not there afore he's back here again. . . . Oh, ta.' He turned to the assistant who was handing him a small paper bag. 'How much?'

'Twopence, sir.'

'There, and thanks.'

As they walked into the street Fred said, 'Shall I carry the bairn for you, Tilly?' and she answered, 'No, but you can take this bag, Fred.'

'You say Arthur's just at the other end of the street?'

'Yes.'

'Well, after a quick walk round I'll see you to him 'cos you've got enough to hump with that 'un.' He thumbed towards the child, and Tilly, laughing said, 'Yes, this 'un's no light weight.'

They had entered the market square now, Fred walking a little in front of Tilly wending his way between the fish stalls, the meat stalls, the hawkers' baskets and the people milling all around them.

When above the usual cries of the market there arose some shrill screams, Fred turned to Tilly and, pulling a face, said, 'Look out! Look out! We'd better keep clear; there's a fight going on ahead. Oh my!' He caught hold of her arm as the people before them, most of then laughing and jeering, backed away from the combatants. But when Fred went to turn Tilly about and make their escape they were checked by the throng behind them who, although not wanting to be brought into the fight, were still interested in the progress of the two women who were tearing at each other's hair, while a man and a boy tried to separate them. The boy had a stout stick in his hand and he was belaying the buttocks of one of the women with it. When at last the viragoes were parted and only their screaming

113

filled the air, Fred remarked, 'Tight as drums. They've started well afore Christmas those two. Come on, let's get out of here.'

Being unable to go back, he now led her towards a gap between two stalls, and it was just as they neared the opening that the larger of the two women turned about. Over the distance of a few yards she stared at Tilly; then grabbing at the shoulder of the boy by her side, she cried, 'Bloody well look at that! This is a day of bad luck all round I'll say. No wonder that whore stole me purse. An' after me standin' her a drink an' all, 'cos look at that, will you! Will you look at that!'

A number of people had gathered in the opening between the two stalls and before Fred could pull Tilly forward Mrs McGrath was upon her, screaming now, 'The bloody witch who killed me son!' Even as she spoke she grabbed the stick from the boy's hand and seemingly in one movement struck out at Tilly's head. Instinctively as Tilly jerked her head away, Fred's arm came upwards to ward off the blow, but too late, it missed both Tilly's head and his arm and caught the child across the forehead.

The cry that went up from all sides drowned that of the child's scream, and when its blood ran over Tilly's hand she, too, screamed. 'Oh my God!'

'She's knocked the bairn's brains out.'

'Eeh! where's the polis? They're never here when they're wanted.'

'She's as drunk as a noodle, but why had she to go and do that? The poor bairn.'

'Oh my God! My God!' Tilly was trying to quench the blood flowing from the gash in the child's brow. There was so much blood that she didn't know exactly where the cut was.

'Here, give him to me. There's an apothecary along the street, he'll do something.' Fred grabbed the child from her arms now and pushed his way through the crowd. Once clear, he ran down the main street, Tilly at his side holding a sodden handkerchief to the child's brow.

The apothecary said, 'Dear! dear!' as he swabbed the child's forehead. Then looking at Tilly, he said, 'There's very little I can do, you must see a doctor. At a pinch I could cauterize it;

then again the cut is much too long and it requires stitching. Look, I will bandage it up temporarily but I think you must get him to a doctor as soon as possible.'

'Which . . . which is the nearest one?'

'Oh . . . let me see.' He scratched his forehead, then said, 'It isn't the nearest one you want but the best one. Now there's a Doctor Simpson. He lives in Prudhoe Street, that's just before you get to Westoe. It's a tidy step but I know he's used to stitching people up.'

'Thank you. Thank you. How much do I owe you?'

'Nothing, nothing, my dear, nothing. I only hope the little man is no worse for this accident.'

Accident. Accident. Those McGraths, they'd be the death of her and her child; nothing they ever did was an accident. Oh God! Oh God! where was it going to end?

Fred picked up the child once more and they hurried out, and in the street he said, 'I'll take you to Arthur and he'll run you along, Tilly, 'cos I'll have to get back to his nibs. He'll be playing hell as it is, leaving the coach in charge of a runner and him but a lad.'

'Yes, yes, Fred. And thank you, thank you. I don't know what I would have done if you hadn't been there. Oh that woman!'

'You'd likely not gone into the market at all.'

'Oh, yes, I would; I intended to go round. He's quiet, is he all right?'

'Aye, he's all right. Don't worry.'

'In the name of God!' The long drawn out exclamation came from Arthur as he saw them hurrying towards him, the child lying limp in Fred's arms, the bandage heavily blood-stained and both he and Tilly bespattered with blood.

After Fred had explained briefly what had happened, Arthur looked at Tilly and, shaking his head, said, 'Eeh! them McGraths. They're devils. Males and females, they're devils. Eeh! By! wait until our Sam and Henry hear of this, they'll deal with the buggers, her an' all. Oh aye, her an' all.'

All Tilly said was, 'Hurry! Arthur. Please hurry.' Then as they moved away she looked down from the cart on Fred, saying again, 'Thank you, Fred. Thank you.'

The cart gone, Fred now took to his heels and ran back the length of King Street, across the market and towards the Mill Dam end, there to see his master mounting the carriage, definitely intent on driving it back himself and, as Fred said later, it was only the sight of the blood on him that stopped him from taking the horses off at a gallop.

'What's happened to you? Been in a fight? Well, it looks as if someone has given you what I would like to give you this minute. Don't you ever dare leave my coach in charge of a boy again, because I promise you it'll be the last time you handle it.'

'Sir, it's . . . it's Miss Trotter.'

'What! What did you say?' Matthew's hands slackened on the reins.

'I . . . I met her while shoppin'. She . . . she was carryin' the child. She . . . she wanted to . . . to. . . .'

'Yes! man. What's happened to her?' Matthew had got down from the box now and was standing facing Fred.

'It isn't her, sir, it's the child. She was carrying the boy an' she met up with Mrs . . . Mrs McGrath. The woman was figthin', and then she saw Tilly . . . Miss Trotter, and she went for her with a big stick.' His hands made an involuntary motion as if measuring the size of the stick. 'But it missed her and struck the bairn's head open.'

'No! Where are they?' The words were quiet, flat sounding.

'I took him to the apothecary's but he advised a doctor and so Arthur . . . Drew, sir, he was in the town collecting stores and I . . . I asked him to take her along.'

'Which doctor, man? Which doctor?'

'Someone near Westoe, Prudhoe Street, a Doctor Simpson.'

'Get up. Let's get off. Go there.'

As Fred scrambled up on to the box, Matthew entered the coach. McGrath. McGraths, those were the people that hated her. One of them who had wanted her had died, stabbed. He remembered his grandmother coming back with some tales about that being the second man who had died through her.

His grandmother had never liked her. But then very few women would. Yet the women of that Drew family adored her. She seemed to court tragedy. What was it about her? Oh God! need he ask? He knew what it was about her; only too well did he know what it was about her. He wished she had never been born; or having been born, she hadn't come to dwell on the estate and enchant his father, because that's what she had done, enchanted him.

He put his head out of the carriage window, saying, 'Can't you make them move?'

'Too much traffic, sir.'

'Aren't there any short cuts?'

'Not to Westoe, sir. . . .'

Fred had no difficulty in finding Doctor Simpson's house in Prudhoe Street because there was the cart standing outside the iron gate and sitting in it rocking the child was Tilly.

When Matthew reached the tail board he began without any leading up, 'Why are you sitting there?'

Tilly showed no surprise at seeing him, she simply answered, 'He's not in, he's not expected for another half hour.'

'Come out of that.'

'He's . . . he's quiet; as long as I rock him he's quiet.'

'Look, give him here!' He almost grabbed the child from her arms, then said, 'Come!' and with that he marched towards the small iron gate, which Arthur, as quickly, jumped to open, then strode up the pathway leading to the front door, to the side of which was a brass plate with a simple statement on it: Arnold P. Simpson, Physician and Surgeon.

'Ring the bell!' He had glanced over his shoulder at Tilly and when she obeyed his command and the door was eventually opened, he stepped forward, almost thrusting the maid aside, saying, 'You have a waiting-room?'

'Doctor ain't in, won't be for. . . .' The girl looked from Matthew to Tilly, then said, 'Aye, there's a waitin'-room, but it's for specials like.'

'Then may I inform you that we are' — he thrust his head forward over the child — 'specials like. Take us to this room immediately.'

The girl went hastily across the narrow hall and opened a door, then watched the gentleman place the child in the woman's arms before turning and saying, 'Fetch a dish of cold water and some hand towels.'

'Eeh! can't do that, mistress wouldn't have it.'

'Is your mistress at home?'

'No, sir, she be out visitin'.'

'Then, my girl, you bring me that water and hand towels or else I shall get them myself. Now away with you!'

When he turned to Tilly he smiled gently at her as he said, mocking himself, 'Terrible man. Terrible man.'

She looked at him but could say nothing, and now he bent over her and his voice was unusually gentle as he said, 'Don't worry. Children are very resilient and, you know, a little blood goes a long way. One thing you must be thankful for, the blow did not touch his eyes.'

Yes, she should be thankful for that. At first she really had thought he had been blinded.

When the maid returned with a bowl of cold water and two towels, she deposited them on a side table, then scampered from the room, and he remarked again with a smile, 'She thinks I'm the devil. Now let's see the damage.'

She was hesitant in unwinding the blood-soaked bandage, and so he, taking it from her fingers, slowly unwound it to reveal the gash still oozing blood, but not so heavily now. The cut went across the middle of the forehead, extending from the outer corner of the child's left eye to a point above the middle of his right eye. Dipping the end of a towel in the water, he gently sponged the blood away from the surface of the brow. Then he dipped the whole huckaback towel in the water and wrung it out before folding it into a narrow length and placing it over the child's brow, saying, 'There, that should quell the bleeding; and it will be ready for him to start on when he comes . . . when he comes.'

He now opened his coat and took out his watch from his waist-coat pocket, saying, 'It is almost four o'clock.' Then standing and looking around the sparsely furnished and dimly lit room, he said, 'If that girl has any sense she'd tell the cook or

118

whoever is in charge to bring you some refreshment. I'll. . . .'

'Please! Please, don't trouble anyone; I'm . . . I'm perfectly all right.'

As she finished speaking there was a slight commotion in the hall and the sound of a chattering voice; then the door opened and the doctor entered. He was a small squat man with a bald head and his appearance would have shattered all preconceived ideas of doctors or surgeons except that his manner was brusque. 'What's this?' he demanded. 'What's this?'

'The child has been hurt, sir.'

The small man looked at the larger one and seemed to take him in at one glance. This was the fellow who had demanded waiting room, water and towels. Evidently a gentleman and one who was used to throwing his weight about.

'Well, let me have a look at the patient.' He took the wet towel from the child's brow, then said, 'H'mm! h'mm! Nasty but fortunate, very fortunate. Another fraction and it would have got his eyes. How did this happen?' He looked from one to the other, but it was Tilly who answered, 'In the market; a drunken woman aimed a staff at me. It missed and hit the child.'

'A drunken woman in the market is nothing new. Locked up half of them; chained up some of them. Wild cats, fish wives, trollops.' The words came out in staccato fashion as he went to the end of the room, opened a glass-fronted cabinet and took out a small box of implements. Then coming back towards them, he looked at Tilly, saying, 'You'd better let your husband hold him, he'll have more stomach for this.'

She opened her mouth twice to speak while the colour seeped temporarily back into her pallid face, and it was Matthew who answered stiffly, 'She is not my wife, she is a Miss Trotter, an old friend of my family. My coachman happened to find her in distress.'

'Oh!' The doctor blinked first at Matthew and then at Tilly, and again he said 'Oh! Well it makes no difference to the stitching, does it? You can still hold the child I suppose.'

Tilly, getting to her feet, placed the baby into Matthew's outstretched arms, and why she should shudder at the contact

119

with him she didn't know, but shudder she did.

'There you are, little fellow. Now we'll put this on first to take some of the sting away. It won't stop you from howling, but you'll have forgotten all about it in a few minutes' time. Although you'll remember it later on because you're going to have a scar here for life. If you're ever lost they'll be able to find you all right.'

Tilly was standing facing the long window that looked on to what appeared to be a back garden and she closed her eyes when the child gave a sharp cry and continued to cry for what seemed an endless time, and she kept them closed until she heard the brusque voice say, 'There, that's done. It took more than I thought. Now a nice little bandage round that and you can face the world again.'

The bandaging done, he now turned to Tilly and said quietly, 'Let him rest for the next few days. No jogging up and down.' He gave her a demonstration. 'No chit-chat, pretty boying, just let him be quiet. He has sustained a shock and that will take time to heal, as well as the cut. Anyway, bring him to me in a week's time. Have you far to go?'

'Quite a way.'

'She . . . she will be here when required, sir.'

The doctor looked at the broad individual with the granite face as he thought to himself, Yes, if he says she'll be here she'll be here. One of those: I speak, you obey. Well, it took all types to make the world go round. He was tired and hungry, and he'd had a day of it. He had drawn splintered bones together, he had stitched up the throat of an unsuccessful suicide, and lastly he had just over an hour ago pushed a man's guts back, and put enough stitches in him to hold a feather tick together. But even so the fellow would likely die, having been at sea three days with part of a spar stuck in his belly.

'Good-day to you.'

'Good-day, doctor. Thank you very much.'

'Good-day, sir, I too thank you.'

He nodded from the man to the woman and blinked at them as he thought, Funny couple this, not man and wife, yet he shows the concern of a husband and she the reserved indifference of a wife. Looking at Matthew, he said, 'I did not get your name, sir.'

'I didn't give it to you, sir, but it is Sopwith, Matthew Sopwith of Highfield Manor. You can send your bill there.'

Sopwith? Oh yes, yes. Now he had the picture clear and bright in his mind. This was the son come back from abroad. Blandford had mentioned something about them. Senior had a mistress who had been a maid or something. Oh yes, yes. Well, well, he could understand it now; she was a beautiful woman. He could also understand the gentleman's concern for the child, his half-brother. Yes, yes. And he had put his foot in it, hadn't he, thinking they were husband and wife? Dear! Dear! 'Good-day to you.'

'Good-day to you. . . .'

Tilly did not protest when Matthew insisted that she get into the coach for all she wanted to do was to get home. . . .

Not until she felt Fred pulling the horses round to enter the gates of the Manor did she speak, and then quickly she said, 'I'll . . . I'll get off here, I can find my way.'

'Don't talk nonsense!'

'Please, I insist.'

'Go on insisting.'

She remained stiff in the seat for a moment until he bent towards her, peering at her in the dim gleam from the carriage lamps as he said, 'Look, Trotter; forget your feeling towards me, at least for the present, the child needs care. You heard what the doctor said. And you yourself need care after the shock you've had. Now you can't look after yourself and the child properly back in that cottage. The weather is vile. Let's be practical; you've got to go out for kindling, what happens if you take ill, who is going to see to the child then? It would have to come here if that happened, wouldn't it?'

She couldn't say, Why should it? And he was right, for what would happen to it if she took ill? She felt tired, weary. Again she had the desire to lay her head down somewhere and cry, but that had become too much of a pattern lately and had to be resisted.

When she remained quiet he said, 'That's it then, that's

settled. There's one thing certain, it will be as good as a Christmas present to your friends, the Drews; they'll have rooms prepared for you in the shake of a lamb's tail.'

She knew that he was smiling and she knew that what he said was right. Of a sudden there was no protest in her, she had the feeling that she was going to float away . . . she was floating away.

She had never before really fainted in her life. As a young girl she had told herself that fainting was the prerogative of ladies and that they usually did it in church or in their drawing-rooms. Even when McGrath and the others had put her in the stocks and pelted her with rotten fruit she hadn't actually fainted.

She opened her eyes to find Biddy bending over her, saying, 'There now. There now.'

'Bring some brandy.' She couldn't see Matthew's face but she recognised his voice and for a moment she wondered where she was. Then she remembered the child and, aiming to rise, said, 'Willy.'

'He's all right. He's all right. He's warmly tucked up and asleep. Don't worry.'

As she closed her eyes again she had the feeling it wasn't Biddy he had asked to fetch the brandy. A moment later when Biddy said, 'Can you raise yourself, lass, and take this drink?' she looked from her to John, who was holding the glass in his hand, and when he said, 'Poor, Tr . . . Trotter,' there was so much kindness in his voice that she had to press her lids tightly closed again to stop herself from crying. She had never felt so weak or so tired, not even when the child was being born; it must be the shock and the knowledge that the McGraths were on her horizon again. Yes, yes, that was it, the McGraths were on her horizon again.

She choked on the brandy and when John said, 'Dr . . . Dr . . . Drink it all up, Trotter, it'll d . . . d . . . do you good,' she drank it. Then she made to rise, saying, 'I'm all right now.'

'Stay where you are, there's nothing to rush for.' Matthew was standing at the back of the couch now looking down on her. 'As Biddy said, the child is all right. Your room will be ready for you in a little while, then you can retire to bed and have a meal there.'

'Thank you, but no.' She pressed Biddy gently aside and, swinging her feet from the couch, she managed to sit upright in spite of still feeling she needed some support. 'I cannot put you to this trouble, and there is no need.'

'Whist! now. Do what the master says and be sensible.' Biddy's tone sounded almost like her master's at the moment. 'The child needs attention, and you an' all. Go tomorrow if you must, but for the night, you stay put.'

'B . . . B . . . Biddy's right, Trotter. B . . . B . . . Be a good girl now.'

As John backed from her she wanted to smile at him.

Be a good girl now. He was a sweet creature was John. If only some of it had rubbed off on to his older brother.

She turned her head and saw them both going from the room, and when the door had closed on them Biddy, pulling a foot stool up to the couch, sat in front of her and, taking her hands, gripped them tight, saying, 'You have some sense, lass, if not for your own sake then for the child's. You're back here, so stay.' She leaned forward until her face was almost touching Tilly's and she whispered, 'From what I gather he'll be off to the Americas again shortly. He's like a cat on hot bricks; he can't find enough to occupy him here. Even since he's taken on opening the pit he's still looking for something to use his energy on. I've never seen a creature so full of unrest, he's never still a minute, so it's my belief he won't be here much longer. He'll leave Master John in charge and then things will run as before. And then the way things are going I'll be surprised if Master John and Miss McGill don't make a match of it. She thinks highly of you that girl. Katie heard her speaking of you to Master John, and his nibs was there an' all. He didn't say a word, Katie said, although I'll give him this 'cos she said he was very nice to the lass. I suppose you've noticed she's got a birthmark? Aye, well, we've all got things to bear. She's got a nice nature and she's sweet on Master John, you can see that, anybody with half an eye can see that. So now, you take my

123

advice. I've never given it you wrong since we met, now have I?'

'No, Biddy.'

'Then, lass' — Biddy's voice dropped to a soft whisper — 'do this for me, stay on. And it's Christmas and we could have a lovely time because I'll not know a minute's peace if you're back there on your own and the sky outside there laden with snow, and if it falls like it did last year we won't be able to get through to you for days, perhaps not for weeks. It happened afore, it could happen again. I worry over you, lass, just as if you were me own; in fact' — she looked downwards now — 'I feel guilty at times 'cos I think of you more than I do me own.'

'Oh, Biddy. Biddy. Do you know something?' Tilly was smiling faintly now, 'You shouldn't be in ordinary service, it is the diplomatic service you should have gone into.'

'And what kind of service may I ask is that?'

'Well, it's for people who have the powers of persuasion.'

The door opened and Katie came stealthily into the room. 'It's all ready, the fire's burning nicely, bed warmer in, and Peg's got your tray all set.'

'Oh dear me!' Tilly drooped her head and Katie, looking at her mother, said, 'What's wrong now? Starting to be contrary again, is she?'

'Less of your cheek,' said Biddy, getting to her feet; 'and get about your business.'

Instead of Katie going about her business she came up to Tilly and, dropping on to her hunkers in a fashion they had both used whilst working side by side down the pit, she said with a grin, 'Eeh! it's like old times, isn't it, Tilly? And we'll have some Christmas jollification an' all that, eh? I wasn't going to decorate our hall but I'll do it the morrow. I'll get the lads to bring some holly in. And I wonder if his nibs will let us do something to the main hall now 'cos he said we hadn't to bother. Didn't he, Ma?'

'Yes, he did,' said Biddy nodding; 'but now, there's a bairn in the house an' that makes the Christmas, a bairn, so go ahead and decorate the main hall an' all, and put some holly in the dining-room.'

'And what about some mistletoe?' said Katie, now smiling broadly. 'Master John might take a nibble at Miss McGill. That would be good to see. But I can't see his nibs kissing anybody, can you, Ma? That would turn them to vinegar right off.'

'Look.' Biddy pointed her finger at her chattering daughter whom, although only a year younger than Tilly, she still treated as a girl. 'What did I tell you? Get yourself away about your business afore I skelp your lug for you, and you'd need some vinegar to put on that!'

Katie went out laughing and Biddy remarked, 'That 'un 'll never change: chatter, chatter, chatter. 'Tis well she hasn't married, she'd drive a man to drink. Come on, lass; let's get you upstairs.'

As if Tilly was a real invalid, Biddy helped her up from the couch, but as they made their way towards the drawing-room door Tilly stopped and said, 'Where are they putting me?'

'In your old room of course.'

She remained staring at Biddy. Which old room? The room that she and Mark had shared or the one at the end of the corridor that she had rarely used?

And Biddy added bluntly, 'The one you started with.'

Tilly turned away and, unaided now, walked across the hall and up the broad stairs, over the gallery and down the long corridor. She did not even glance towards the main bedroom but went on past it, past the dressing-room, past the closet and into the end room, and as she entered it she knew that she had come back and to stay; but at the same time that strange fear mounted in her again, the fear that she was afraid to put a name to, the fear that wasn't connected with either the McGraths or the villagers.

PART THREE

The Child

1

She had fallen into the routine of the house as if she had never left it. Christmas had been a gay affair, although the Christmas dinner was the only time she had allowed herself to sit in the dining-room and eat. From the day following her entry back into the house she had refused Matthew's order that she must eat with him. It was only on John's plea that Miss McGill would feel a little out of place, there being one lady and two men, that she consented to have her Christmas dinner in the dining-room instead of in the servants' hall. She had also said firmly that if she were to stay then she must make her rooms, as in the early days, on the nursery floor for now she had a child to see to.

Matthew raised no objection to this, and things went smoothly between them until the second week of the New Year when, returning from the town late one afternoon he called her into the library, and there without any preamble he said, 'I am sure you'll be pleased to learn that the McGrath woman will shortly get her deserts.'

'What do you mean?' She peered at him through narrowed lids.

'Well, what I've just said.' He nodded towards her. 'The matter has been in the hands of my solicitor since shortly after the incident. She is to appear in court the day after tomorrow. Leyburn will testify, as will you yourself.'

'*No! No!*' Her voice was loud. 'I won't. I won't go into court again! You should not have done this.'

'Not have done it? She could have killed the child and you say I shouldn't have done it!'

'Yes; I repeat you shouldn't have done it, it's none of your business.'

'Trotter!' His voice was low and his tone cold. 'I don't want to remind you again that the child is my half-brother. There is the question of blood, I have an interest in him, he will carry that woman's mark to his grave.'

'He is my child, you have no claim on him, none whatever. And I would like you to get that firmly in your head: *You have no claim on him.* What is more, you have no right to do this.' She choked and hunched her shoulders up around her neck; then she bent her head forward and placed her hand on her brow as she said, 'You don't understand. Even if she had murdered him I . . . I could not have gone into court. I have been in a court. I was accused in a court of being a witch and of being the instigation of causing a man's death. The scene has never left me. You may have nightmares about frogs but' — she swung her head from side to side — 'there are periods when I'm back in that courtroom night after night.'

She now raised her head, and they stared at each other; then, her voice soft, her tone flat, she said, 'I . . . I appreciate your concern, I do really, but believe me I don't want this matter to go to court. She was drunk else she would never have done what she did, as bad as she is. And . . . and another thing, that family has known enough trouble inadvertently through me. If . . . if that woman were sent to prison I . . . I wouldn't know a moment's rest. And I can tell you this, if that family were to suffer again through me it would cause such bad feeling in the village I would be afraid to move out of these gates. One of her sons died in . . . in strange circumstances.' She lowered her eyes now. 'I . . . I was held responsible for it, although the matter never came to court. The youngest son, who incidentally was different from all the rest and . . . and was kind to me, he left home never to return. A third son went into the army and was killed. She has one son left now and one grandson.'

As her head drooped again a silence fell between them until he said, 'It will be as you wish. I . . . I imagined that you would have liked retribution, but I can see that I was wrong.'

He walked now the length of the room towards the window,

and there he stood looking out for some moments before he said, 'There was another matter I wanted to speak about. In about two weeks' time I would like you to prepare a small dinner party. It will be for six. Just an ordinary affair, nothing too elaborate. The guests will be Mr and Mrs Rosier and a Miss Alicia Bennett, Mrs Rosier's cousin. And then, of course, John and Anna and. . . .'

'The Rosiers?' The name escaped her.

He turned now and walked back towards her, saying, 'Yes, the Rosiers. He is going into partnership with me in the mine.'

'Partnership! . . . Your father. . . .'

The change in him startled her for he almost yelled at her now, 'What my father did and what I want to do are two entirely different things. My father had a personal prejudice against the Rosiers. I have no feelings for them one way or the other, but I need his expertise. He knows all about mines, I unfortunately don't as yet. And if I return to America . . . I should say, when I return to America, John will be left in charge, and he knows less than nothing about mining. I am putting a great deal of money into this concern, and Mr Rosier has enough faith in the project to add more to it. Moreover, he has the experience to pick men with the ability not only to manage but to work the mine. . . .'

'Yes, and drive them like slaves and house them in hovels, and dismiss them at a moment's notice if they dare attempt to read and write, put them on to the road in effect.'

'That was some years ago' — his tone had altered now — 'things have improved.'

'Oh no they haven't, not by what I hear.'

'The Drews still keep you supplied with pit news then?'

When she didn't reply he said, 'By all accounts my father wasn't any better an employer than Mr Rosier. He allowed you to work in his mine, didn't he? And the little girl who was killed beside you in the fall, how old was she? And speaking of cottages, I was through his row yesterday, and although they have become more dilapidated with the years there is still evidence of what they would have been when inhabited; and let me tell you this, some of the rough-necks I met in America would have preferred to sleep outside in the open and braved the elements and wild animals rather than bunk down into those hovels. . . .

'So —' he moved nearer to her until she was only an arm's length from him and, looking straight into her face, he said, 'If you would be kind enough, Trotter, to oblige me by arranging, as I said, a small dinner party for the twenty-eighth? Thank you.'

She was left standing, her hands tightly gripped in front of her waist.

Why was it he always seemed to put her in the wrong? And why was it she always had the desire to go against him, argue with him? And it wasn't her place. But what was her place? As her granny would have said, she was neither fish, fowl, nor good red meat. Left to herself she felt as if she were mistress of the house, but in his presence she became a servant. Yet the odd thing was he never treated her as such, rather, more as an equal.

But this Rosier business. Well, she supposed he was right in all he had said: he had no knowledge of mines and if he was going back to America he'd have to leave someone in charge. She wished he were going back tomorrow. Oh yes, tomorrow. The sooner the better.

It was a blustery day towards the end of April when the wind seemed to be trying to obliterate the sun by sending scudding clouds across the sky. Tilly was in the nursery; she had the child in her arms and was standing before the window pointing upwards, saying, 'Look! birdie. . . . Look! Willy, birdie.'

But the child didn't follow her pointing finger, he made an unintelligible sound and stroked her cheek with his plump hand, and she stared into his eyes, large soft brown eyes; then she traced her finger above the jagged scar running across his brow. It hadn't faded as the doctor had said it would, it still showed as a narrow red weal; and on each visit he still assured her that as the child grew older the weal would flatten; he would always carry a scar but it would be hardly noticeable in later life as his skin grew tougher.

The doctor had insisted that she take the child to him every month. He would look into the child's eyes and mutter, but make no comment other than to say jocularly, 'He's a healthy little beggar, is our Willy.'

The nursery door opened and John peeped round into the room, saying, 'C . . . can I have a w . . . w . . . word with you, Trotter?'

'Yes, of course.'

'I know I sh . . . sh . . . shouldn't disturb you in your r . . . r . . . rest time but I w . . . w . . . wanted you to be the f . . . first to know.'

She smiled at him as she seated herself at the corner of the nursery table and pointed to the seat opposite. She knew exactly what news he was about to divulge but she waited, saying nothing.

'Tr . . . Trotter —' he blinked his eyes, screwed them up tight, then opened his mouth wide before he brought out, 'I . . . I don't know whether y . . . you've s . . . s . . . seen it or not, but I'm in lo . . . lo . . . love with Anna.'

'Well, I had noticed something different about you.' She now burst out laughing, and he put his head down and covered his eyes with his hands for a moment before he said, 'I'm going to her gr . . . gr . . . grandmama today to ask p . . . per . . . mission to marry her.'

'Oh, I'm so glad, John, so glad.' She put her free hand across the table towards him, and he said, 'I th . . . thought you m . . . might be, and I know you like Anna. She . . . she . . . she dotes on you. But I'm r . . . rather wor . . . worried, her gr . . . grand . . . grandmama is a very stiff old girl.'

'Oh, you'll soften her up, never fear, John. You'll soften her up.'

'I'm n . . . not so sure, in some . . . some ways she p . . . puts me in mind of my gr . . . grandmama. You remember, sh . . . she . . . she didn't like me just because I . . . I stammered.'

'Well, she wasn't a nice person and very few people liked her.'

'You kn . . . know, Trotter, it w . . . was you who brought

133

us together. We'll never forget that, never.' He moved his head slowly as he looked at her, then said, 'And now I must g . . . go and f . . . f . . . find Matthew. He went out r . . . r . . . riding about an hour ago, but I don't know whether he's gone to the m . . . m . . . mine or gone riding with Miss . . . Miss Bennett.' He rose to his feet and bending towards her said in a mock whisper, 'Wouldn't it be f . . . f . . . funny if we had a d . . . double engagement, Trotter? Wouldn't it?'

She made no answer but watched him walk to the door, and as he opened it she said, 'Is Matthew thinking about going back to America shortly?'

There was a broad grin on his face as he answered, 'Never heard a w . . . w . . . word of it recently, not s . . . s . . . since he met the d . . . divine Alicia. She scares me a b . . . b . . . bit. I think Matthew has met his m . . . m . . . match. What do you think?'

She didn't say what she thought, she just shook her head and he went out. She rose and placed the child on the rug before walking to the window again and looking out. Well, there was one thing certain, if the divine Alicia became mistress of this house she herself would once again pack her bundle and depart.

Later that day John and Anna came running through the house like two children, calling, 'Trotter! Trotter!' and after being directed to the servants' hall they stood before her, and she held out her hands to both of them and said, 'I'm so glad.'

It was Anna who spoke first. Her voice full of meaning, she said, 'Thank you, Trotter.'

John, leaning towards her, his eyes sparkling with happiness, exclaimed on a laugh, 'W . . . W . . . Wouldn't believe it, Trotter. I n . . . n . . . nearly fainted, her gr . . . grandmama k . . . k . . . kissed me.'

Tilly watched them lean against each other. Then John turned towards Biddy, and she came forward and said, 'I'm happy for you, sir. I'm happy for you both. I'll make the grandest spread for you in the county on the day it happens.'

'Thank you, Bi . . . Biddy.'

134

'Oh, thank you, Biddy.'

Katie now came forward and dipped her knee to the young girl, and Fanny, Peg and Betty followed.

'Ha . . . have a drink at d . . . d . . . dinnertime to us.' John nodded from one to the other. 'Will you br . . . br . . . bring a bottle up, Trotter?'

'Yes, I'll do that.'

As the two of them turned hand in hand and ran from the room the girls all put their hands over their mouths to still their laughter, and Biddy said, 'There's two that'll make it.'

It was Katie who turned to her mother now and said, 'An' I wonder if the master will make it with Miss Bennett. What do you think?'

Biddy's answer was abrupt. 'I'm not paid for thinkin', I'm paid for workin', and so are you. Now you've finished your tea get on with it.' And as Katie's hand went out to the last cake left on a plate her mother slapped the hand aside, saying, 'Go on, leave that alone; you're always stuffin' your kite. You never see green cheese but your mouth waters.'

'Aw, Ma, you!' Katie replied and pushed Fanny before her.

As Biddy turned and walked towards the door leading to the kitchen she said, 'What's your idea about him and the horse-mad heifer?'

Tilly paused before answering, 'I haven't really thought about it,' at the same time reminding herself that very little passed Biddy's nose. 'If he wants her, he'll have her, I suppose; he's that kind of man.'

'I wish he'd get himself off back to the Americas, that's what I wish.'

As Tilly now walked up the kitchen she answered quietly without looking in Biddy's direction, 'You're not the only one, Biddy. You're not the only one.'

2

The engagement party was being held in honour of Willy's forthcoming birthday too. The day had been very hot and the evening promised no relief until the moon should come up.

The preparations in the house during the past two weeks had been on from early morning until late at night. John and Anna had wanted a small private engagement party, but Matthew had shouted them down, saying that as he was the first of the three to put the halter round his neck, it must be done at least with a little ostentation, not too much, but just a little.

The meal was to consist of a cold buffet supper, and concerning this Matthew had annoyed not only Biddy but Tilly also, for apart from the cold game, porks, sirloins and hams, and the pastries and cakes, the roasting and baking of which Biddy had perfected over the years, he had ordered from a Newcastle firm a large iced three-tiered cake that was to be the centre of the main table, as well as trays of fancy tit-bits.

Then at the last moment, only two days ago in fact, he had informed Tilly that he was engaging six male servants from Newcastle, one to act as butler, two as first and second foot-man, and three as wine waiters. There was also to be a quartet to provide music.

When she had shown her surprise and open displeasure at the engaging of the male staff, he had turned on her, saying, 'I do it to relieve you of the responsibility of the staff on that evening. You manage the household, in fact act as its mistress, so I want you to put on your best dress and help receive the guests . . . as its mistress.'

She recalled the scene, the open quarrel that ensued when she cried at him 'Oh no! No! Do you wish to humiliate me? You have given me the list of guests, and in it I notice three names, supposed friends of your father, the Fieldmans, the Tolmans and the Craggs. I remember just how their wives considered me the last time they were in this house. To them I was merely a servant, and rightly so, but there are ways and ways of treating a servant. Apart from Miss Bennett I don't know any of the other names on the guest list, but I know those three ladies. There is a name for them. I remember applying it to them all those years ago, it still remains vivid in my mind, and that name is bitch. They were three bitches then, so imagine their reaction to me if I should be in the hall to receive them, as you say, mistress of the house. . . . Oh, you know the correct procedure better than most, so why are you set on subjecting me to this humiliation? Anyway, the rightful people on this occasion to receive the guests are John and Anna. And my part, I can assure you, will be that of the housekeeper, because after all that is what I am, the housekeeper, and I would thank you to remember that and not embarrass me with such ridiculous suggestions.'

'God!' He had gripped his unruly hair with both hands and swung round from her as he exclaimed, 'Of all the bloody aggravating women on this earth, Trotter, you'd be hard to beat! All right' — he had turned to her again — 'you want to be a housekeeper, from now on I'll see that you are treated as a housekeeper.'

She had glared at him, returning a look similar to that in his eyes and stretching her neck upwards and so, outreaching his height, she had said, 'Very good, sir,' then turned and walked out of the drawing-room. But as she went to close the door she had paused for a second as his muttered oath came to her, saying, 'Damn and blast you!'

That night she had hardly slept, and the next morning John had come to her and said without any lead up, 'Now, Trotter, you are to c . . . c . . . come to the p . . . p . . . party, M . . . M . . . Matthew is furious, like a b . . . bear with a sore skull.' And he had put his head on one side as he added, 'I . . . I don't

137

know how it is, Trotter, b . . . b . . . but you know you g . . . g
. . . get under his skin . . . skin more than anyone else I know. I
c . . . c . . . can't understand it, you who are s . . . s . . . so good
and tactful with everybody, but you s . . . s . . . seem to an . . .
annoy him. Why? Why, Trotter?'

'I don't mean to, John; but I don't think he's ever forgiven
me for being your father's mistress.'

'Oh, I th . . . think he has, Trotter; in fact, I know he's v . . .
v . . . very concerned for you and li . . . li . . . little Willy. He's
very f . . f . . . fond of Willy, as we all are, and as he said the
party c . . . c . . . could be a celebration f . . . f . . . for his first
birthday too. Oh, come on.' He put his hand on her arm. 'After
all, Tr . . . Trotter, both Anna and I know that you . . . you m
. . . made our engagement possible.'

'Don't worry.' She smiled at him. 'Just leave it, we'll see.'

'You m . . . m . . . must, Trotter.'

'All right, all right.'

'Good! Good!'

John went out of the room, down the stairs taking them two
at a time, almost upsetting Katie who was carrying a tray of
dishes from the morning-room. As he steadied her and the
tray, he said, 'M . . . M . . . Matthew. M . . . M . . . Master
Matthew, has he gone?'

'No, he's still in there, Master John.'

John entered the morning-room almost at a run, to see his
brother standing looking out of the window on to the side
lawn, and he said immediately, 'I've s . . . s . . . seen her. She'll
c . . . c . . . come as the f . . . family. You kn . . . know,
Matthew, you are too rough with p . . . p . . . people and
Trotter is a s . . . s . . . sensitive p . . . person.'

'*Sensitive!* . . . *Sensitive!*' Matthew swung round from the
window. 'When she decides she's not going to do anything
she's about as sensitive as a long-horned bull.'

John laughed at this, then said, 'Well, I would have f . . . f
. . . felt awful if she just t . . . took up the position of a s . . . s
. . . servant to . . . tomorrow night. You see I cannot help it,
Matthew, b . . . but I feel she is something sp . . . sp . . .
special in a way, and both Anna and I owe her so much. You s

'...s...see, Anna went to her in the first place thinking she was a wi...witch and that she might be able to remove the b...b...birthmark. And you know, I...I somehow think she is a bi...bit of a witch because....'

'Don't say that word, and don't couple it with her! Do you hear me? Don't ever couple it with her!'

'Oh, Ma...Matthew, I'm s...s...sorry but I didn't m...m...mean it in a nas...nasty way, you know that, it was a s...sort of a com...compliment.'

'There's no compliment in being called a witch. I know of places in America where people bow their heads when that word is used, some in shame, some in sorrow; those in shame because their ancestors were not ignorant scum but class people, who would have been known as gentry here, and it was mainly they and the clergy who condemned innocent people to be hung and just from hearsay.'

'Oh.' The syllable sounded placating but lacked a note of interest. 'They were as b...bad as they w...w...were here then?'

'Worse, I should say. There was a time towards the end of the sixteen hundreds when people in Massachusetts, and other states too, went crazy in witch hunts. Some young clergyman wrote a book about an old woman in Boston who had been executed for being a witch. The story goes that the book got into the hands of three silly girls and they accused someone of being a witch, and to save her own neck the victim implicated others. It got so bad that there were special courts appointed to try the supposed witches. The frightened victims confessed to all kinds of things, saying that some travelled on broomsticks and held conversations with the devil. Those who dared raise their voice against the courts were immediately accused of being the devil's tongue. Some of the victims were hanged and one man, so I heard from a descendant of his, was pressed to death. I tell you, John' — Matthew pointed at his brother, his voice harsh, and his face red — 'although it's a long time since a witch was burnt in this country the fear still prevails. You've only to go back to what happened to Trotter because she danced with the parson's wife. You won't remember it, except by hearsay, but they put her in the stocks. And when the parson's wife accidentally killed one of Trotter's persecutors they burned down her grandmother's cottage. Although the rubble has all been cleared away the foundations still remain as a grim reminder at the east end of the estate.'

'I d . . . d . . . didn't understand. I never meant. . . .'

'Oh, I know you didn't.' Matthew made a conciliatory movement with his hand. 'I never thought much about witchcraft myself until I went to America. I knew people here referred to Trotter as a witch, but to me then the word simply meant somebody bewitching as she undoubtedly was. But when I came across two families who, I understood, had hated each other for more than a hundred years and was told the reason why, well, since then, the very word is anathema to me, because hatred caused the death, supposedly accidental, of the son of one house and kept the daughter of the other house separated. They had fallen in love. The result was, one grew into a sour old maid and the other was killed. And this all came about through the word witch. And the sour old maid happens to be Uncle's daughter.'

'Oh! Oh! R . . . really? I'm sorry, Ma . . . Matthew. I understand how you f . . . f . . . feel so strongly about it. R . . . R . . . Rest ass . . . assured I'll n . . . never apply that name to Trotter again. In fact, I d . . . d . . . don't think I'll ever use it again in . . . in . . . in any way.'

Matthew drew in a long breath, lowered his head and shook it from side to side before saying, 'You must think me odd at times, John, a little crazy, but living over there has changed my views on everything and everyone. There's a rawness about it that . . . that finds its counterpart inside me. When I left England for the first time I felt capable of holding my own with anyone, gentry or commoner. Well, I found I could hold my own with the so-called gentry, they were no different as I said from what they are over here, except perhaps a little more ruthless, for they have more to gain and more to lose; but it was the common man, the ordinary fellow who stands up to you and tells you that he's as good as you, boy. They don't do it in so many words, it's by looks and actions, it's more of what they leave out than what they put into their attitude towards you that brings you down. What you value they laugh at, they spit at; oh yes, literally. It turns your stomach at first, because everybody spits; no matter where they are, who they are, they spit. They chew tobacco and spit. I found it so nauseating that I actually wanted to vomit at times. Really, I did.' He nodded his head now as he smiled at John. 'Then you get used to it. You have to. In fact, at times you're even tempted to copy them instead of swallowing, especially if you're smoking a pipe. Good lord!' He laughed now as he put his arm around John's shoulders, saying, 'I have gone on, haven't I? America, first lesson, from witches to spit!'

'It was in . . . inter . . . interesting. I wish you would talk more, Matthew. You've told me v . . . v . . . very little about Uncle; I don't even know what he looks like, this uncle. I only hope he doesn't t . . . t . . . take after Gr . . . Gr . . . Grandmama. He was her half-bro . . . brother, wasn't he?'

'Yes, but I can assure you there's nothing of Grandmama in Alvero Portes, except perhaps his determination to have his own way; but unlike Grandmama, he tempers this with a great deal of tact. Anyway, we'll talk about him later; but now, to get back to the present and my bone of contention, namely Trotter. You succeeded where I failed, and when I come to think of it, you always did have a better effect on her than I had. Well now, I think you'd better go and carry out your charm in the kitchen because the wind there I fear is against me. If they had any sense they'd know they couldn't cope with everything tomorrow and that I was thinking of them when I ordered the additional staff.'

'N . . . n . . . no, you weren't.' John pushed Matthew none too playfully now in the shoulder. 'Y . . . you know you weren't. Os . . . os . . . ostentation you said, a bit, not too much. Are you ins . . . ins . . . insisting on them wearing s . . . s . . . satin breeches and g . . . gaiters?'

'No, kilts like the Scots in order to placate your future wife's grandmother who, I understand, hails from over the Border.'

'Oh.' John put his head back and let out a free peal of laughter, and they were both laughing when they crossed the hall and picked up their tall hats and coats and went out of the door and to the stables.

A few minutes later, as Tilly watched them both riding down the drive, she thought how unlike their temperaments were. If only Matthew had been born with a little of John's kindness and softness. But what about the other way? Yes, she supposed it would have helped John if in his turn he'd had a little more self-assurance; but not so much that it amounted to bombast.

She repeated the word to herself, bombast. But could that word be correctly applied to Matthew? What did it mean? She was thinking in the way of Mr Burgess as she said to herself: Stuffing, padding, loud assertiveness, over-stressed eloquent phrasing. Well no, bombast was the wrong word, there was no padding about him, he was too forthright. . . . Loud assertiveness? Yes; he yelled more often than not, especially when he was angry. And of course, he did assert himself, but not with high-falutin phrases. . . . Oh, why on earth was she standing here dissecting his character? Didn't she get enough of him when they were face to face? She was becoming daily more irritated by his very presence. And then the party tomorrow. He had taken as much trouble over it as if it was to celebrate his own engagement. Hm! Perhaps it was, too. Well, the sooner the better. She turned from the window and went about her duties.

As Biddy remarked later to Katie, 'She's going round lookin' like I feel, as if the only thing that would ease her would be to slap somebody's lug.'

It was many a year since the house had known such gaiety, and the almost full moon and the soft night together seemed to lend enchantment to the whole affair.

At ten o'clock Matthew's eloquent but brief speech, followed by the drinking of the health of the happy couple, was over and most of the guests had dispersed into the grounds, which gave Matthew the idea to have the quartet brought from the gallery on to the terrace. The young people were dancing on the sunken lawn; and not only the young, for the wine seemed to have loosened the stiffness in the legs of their parents and many were showing their paces, dancing not only the minuet, but the schottische, and even the faster polka.

The waiters, too, were kept busy, moving among the guests handing plates of sweetmeats and even more substantial cuts; and it was nothing to see a velvet-coated gentleman gnawing at a chicken leg, or another holding his head back as he dangled a slice of sirloin above his gaping mouth.

The lamps on the terrace and the lights from the house assisting the moon showed the scene up almost as if it were being enacted in daylight. Tilly was standing just within the open window of the morning-room at the end of the terrace. The shadow cast by the cypress tree fell across the window and so hid the expression on her face, a mixture of anger and disdain as she looked down on the scene. Her eyes were focussed on a small group of women.

Those three! She felt that she had jumped back thirteen years. As on that night years ago Mrs Tolman, Mrs Fieldman and Mrs Cragg and their parties had all arrived together, and just as on that night they had made a point of speaking about her as if she weren't present, so they had done tonight but with a difference. On the previous occasion when they had discussed her they had not been certain of her position in the house, but tonight they were, and as if prior to their arrival they had together decided what form their attitude towards her was to be, they had all stared boldly at her as they stood side by side like three ravens: one was dressed in blue taffeta, one in dark green silk, and the other in black lace, and the colours combined were like the sheen on a raven's back. What was more, they had pointedly ignored John's introduction of her, and his 'Miss Trotter, a friend of the family' brought a sound like a hoot from Mrs Bernice Cragg. But the final insult was when Alice Tolman, the eldest of the four Tolman girls, who, although being twenty-eight years old and plain, was of a pleasant nature, had stopped to speak to her, for it was then her mother sailed towards them and, without looking at either of them, said, 'You should know your place, Alice, even if others forget theirs.'

143

She should never, never have allowed herself to be persuaded to act as hostess tonight. She looked down at her dress. It was pretty, simple but pretty, made of yellow cotton with a pale blue forget-me-not sprig. She had purchased it in Newcastle at the last moment. The bodice was close fitting and the skirt not entirely fashionable, for it wasn't over full; the neck was square but not low enough to show the dip between her small breasts. The sleeves were elbow length with an attached loose frill that came half way down her forearms. Her hair, swept upwards from the back and the sides, made her appear even taller than she was. She wore neither powder nor rouge and therefore in comparison with most of the ladies present looked a tall, willowy pale thing.

All the Drews had exclaimed aloud when they saw her. But then they would, wouldn't they? They were like her family and real families never decried their own. But Anna, too, had said she looked nice, only she had used the word beautiful. And John had endorsed her remark. Matthew had said nothing, he had merely looked her up and down. But he had said nothing.

He had, she noticed, been drinking heavily during the evening. They all had, the noise from the garden proclaimed this, and the merriment had, in some quarters, turned to vulgarity, fathers chasing young girls who weren't their daughters, men guzzling meat like market day yokels. In fact, the whole scene had now taken on the appearance of a fairground. She turned into the darkened room and peered at the clock on the mantelpiece. Ten minutes to twelve. She was tired, weary. She wished she could go to bed, but this she wouldn't be able to do until the last of the guests had gone, and as yet no one had shown any sign of leaving.

She made her way out of the room into the hall and as she went past the foot of the stairs on her way to the kitchen she was almost knocked on to her back by one of the Fieldman boys chasing Miss Phoebe Cragg. Neither stopped to apologise, and she stood for a moment watching them racing out of the front door and down the steps on to the drive.

When she reached the kitchen it was to see Biddy still busy

at the table packing plates with pies and tarts and handing them to the girls, who in turn would take them out the back way to supply the waiters, who had set up a long table, near the end of the terrace.

Without looking up, Biddy said, 'They've gone through the fancy tit-bits an' now they're startin' on the real food.'

'Will you have enough?'

'I should say so; we've baked two hundred pasties and a hundred big tarts in the last four days. But I can tell you something, Tilly, I'm droppin' on me feet.'

'Yes, I know you are, Biddy; I wish you'd let me help.'

'What!' Biddy turned and looked at her and smiled wearily now, saying, 'Your place is in there. Get yourself back. How's things goin'?'

'Oh, very well I should say.'

'Aye, by the sound of it I should say that an' all. As Katie said, it's more like a harvest do than an engagement party. It'll surprise me if the rabbits don't start breedin' after this.'

'Oh' — Tilly managed to laugh — ' 'tisn't as bad as that. They're all very jolly, wine jolly, mostly.'

'Aye, well, when drink's in wits are out, as they say. An' when the men reach that stage it's no use warnin' the lasses to keep their eyes open and their skirts down. As the saying goes, there's no difference atween a lord and a lout when they are both without a clout.'

'Oh Biddy!' Again Tilly laughed; then she added, 'I'll slip up and see how Willy is. He was as sound as a top an hour ago but the narration might have woken him up.'

As Biddy turned away to hand two plates to Peg, she said, 'You're not enjoyin' it, are you?'

Tilly half turned now and looked at her, but Biddy was busily filling more plates and she answered, 'About as much as you are.' Then she went out; but she did not go into the hall, she took the back stairs and entered the gallery from a side door, and as she crossed it to go up the corridor Matthew came out of his father's room accompanied by Alicia Bennett.

Her pause was hardly perceivable, only long enough to glance at them and as Matthew went to speak she was already some steps away from them.

Inside, she was ablaze. How dare he take that woman in there! Whatever he wanted to do with her, why didn't he take her to his own room?

She reached the night nursery and stood for a moment looking down on the sleeping child. She was gripping the side of the cot as much in anger as for support as her thoughts reminded her that after all it was his room. Every room in the house was his room; that's what she kept forgetting. He was the master here, Mark was dead, and she herself had no position other than that of housekeeper.

She sat down on the low nursing chair near the banked-down fire which, in spite of the heat, was always kept alight, and she asked herself what was the matter with her? She felt so unhappy, so lost. She had felt unhappy after Mark died, but then the companionship of Mr Burgess and the waiting time whilst she was carrying the child she saw now as a time of peace. Even in her loneliness there was a certain kind of happiness, but she had never known a moment's happiness since she had come back into this house.

Pulling a small table towards her, she leant her arms on it and dropped her head on to them. . . .

She jumped with a start when a hand came on her shoulder, then gasped as she looked up into Katie's face.

'Eeh! I'm sorry to wake you, Tilly, but we wondered where you were. They've nearly all gone.'

'*What!*'

'Well, it's half past two.'

'*No!* Oh dear, dear!' She rose to her feet. 'I . . . I must have fallen asleep.'

'Well, it'll do you good. An' that's what I want to do, fall asleep, I'm nearly droppin' on me feet.'

'You say they've nearly all gone?'

'Aye; the Rosiers have just left, and the Tolmans and the Craggs, at least the old 'uns of that lot have. But some of the young 'uns are hangin' on, especially the fellows who came on horseback. One went off with a lass up afront of him. I don't know who he was but all of them on the drive were splittin' their sides.'

'What about Mrs McGill?'

'Oh, she went off about an hour ago, and the aunt an' all. I liked her. She spoke to me, they both did. They're sort of gentry, good gentry those two, not like some of them there the night. Coo! the Bull an' Pen on a Saturday night is nothin' to some of the things I saw goin' on. Lordy. . . !'

'What about Miss Anna?'

'Oh, she went along of them, and Master John, he rode aside the carriage. A lot of the young 'uns ran alongside as they went down the drive, cheerin' and laughin'. That was nice.'

'I'll come down.'

'Me ma's dead beat.'

'I should think she would be. You must make her lie in tomorrow morning; I can see to things here.'

'Oh, I doubt if she'll stand for that.'

Before leaving the nursery, they both went and looked at the child. He was lying with his thumb in his mouth and Katie said, 'When he looks like that I could eat him.'

They went quietly out and down the stairs on to the main landing. The house was strangely still now.

In the kitchen Biddy was sitting with her feet up on a cracket and, turning and looking towards Tilly, she said, 'I thought you were lost, lass.'

'I'm sorry; I fell asleep.'

'Nowt to be sorry for. Anyway, it's all over except payin' the bill. An' I bet this's cost him a pretty penny the night.'

'The waiters. . . ?'

'Oh, they went off in the brake with the band about fifteen minutes ago. And you know something?' She turned her head and looked up at Tilly. 'They were for taking the remainder of the stuff that was left outside. Aye, they were. . . . Aw, I told them where to go to. By! I did. They said it was the rule. Well, I said to them, there's a first time for everything an' this is the first time your rule's gona be broken, an' I hope it won't be the last. . . . Five bob a night each and all they could eat . . . and drink, and then they wanted to take the foodstuff. My! some people get their livin' easy.'

'Come on. Get off to bed. And you an' all, Katie. I'll see to things here.'

Biddy got slowly to her feet, saying, 'Yes, lass, I think I will. We've cleared up as much as we can, we'll do the rest in the mornin'. But look, how are we gona get down the drive without bumping into somebody? There's still young 'uns kickin' about in the garden.'

'Go round by the orchard and the water garden.'

'Oh, I don't like that way,' Katie put in now; 'it's dark round there, you've got to go under them cypresses.' And when Fanny and Peg endorsed this by saying together, 'Me neither,' Tilly said, 'Well, go and ask Arthur to go with you, or one of the others can leave the stables now the carriages are nearly all gone. Anyway, Fred may still be about; he's nearly sure to be.'

'Oh, don't bother them; they've had enough on their plates the night.' Biddy flapped her hand towards the girls, saying, 'Don't worry; there's none of the young sparks going to break you in.'

'Oh, Ma! The things you say. She's awful, isn't she, Tilly?'

Tilly smiled at Fanny as she said now, 'Come on, I'll walk with you, I could do with a breath of air.'

Biddy gave one last look around the kitchen; then motioning to her daughters, she waved them out of the door before following them; and when in the yard she stood and looked up towards the moonlit sky, she said, 'Well, if he had paid to have a night like this he couldn't have got better value for his money, could he now?'

'You're right there, Biddy.' Tilly smiled at her. 'It's a most beautiful night, almost like day. I don't remember ever seeing a brighter one. And it isn't a full moon yet.'

They met no one on their journey back to the lodge but they heard laughter and running footsteps here and there in the garden, and when Biddy remarked, 'Somebody's still loose. I hope he hurries up an' catches her so we can settle down,' the girls smothered their giggles.

With the back of the lodge in sight Biddy said, 'Well, here we are. Thanks, lass. And good-night, or good-mornin'. See you later on.'

'Good-night, Biddy. . . . Good-night, Katie. Good-night, Peg. Good-night, Fanny.'

148

'Good-night, Tilly. Good-night, Tilly. Good-night, Tilly. Good-night, Tilly.'

The whispered farewells over, Tilly turned slowly and made her way back to the cypress walk.

There were no sounds coming from the garden now; that was until she had almost reached the end of the walk. Then she was startled by the sound of laughter, and it brought her to a dead stop for she recognised that laugh, and she knew that if she continued on for the next few yards she would come up with the owner of that voice and his companion, and so, taking two cautious steps to the side, she stood in the deep shadow of a cypress tree. Then again she was startled by the fact that whoever was on the other path had also stopped, for now the laughter seemed to be almost in her ear.

Then the woman's voice came to her, saying, 'You know something? You are drunk, Matthew Sopwith, you are drunk'; and Matthew's voice answered on a throaty laugh, 'And you are not a kick in the backside from it, Miss Bennett, not a kick in the backside from it.'

Alicia Bennett's laughter now joined his, and Tilly had the impression that they were leaning against each other.

Now Alicia Bennett was saying, 'Why were you so mad a while back? Come on, tell me, why were you so mad?'

'I wasn't mad.'

'Oh-yes-you-were. And all because I wanted to see the nursery floor.'

'Well, as I told you, it's private up there.'

'*Private? Housekeeper's quarters, private! When were housekeeper's apartments private?* No servants' quarters are private. I know what it was, you didn't want me to see the child, did you? Is anything wrong with it? Two heads? Has it two heads? Or water on the brain? I once saw a child with water on the brain. It was so big they propped its head up in a cage.'

'Don't be silly, water on the brain! You have water on the brain. I don't care if you see the child; anybody can see the child. Anyway, forget about it. Come on.'

'No, listen. Stop it. I want to know something. Why do you

have that one as your housekeeper?'

'Why shouldn't I have her as my housekeeper?'

'Oh, you know as well as I do. . . .'

'Look, I don't want to discuss this with you, Alicia. Anyway, I want a drink, come on.'

'It's the talk of the county.'

There followed a pause.

'What's the talk of the county?'

The tone of Matthew's voice now caused Tilly to press her hand tightly over her mouth.

'You know as well as I do: your father's mistress, now your housekeeper. As my pa always says, have your fun on the side but should there be results keep them on the side too.'

There was a longer pause now before Matthew's voice came thick and fuddled: 'Well, your pa should know what he's talkin' about as he's done a lot of work on the side, hasn't he, Alicia? His sidelines run right through his four farms, an' away beyond, so I understand. I've only one little half-brother but you must have enough to fill a workhouse, 'cos that's where they go, don't they, the maids with their bellies full?'

Now Alicia Bennett's voice came harsh, the words spitting, 'That isn't funny; I don't find you amusing. You're acting like a swine.'

'Only because you, my dear Alicia, are acting like some cheap hussy.'

'Cheap hussy, am I? Huh!' She gave a short laugh now before saying on a high sarcastic note, 'Oh, do please forgive me, Matthew, for daring to criticise your father's whore, I. . . .'

There followed the sound of a ringing slap, a gasp, then a long drawn out 'O . . . h!' Then Alicia Bennett's voice, deep and sober-sounding, came through the thicket of the trees like barbed prongs, saying, 'You shouldn't have done that, Matthew Sopwith. That was no slap, that was a blow. You are the first man who has ever dared lift his hand to me. You'll be sorry. You mark my words.'

Tilly stood as if she had become rooted to the spot. She heard one set of footsteps running into the distance but she dare not move because she knew that Matthew would be still standing where Alicia Bennett had left him. Then she almost cried out aloud as the trunk of the cypress which she was facing began to shake, and she knew that he had hold of it and that his hands were within an arm's length of her face. And when, as if he were speaking to her, his voice came on a groan, saying, 'Christ Almighty!' she closed her eyes tightly and gripped her mouth until the pressure hurt.

When at last she heard him move from the tree, she held her breath wondering if he would turn at the end of the path and come down the cypress walk. And when he did just that she prayed, 'Oh God! don't let him see me.'

When he came abreast of her his head was down, his chin almost on his breast, and his walk was not that of a drunken man, but rather that of an old one.

Presently his footsteps faded away in the distance, and she came from out of the shadows.

She didn't run back to the house, she walked slowly, but her whole body was shaking, and she was asking herself the question that she had asked a number of times in her life, Was it starting again?

3

By lunchtime the following day the house was back to normal, at least as far as clearing up was concerned; but there seemed to be a tension running through every member of the household. Katie, Peg, Fanny and Betty all grumbled about the mess left by the hired waiters; Biddy hadn't a civil word for anyone; the men outside hadn't been able to go to bed until the last horse had gone from the stable, and that had been nearly four o'clock; the master himself, Arthur said, mustn't have slept at all because he was dressed and out on his horse by seven, and he must have harnessed the animal himself.

The only one who seemed happy was John, and it was around one o'clock in the afternoon that Tilly met him as she went through the main gates. He was riding back from having paid a brief visit to the mine. He stopped and, looking down at her, said, 'You off for a w . . . w . . . walk, Trotter?'

'I'm going to the cottage.'

'Oh, that's a l . . . long tr . . . tr . . . trail. Why don't you t . . . t . . . take the trap?'

'I want to walk.'

'Oh, yes. Well I . . . I understand: I, too, f . . . felt I had to g . . . g . . . get out this morning after the r . . . rumpus of l . . . last night. Went off won . . . won . . . wonderfully, didn't it?'

'Yes, it did, John; a great success.'

'It was d . . . d . . . dawn before the l . . . last ones left and I slept late. Then Arthur t . . . t . . . told me that Ma . . . Matthew had been up and gone since s . . . s . . . seven, so I've just b . . . been along to see him, and he's l . . . l . . . like a bear with a sore scalp. I don't think he r . . . really cares much for

152

parties and such. Being in America has ch ... changed his taste about many things. Did you know he was in a p ... p ... paddy, Trotter?'

'No.'

'Well, something or some ... somebody has upset him. I asked him if he was c ... c ... coming back to dinner and he said no, he was going into New ... New ... Newcastle.' He bent further towards her and grinned now as he said, 'Likely had w ... w ... words with the Lady Alicia, eh?'

She swallowed deeply before she answered, 'Yes, likely.'

'Well, bye, Tr ... Tr ... Trotter. Have a nice w ... w ... walk.'

As he urged his horse on she turned away and went into the main road. John was in love. His world looked rosy.

But his brother wasn't the only one who couldn't bear the house today; she had been longing from early morning to get out of it, and now the nearer she came to the cottage the more she wished with all her heart that she was living in it again, just her and the child.

When she reached it the first thing she did was to open all the windows. Unless the fire was kept on the musty smell from the old books permeated the house. After taking off her light dust coat and hat she sat on the couch near the empty fireplace and looked about her. There was nothing to stop her coming back here; she was independent, she didn't need to work. But what excuse could she give to him for leaving the house? Did she need to give him any excuse? Couldn't she just say she wished to return to the cottage? Then what would happen? She couldn't give herself an answer to this, but in her mind's eye she could see him stalking round the room yelling; she could see his face hovering above hers, his eyes fierce with a light that created an inward shaking in her. What was she to do? She must do something, and soon, because if she didn't it would be too late, and then she wouldn't be able to do anything about it. She didn't explain to herself what it was she'd be unable to do anything about, it was something she hadn't as yet had the courage to put into words because once she admitted it that would be the end of her and the beginning of

153

something that couldn't be countenanced.

She rose to her feet. She was thirsty, she could do with a cup of tea. But it wasn't worth lighting the fire for that; the well water would be cool. She went through the room and the scullery and unlocked the back door, and taking the water bucket that was hanging from a hook in the ceiling, she went out to the well.

She took the wooden lid off the top of the well, attached the bucket to the chain, then allowed it to drop slowly down. It had a cool sound as it hit the water.

As she wound it back again and pulled the bucket on to the stone rim of the well she had the odd feeling that there was someone watching her, and, the old fear of the McGraths acting like a spring, she swung round and the bucket toppled back into the well again.

A man was standing by the corner of the cottage. He was staring at her with as much surprise on his face as was on hers. It took more than a moment for her to recognise him; the last time she had seen him he had appeared but a boy, he was eighteen years old and was pressing her to marry him. Almost his last words came back to her, 'I killed me brother for you, Tilly,' he had said. But there was hardly any resemblance in the Steve McGrath of thirteen years ago and this man. Yet it was he, but he seemed twice as tall, twice as broad, and there was no sullen, sad look about his face. It was a good-looking face, even a handsome one; but even if she hadn't been able to recognise him his left forearm held at that odd angle would have been evidence enough of his identity.

It was he who spoke first. 'Why, Tilly, I . . . I never expected to see you here.'

'Steve! Oh, you did give me a fright. The bucket's gone.' She looked down the well; then turned to him, laughing now, and he, coming up to her, smiled into her face before bending over and looking down to where the bucket was bobbing far below on the cool water.

'Have you got another bucket?'

'Yes, but not a special one; this is the one I used to keep for the water.'

154

'Well, let's see if we can get it up.'

She watched him as he wound down the chain, and when it was at its full stretch he began to manoeuvre it gently until of a sudden he gave it a jerk, then glanced at her, saying, 'Got it!'

When the bucket was once more standing on the stone surround he took it off the hook; then lifting it up, he said, 'I could do with a drink of this myself.'

'Well, it's cheap.' She laughed at him before turning away and walking towards the cottage.

A minute later, after they had both drunk a mugful of the ice-cold water, she said, 'Sit down, won't you, Steve. Oh, I'm still amazed. I can't believe it's you. You know, you have changed.'

He was about to sit himself on the couch when he turned and glanced at her as he said, 'Can't say the same for you, Tilly.'

She blinked and flushed slightly, then said, 'Where've you been all this time, and what are you doing back here now?'

'I . . . I was looking for a cottage and I understood this one was empty.'

'Really? Well, you see' — she spread her hands wide — 'it isn't empty, but it's mine.'

'It's yours, Tilly?'

'Yes. Oh, it's a long story, but you remember Mr Burgess?'

'Oh yes, I remember Mr Burgess.'

'Well, I' — she looked downwards for a moment — 'when I left the house, I came and lived with Mr Burgess for a time and he bequeathed it to me.'

'You're living here then?'

'No, no; I'm housekeeper back at the Manor.' Her words were spaced and it was he who blinked his eyes now and looked away as he said, 'Oh aye. Aye, I see.' Then more brightly, 'But you still own this?'

'Yes.'

'Are you thinking of selling it?'

'No, no; I don't think I'd ever sell it, it's got a sentimental value for me.'

'Would . . . would you let it then?'

She stared at him. 'You'd want to take it? But . . . but are

155

you working round here? What about your mother?' Even the word brought a tightening of her stomach muscles.

His voice as he answered her was grim. 'Answering your last question, Tilly, I want nothing to do with me mother, or our George. They don't know I'm back and it'll make no difference when they do. I haven't seen them since I left home thirteen years ago. Anyway, I'm now engaged at the Sopwith and Rosier mine as under-manager.'

'*Under-manager!*' the words came out on a high surprised note and he nodded, a pleased expression on his face. 'Aye. Would you believe it, the pitman an under-manager? It's a long story. I suppose you could say I've been lucky. When I left here I went on the road for a time, then landed up at a Durham pit and I lodged with a Mr Ransome. He was a deputy, and his wife was a canny body, they made me feel at home. Well, it was the only real home life I'd ever experienced and Mr Ransome was very taken up with his job, and he had a ready listener in me, so just listenin' to him I learned more things in a year than I would have done in a lifetime otherwise, I mean about the workings of the pit. Well, he got me so interested that I started to study an' for once no opposition to the fact that I could read and write. Well, after a lot of night work, burning the midnight oil ... and candles' — he laughed — 'I got me deputy's ticket. And I thought that was the end, but it was only the beginning. I went on from there, and last year I passed for under-manager and when I heard they were wantin' one here I applied, and with a little push from Mr Ransome and Mr Burrows, the manager, I was accepted. At first I was hesitant about coming so near the village an' me mother again, but it was the only post going. And you've got to be an under-manager afore you can become a manager. So there you have it, Tilly.'

'Oh, Steve, I'm so glad for you. And nobody deserves success more than you do.' She now hesitated before asking a very touchy question and when it did come out she tried to make it sound ordinary, conversational. 'Are you married, Steve?'

He looked straight at her for a second before he said quietly,

'No, Tilly, I'm not married.'

'Oh.' She lowered her gaze from his. 'You know I have a son now, Steve?'

'Aye' — he nodded at her — 'I heard you had, Tilly. I hope he's in good fettle, I mean I hope he's fully recovered. I also heard what happened to him because of me mother, and how you stopped the case and her going along the line.'

She ignored the last and said, 'Yes, he's fully recovered, well, at least' — she shook her head in small movements before she said — 'I've still got to take him to the doctor's every month. I think it's in case his eyes become affected.'

'Eeh!' He now got to his feet and walked towards the table, his back towards her as he said, 'The things our family have done to you, it's unbelievable.' Then turning abruptly towards her again, he asked pointedly now, 'What made you go back there, I mean after' — there was an embarrassed silence before he ended — 'after you left?'

She returned his questioning look as she said, 'It happened the day he was struck. It was fortunate that Mr Matthew was in town and . . . and he saw us to a doctor; then I think the shock had been a little too much for me and I collapsed, and it was natural I suppose that he took me back to the Manor, and just as natural that I should take up my old post again.'

'Oh.' His chin jerked upwards on the word. 'He's a funny fellow, isn't he?'

'Who?'

'Mr Matthew, quite a lad. Perhaps that's the wrong word. I don't mean with the women, though I don't know anything about him in that line, but he's not bothered about getting himself mucked up, he'll crawl with you side by side and talk to you man to man. Then when he's above ground he's like a different being, closes up like a clam, as if you might take advantage like.'

'You've worked with him?'

'I've been down two or three times along of Mr Rowland when he was showing me the layout. They say he's got a temper like a fiend, an' I can well imagine it. I wouldn't like to cross him.' He smiled wryly now.

'Well, by the size you've grow into, Steve, I think you'd be able to hold your own.' She smiled and he lowered his head as he said, 'Aye, all the years I lived around here I seemed to be stunted in all ways, but once I got away I sprouted. I think Mrs Ransome's good food and care helped more than a bit. But well now, about this place.' He now moved his hand widely, taking in the room. 'Will you let it to me, Tilly?'

She rose from the settle, considered a moment, then said, 'I don't see why not, Steve. It'll save me having to send someone along every week to keep it aired. Have . . . have you any furniture?'

'No, not a stick.'

'Would you like to take it as it is?'

'Oh, that would be grand, Tilly, grand.'

'There'd be one stipulation. The loft bedroom upstairs is half full of books, I'd want them left as they are. They are Mr Burgess's and he valued them greatly, and I do too.'

'Nothing'll be touched, Tilly. It's fine and comfortable looking as it is. You have my word for it, nothing'll be touched, except I might be glad to read some of them books.'

'You'll be very welcome to do that, and I'm sure he'll be pleased to know that they are being put to use again.'

'Then that's settled. How much will you want a week?'

'Oh, I don't know.' She shook her head. 'I really don't want anything. Let's say rent free for old time's sake.'

'Ah no, Tilly. No, no. If it's a business deal it's a business deal. What about three shillings a week, how's that?'

'Oh, if that'll suit you it'll suit me.'

'Well, we'll shake on it.' He held out his hand, and she hesitated a moment before she put hers into it. His grip was firm and warm.

She had to withdraw her fingers from his and she turned from him, saying, 'I'll leave the key with you then, Steve; I've got to go now.'

'Aye. Aye.' He followed her to the door, where on a laugh he said, 'By, life's funny. When I came off that road I never thought that within the next hour I'd have a home of me own, your home. It makes me glad to be back, Tilly.'

Outside the door she turned to him and out of politeness she said, 'It's nice to see you back, Steve. Good-bye now.'

'Good-bye, Tilly. We'll be knocking into each other I've no doubt.'

She looked over her shoulder at him as she answered, 'Yes, yes, of course, Steve.'

She was well out of sight of the cottage when she stopped. Nice to see him back. Was it? No! No! The Steve of thirteen years ago had altered physically, but the Steve underneath she could see through the light in his eyes was still the same Steve, and because he hadn't married she knew he had brought back with him all the old complications.

Yet need they be complications? He could offer her a way out. She liked him, you couldn't help but like him, and he'd always been so kind to her; and he would continue to be kind to her, no matter what happened. Yes, here was a way out, a loophole, an escape from that fear that must soon take shape and spring upon her; it was in the atmosphere; it pervaded the air. Up till last night she had imagined she could ward it off, fight it with a manner of aloofness, call up propriety to her aid, but after hearing the sound of that blow in her defence when she was called a whore, she knew that neither aloofness nor propriety would be strong enough to withstand the onslaught of the fear when it did take shape and gave voice.

Perhaps God had sent Steve at this opportune time to save her.

4

'What's this I hear, Trotter?'

'What do you hear?' She had just descended the front steps to the drive and at the sight of her he had dismounted from his horse, slapping it on the rump as he did so and sending it towards the yard.

'That you have let your cottage.'

'That's right.'

'I hope you know what you've done.'

'Yes, I think I do.'

'He's a McGrath.'

'I know that too, but he's a good McGrath, the only good McGrath. He's been a friend of mine since childhood.'

'Really! Suppose his parents start visiting him?'

'For my part they're welcome to, as I shan't be there. But I doubt if he'll welcome any visit from them seeing that he cut adrift some years ago.'

'You know he's to be my under-manager?'

'Yes, he told me so, and I think he'll be a very good one.'

'That remains to be seen.' He now struck the top of his leather boot with his crop as he said, 'What if you at one time should wish to return to the cottage?'

'I can't see that offering any problem, I could give him notice.'

They stared at each other like two combatants waiting for the other to thrust and he made the final move when he said, 'By what I recollect from one and another you may not need to give him notice.'

She felt herself rearing inside but she warned herself to keep calm, and when she spoke her words came without a tremor as she said, 'That could be quite possible, and if it should happen it could realise his long-felt wish.'

She did not step back from him but her shoulders receded and her chin drew into her neck pulling her head slightly to the side for a moment as he again struck his leather gaiter with his whip. Then after staring at her, he passed her and went up the steps towards the door. Strangely, as one would have expected from the look on his face, he did not run up them, or even hurry, but he took each step slowly and firmly, and he had passed through the doors and into the hall before she herself felt able to move; then she went on towards the lower garden and the greenhouses, there to see what fruit was available for dessert.

Twenty minutes later when she returned to the house by the kitchen Biddy met her at the door, saying, 'There's hell going on in the library. That Mr Rosier's there, and it's who can shout the loudest. You can hear them all over the house. Peg says it's about Master Matthew hitting that Miss Bennett. I can't believe that, can you? He's got a temper I know, but he's a gentleman at bottom an' he's gone on her, at least he was. There was all the signs of it, wasn't there? Out gallopin' the countryside together!'

Tilly put the skip of fruit on the table and she surprised Biddy by making no comment at all but instead hurried up the kitchen, along the passage and into the hall. But after closing the door she went no further. She stood with her back pressed to it as she watched the library door burst open and Mr Rosier come stalking out, crying as he did so, 'If it wasn't that we are linked in business I'd have you up. Begod! I would. And her father might yet, so don't think you're out of the wood. There's such a thing as defamation of character.'

'Go to hell! And take Bennett with you, and his bastards. They could fill it up. Tell him so from me.'

Tilly watched Mr Rosier turn back towards the door and, his voice lower now but his words deep and telling, brought the particular fear that she kept buried in the dungeon of her mind tearing up through her being, bringing her hands to cover her ears but unable to shut out his voice as he said, 'You talk of a man's bastards, you of all people! Thou shalt not covet thy neighbour's wife or . . . thy father's whore. Alicia wasn't blind.'

Although she wasn't aware of pressing her back against the green-baized door and so opening it, she was vitally aware of Matthew standing like a stone image and as speechless.

When she managed to get round the door and into the passage, there was Biddy standing, and that she had heard every word was evident, because her face at this moment was so stretched all the furrows and wrinkles in her skin were smoothed out.

When Tilly gasped and put her hand to her throat Biddy made no move towards her; not until Tilly closed her eyes and drooped her head forward did her hand come on to her shoulder. But she said nothing to her, just turned, went into the kitchen and, looking towards where Betty Leyburn was chopping up vegetables at the long table, said to her, 'Go and see if Peg wants any help upstairs.'

'Me, Mrs Drew?'

'Aye, who else? There's nobody here but you, is there? Go on; get yourself away. Go out the back and up the side stairs.'

When the girl was gone, Biddy pulled Tilly from the door against which she was pressed and led her down the kitchen, and having sat her down in a chair she dragged the end of the form from under the table and seated herself before saying, 'Aw, lass, is this true?'

'Oh, Biddy.' Tilly's head drooped further. 'I don't know. I don't know.'

'Aw, you're bound to know, if it's got outside an' roundabout, you're bound to know.'

Tilly's head now jerked upwards and she said stiffly, 'He's never said a word to me along those lines, not one word.'

'Yet you know he wants you?'

Her head went down again, but she remained quiet, and Biddy let out a deep-drawn sigh as she said, 'God above! what a state of affairs. How long have you known?'

'I . . . I don't really know. Truthfully I don't really know.'

'What brought it all out, I mean why did the Rosier man come this morning?'

Tilly, turning her head, now muttered, 'Because Matthew did strike Miss Bennett. It was after I left you. I heard them on the other side of the walk and I hid amongst the trees. Apparently she had wanted to go up into the nursery and he wouldn't take her, and . . . and so she taunted him and he struck her. They were both drunk.'

'Well, the blow must have sobered her up, lass, an' she's put two and two together. Now where do you go from here?'

'Don't ask me, Biddy. But if I hadn't let the cottage to Steve, I'd go there this very day.'

'Well, as far as I can see that wouldn't make much difference, you'd be more open to him there than you are here. Tell me something, how do you feel about him?'

'Again I say I . . . I don't know, Biddy, and that's the truth. I wish I did know.'

'Father, then son. 'Tisn't right, lass. 'Tisn't right.'

'I know that, Biddy, I know that, nobody better.'

'And the child his half-brother. It's a complication, lass. If ever there was one it's a complication. There's only one thing to be thankful for now, as far as I can see, an' that is that you didn't marry the father, for from the little I've seen of this one's character if he does a thing he does it, he wants to go the whole hog. I can't see him havin' you on the side and. . . .'

'Oh Biddy! Biddy!' Tilly ground the words out as she got to her feet. 'Don't suggest such things.'

'Don't suggest such things, you say? Well, it looks to me that the time's almost past for sayin' such things when the stage is set for action.'

'Oh . . . dear . . . God!' Tilly brought the words out on a long shuddering breath, and Biddy repeated them, saying, 'Aye, oh dear God!' Then she asked, 'Did he see you out there? Did he know you heard?'

'No; the last he saw of me was I was going into the garden. Yet' — she moved her head with a jerk — 'that was some time ago.'

'Well, get into the garden again because it's my bet he'll come rampaging through here. He knows we've all got ears like cuddys' lugs, and as long as he thinks that you haven't got the gist of what's in his mind you've got time to pull yourself together and by! lass, you'll need to pull yourself together.'

As if she was a child again obeying an order, Tilly went from the kitchen, across the yard, under the arch and into the garden, and she came to a stop by the high stone wall, just where she had stood all those years ago when Steve had said to her 'Will you marry me, Tilly?'

Steve. There was an escape route, and the sooner she took it the better.

When she returned some time later to the house she did not see Matthew nor, as Biddy had prophesied, had he come rampaging through the house looking for her, but he had left the yard, apparently bent on going to the mine. What Biddy said to her straightaway was, 'Young Betty brought the bairn down, he was screaming his head off, he had bumped into something. . . . Now, now, it's all right, he hasn't cut himself or anything, just a little bump on the head. I put some butter on it. You're takin' him in the morrow, aren't you? Well, I'd ask them to have a good look at his eyes. That's not the first time in the last few days he's bumped into something. Now, now, don't go off like a divil in a gale of wind.'

But Tilly was running across the hall and up the stairs. When she reached the nursery floor it was to see Betty bouncing the child on her knee, and the child laughing. Grabbing him up into her arms, she looked at the small bump in the middle of his forehead a little above the scar, and Betty said, 'He went into the leg of the table, Miss Tilly. It wasn't my fault.'

'It's all right. It's all right. Don't worry.' She glanced at the girl. 'Bring me his grey coat and bonnet, we're going out for a walk. . . .'

Half an hour later, carrying the child, she turned off the coach road on to the lane leading to the cottage. Coming upon a fallen tree, she sat down on the trunk and asked herself if she

164

knew what she was doing. And whether it was fair to Steve. She could give him only affection, a respectful affection, for he would never be able to touch the burning want in her. It appeared that only a Sopwith could allay that feeling in her. Oh dear, dear God! She stood up, moved the child from one arm to another, then went on, and it wasn't until she came in sight of the cottage that she said to herself in Biddy's colloquial way, 'You must be up the pole. It's three o'clock in the afternoon, under-manager or not he's a workman, he'll be at the pit.'

But there were shifts, and managers and under-managers rarely worked in shifts. As she expected, the door was locked. She put the child down on the grass to the side of the path, then looked through the window. The room was tidy. She could see that the fire had been banked down, and right opposite to her in the middle of the table was a jar full of wild flowers. It was the sight of these that made her straighten up, turn her back to the window and, resting her buttocks against the window-sill, bow her head down. There was something nice, something good in Steve. It wasn't fair to make a fool of him. Nor could she now ask him to leave the cottage. What was she to do?

The child had turned on to his hands and knees and was crawling over the grass; then when he was almost opposite to her he lumbered to his feet and, swaying, he held out his arms to her, saying, 'Mama, Mama.'

Swiftly she gathered him up and pressed him tightly to her, and as swiftly she left the cottage, went back down the lane and on to the coach road again, there to see not a hundred yards from her Matthew and John.

It was John who turned and cried, 'Why, Tr . . . Tr . . . Trotter!' Then they both reined their horses until she came abreast of them, and after a moment they dismounted and it was John who said, 'Wh . . . Wh . . . What are you doing out here?'

'I've been to the cottage.'

'Oh, I . . . I thought you had l . . . l . . . let it to the . . . the under-manager?'

'Yes, I have, but he's an old friend of mine, I just wanted to see how he was faring.'

She was walking by John's side. Matthew, leading his horse, was walking between the two animals and because of their bobbing heads and the fact that he didn't turn and look at her she couldn't see the expression on his face as he said, 'Very good fellow, McGrath. I think he'll turn out to be valuable. As you remarked the other day, the only good one of that particular bunch.'

She stared past John and over the horse's back; her eyes were wide, her mouth slightly open. If he had said to her, 'You are to go ahead and marry this man,' he couldn't have made it any plainer. It was evident in this moment that he wanted to be out of this situation as much as she did. Well now, at last she knew where she stood.

It was a full minute later when she said to John, 'Do please mount.'

'N . . . no, Trotter; we . . . we can't leave you w . . . w . . . walking along with that heavy bu . . . bundle.' He poked the child in the chest gently with his fingers. 'I t . . . tell you wh . . . what I'll do, I'll . . . I'll ride him home. He'll . . . he'll like that, f . . . f . . . first ride on a horse.'

'No! No!' She stepped to the side, but he pulled the horse to a standstill and mounted, then held out his arms, saying, 'All right. Trotter, I w . . . w . . . won't drop him.'

Matthew, too, had stopped. He was looking across at her now and she couldn't fathom the expression on his face, in fact it seemed utterly expressionless, just blank. But when John laughingly looked down on her, saying, 'W . . . w . . . would you fe . . . feel he was safer w . . . w . . . with Matthew?' she immediately handed her son up to him and he, seating the child on the front of the saddle, cradled him firmly with one arm, while jerking the reins with the other, and he moved forward leaving an empty space between herself and Matthew.

When she turned to follow John, Matthew did not mount his horse but led it forward and walked by her side; and they never uttered one word for the remainder of the journey, nor did he look at her when, having reached the house steps, they parted, he going on towards the stables and she reaching up to take the child from John.

It was, she felt, the end of something that had not yet begun.

5

She had other things on her mind when she returned from Shields after seeing the doctor the following day, for she had been given a letter to take to a Dr Davidson at the Newcastle Infirmary in four days' time. Apparently Doctor Simpson was not entirely satisfied about the child's sight. He had assured her there was really nothing to worry about but that this particular Dr Davidson had had a great deal of experience with regard to eyesight and that perhaps all the child would need in the future would be spectacles.

There was a feeling of unrest in the house, not, as Biddy said, that you could put the blame down to his nibs rampaging, but quite the reverse, for during the last few days he hadn't appeared as his natural self at all; in fact the house had hardly seen him. If he wasn't at the mine he was away in the city, where he had been from early morning yesterday until late last night. And she didn't voice what she was thinking: What do men want to spend all day in Newcastle for? for she would have answered herself by saying, 'Well, what do young bucks like him go to the city for in any case, their kind of business doesn't need a board room.'

But this morning he hadn't gone to the mine, and he hadn't gone to Newcastle, he had come down to breakfast and was now closeted with John in the morning-room, and at this moment John was gazing at him sadly as he was saying, 'B . . . B . . . But why do you w . . . want to go back so s . . . s . . . soon? Anyway, Matthew I don't think I'm ca . . . ca . . . capable of man . . . managing the mine on my own.'

'You won't have to manage on your own, you'll have two good men, Rowland and the new one, McGrath; he . . . he shows to be very promising.'

'But . . . but . . . but what has happened b . . . b . . . between you and Mr Ro . . . Ro . . . Rosier that he w . . . w . . . wants to sell out now? He was so k . . . keen, it was he who p . . . p . . . put you on to opening it. There must be a se . . . se . . . serious reason.'

'There is.'

'Well, I f . . . f . . . feel I'm enti . . . enti . . . entitled to know what it is.'

'I struck Alicia on the night of your engagement party.'

'Y . . . Y . . . You what!'

'You heard me, John, I struck Alicia, if you can call slapping her face striking her. She was bent on finding out all about Trotter, and when I wouldn't go along with her she insulted her. My only excuse is that I was drunk, and so was she. The blow must have sobered her up.'

'G . . . G . . . God! that's why she t . . . t . . . turned down Pl . . . Pl . . . Platt's Walk when she saw me c . . . c . . . coming the other day. I w . . . w . . . waved to her but she . . . she galloped off. Oh my G . . . God! Matthew, that was an awful thing t . . . t . . . to do. I thought you liked her . . . well m . . . m . . . more than liked her.'

'I liked her but I didn't more than like her, John, and I never had any intention of letting the liking grow; nor did I give her to understand this. That, I fear, is what piqued her.'

'Aw' — John wagged his head from side to side — 'and I imagined it was a l . . . l . . . lovely party. So did Anna.'

'It was a lovely party. That incident was private. . . .'

'And it's having it . . . it . . . its repercussions' — John was nodding his head grimly at Matthew now — 'and driving you off b . . . b . . . back to America.'

'I intended to go in any case.'

'But not so s . . . s . . . soon. Oh, w . . . w . . . wait a little longer, say three m . . . months until I g . . . g . . . get more used to it.'

'You'll never be more used to the mine, John, until you have

168

to take full responsibility. The thing to do is to get married and bring Anna here. You could both be very happy here.'

'I . . . I have n . . . n . . . no doubt of that, Matthew, b . . . b . . . but I'd be happier if I knew that you were . . . were . . . were about, at least at the m . . . mine. You can manage m . . . m . . . men, you . . . you've got a w . . . w . . . way with you that . . . that I'll never acquire.'

Matthew smiled weakly as he said, 'I shout more, but men can see through that. If they respect you they'll work for you, and you're highly respected.'

'Oh! Matthew.' John now walked towards his brother and, putting his hands on his shoulders, he looked into his face and like a young boy, that he really was at heart, he pleaded, 'M . . . M . . . Must you go? Must you go, Matthew?'

'I must, John. Yes, I must.'

'The f . . . f . . . fourth of July, it's like tomorrow, just over f . . . f . . . four weeks. There's something I don't quite understand, I wouldn't have thought that thi . . . thi . . . this business with Ro . . . Rosier would have m . . . m . . . made you turn tail, more like stand up and f . . . f . . . fight him when he's b . . . backing out.'

'Don't try, John. As for him backing out, it isn't like that. If it meant a fight and I couldn't afford to buy him out and wanted him to stick to his contract then I likely would have stayed, but as it is I want him out and I can afford to pay the damned exorbitant percentage he's asking. So now' — he put out his hand and ruffled John's straight hair — 'what we've got to do, boyo, is to get you to that mine every day, and not just on the top but down below. Your training is going to be intensive during the next few weeks.'

'Have . . . have you t . . . t . . . told Trotter?'

Matthew turned away now and went towards the mantelpiece and lifting up a long-stemmed wooden pipe, he bent down and knocked out the dottle into the empty grate before he said briefly, 'No.'

'She's g . . . g . . . going to be very upset.'

'I don't think so.'

'Oh, she w . . . will be.'

169

Matthew now turned and smiled wryly at his brother as he said, 'It would be nice to think so, but I think she will be as relieved as many others when I depart from these shores.'

'You have a very p . . . p . . . poor opinion of yourself, Matthew. You. . . .'

'On the contrary' — Matthew's voice took on its customary arrogant tone — 'I've a very high opinion of myself, let me tell you, John; in fact, inside I don't think there's anyone to come up to me. Of course, outside' — he pulled a wry face now — 'things are a little different. Men don't see me with my eyes . . . nor do women. I'll have to do something about the latter.'

'Oh! Matthew.' John was laughing now but sadly as he said, 'You're a c . . . c . . . case, L . . . L . . . Luke always s . . . said there was only one of you and it would have been dis . . . disastrous had there been twins and. . . .' Of a sudden John stopped and, his head bowed, he added softly, 'Oh, M . . . Matthew, I'm g . . . g . . . going to m . . . miss you. You don't know how m . . . m . . . much I love you.'

Swiftly now Matthew went to his brother and put his arms about him, and they clung together for a moment before Matthew, thrusting him away, turned and went hastily from the room.

6

It was five o'clock in the afternoon. They had both returned from the mine dirty and almost wet through for their capes hadn't succeeded in keeping out the heavy rain. It had rained for the past two days, the heat of the earlier June days being but a faint memory now; the roads were like bogs, the sky low, promising more rain to come.

They dismounted and after handing their horses to Fred Leyburn John said, 'I w . . . w . . . want a bath, hot, steaming. I'll t . . . t . . . toss you for which one gets prepared first.'

At the top of the steps, Matthew turned and, thrusting his hand into his breeches' pocket, pulled out a coin, saying, 'Tails,' and they were entering the hall as he flicked the coin; then lifting the palm of his hand up quickly from the back of his other hand, he said, 'You win.'

'Good. W . . . W . . . Why is it you don't mind being wet, Matthew?'

'I suppose it was because I was dry, so dry during those three years over there when at times I would have given half my life to stand in the rain.'

Peg was in the hall to meet them. She took their sodden cloaks and hats from them, and as John dashed towards the stairs, crying, 'Hot w . . . w . . . water, Peg. Hot w . . . water,' she said, ' 'Tis all ready, sir, 'tis all ready. It'll be up in your room in a minute.'

It was something in her voice that made Matthew turn and look her full in the face. It was evident that she had been crying; her eyes were red, her lashes still wet. His voice holding a

171

hearty tone, he said, 'Ho! ho! what's this, isn't there enough water outside?'

She blinked now and, her head drooping further, the tears ran down her cheeks which made him ask, his tone more sympathetic now, 'What is it, girl? What's happened? Are you in trouble? Your mother?'

'Not me, sir, nor mam, 'tis the child.'

'What! What's happened to the child?'

'Tilly . . . Miss Tilly, she took him to Newcastle to see the eye man. He says the child is to go blind.'

He screwed up his face, his eyes narrowing and his lips moving silently on the word blind.

'Miss Tilly's in a state, she's. . . .'

He did not wait to hear what more she had to say but, taking the stairs two at a time, he ran across the gallery, along the corridor and up to the nursery floor where he thrust open the schoolroom door, only to find the room empty. He remained standing now and looking from one door to the other; he had not been up on this floor since she had taken possession of it. His eyes became focused on the second door to the left of him. That had been her room when she first came here.

Quickly he walked towards it, but gently now he turned the handle and pushed it open. She was lying on the bed, her back to him, her arm round the child. She did not move, likely thinking it was one of the Drews, but when he placed his hand on her shoulder she swung round as if she had been stung, and lay staring up at him.

There was no sign of tears on her face, there was no colour in it; it was even no longer fleshly pale, it was more the colour of a piece of bleached lint. Her eyes were dark pools of pain, her mouth was slightly open, her lips trembling. He took his hand from her and, bending over her, he lifted the child up and, taking it to the window, looked into its eyes. They were deep blue.

The child smiled at him and grabbed at his face.

'What did he say?' He was still looking at the child as he asked the question, but when she didn't answer he turned his head towards her.

172

She was sitting on the edge of the bed now, her body bent forward, and, her voice low, she answered, 'He said he didn't think there was much could be done. The . . . the sight of the left eye is already gone. Spectacles may help for a short time with the other but he doesn't. . . .' Her voice choked and when she turned her body round and buried her face in the pillow he quickly went to the bed and laid the child down again; then coming round the foot of it he dropped on to his knees by her side and, putting his arm around her shoulder, he brought her towards him, looking into her face as he said, 'Don't . . . don't cry like that.'

When her head drooped further and the tears flowed down her cheeks he implored, 'Please, please, Trotter, don't, it will be the undoing of me. Don't.'

When there erupted from her throat a strangled cry, he closed his own eyes tightly and brought his teeth clamping down on his lower lip and what he said now was, 'You should have let me prosecute that woman.'

Her breath was choking her, the tears seemed to be oozing out of every pore in her body. If the restriction in her throat didn't ease she would die. Oh, if she could only die this minute and take the child with her.

'Tilly! Tilly! Oh my God! Tilly.' His arms were about her. He was sitting on the side of the bed now beside her. It was even more difficult to get her breath because her head was pressed tight into his neck, and he was talking, talking, talking. Now his hands were in her hair, lifting her face up towards him. She couldn't see him, she could only hear him, hear him repeating her name, 'Oh Tilly! Tilly!' His father had said it like that, 'Oh Tilly! Tilly!' She must get away, push him off, this was wrong, she was going to marry Steve. Steve would be her salvation. But she didn't want salvation; she wanted two things at this moment, she wanted her child to be able to see and she wanted this man's arms around her. She wanted to feel his lips forever on her face as they were now. But it was wrong, wrong, in all ways it was wrong. And she was so much older than he but she looked so much younger; he wasn't a young man, he had never been a young man. He was strong, deter-

173

mined; she would be safe with him, wherever she went she would be safe with him. And he was still talking, talking, talking.

Now he was wiping her eyes and her face with his handkerchief and whispering all the while, 'Oh, my love! My love! You know, don't you, you've always known? When I hated you I loved you; when I knew you had given Father a child I think I would have murdered you if I had been near you. Now I love the child' — he glanced towards it — 'but I don't love you as I love the child. What feeling I have for you is past love, Tilly, it's like a rage, a mad consuming rage; it has grown with the years, it's been like a malignant disease. I've feared at times I would die of it, and if I don't have you, Tilly, I will die of it in the end. But I know that before I do I'll make so many people miserable. That's me; if I'm not happy I make other people unhappy too, I hate suffering alone. I have the power to make people miserable; I can be one big bloody swine. I know myself, Tilly. There is something in me that is mean. I knew this when I was a boy. You knew it too, didn't you? Yet, once you put the weight of your love on the scales I could become a saint, at least a lovable, generous individual. Oh my dearest, dearest, Tilly.'

His lips were moving over hers gently, gently backward and forward. Then he was talking again, talking, talking. 'The effect you have on a man, the effect you've always had on me. I even loved my nightmares because you gave them to me, Trotter, Trotter. From the first moment you stepped on to this floor you had me, all of me, the good, the bad, the rotten. Oh Tilly! my Tilly! I adore you. If God was a woman then you would be my God, you are my God . . . my God, the only God I want. Oh my dearest, don't push me away, please.'

'Matthew.' His name came out as if it were weighed down with lead; then again, 'Matthew, we mustn't, we can't.'

'We can and we will. Do you hear me, Tilly Trotter?' He was holding her face between his hands now. 'We can and we will. We must come together; there will be no meaning in my life if we don't. You were in it from the beginning. I wasn't born until I was ten and that was the moment I saw you bend-

174

ing over me in the bed across the landing there.' He pointed his arm backwards. 'And from that moment until now I've never known any release from you. When you went to Father I went to hell.'

'But . . . but it doesn't seem right, clean. . . . I can't. . . .'

'Don't say that!' His voice was harsh now. 'There is nothing unclean about it. It was only by chance you went to Father and more out of pity and compassion I guess than anything else, and of course his need for you, for what man being near you wouldn't want you. I don't blame Father now, I don't blame you, but you were mine before you were Father's. Tell me, look me straight in the face. Come on, lift your lids, Tilly Trotter, and look into my eyes and tell me that you don't love me.'

She lifted her lids and she looked into his eyes and what she said was, 'Oh Matthew! Matthew!' and then she was in his arms once more; and now the fear in her was gone and in its place was a feeling akin to anguish, and when she returned his kiss with a fierceness that his father had never evoked in her she knew that at this age of thirty-two she was for the first time really experiencing young love, not the kind of love she'd had for Simon Bentwood, nor that tender love she'd had for Mark Sopwith, but the love that should come to every woman in her youth. And she was in her youth again and the six years between them was as nothing.

When their lips parted and they looked at each other she knew she'd remember the expression on his face until the day she died. It was such that would be seen on the look of a man given freedom after years of confinement. There was such a light of love in his eyes that she bowed her head against it.

'We'll be married before we sail for America.'

'What!' Her head jerked up.

'I'm due to sail on the fourth of next month.'

'But . . . but, Matthew. . . .'

'No buts. No buts.' He put two fingers on her lips.

She moved slightly away from him. 'But yes, I must; there is your position, the county.'

175

'Damn and blast the county!'

'Oh Matthew!' She shook her head slowly. 'You can damn and blast the county as much as you like but . . . but you would never live this down.'

When she turned her head away he cried at her, 'Oh no! no! not another situation like with Father, not for me and you, oh no! no! You marry me, Tilly. I want you for mine, I want to own you, yes, own you. You are to be mine legally. Now get that into your head, you are to be mine, to belong to me. And what do I care for the county? Blast the county to hell and all in it! Even if we were staying here, but we're not, we're going to America where nobody will know anything about us or him.' He thumbed towards the child. 'I have married a widow with a young child. That's all that need be known. Anyway, I wonder why you put so much stock on the damn county, what do you care for the county? Look' — he got hold of her hands — 'I know you are thinking only of me, as you thought of Father when you refused to marry him, but I'm not having you other than as a wife, and I mean to have you as a wife if I've got to drag you to the church, or even to a registry office, anywhere we can be signed and sealed before sailing. *Now, is that clear. . . . Trotter?*'

She smiled wanly at him now as she said, 'Yes, Master Matthew.'

'Oh my dear, dear Tilly.' Gently now he drew her towards him as he said, 'You know I've never liked the name Trotter or even Tilly; I think from the day we are married I shall call you Matilda. It has a good homespun sound, Matilda. It will deny that you are beautiful and alluring, and no other man will be very interested in anyone called Matilda Sopwith.'

Her smile was wider now as she said, 'Then the day you call me Matilda I shall call you Matt.'

'Good! Good! I like that. . . . Oh my love. Oh my love.'

They were enfolded again tightly, her face lost in his, when the door burst open and Katie almost left the ground in amazed surprise which brought from her the high exclamation of 'Oh my God!'

As she made to dash from the room Matthew sprang from

the bed and pulled her forcedly back, then pushed her towards Tilly, saying, 'You are the first to know, Katie Drew, that your friend has promised to become my wife.'

'*Wh. . . . What!*'

Tilly had to bow her head against the look of utter incredulity on Katie's face and her stammer that sounded so much like John's.

'Yes, wh . . . what! And now, Katie Drew, you may go downstairs and tell your dear mama the news, and anyone else you come across. You may also tell them that on the fourth of July you are sailing with your master and mistress to America as nursemaid to the young William there.' Again he thumbed towards the child, and when Katie's mouth opened again to say, 'What!' he checked her with a finger wagging in her face, saying, 'And get out of the habit of that syllabic silly What! and replace it with pardon. Now go.'

Katie backed from him, she backed from them both until she reached the open door, and there all she could say after looking from one to the other was, 'Eeh!'

When the door had closed on her they gazed at each other and Tilly asked, quietly now, 'You meant that, you weren't joking, you'll take her with us?'

'Yes, of course. You'll want someone to help look after the child, and I'll want my wife to myself now and then.' Again he was cupping her face and she turned and looked down towards the boy, who was lying quite peaceably sucking his thumb, and the joy going from her face, she muttered, 'Blind. How will he bear it?'

His voice was soft, his tone compassionate as he said, 'He'll become used to it and he'll always have us. But' — he squeezed her face tightly now — 'these eye men can work miracles today, they put lenses in spectacles that can enlarge a spot as if the wearer were looking through a telescope. Look, I'll go tomorrow and see him. We'll have the best advice in the country. Don't worry, as long as he has partial sight of one eye he'll be all right.' And now he paused and staring into her misted eyes, he said, 'Do you love me, Tilly? Really love me? I feel you do but I want to hear you say it aloud. I've made you

177

say it in the night; I've made you say, "Matthew, Matthew, I love you." And at those times when we've been going at each other's throats, part of me has been crying, "Say it, Tilly. Oh, say you love me." And now I want to hear it from your lips.'

It was she who put her hands out now and, covering his rough bristled coal-dust and rain-smeared face, said gently, 'I love you, Matthew Sopwith. I love you. I don't know when it began, I only know I feel for you as I've felt for no other, not even your father.'

'Tilly! Tilly!' There was a break in his voice and he drew her to her feet, and now as he held her close her slim body seemed to sink into his and she knew that for good or ill she'd always want it to remain there.

Biddy couldn't believe it; Katie couldn't believe it; none of the Drew family could believe it; and least of all could Tilly believe that she was to be married and would be going to America, to that strange wild, new country.

But the villagers said they could believe it for anything that was a sin before God could be attributed to that witch. Some of the more godly even went as far as persuading the parson to go and see her. He came but he was confronted by Matthew, and his exit from the house was much more hurried than his entry. As he later said to his housekeeper, he did not blame the woman so much as the man, because well-born he might have been, but he had certainly not grown into a gentleman.

Did the county believe it? Oh yes, the Tolmans, the Fieldmans, and the Craggs all said they had known about it all along, since he had first come home in fact; they knew that that piece, having lost the father and thereby her place in the house would leave no stone unturned until she could regain it. And what would be the best way to do that? To entangle the son in her snares. It was a disgrace, obscene. Oh yes, gentlemen had married servants before today, they all said, they were well aware of this, but the father and son to share a mistress, well! that was something different. It was just as well they were leaving the district; if not, the place would become too hot for both of them.

And they were leaving that young stammerer in charge of the mine. Well! they knew what would happen to that now it was deprived of Mr Rosier's expert advice and control. Mr Rosier had shown himself to be a man of high morals; immediately he had heard about this scandalous affair he had cut adrift from all connection with the Sopwiths. . . . Really! the things that happened.

When the last words were also reiterated in the village, it was Tom Pearson who brought censure upon himself by ending it with, 'They've been unfortunate, they've been found out. If all the things that happened, not only among the county lot, but in this very village were aired the devil would be declared head-man.'

Tom Pearson, the parson again confided in his housekeeper, wasn't a good influence in the village; he would have to arrange that the man got very few orders for painting or odd jobs for this might induce him to seek a habitation further afield.

No one knew what Steve McGrath thought or had said about the scandalous affair, but it was known that his mother had visited him at the cottage and when he wouldn't allow her entry she, like her grandson, had thrown a brick through the window.

When lastly it was rumoured that Trotter's child was going blind few, if any, attributed any blame to Mrs McGrath except to say that God had a strange way of dealing out punishment, and who was to blame Him for the instruments He chose.

Although no one mentioned the villagers or any member of the county to Tilly she was well aware of the seething hostility surrounding her and she knew that she would never have survived it if Matthew had decided to stay on here.

They were to be married by special licence on the third of July and were to sail from Liverpool on the evening of the fourth. It had been arranged that Katie, accompanied by Arthur, would take the child and travel to Liverpool on the morning of the wedding, there to await Matthew's and Tilly's arrival.

The marriage was to take place in Newcastle attended only by John. Luke and Biddy; and following this, the couple would board the train and so begin their journey.

So there was to be a farewell family party on the Saturday evening. Biddy had suggested that the master, and Mr John

180

and Mr Luke should be present, but Tilly had said no, it was just for those who for years she had considered her family, together with Phyllis and Fred and Sam and Alec and their families, because it was not only a farewell to her but also a farewell to Katie.

That Katie was the envy of her sisters was plain to be seen, but that she herself was also fearful of the journey and of the new life ahead of her was equally evident, for as she said to her mother as she stood by the table laden with the fare they had been cooking for the last two days: 'What if I don't like it, Ma?'

'You can always come home, lass. They'll see to it. You can always come home.'

'Yet I wouldn't want to leave her.'

'Well, what you've got to remember, our Katie, is that she's got a husband and as yet you haven't, so if the place doesn't suit you or you don't suit it, come back to where you belong.'

'I'm all excited inside, Ma.'

'I'm all sad inside, lass.'

For the first time that Katie could remember, her mother enfolded her in her arms and so warming was her mother's embrace that she began to cry and said, 'I don't know whether I want to go or not, Ma.'

Biddy pushed her away, saying, 'You're goin'. Your bags are packed, your ticket's got, and, who knows, you might find a lad out there who'll take a fancy to your face.'

'Oh, our Ma! . . . I'm going to miss you our Ma.'

'And I'll miss you, lass. And I'll miss her an' all because she's been like one of me own. You know that.'

'Aye, I do. Sometimes I've thought you even think more of her than you do of any of us.'

Biddy didn't answer this; instead, she said, 'I'd be happy to know that she's got you with her because there'll be times when she'll need a friend and comforter.'

'Oh, I can't see that, Ma, not having him.'

'Aye, me girl, it's just because she does have him for, as I see it, he's gona be no easy packet is Master Matthew. Jealous as sin he'll be of her, you mark my words, an', like the devil, he'll hold on to what he's got; and she being who she is, 'cos she's of a proud nature, there'll come times I'm sure when he'll hold the reins too tightly and she won't like the bit in her mouth. Then the skull and hair'll fly.'

'Oh, Ma, you sound doleful.'

'No, no, I'm not, lass' — Biddy shook her head — 'but I've been through life an' I've seen a bit an' it's taught me to read a character, an' as I said, there'll come a time when she may need you.'

'Aye, well, I hope you're wrong there, Ma, in that particular way anyhow. Oh! there's the carriage.' She ran to the kitchen door and craned out her neck. 'It will be Master Luke. I wonder what he thought about it all when he heard. By! I bet he got a gliff.'

The three brothers were seated in the drawing-room. There had been very little talk during the journey from Newcastle and no mention at all of why Luke had been asked to get leave, and so John, aiming to ease what he imagined to be a rather embarrassing situation, said, 'That uniform's s . . . s . . . so smart, L . . . Luke, that I think . . . think I'll join up myself.'

'Good idea; they can do with fellows like you in the cook-house.'

'Oh you!' John tossed his head.

There followed another short silence; then when they both looked at Matthew where he was standing with his back to the fire, he, looking back at his brothers, said briefly, 'Well! out with it.'

'Out with what?'

'Don't hedge, you know why you're here. Didn't my letter surprise you?'

'No.' Luke pursed his lips, then moved his head from side to side before repeating, 'No; why should I be surprised about something I've known all my life?'

Both John and Matthew stared at him now.

'She turned you crazy the first time you set eyes on her, she did the same to me. She didn't affect John there' — he turned and laughed at his younger brother now — 'he wasn't old enough, but you remember the incident when we came from Grandmama's that time and I said I was going to marry her when I grew up . . . you do remember, don't you?'

'Yes, I remember it.'

'Well then, you know what happened, you nearly knocked the daylights out of me. She had to come up and separate us.'

Matthew lowered his head and gave a short laugh.

'I used to envy you,' said Luke now, 'because you were bigger than me and therefore, I thought, she would show you that much more affection.'

Matthew smiled across at Luke as he asked, 'Do you envy me now?'

'No, no, I don't Matthew.' Luke's tone and expression were so solemn that the brothers stared at him as he went on, 'I wouldn't want to love anyone like you do, Matthew. I'm all against self torture. Your kind of love is. . . .'

'Is what?' The question was flat.

Luke now got to his feet and, pulling his tunic down round his hips, he shook his head slowly, saying, 'You know, I can't find a word to explain it. Don't be mad at me. Come on, don't look like that, but . . . but your feelings have always been so intense, Matthew, where she's concerned, as if she had. . . .'

'Don't say it, Luke. Don't say it.'

'What was I going to say?'

'Bewitched me.'

'Yes, I suppose I was, but there's no harm in that. In a way I wish I could find some woman who would bewitch me. They love me and leave me and I get a bit pipped about it, but I don't suffer any agony. Yes, that's the word.' He pointed to Matthew now as he laughed, 'That's the word to describe your love, agony.'

'Oh, don't be so bloody silly, Luke! The feeling I have for Tilly is anything but agony.'

'Well, I'm glad to hear it at last, I'm glad to hear it.' Luke walked across to Matthew now and, thumping him in the shoulder, said, 'Where is she anyway? And you know something?' He poked his long face towards his brother. 'I'll tell you a secret, I've always wanted to kiss her and now I'm going to do just that; and you stay there, big fellow, you stay there.'

He pushed Matthew hard in the shoulder, almost over-balancing him into the fire; then laughing, he went hurrying down the room, calling, 'Trotter! Where are you, Trotter?'

As Matthew now made to follow Luke, John pulled at his arm, saying quietly, 'L . . . L . . . Let him g . . . go, Matthew. L . . . L . . . Let him go.'

'But why is he acting like this, he's being almost insulting?'

Now it was John who poked his face forward and said, 'D . . . D . . . Don't you know?'

'No. I don't.'

'Well, I'd b . . . b . . . better tell you, big . . . big . . . big brother, he's j . . . jealous.'

'Don't be silly.'

'I'm not. He has l . . . l . . . lots of women has L . . . Luke. They all trip . . . trip over themselves f . . . for him; but he's never found one like Tro . . . Trotter . . . he's jealous.'

'Huh!' Matthew's eyes crinkled in laughter now and again he said, 'Huh!' then putting his arm around John's shoulder, he pressed him close, saying, 'You know, besides being the best of our particular bunch, you're also the wisest.'

8

'*Matthew George Sopwith, wilt thou have this woman to thy wedded wife, to live together after God's ordinance in the holy estate of Matrimony? Wilt thou love her, comfort her, honour, and keep her, in sickness and in health; and, forsaking all other, keep thee only unto her, as long as ye both shall live?*'

'*I will.*'

'*Matilda Trotter, wilt thou have this man to thy wedded husband, to live together after God's ordinance in the holy estate of Matrimony? Wilt thou obey him, and serve him, love, honour, and keep him, in sickness and in health; and forsaking all other, keep thee only unto him, so long as ye both shall live?*'

'*I will.*'

She couldn't believe it was happening, it was so unreal. She was cold, yet she was sweating. Was she really standing here being married to Matthew? Her hand was in his and he was saying:

'*I Matthew take thee Matilda to my wedded wife, to have and to hold from this day forward, for better for worse, for richer for poorer, in sickness and in health, to love and to cherish, till death do us part, according to God's holy ordinance; and thereto I plight thee my troth.*'

'*I Matilda take thee Matthew to my wedded husband, to have and to hold from this day forward, for better for worse, for richer for poorer, in sickness and in health, to love, cherish, and to obey, till death do us part, according to God's holy ordinance; and thereto I give thee my troth.*'

'*With this ring I thee wed, with my body I thee worship, and with all my worldly goods I thee endow: In the name of the Father,*' *and of the Son, and of the Holy Ghost. Amen.'*

Not until later in the vestry did the full impact of the ceremony and realisation of its meaning affect her. The ring was on her finger. She was married, married to Matthew. She was no longer Tilly Trotter, she was Mrs Matilda Sopwith. She felt faint. His lips were on hers, his eyes looking deep into hers. She heard John laugh and Luke say, 'It's my privilege to kiss the bride'; and she wasn't really aware that he kissed her hard on the lips.

John's face was now hovering close to hers. He looked at her for some seconds before placing his lips against her cheek, saying softly and without any stammer, 'Now I've got a sister whom I can love.'

The word sister brought back the scene of a week ago when Jessie Ann had descended on the house merely to tell her brother what she thought of him and to order him not to go through with this thing that was almost sacrilegious in her eyes and, she had added, in those of everyone else.

She hadn't come face to face with Jessie Ann, she had only heard her voice and seen Matthew escorting her almost forcibly to her carriage. Oh, she was glad she was leaving and going to America to a new life. Oh she was. And she was happy, so happy she couldn't believe it. But she wouldn't be able to let that happiness have full rein until she saw the shores of this country receding from view; then, and then only, she knew she would feel free because then no one would know about her except Matthew, her beloved Matthew. And he was her beloved Matthew. She felt no shame now in her love for him. Nor did she feel guilt for the part she had played in his father's life.

And then there was Katie. Katie would be a comfort. She would never feel that she had lost all the Drew family as long as she had Katie. . . . And her child. Well, he would grow up in a new country, free; even if his sight was impaired there would be no one to shout after him 'Witch's spawn!' She was leaving this country without one regret. Well, perhaps just one. She wished she hadn't to carry the memory of the look on Steve McGrath's face. They had met only once after the news of her impending marriage had set the village and the district aflame. She had met him on the main road and they had stopped and stared at each other; and as she looked into his face she had longed for words that would bring him some kind of comfort, for the look in his eyes had been the same as on that day when, a boy, he had asked her to marry him.

There had been no lead up to their brief conversation. 'Do you still want to stay in the cottage, Steve?' she had asked him quietly, and after a moment he had answered, 'Why not? One place is just the same as another.'

As she nodded at him and made to move away he had added, 'In spite of what I feel, Tilly, I still wish you happiness,' and to this she had muttered, 'Thanks Steve, thanks. That's . . . that's kind of you. . . .'

She was outside in the street. Matthew had helped Biddy up into the carriage, and when he turned to her, after a moment's pause he put his arms about her and almost lifted her in. Then Luke entered and John climbed on the box beside Fred Leyburn, and Matthew cried, 'To breakfast!' and seated himself beside Tilly.

His hand gripping hers, he looked across at Luke, asking now, 'How long have we got before the train goes?'

'Oh.' Luke glanced at his watch. 'An hour and a half, ample time.'

Following this there was silence except for the rumbling of the wheels over the cobbles. Nor was there much merriment at the breakfast except that which was supplied by John. His stammer much in evidence again, he kept up an almost one-sided jocular conversation during the meal.

Little over an hour later they were all standing under the awning of the station. The train was in, the engine noisily puffing out steam, their personal luggage was on the rack, and now the actual moment of parting had arrived.

When Biddy and Tilly put their arms about each other there were no words spoken. Their eyes were wet and their throats were full. Then Luke was kissing her again, a soft kiss now, his face straight, his eyes thoughtful, and what he said was, 'Be good to him, Trotter.'

187

Next came John and what he said was, 'I'll ha . . . have a w . . . w . . . wife shortly, Trotter, b . . . b . . . but I'll never have a fr . . . friend like you.' He touched her cheek gently with his fingers, then turned her round towards where Matthew was waiting; and Matthew, silently now and soberly, lifted her up the high step and into the compartment. Then he was saying good-bye to his brothers.

At one moment he was holding both their hands, then they stood close, their arms about each other's shoulders like triplets, and like triplets about to be severed there was pain on each face.

And lastly, Matthew stood before Biddy and, bending over her, he put his lips to her wrinkled face and what he said to her under his breath was, 'Look after the house and all in it, for who knows, we may be back some day. . . .'

They hung out of the window until those on the platform were lost by the curve of the rails and the steam from the engine, and then for the first time they were really alone.

Sitting close now, their fingers linked tightly, they looked at each other; but it was some moments before any words came. Gently withdrawing his hands from hers, he put them up to her head and there slowly pulled out the pins from her hat and laid it on the seat opposite; then putting his fingers into her hair he brought her face close to his and his gaze was soft and his voice tender as he said, 'You're beautiful, Mrs Matilda Sopwith, and you're mine. At last you're mine, all mine for life.'

Mrs Sopwith. Tilly Trotter was no more. She had turned into Matilda Sopwith and she knew that Matilda Sopwith would be loved as Tilly Trotter had never been, and that as Matilda Sopwith she would love as Tilly Trotter had never loved. She put her arms about his neck and all she could find to say was, 'Oh, Matthew! Matthew!'

PART FOUR

Tilly Trotter Wed

1

As Matthew helped Tilly down the gangway at Galveston she prayed silently and fervently that she wouldn't be called upon ever in her life again to board any kind of boat.

The crossing of the Atlantic had been such that during it she had longed to be back anywhere in England, even in the village, anywhere but on the heaving, rolling, stomach-erupting sea. That she had got over her bout of seasickness within the first week hadn't helped for there were the cramped quarters to contend with, and Katie who was in a bad state for the whole of the following two weeks of the journey; and then the child. At one time he had been so ill she thought she was going to lose him.

One thing the journey did teach her was that the heat of love, rising from no matter what depth of passion, could be cooled by the physical weaknesses of the body. Constant retching and the efforts of will it took to attend to Katie and the child caused her to ask herself more than once why she had done this mad thing. To marry a man six years her junior and follow him across the world would have been test enough for a young girl with an adventurous spirit, but she was no longer a young girl, she was thirty-three years old with the responsibility of a handicapped child and an almost equal responsibility for Katie who, from a tough little woman when on land had, from first setting foot on the ship, disintegrated into a bundle of nerves, and the ship was then still in dock.

That Matthew experienced no seasickness, in fact seemed to enjoy every minute of the voyage, did not help in the least; nor did the fact that he did all he could to alleviate their sufferings;

191

his very heartiness became an irritation.

But now it was all over. They were on dry land, standing amidst smiling faces, black faces, brown faces, white faces, most of the latter seeming to be bearded. There was bustle and talk all about her, deep guttural laughter, hand-shaking, people being met, all except them apparently.

Matthew was looking about him. He turned to her and smiled, saying, 'They'll be here somewhere. Look; stay there, sit on that trunk.' He pressed her down. 'I'll be back in a minute.'

As she watched him making his way among the throng, she felt a sudden pride rise in her and with it an onrush of love that the sea seemed to have washed away. He was a fine, upstanding figure of a man, handsome, and he looked older than his years, for which she was glad. She turned to Katie who was sitting on the trunk beside her holding the child in her arms whilst staring about her in bewilderment, and she said, 'We'll soon be home.' It sounded so natural to say, 'We'll soon be home.'

When Katie, bringing her white peaked face towards her, said, 'Aye, well, thank God for that,' she laughed out aloud, which brought the eyes of two strange-looking black men upon her. They were carrying big hessian wrapped bales on their shoulders and they twisted their heads towards her, pausing for a second before going on.

Her hand still over her mouth, she looked at Katie and said, 'You sounded just as if we were back in the kitchen.'

'Aye, well, I've got to say it, Tilly, I wish I was at this minute.'

'Oh, it's going to be all right.'

'You think so?' There was a tinge of fear in the question, and Tilly, her face straight now, said, 'Of course it is.'

Katie moved her head to gaze beyond the child's face towards the end of the quay, then turned it slowly to take in the buildings, some that looked like warehouses, others squat-shaped huts, and what she said was, 'Everything looks odd. An' the faces, some of them would scare the daylights out of you.'

Tilly now leaned towards her and muttered, 'You're in a different country, Katie,' and Katie, nodding her head now, replied tartly, 'There'll be no need to keep tellin' me that, I've got eyes.' Then lowering her glance, she spoke under her breath, saying, 'There's a fellow just to your right starin' at us. He's comin' this way.'

Tilly turned her head sharply and saw coming towards them a tall, gangling young man wearing a wide hat that looked as if it was about to fall off the back of his head, or perhaps it had been pushed there to show off an abundance of red curly hair. He wore an open-necked shirt, tight breeches that disappeared below the knee into high leather boots. His face was long and clean-shaven, his open mouth showed a set of big teeth, from which one only seemed to be missing. This left a gap in the middle of the lower set through which now he seemed to whistle as he scrutinized Tilly. After a moment he walked behind her and looked at the name on the trunk; then he rounded the remaining pile of luggage before stepping in front of her again, saying, 'Doug Scott, ma'am.'

Tilly slid to her feet as she said, 'How . . . how do you do?'

'I'm fine, ma'am. Where is he?'

'He's. . . . Well' — she moved her head — 'I think he must be looking for you, Mr Scott.'

'Doug, ma'am, if you don't mind, Doug.' He grinned widely at her.

Tilly swallowed, made a motion with her head but said nothing, until Mr Doug Scott turned his attention to Katie and the child, when she put in quickly, 'This is my friend, Miss Katie Drew, and my son, Willy.'

'Son?' Doug Scott's eyes were narrowed now as he stared at Tilly. 'You are Matt's missis, aren't you?'

'Yes; yes, I am.'

'Oh!'

She smiled at his perplexity and repeated what they had arranged to answer in just such circumstances. 'I was a widow when I married Mr Sopwith.'

'O . . . h. Oh yes, ma'am. Yes. Yes.'

'*Doug! Why Doug!*'

At the sound of his name Doug Scott swung round. Then they were striding towards each other, Doug Scott and Matthew, their hands outstretched, then shaking and thumping each other, as Tilly thought, like long lost brothers. When they came towards her Doug was saying, 'Bloody axle broke just passing through Hempstead. Should have been in yesterday by rights. God! was I sweatin'. Heard the boat was sighted. Anyway, got two fresh horses from Lob Curtis. Boy! was he pleased to know you're comin'. An' the girls. But their noses are put out now you've got yourself a spicy piece.'

Matthew was smiling widely. He looked relaxed and happy as he put his arm round Tilly's shoulders, saying, 'You've met this bloke already. He's the only articulate ranger in the whole of the frontier.'

'What do you mean, articulate, you little islander?'

Matthew again hugged Tilly to him as he said, 'He's the only Texan I've ever met who never stops talking. I've told you, haven't I? You can sit for days with some of them and they never open their mouths, but not our Doug here.'

'Aw, don't make me out to be a blatherer. Come on with you, I've got you rooms in the tavern a little way out. You'll be more comfortable there for the night. It'll be like barbecue night at the hotel here, so many comin' in and none leavin'; we'll soon won't be able to move.' He laughed at his own joke. Then beckoning a tall negro towards him, he said, 'Give a hand here,' then added, 'You take the ladies on, Matt; the buggy's at the end of the row. Diego is drivin'. See you in a few minutes.'

The buggy was like a cab that was a common sight in Newcastle, only it was bigger and was driven by two horses, not big strapping looking animals but more like the horses that had been used down the pit, not the ponies but the ones who pulled the wagon sets. Yet these looked thinner and unlovely beasts. Matthew had told her that this was horse country, that most of the wealth had lain in horses and cattle until the gold rush started; and then in some cases a horse had become as precious as the gold dust itself.

During the voyage Matthew had talked endlessly about this country. He had tried to take her mind off the heaving seas by telling her about the ranchers, the homesteaders, and the Indian tribes. He hadn't dwelt much on the Indians, just to give them names, strange sounding names like Tonkawas and Wichitas, and some that he called the Comanche. The Indians, she understood, were people who lived by hunting the buffalo, the deer, and such animals, and the ranchers lived by trading horses and cattle called shorthorns, while the homesteaders were what she surmised to be like English farmers. They ploughed the land, grew corn, they built their own houses and lived mostly by means of the exchange of goods. But nothing he had told her had fitted in with anything she had seen so far. But hadn't she just landed! She chastised herself.

'Hello, Diego. Hello there. How are you?'

The half-breed Mexican Indian smiled widely at Matthew; but Matthew did not extend his hand, nor did the man seem to expect it, but that he was delighted to see Matthew was evident.

'Wel . . . come back, boss-two.'

'Good to see you, Diego. How is Big Maria and Ki?'

'Good, very good. Ki shoot well . . . own gun now. Eight years old.'

'Oh, that's good, that's good. . . . This is my wife, Diego, and my stepson.'

The man gazed at Tilly for a moment; then slowly touched the brim of what she took to be a bowler hat, which was set ludicrously on top of his long straight black hair, and what he said was, 'Good'; then turning his gaze on to Katie and the child, he looked them over before repeating 'Good,' before once again letting his eyes rest on Tilly. Now he spoke in a strange tongue while he moved his hands over his face, then swept one hand down the length of his body, and his actions caused Matthew to laugh and say, 'I will tell her, she will be very pleased,' and turning, he said, 'Ah, there comes Boss Scott. Give him a hand, Diego.'

The man turned away but he did not hurry towards Doug

Scott and the negro who were holding the luggage, his step was slow if not stately, and as Matthew helped Tilly up into the buggy he said, 'Diego's a character. He's a half-breed, he speaks mostly Mexican. He paid you a fine compliment, he said you were beautiful like the land beyond the plains where it towers high.'

As she sank down on to the hide-covered straight-backed seat she made a slight face at him, saying, 'And that's a compliment?'

'Indeed! Indeed!' He turned now and, taking the child from Katie's arms, he lifted it on to Tilly's lap; then putting his hands under Katie's oxters, he said, 'Up you go! and take that frightened look off your face, nobody's going to eat you, not yet at any rate.'

Presently the sound of thumping coming from the back of the buggy caused both Tilly and Katie to look round. The luggage was being stacked, but now Doug Scott's voice drowned the noise as he shouted, 'Great sport next week. 'Tis all arranged, a bear hunt. Lob Curtis, Peter Ingersoll, the Purdies. . . .'

'Quiet, man! Quiet!' That was Matthew's voice, and both Katie and Tilly now exchanged glances as Katie's lips silently formed the word bears.

Tilly said, 'Well, there's bound to be wild animals here, it's a big country.'

'But bears! Tilly.'

'Aw, for goodness sake, stop worrying, Katie. Look, we haven't got there yet.' There was a note of impatience in her voice now. 'There'll be plenty of time to start worrying when there's something to worry about.'

'Aye, perhaps you're right. But somehow I don't think that'll be very far ahead.' Katie sounded so like her mother as she made this terse remark that Tilly knew a moment of homesickness while at the same time seeming to take into herself the dread that Katie had expressed, and she recalled the words she had said to Matthew on the last night of the voyage, 'What if I don't turn out to be made of pioneer material?'

* * *

They were on the road again, bumping and jostling. At times they were thrown from one end of the seat to the other. What seemed to make things worse for Tilly was being alone in the buggy with Katie and the child, no longer having Matthew's support. He was riding alongside Doug Scott. From time to time she caught sight of them galloping away into the distance; then Matthew would turn about and ride back to the window, laughing in on her, nodding and gesticulating. He was happy as she had never seen him happy. This was a different Matthew; he seemed to be one with the people and the surrounding countryside.

For a time the buggy rolled along smoothly and she had time to look out at the landscape. It was nice in parts, tree-lined slopes, the thin line of a river far away; but as yet she had seen no houses since leaving the tavern.

. . . And the tavern, so called, she had seen as merely a large wooden hut. Every part of it was wood, the walls, the floor, the furniture; and all rough hewn, no polish on anything. The bed was a wooden platform set in the middle of four posts but, unlike a four-poster bed, it had no canopy and no drapes. Still, she had slept well, and she had eaten well; the food had been roughly served, but there had been plenty of it.

It had been their first night in a real bed and they had loved and laughed, and she had gone to sleep in his arms.

She awoke to find herself alone; and when she did see him he was fully dressed and had already been outside with the men.

She discovered that he had enormous energy. It seemed that he must always be up and doing; and she understood now the sense of frustration he must have felt during the time he had spent at home.

Home. He spoke of this place for which they were bound as home. When she had asked him how far it was he had said, 'Oh, we'll be home by tomorrow nightfall at the latest.'

They had already made two stops, one at Houston, then at a place called Hempstead. They had made another short stop between these two places at a kind of crossroads, where Matthew had walked her around and pointed into the empty distance naming places, San Antonio away to the left,

Huntsville to the right, and vaguely somewhere in between the place for which they were making. And all the time referring to a man named Sam Houston. Then, of course, the river that they were travelling beside was the Brazos. One day soon, he promised, he'd take her to the falls of Brazos where there was a trading post; and oh, she would enjoy seeing Indians bringing in the pelts, and listening to the subsequent bargaining, mostly by signs, which he had demonstrated.

She had gazed at him in amazement as he talked. He spoke like a man who was walking on land that he owned. She also knew that he had become lost in himself, that he wasn't so much explaining to her but telling himself of its wonders, its charm. She had, since landing in this country, become aware of yet another facet of his character, a new facet, and with the awareness had come the knowledge that she really knew very little about this husband of hers. He appeared as strange to her now as the land about her; but one thing was evident, he was at one with this land, it was as if he had been born here, reared here, for he obviously loved it. She was already realising too that, with the exception of Houston, what the men referred to as towns were little more than villages; in fact the village at home was bigger and certainly looked more substantial, the houses being brick and stone built.

At the last wayside tavern where they had stopped she had listened to the garrulous Mr Scott talking about places which all seemed to be preceded by the word Fort: Fort Worth, Fort Belknap, Fort Phantom Hill, and when he seemed about to enlarge on the fact by saying they had rounded the beggars up there, she knew that the only reason why he stopped was because of some signal he had received from Matthew, who at the time had his back to her.

She knew there had to be forts to protect people from the Indians. She had learned from Matthew all about the Indians and their raids on the settlers, but all this, she understood, took place in a distant part of the country. Anyway, the rangers saw to it that the Indians toed the line. These were Matthew's words, this was Matthew's explanation. But strangely from the very moment they landed and had met up with Mr Scott, she'd had the strong feeling that Matthew's statements were not quite accurate, but that he made them light in order to alleviate any fears that the true situation might arouse in her. She felt that she wouldn't have to be long in Mr Scott's company for the true state of affairs to be made clear, absolutely clear.

The distance before the next stop was comparatively short, and at Washington-on-the-Brazos she sat at a table in what for the first time she considered a real house, but again one made entirely of wood, yet artistically so this time. It was a private house owned by a Mr Rankin. He was a small, spare-framed man, whose wife seemed to have been cut out of the same mould. They had two sons. The family had a chandler's store in the town which the father and the eldest son appeared to run, but the younger one's business seemed to be with horses, and the conversation at the dinner table revolved generally around horses, particularly mustangs.

Although the men talked and the mother listened she knew that the family were all covertly weighing her up. Their greetings to her had been friendly but not effusive as they had been towards Matthew, yet even that had been expressed in hand-shakes and slapping on backs accompanied by very few words.

No one asked her any questions. They had merely nodded at Matthew's explanation of the child's presence; Katie they took for granted, she was a nursemaid.

They, too, had servants, many more than a house of this size would have entailed had it been in England: one Mexican waited on table, with another hovering in the background, while earlier in the yard she had seen three negro slaves.

She had yet to take in the fact that people who kept slaves could be nice, friendly creatures. Years ago the parson's wife had talked about slaves and the hard cruel people who owned them, but as yet she had seen no sign of cruelty, but as yet, too, she told herself she had barely set foot on this land; then wryly she thought, she might barely have set foot but her back and buttocks were feeling as if they had been bumping along these roads for years.

She noticed with this family too that the men either talked a lot or they talked little, that there seemed to be no happy medium.

The meal over, they sat on the verandah and watched the night creeping into the great expanse of sky, but it was much as Tilly could do to remain seated in the slat-back wooden chair and not run to the closet, which even in this house was an exposed hut at the end of the yard. All her life she had seen men spitting. The roadways and pavements of Shields, and Jarrow and Newcastle were covered with sputum and the fireplaces of the poor were often tattooed with it, but to hear the constant pinging aimed into an iron receptacle set between the chairs became almost too much to bear, especially on top of a meal of pork, but the three Rankin men sucked at their pipes, coughed, then spat until the sound almost created a nauseating melody in her head.

Matthew was smoking, but like his father he didn't spit, except into a handkerchief, and for this she was thankful.

Making the child an excuse to leave the company, she rose to her feet. Matthew, too, rose, and smiled and nodded towards her before resuming his seat.

As she walked along the verandah to go into the house she heard the young son laugh as he said, 'Long spanker there, Matthew man. A horse like that and. . . .' She passed out of earshot, but when, on her way along another corridor towards their room, she saw through an open door Katie sitting at the end of a table with Doug Scott, and the two of them laughing, she had an overwhelming urge to join them. But here she recognised another obstacle facing her in this free country, there was status to be considered. As Matthew had said laughingly, although they wouldn't have it said they were more class conscious here than they were in England, for here there were more divisions of class. There were the slaves at the bottom of the grades, then the half-castes, which could be Mexican Indians or Mexican whites or even Indian whites; and there were the homesteaders, the majority of them respectable but others who were slackers; then there were the whites who set the standards, the tradesmen, the bankers, the lawyers. It was from these came the offshoots, the politicians and, one mustn't

200

forget, the army. Some of the officers were class, mainly those, Matthew had added, who had come over from England; but a number of them were mere mercenaries, no better than the men they controlled, the majority of whom were scum who had merely joined up to escape punishment of one kind or another, not realising that life in the so-called forts was a punishment alone to outdo all others.

He had spoken of this so lightly, much as Mr Burgess would have done in giving a history lesson, like something that had happened in some bygone time. The only difference was the bygone time was now and she was experiencing the happening.

Katie, glimpsing her, got to her feet as she said, 'Do you want me, Ti . . . ma'am?'

'No, no,' she called back; 'it's all right,' and Katie resumed her seat.

That was another thing; she must be ma'am now all the time to Katie, and she smiled to herself as she recalled the difficulty Katie had in remembering this form of address.

The child was asleep. He had kicked the clothes down to the bottom of the rocking cradle. She had been surprised when first shown the cradle; then Mrs Rankin had informed her that she had three married daughters and a number of grandchildren. Willy had the fingers of one hand in his hair as if he were scratching his head, his other small fist was doubled under his chin. He looked funny, amusing and beautiful. Whenever she looked at him like this she always wanted to gather him into her arms and press him into her, he was so precious and so loving. If only his eyes. . . . She shook her head. She mustn't start whining about this, she had got to face up to it, and help him to meet it too. He could still see out of one eye. They could but hope he would continue to do so until he was old enough to be fitted with spectacles.

She turned now quickly from the crib as the door opened and Matthew entered, and moved swiftly towards her. With his arm about her, he stood looking down with her on the sleeping child. She found it strange that he should care so much for the child, that there was no trace of jealousy in him, it

201

was as if the child were his own.

When they turned from the cot he peered at her in the fading light, and taking her face between his hands, he said, 'They like you,' then jerking his chin upwards as if in annoyance at an inane remark, he repeated, 'They like you. What I mean is, you've knocked them flat on their faces.'

She opened her eyes wide as she lowered her head while still looking at him, and she said, 'It wasn't apparent to me.'

'Because they don't talk? You can't go by that; it's something one detects in their manner, in their look. You've got to wait a couple of years before they speak to you.'

'Well, that's something to look forward to.'

'Oh, darling! Darling!' He pulled her into his arms and they kissed and clung tightly together; then after a moment, as he released her, she asked, 'How much further, really?'

'If we make good time, no hitches, we should be there by noon tomorrow.'

She looked at him soberly now as she said, 'I'm a bit scared, Matthew.'

'Of the country?'

'No.'

'The Indians?'

'No, no; although' — she nodded — 'I wouldn't want to meet any Indians. No, it's meeting your uncle and his daughter. You said he looked upon you as a sort of son. Well, he may not like his son having taken a wife.'

'Nonsense! Nonsense! He's a fine man, a most understanding man. About most things that is. One thing I've never fathomed about him is the fact that he doesn't seem to understand his own daughter; nor for that matter does his daughter understand him, although I must admit she's got a point. Oh yes, yes; she's got a point.'

She waited but he did not go on to explain what the point was.

'Anyway, come on; they're talking about a barbecue they're putting on in a fortnight's time.'

'A barbecue. What's a barbecue?'

'Oh, well, now' — he scratched his head — 'it's a cross

between a county ball and a barn dance, somewhere in the middle.'

'Oh, I'll have to see this.'

'Yes, you'll have to see this.' He again pulled her into his arms. 'And they'll all want to see you because you'll be the belle of the ball. There's been nothing like you around here for a long, long time. I'll lay my last dollar on that.'

She looked at him in silence now. He was so proud of her; yet she knew it to be a strange pride, one of possession. And he endorsed this as he now said, 'I've always believed that if you want a thing badly enough you'll get it in the end, yet there were times when I doubted it, but not any more. Tilly Trotter that was, you're mine, mine!' His lips pressed so hard against hers that the kiss became painful, but she endured it.

2

They seemed to have left the tree-lined country miles and miles behind them. They had passed dwellings, poor make-shift affairs, but each passing had always been greeted with wavings and calls from both sides. At one such place they had stopped for Tilly and Katie to get out to stretch their legs and the men to water the horses in a brook nearby. The family had stood gaping at her: the woman of indeterminable age, a girl of about twelve, and two small children, their sex hidden under long skirts. Neither the woman nor the children spoke, they just gaped at her as if she were a mirage dropped from the sky.

What had simply amazed Tilly and sent her mind question-ing was the sight of a man running from a far field accom-panied by a small boy who could have been no more than seven years old, for both of them were carrying guns. The man hailed Doug Scott enthusiastically and nodded in a friendly fashion towards Matthew, but when he looked at her it was some moments before he spoke, and then he said, 'How-do, ma'am?'

The boy with the gun slung across his shoulders stared at her, his mouth partly open, his eyes wide and smiling.

She wanted to say to the boy, 'Why are you carrying a gun?' but then she asked herself, why not? At home young boys shot rabbits. Yes, but not a boy as small as this one. And another thing, from the condition of his boots and his hands it was evident that he had been working in the fields.

She turned to Matthew, but Matthew was now preparing to leave and he called to her, 'Come along'; then to the family he said. 'Good-day.'

All nodded towards him, and she, looking at the woman, said, 'Good-bye.' Still the woman didn't speak, she merely inclined her head towards her.

The poverty, the almost squalid poverty of the family depressed her. It was Katie who voiced her thoughts, saying, 'I've never seen anybody as poorly off as that, not even in the pit row. I thought we had reached bottom there. And that little lad. Did you see he was carrying a gun? Why was that now, do you think?'

Tilly shook her head as she answered, 'Likely for game. There's a tremendous amount around; you saw for yourself a way back.'

'Aye, but there's no trees here for them to live among. Would it be to shoot them Indians do you think?' It was a fear-tinged question and Tilly was quick to respond, 'Oh no, of course not. The rangers see to them. In any case, they're miles away, two hundred, three hundred, four hundred. So Matthew says.'

'Well, that's something to be thankful for.'

They smiled at each other. Then Katie put a question to Tilly that she couldn't answer. What she said was, 'Do you see how they treat Diego? Mr Scott speaks to him all right and, of course, the boss, but them we just left, and them last night took no notice of him. Is it because he looks a bit like an Indian?'

Tilly considered for a moment before she said, 'Well, Katie, we've got to face it, it's likely the servant question over again.' She finished this on a laugh, and Katie, laughing with her, said 'Aye, you could be right. Although I wouldn't have thought we would have come across anything like that out here where everything's so rough.'

Yes, where everything was so rough. The land was rough. Beautiful, yes, but rough and dangerous. They had spoken again of bears last night. And the people. Even those one expected to show some refinement had a roughness about them. Oh, she wished she was settled in to the new home. She wished she knew what was facing her. She had a strange, even a weird feeling of premonition hanging over her. Well, she would soon know. Less than a couple of hours now and she would know.

She saw the homestead when still some way off. It was what she termed the railings she saw first surrounding what appeared to be a large farm. She was leaning her head slightly out of the window and through the dust from the galloping horses' hooves she saw Matthew and Doug Scott riding ahead. They were shouting as they rode, their voices coming back to her in an unintelligible sound. Diego was yelling too, and his cry she made out to be, 'Hi-hi! . . . Hi-hi!'

Then the buggy was rolling between the high fences and into a big open space, and the horses suddenly seeming to skid to a stop brought her, Katie, and the child into a heap on the seat.

They were disentangling themselves when the door was pulled open and Matthew, his face alight, said, 'Come.'

Tilly straightened her hat, took a handkerchief swiftly around her face, and pulled down the skirt of her long blue coat before holding out her hand to him.

Then they were in the compound and he was leading her towards the tall grey-haired man who was standing at the bottom of a set of steps that led to the long verandah fronting the wooden house, which appeared quite imposing in its style.

'Well, Uncle, here we are.'

Matthew still kept hold of her hand as he held out his other to Alvero Portes, and the man, taking it, gripped it hard as he said simply, 'Welcome home, Matthew. Welcome home.' Then turning his attention to Tilly, he looked her up and down; and she returned his gaze, and as she did so she knew immediately that this man resented her presence. Even when he smiled at her and said, 'And welcome to your wife,' that innate knowledge which she possessed that had not been born of experience but which she had inherited from some ancestor who had been wise in knowing told her that a smile, no matter how oiled, could not hide the truth that lay deep in the eyes.

'Come in, come in; you must be tired. Oh.' He paused and looked towards where Katie was standing with the child in her

206

arms and he said, 'Ah, your stepson. I was prepared; I got your mail yesterday.' He did not give any more attention to the child but turned and went up the steps, and Matthew, gripping her hand tightly, drew her with him, and thus she entered the house.

The house itself was a surprise. The door from the verandah led into a large room, which she guessed to be thirty feet or more long and two thirds of its length wide. To the far right of her a table was set out for a meal, the glass on it glinting in the shaded dimness of the room. To the left of her in the end wall was a stone fireplace, the open area being almost concealed by a huge jug of dried grasses. At right angles to the fireplace was a couch covered with various animal skins lying loosely on it. There were a number of chairs in the room, one large and hide-covered; the others she took to be wooden chairs, but with one noticeable difference from those she had seen beforehand, these were all polished.

There were three doors in the room, one by which she had entered, one almost opposite leading into a passageway, the third at the end of the room where the dining-table was. The whole atmosphere gave off a sense of comfort touching on elegance. This last was created by, of all things, a diamond-paned china cabinet standing to the right of the doorway that led into the corridor. There were four windows giving on to the verandah, which shaded the light that would otherwise have penetrated the room.

'Isn't it a lovely room?' Matthew threw his arm out in a wide sweep, and she nodded at him, smiling as she said, 'Yes, indeed it is.'

'Never mind about admiring the room. Take your wife to your quarters; I'm sure she needs to freshen up after her little jaunt.' Laughter accompanied the last words and the sound was high, unexpected coming from the full-lipped wide mouth.

As Matthew led Tilly towards the corridor Katie was about to follow with the child in her arms when for a moment she imagined that the tall man was going to stop her passage for he made a movement with his hand, then checked it. Following this he inclined his head slightly towards her: it was permission that she could cross the room and follow her mistress.

The apartments were two rooms at the end of the corridor. The bedroom was comfortably furnished, the window looking out on to an open space where a number of horses were standing as if asleep. The other room was a kind of dressing room-cum-study; in it was a wash-hand stand holding a jug and basin, and clean white towels hung from a rack beside it.

As she took off her coat and hat she let out a long sigh which brought Matthew to come and stand in front of her, and there was a note of slight anxiety in his voice as he said, 'Well, this is it. What do you think?'

She did not return his smile as she answered, 'I think it's too early to say.'

'Oh, Matilda! You're going to like it, you must, it's going to be our home.'

'Always? In this house with . . . with your uncle?'

'Don't you like him?'

She turned her head slightly to the side. 'I've hardly met him. I glimpsed a tall, aristocratic man who was delighted to have you back but would have preferred you to have come alone.'

'Oh now! Now!' He wagged his finger in her face. 'If you've only glimpsed him for a moment, as you say, how can you make that out? Be fair. I'd wait a little while before you pass judgment on him. He's a fine man. He has his faults, haven't we all, but you'll come to like and respect him. You'll see.'

'Where is his daughter?'

'Oh, she's likely in the dog run.'

'*The what*!' She screwed up her face at him, and he now said, 'Oh, that isn't as bad as it sounds. It was the original house built here years ago, it's a kind of log hut with an open runway going through it. Anyway, we'll see it all later on.'

'But why does she live there?'

'Oh, it's a long story and interesting, and I'll tell you about it later. . . . Come now.'

'Wait.' She pushed him gently aside. 'I must see to Katie and the child; I'd forgotten. . . .'

'Oh yes, yes, of course.'

Tilly opened the door to see Katie, her face straight, standing holding the child, and she took the boy into her arms, saying, 'I'm sorry. I'm sorry, Katie. We'll get settled shortly.' She now turned towards Matthew. 'What . . . what about Katie and a room for the nursery?'

He stood looking at her for a moment gnawing on his lip, a look of perplexity on his face; then going past them, he said, 'Just wait a moment, I'll see Uncle.'

'Come in and sit down.' Tilly motioned Katie into the room, and Katie came in but she didn't sit down. Looking at Tilly, she said, 'He wasn't going to let me across the room.'

'What do you mean?'

'That man, his uncle, he was for making me go round the back, wherever that is.'

'Oh no!'

'Oh aye, Tilly, I saw it in his face: What is the meaning of this! Wrong door, tradesmen's entrance. You know what it was like back home.'

Tilly bowed her head for a moment before she said, 'It's all going to be so different from back home, Katie; we've both got to understand that.'

'Oh, I understand it, never fear. Don't worry about me.' Katie smiled at her now, but it was a tight smile. 'Only you can't help noticin' things, an' some of them pip you. You know what I mean?'

'Yes. I know what you mean.' They looked at each other and nodded, and they both knew that the servant-mistress association was going to be much more difficult in this home than it had been at the Manor. . . .

They had taken the child's dust-covered outer clothes off, washed his hands and face; Tilly had also freshened herself with a wash and told Katie to do the same; following this, they sat waiting for another five minutes before Tilly, rising impatiently to her feet, said, 'I'll go and see what's happening.'

Leaving the room, she went along the corridor and through the open door that led into the main room. There was no one in the room except a Mexican, who looked very like Diego. He had been attending to the table and he glanced towards her and in stilted English said, 'Ma'am, I . . . I Emilio.'

'Hello, Emilio.' She inclined her head towards him, and he bowed slightly before turning and walking towards the door beyond the table.

Alone, she could now hear voices coming from beyond the fireplace end of the room. There was no door there, just a heavy embroidered curtain hanging on the wall. She had earlier taken it to be a piece of tapestry but now she realised that there must be a room beyond. She was nearing it when she stopped as the old man's voice came to her, saying, 'As I said, I'm not against you marrying, my dear boy, but a widow with a child! You say her husband was a gentleman?'

'Yes.' The syllable was curt.

'Landed?'

'Yes, the owner of an estate, and a mine.'

'Did he leave her well off?'

'She has an income.'

'It must have happened very quickly.'

'No, not at all, Uncle. I've been in love with her for years.'

'As a married woman?' There was a shocked note in the question.

'Yes, as a married woman; and before.'

'You must have been a mere boy. How long was she married?'

'Oh, I don't know, two or three years, five perhaps.'

'Well, I'm sorry to say it, Matthew, but she doesn't on first appearance seem to be the type that will settle for this kind of life; she is dressed and certainly looks like a town woman.'

'You don't know anything about her as yet, Uncle. She's had a strange life, a hard life in some ways. She. . . .'

'Hard? But you said she was married to a gentleman?'

There was a silence now and during it Tilly turned away, but as she did so Matthew's voice came to her, saying, 'And he was a gentleman, very much so. I . . . I shall tell you about him some day perhaps. In the meantime, Uncle, as I asked earlier, can you tell me where I can house the child and the maid?'

When she returned to the room at the end of the corridor she paused before opening the door and drew in a long shuddering breath, she mustn't let Katie see she was upset.

On entering the room, she said, 'He's talking to his uncle; they must be arranging something.'

'What's the matter?' Katie got to her feet; 'you look white.'

'I feel white; it's been a long journey.'

'Aye, you could say that.'

Of a sudden Tilly put out her hands and grabbed those of the dumpy young woman facing her, and her voice had a break in it as she said, 'Oh! Katie, I'm glad you came with me, and never more than at this minute.'

Within an hour the space with the dormer windows under the roof had been cleared by four negroes, one a man with white hair, another in his middle years, the other two in their early twenties.

While this was being done, Matthew escorted Tilly around the homestead, and she made the acquaintance of Luisa Portes.

They had left the house by the door at the end of the main room, walked across some duck boards and into a room that Tilly took to be a kitchen, for it was fully equipped with all that was needed in a kitchen including a table and a wood oven stove, besides rows of pans and kitchen utensils hanging on one wall and a rough-hewn dresser flanking the opposite one.

Emilio was in the kitchen. He was grinding meat through an iron sieve bolted to the corner of the table, and he stopped his work and smiled at them, but waited for Matthew to speak. 'Good to see you again, Emilio,' Matthew said.

'And you, young boss.'

'How are the children?'

'Very well, thrivin' . . . that is right? thrivin'?'

'Yes' — Matthew laughed now — 'that is right, thriving. . . . Where is Miss Luisa?'

'In quarter.' The man jerked his head backwards.

'Thank you.' Matthew took her arm now and led her out of another door where there was another set of duck boards leading to a door opposite, but he didn't take her through this door;

211

instead, stepping off the boards on to the rough ground, he guided her to the front of the house and on to yet another layer of duck boards. These fronted a doorless space, through which she could see to the far end and out to where a tree was growing.

When she glanced at him enquiringly he said, speaking under his breath now, 'This is called a dog run. It was at one time used for sheltering the animals; it also serves another purpose, it forms an air tunnel in high summer, and you need it, I can tell you.'

Tilly followed him into the open space which had two doors on either side and when he tapped on one of them it was opened almost immediately and Tilly found herself looking down on a woman whose age puzzled her at the moment. The woman was small and sturdily built; she was wearing a long faded serge skirt and a striped blouse over which was a fine fur-skin waistcoat. Her hair was drawn tightly back from her forehead; it was black without a trace of grey in it. Her face appeared square owing to the width of her jaw, her skin had a warm olive tint and her eyes lying in deep hollows appeared black, but a fiery black.

'Hello, Luisa.'

The woman looked from Matthew to Tilly and into her eyes for some seconds before answering Matthew's greeting, saying simply, 'Hello.' Then standing aside, she allowed them to enter the room.

Tilly had no time to take in more than a fleeting impression of the room but that was enough to tell her that the place looked comfortless, even stark in its furnishing, which was so utterly in contrast to that in the big room across the yard.

When Matthew said, 'My wife, Luisa,' Tilly held out her hand, saying, 'I'm very pleased to meet you.'

It was with some hesitation that Tilly's hand was taken. She was surprised at the hard firmness of the grip; then she was more surprised, even startled when the woman gave a laugh and, looking her up and down, she said, 'You'd be anything but a welcome surprise to him.'

'Come, come, Luisa.' Matthew caught hold of her arm. 'Don't tell me things haven't improved; you promised you would try.'

'I promised no such thing.' Luisa withdrew her arm with a jerk from Matthew's hold. 'And as for improving, you know that's an impossibility; things don't improve with him, they only get worse. Oh . . . oh' — she now shook her head from side to side — 'this isn't done I know.' She was looking at Tilly now. 'One should be polite and greet the guests, but as you're going to live here you might as well know how things stand from the start. So I can tell you I hate that man across there and always will. I cook for him, and that's as far as it goes. I don't enter his house, but you' — there was a suspicion, just a suspicion of a smile on her face now as she added, 'you're in a different position, you'll be living under his roof and you'll make up your mind for yourself. And I can tell you this right away, if he decides to put on a good face for you now that he has partly lost his adopted son to you' — she jerked her head towards Matthew — 'you'll find me in the wrong. My attitude you'll put down to that of a crabbed old maid. Well, so be it, time will tell. Anyway, I'm glad to see you. It's good to see another woman's face about the place, a white woman's, and if things get too hot for you over in the . . . palace, then you'll always be welcome to use this' — she made a flicking movement with her hand — 'as a fort.'

'Thank you.' Tilly smiled at the woman and she knew immediately that she was going to like her, she did like her, whereas she doubted if she would like her father.

'I'll take you at your word,' she said; and with her next words she didn't consider if she was vexing or pleasing Matthew, but she added, 'And I'll bring the baby and my friend too.' She made a 'Huh!' sound in her throat now as she ended, 'She's supposed to be nursemaid to the child but we've been friends for many years.'

As she ended she cast a glance at Matthew. He was looking at her quizzically but he said nothing.

'Sit down and have a drink. What is it for you, the same as usual?'

'Yes, Luisa, the same as usual.'

'And you? By the way, what must I call you?'

'Ti . . . Matilda.'

'Matilda. Well, Matilda, what's your drink? I can offer you one of three, Spanish wine, brandy or whisky.'

'I'll have the wine, please.' Tilly watched the small woman go to a cupboard in the wall and take out two bottles and three glasses, and when she had poured out the drinks she handed Tilly the wine, and as she gave Matthew the glass of brandy she said briefly, 'Bear hunt next week. Far better if they joined the rangers; ten bears ain't half as troublesome as one Indian. Mack's out you know.'

'Where?'

'Waco, beyond the falls, bloody Comanches. It's been quiet for too long. More families have settled up there now and that's drawing the bloody barbarians out again.'

'Which group is he riding with?'

'O'Toole's.'

'O'Toole's? When did they leave?'

'The day before yesterday. And — ' she nodded now, a sneer on her face and in her voice as she said, 'You won't believe it, you know what that Jefferson Davis has gone and done?' She waited while Matthew stared at her. 'Supplied the army with camels. Huh! Huh! did you ever hear anything like it? Camels! If he spent the money on reinforcing the rangers instead on humpty-backed camels we'd likely get somewhere. They make me bloody mad these politicians.' On this she lifted the glass to her mouth and threw her drink off in one gulp; then banging the glass down on a rough wooden table to her side, she said, 'Forts, forts, forts! They'll soon have as many bloody forts as they have buffalo; they're springing up all over the damn place.'

'Well, as I see it, Luisa, that isn't a bad thing.'

'New one up river, near the Brazos Reservation, Fort Belknap. But they opened that before you left, didn't they? Then the fellows tell me there's another one below Brazos Reservation, Phantom Hill they call that one. Oh my God! we won't see the wood for the trees shortly. Another drink?' She looked from one to the other, and Matthew, getting to his feet, said, 'No thanks, not at the moment, Luisa; we're just going round the rest of the standing.'

At the door, Luisa looked up into Tilly's face as she said quietly, 'If you're going to stay, make him' — she now thumbed towards Matthew — 'build you a house outside.'

'I'll . . . I'll see he does that.'

'Don't wait too long.'

'I won't.'

'Come on. Come on.' Matthew gave her arm a sharp tug that caused her almost to jump off the step on to the duck board and to reprimand him, not actually in the words but in the tone that she gave to them as she said, 'Please, Matthew, careful.'

He was walking a little ahead of her as he remarked coolly now, 'You won't have to listen . . . at least you won't have to believe all that Luisa says.'

'Then I shouldn't insist on us having a home of our own?'

'Not yet at any rate.'

'And this talk of Indians and raids, you haven't told me any of this, Matthew; you indicated all this happened miles away.'

He slowed up and walked by her side now, his head slightly bent, and his voice was low but had a forced patient note to it as he said, 'This is a new country, there's always skirmishes. Most of the Indians have become friendly but there are some who won't toe the line. They've got to be made to fall into place, the place allotted to them by the state. So' — he turned and looked at her — 'there'll always be skirmishes but, as I've already told you, they take place hundreds of miles away.'

'Well, why does everyone seem to carry a gun? I noticed guns on each side of the fireplace in your uncle's room and one standing near the door. There was that little boy we passed, he had a gun while he was working in the fields.'

'It was at one time a necessary form of protection, now it has become a habit. That's all.'

They were nearing the long low row of huts now and she stopped and said to him quietly, 'As you are well aware, Matthew, I am no child, so it would be better if you did not treat me as such. If there is danger I would like to know about it, so . . . so that I, too, may become prepared.'

His face slid into a slow smile now and he said, 'Very well, Mrs Sopwith, when we have time to ourselves I shall put you into the picture; what is more, I shall teach you to shoot and to ride, and then' — he chuckled — 'you can be my bodyguard. . . .'

'Well! . . . Hie!'

They both turned to see coming towards them a short-built man who appeared to be so thin his body seemed to be lost within the breeches and heavy coat he was wearing.

'Hello there, Rod.'

Tilly again watched Matthew shaking hands as if he were greeting a long lost brother; then turning to her, he said, 'This is Rod Tyler, one of the best horse-breakers in Texas.'

'Go on with you! . . . How do you do, ma'am? . . . Welcome.'

'Thank you.' She was smiling at the man, who she guessed to be in his mid-thirties, but then again it was difficult to tell the ages of the people she had met in this strange wild land. He had a pleasant face, handsome in a way. His eyes were merry and they seemed to infect his voice and laugh.

They were walking towards the bunkhouse now and Matthew said, 'I hear Mack's gone out.'

'Aye, the silly old fool. We nearly had an up-'n-downer for it, but I let him have it as he knows that district better than me.'

'Are you on your own then but for Doug?'

'No; Pete Ford and Andy O'Brien have stopped along the way. You remember them?'

'Oh, yes, I remember them, and they'll remember me. Remember the nightmare?'

As Rod Tyler was going through the doorway he turned and threw his head back and let out a roar of a laugh as he thumped Matthew on the back, saying, 'Do I remember your nightmare! we thought the horse maniacs had certainly come to say hello. Boy! did you cause a stir that night. God! I'll say.'

Laughing, they entered the bunkhouse which Tilly saw was just that, a long room that held ten narrow cots, and running down the middle were two tables end to end with long forms underneath them. But at one end of the house a door led into what apparently was an extra room, a kitchen she surmised; at the other end a stove dominated the wall with a black pipe going up to the ceiling and through it.

'Well, this is home from home, ma'am.' Rod Tyler grinned widely as he waved his arm from one side to the other. 'And there's many worse I can tell you.' And looking at Tilly, he said, 'We'll make you a hash one night, ma'am, after a hunt. You've never tasted anything like our hash, especially when Doug Scott's got a hand in it.'

'Where's Doug, by the way?'

'He's gone off to the bottom corral with Pete and Andy. We brought in a couple of herds last week but it's gettin' a bit too dry . . . and too cold for them down there, they'd be better up here.'

The room was stuffy, there was a strong smell, a mixture of sweat and smoke and the odd odour that comes from hides and leather, and Tilly was glad when she got out into the air again.

As they stood in the doorway of the bunkhouse Rod Tyler, looking at Matthew, said, 'Good to see you back.' Then turning his glance on Tilly, he added, 'And with such a spankin' lady. . . . You ride, ma'am?'

'No, I'm afraid I don't.'

'I'm soon going to cure that failing.' Matthew nodded at Rod Tyler, and he, nodding back, said, 'Pick you one of the best out.'

Tilly, laughing now, put in, 'You may, but it'll be another job to get me on its back.'

'We'll do that, ma'am, never fear, ma'am. What do you say, eh, Matt?'

It was strange to hear Matthew being called Matt. She had said jokingly that she would call him Matt if he called her Matilda but she had found it didn't come natural, so he was always Matthew to her; but only at odd times did she revert to Tilly to him.

They were now making their way to the far corner of the compound towards a small huddle of huts, four in all, and

Matthew, stopping before the first hut, leant slightly forward as he called, 'Hie there! You in there, Ma One?'

Almost immediately the rickety door was pulled open and the aperture was filled with the figure of a large old negro woman; her face one big smile, she said, 'Ah! young boss come back. Welcome. Welcome, young boss.'

'How are you, Ma One?'

'As best the good Lord sends.'

'Then you couldn't be better.'

' 'S'right, young boss. 'S'right.'

'This is my wife, Ma One.'

'Yes, I see your wife. Tall, great lady. Ah yes! Ah yes! Fine great lady, ma'am.'

All Tilly could add to this stilted conversation was the equally and formally stilted words of, 'How do you do?' and to this the old negress answered, 'Aw, do fine, ma'am, do fine.'

'One, all right, Ma?'

'One all right, boss, One all right.'

'And Two, Three and Four?'

'Two all right, boss, but Three 'n Four' — she laughed now, her huge breasts wobbling as she said, 'They'll never be all right till they reach great age, young never all right. But Three, he better this past time for boss Tyler let him ride.'

'Oh, good, good; I'm glad of that.'

'You find Miss Luisa good, boss?'

'Yes, Ma One, in fine fettle.'

'I keep her well, in fine fettle, look after her well.' The smile had slid from her face and she was nodding her head slowly; and Matthew nodded back at her, saying, 'I know you do, Ma One, and she is very grateful.'

The old woman nodded her head even more slowly now and when Matthew said, 'We are making the rounds, we'll go and see the boys,' the old woman laughed. 'All in the stable make tallow,' she said.

They smiled at each other now and without more ado Matthew turned Tilly about and led her along by the side of the wire fence towards a row of well-built wooden huts, and as they went she, looking straight ahead, said, 'Why on earth do you call the negroes by numbers?'

'Oh, Uncle apparently did this years ago when he bought them and it's stuck.'

'Bought them?'

'Yes, bought them, they're slaves.'

'Slaves?' She drew him to a stop, then pulled the collar of her coat tighter around her neck as she looked at him for a moment before saying, 'Do you condone slavery, Matthew?'

He paused and his face had that straight look that spoke of mixed feelings, and what he said was, 'No, I don't condone slavery, dear. In England I would abhor it, but here I accept it as an economical fact; they were first imported as labour for the plantations.'

'Imported?' She stared steadily at him, and he repeated, 'Yes, imported, like goods, but not as carefully handled as goods I must admit; yet in many cases they were a much more valuable cargo.'

'It's terrible.'

'Well, you're not alone in thinking like that, dear, but one thing I ask of you, don't express your opinions with regard to the slaves or even the half-breeds such as Diego or Emilio in front of Uncle, for you'll be on very swampy ground here and you'll find yourself sinking under his arguments.' He smiled, adding, 'On the importation of slaves, on the keeping in their place of half-castes, and on the absolute extermination of all Indians, Uncle holds himself as an authority.'

She shivered slightly and again tucked her collar tight under her chin before saying, 'You're very fond of him, aren't you?'

'Yes, I'm fond of him, but I'm not blind to his defects nor do I adhere to his opinions, nor keep his petty laws; but again, in spite of all this, I must say I am fond of him. And you'll grow to be fond of him too when you get to know him.'

'His daughter knows him and she's not fond of him.'

His face darkened slightly and again he turned her about and walked her forward, saying now, 'Whatever is between them is a family matter. I've told you I'll explain it to you later, at least my particular knowledge of it.'

They now entered the first block of the stables where three

negroes were working. A tall spare-framed old negro with white hair was stirring an obnoxious-smelling liquid in an iron pot over a wood-burning stove. He straightened up immediately, as did the other two men, and they stood in a rough line as they smiled at Matthew.

Touching his forehead, the old man said, 'Hello, young boss.'

Matthew answered his greeting with, 'Hello, One,' then he nodded at the other two, saying, 'Hello there. . . . How are things?'

'Things good, boss, things good.'

Tilly stared at the ebony faces. Apart from the old man, the other two looked to be at least in their thirties. She learned later that they were not related to him.

As Tilly looked at them she was overwhelmed by a feeling of sadness: an old man and two men in their prime named by numbers and referred to as boys. In some ways the very numbers robbed them of their manhood. They were looking at her and nodding their heads and she had to force herself to smile at them. She was glad when a few minutes later they left the stable, but outside she saw the fourth negro. He was coming from the direction of the dog run. She told herself she'd never get used to calling the house a dog run, it was too akin to a dog kennel, but this negro did not make his way towards them, in fact Tilly thought he went out of his way to avoid them, and when she remarked on this Matthew said, 'Yes, very likely you're right; he's a sour one is Four, and that's been brought about by kindness, Luisa's kindness. He's her house-boy and she made the mistake of teaching him to read.'

'You think then it's a mistake for any human being to be able to read and understand words?'

'Now! now! now! don't get on your old high horse, Tilly Trotter.' He was tweaking her nose now. 'In this case, yes, because the others accept their lot, but the little knowledge he has gained has made him uneasy, groping. It has also prevented him from doing the one thing he wants to do, ride.'

'Why?'

'Well! . . . Oh dear me, it's such a tangled story, it's to do

220

with Luisa. If she'd only be reasonable and go back and live in the house and act as a daughter should, Uncle would give her the earth, literally all this earth that he owns, and that's a few hundred square miles of it, not to mention his other assets, two banks and a factory, et cetera, et cetera. Well, since she won't act normally, he, being the man he is, takes it out on anyone she favours, so Four has a rough time of it. But strangely, the solution lies in the boy's own hands, he could ask for a transfer to the stables or other work, then once he left Luisa and the dog run, Uncle would see that he had a ride now and again; but it seems a toss up between learning to read or riding.'

'And loyalty to Luisa I should imagine.'

'Yes, that must be so. Still, that's the situation. I can't alter it, I have tried, and I would advise you, my dear, not to attempt it. Yet' — his head jerked — 'after having said that I would say that if you could bring Luisa back into the house Uncle would deck you out in jewels, I'm sure of that.'

'I've never had a taste for jewellery.' Quickly changing the conversation now she added, 'Those houses or huts outside the compound, who lives there?'

'Oh, Diego and his wife Big Maria. They have one child, Ki. Emilio lives there also with his two children, a boy and girl. His wife died about three years ago. She, too, was called Maria; there was Big Maria and Little Maria.'

'They look better houses than those inside the compound, quite big in fact for two families.'

'There are really four houses over there and they built them themselves. Two of them are empty.'

'Are we going over to see them?'

'No, not now; we'd better go in to dinner. And, darling' — he pulled her to a stop — 'you won't forget when answering Uncle's questions, and he'll be firing them at you, there's no doubt about that, that you are a widow of an English gentleman named Trotter?'

She answered him quietly, saying, 'I won't forget, but would it be so terrible if he did find out the true facts?'

He looked down towards the hard dry earth and moved a

loose pebble with the toe of his boot as he said, 'I would rather he didn't know.' Then raising his eyes to her face, he added softly, 'This is a new life we're starting, you and I, and I don't want anything to mar it, and nothing or no one to come between us, and if anyone should try — ' His lips went into a twisted smile now and he pulled her arm tight into his waist as they went forward and he ended, 'Remember what I did to Luke in the nursery all those years ago when he dared to say he was going to marry you?' and she answered, 'Yes, I remember. But does the no one include your uncle?'

'Uncle! Don't be silly, dearest, Uncle would be the last person who'd attempt any such thing.'

'But just say he did.'

'Now, now, Matilda; stop it. The question will never arise. And I hate to hear you voicing such opinions before the dust is off your shoes. Really! what's come over you?'

They stopped at the foot of the verandah face to face, a silence between them, until she said, 'It could be called intuition.'

He was about to speak when there was a sudden high neighing of a horse, and the mass of horses in the corral began to move and stamp. At the same moment Alvero Portes appeared at the top of the steps, a gun in his hand, and he didn't look down on them or speak but peered through narrowed lids away to the right to where a thin cloud of dust blurred the skyline. After staring at it for a full minute, he placed his gun by the side of the verandah post and came down the steps towards them smiling. But Tilly didn't answer his smile, she looked at Matthew with her mouth slightly agape and a deep question in her eyes.

3

The days passed into weeks and the weeks mounted to Christmas; and Christmas passed, a strange Christmas, made familiar only by the cold nights. Tilly was surprised at the intenseness of the cold after the heat of the day, it seemed a different cold from that which she had experienced in the North of England. The winters had been severe there and she always felt if you could stand those you could stand anything, but at times here when the wind was from the north, the cold was bone-chilling in the night.

Yet the days passed pleasantly enough and time did not hang heavy on her hands, except when Matthew was out riding with the men; and when their task was to round up a fresh batch of horses he could be away for three or four days at a time, then no matter how she occupied herself, the hours seemed to drag.

Willy took up most of her time. He was running all over the place now and it took a considerable amount of energy both on hers and Katie's part to keep him in check, and to keep him from under the feet of . . . Uncle, because being able only to see out of one eye he blundered into things, and when he came up against a leg he was apt to cling on to it; and Uncle apparently wasn't over-fond of children.

Uncle's first love in life, Tilly thought, was horses. The second, and she hated to admit this to herself, seemed to be Matthew. It was beginning to irk her that Matthew could hardly enter the house before the old man would claim his attention.

She thought of Alvero Portes as a very old man, yet he could only be in his early sixties.

She was sorry to have to admit to herself that she couldn't like the man, but she let this knowledge go no further than her own mind, for if she had expressed her feelings wholly on this matter to Matthew she knew that she would have both troubled and hurt him. She told herself often that if Uncle had been a different kind of man she would have loved every minute of her stay in this strange, wild, beautiful country.

One thing that was giving her delight was the fact that she could now ride a horse. She could actually keep on its back when it went into a gallop, and this seemed wonderful to her. Her prowess was due to the encouragement of Matthew and the patience of Rod Tyler, and not a little to the admiration and slight envy she had for Luisa in her handling of a horse, for Luisa was as expert a rider as anyone on the ranch.

Luisa seemed a different being when she sat astride a horse; the years fell from her, the hard look left her face, and her eyes lost their habitual expression of aggressive weariness and became alight with excitement.

Then there was the shooting. At first, Matthew had had his work cut out to get her to take a gun into her hand. He did not give the reason why it was important she should learn to shoot, treating it more as a game or an added accomplishment for her. It was Luisa who opened her eyes to the necessity for being able to use a gun. Only yesterday Luisa had said to her, 'Matthew treats you as some delicate town lady, someone to be protected from reality, and you're not a town lady, are you? Underneath you're as tough and as stubborn as they come, only he can't see it.'

Tilly hadn't known whether to laugh or to be slightly annoyed, but Luisa decided that she take up the former attitude and said, 'Come on with you; you're nearly twice as tall as me but we're near alike under the skin, at least we will be when you get that doting husband of yours to understand that he's brought you to live on the prairies. Mind, I'm not saying that it's everyone that can be attracted to the prairies for I've known women to turn and run from the sight of land going on to nowhere; and not only women either, this is no place for men with weak stomachs. If we could get Mack talking sometime he'd open your eyes for you. Of course I can't promise when that might be.' She laughed one of her rare laughs. 'He opens up about once every two years and then he's got to be drunk.'

Tilly had discovered that if Luisa had an affection for anyone on the ranch it was for Mack McNeill. Mack, like all the men she had met, seemed of indeterminable age; he could be forty, forty-five or even fifty. He was tall, thin, bearded and walked with a slight limp.

She had said to Luisa, 'How long has Mack been here? And why is he part ranger and part cowboy?'

The conversation had taken place in the cookhouse, the hut that divided the main house from the dog run, and Luisa, punching some dough with her fist as if she had a spite against it, said, 'He rides when necessary. He knows the country right away into the Comancheria; he's a scout, as good as any Indian. The Comanches laugh at the soldiery but never at the rangers. I think he and O'Toole's rangers have been farther north than any of them yet. Up there the Comanches had it all to themselves at one time; they used to ride down from the high plateaus, usually in moonlight, and raid the small ranch-steaders. Years ago they had it all their own way because, give it to them, they can make their horses run swifter than flying birds, and they think nothing of coming three or four hundred miles to carry out a raid. It took time for the rangers to get their measure, but they did. When they invaded the prairies the rangers followed them back to the high plateaus where they imagined no white man could go. Anyway, most of the Indians are under control now, all except the damned Comanches, and if Houston hadn't been so bloody soft they would have been settled, too, long before now. But' — she stopped speaking for a moment and, taking up the lump of dough, she flung it into a great earthenware bowl, then motioned to Ma One who lifted it from the table and laid it down on the hearth before the wood fire, then she said abruptly, 'You were asking how long Mack had been here, the answer is always.'

Tilly repeated, 'Always?' and Luisa had made a deep obeisance with her head as she replied, 'That's what I said, always. This was his place before it was ours.'

'The ranch?'

'Yes, the ranch; not all of it as it stands now, just this house. Father came along. He saw the situation, he liked it, he bought it. Mack's father had died; Mack himself was riding on patrol most of the time, his mother was left here alone. They had previously come out with the idea of herding cattle, but that didn't work out, the cattle ranged too far and it meant men and horses for the round-up. In those days, too, when you got a few horses together if the Indian raiders didn't take them some marauding dirty whites did, so what he had he sold to Father and stayed on between times as a cowboy, because Father had money which could be turned into horses and men, and so they could go ranging for the cattle. But Father wasn't satisfied with ordinary scraggy longhorn cattle; it was shorthorns he wanted to breed, and horses.' She had now leant her hands on the table and stared down towards it as she repeated with a strange bitterness, 'Hundreds, hundreds and hundreds of horses, not just common mustangs either, oh no, not for him, thoroughbred Arabs, Mexican strains. Oh — ' She had suddenly swung round from the table, ending with, 'What does it matter, and why am I jabbering like this? You know something, Matilda, you make people talk, there's something about you that loosens a body's tongue like drink.' Then abruptly changing the subject again, she said, 'What about that house you're going to have built? It should be started by now, at least the planning, for the haulage of the timber and stuff will take weeks in itself; even if they bring it up the river. Get at him.' On this she had turned about and walked abruptly out of the room leaving Tilly nonplussed for a moment, until Ma One came to her side and, smiling broadly at her, said, 'Good 'vice, own house 'n fire, good 'vice.'

That was yesterday, and now she was looking for Matthew to put to him the good advice. Last night he had been in no mood for discussion, he had been out with the hands all day and when he came in was both tired and hungry. A steaming hip bath had not seemed to refresh him and he had appeared preoccupied about something.

This morning he had been closeted with Uncle in the study.

226

This was the small book-lined room behind the multi-coloured curtain.

The break in the morning for coffee was always in the company of Uncle, and this morning after coffee they had gone to the enclosure where some horses were in the process of being broken in. She could never watch this, the taming of a high spirit, the final submission, that look of pain that was in the eyes of all animals once their spirit was broken left something inside her that was too akin to human humiliation to be borne; so she had excused herself, which she knew had annoyed Matthew as he was about to try his not unskilful hand at the breaking.

But now, two hours later, there were few hands about, and she didn't like to ask where he was for it would appear, she imagined, as if she were hanging on to his coat tails. And then she met Alvero. He was making his way towards the house, and she caught up with him at the bottom of the steps.

'I'm looking for Matthew, Uncle.'

'Oh!' He turned and smiled at her. 'Then you'd better mount your horse and go off at a gallop. You should pick him up somewhere between Boonville and Wheelock.'

She paused for a moment on the steps as she said, 'I didn't know he had gone out.'

'Oh, I must tell him to inform you of his movements in future.'

Her face became tight, her shoulders stiffened. They surveyed each other in silence for some seconds before both moved across the verandah and into the room, and there, looking at him fully again, she said, 'I cannot help but say it, Mr Portes, but I don't like your manner.'

'Oh, you don't, madam? Dear! dear! dear!' He turned from her and walked up the room towards the fire. And now taking his stand with his back to it, he folded his arms across his chest as he stared at her walking slowly towards him, and when she was again confronting him she knew a moment of fear, yet it ws overridden by a wave of anger, justifiable anger such as she had never felt for a long time, and she knew that the cards, so to speak, were on the table between her and this man. Her voice was low and deep, her words clipped as she said, 'I have no doubt in my mind, Mr Portes, that you object to my presence here; I've been aware of it from the moment of my arrival.'

'Please be seated, Mrs Sopwith.' As she had given him his full title, now he was giving her hers. As he extended his hand towards a chair she replied, 'I prefer to stand while discussing this matter.'

'As you wish.'

She watched him stretch his thin neck up out of the soft white muffler that he was in the habit of wearing over the high collar of his coat, and his words startled her. 'Are you married to my nephew, Matilda?' he said.

She took in a long slow breath and held it for a moment before she replied, 'Yes, I am married to Matthew. How dare you suggest otherwise! And at this point I will remind you that he is not your nephew, the relationship between you is very, very slight. He is the grandson of your half-sister and the blood tie there is very thin.'

Alvero reached in his pocket for a handkerchief with which he wiped his lips and she saw that his tanned skin for the moment had lost its healthy hue and she realised that he was experiencing an anger that went far beyond her own. Of a sudden she felt in danger. Then in a voice that held a slight tremor, he said, 'Heredity has the power to repeat itself after generations, it only needs that thread to which you refer, and I instinctively know I am repeated in Matthew. He is every inch me under the skin.'

'Never! There is nothing of you in him. I should know, I've known him since he was a child.'

He put his head on one side now as he said, 'You speak like a mother,' and he repeated, 'You've known him since he was a child? You know what I think, Mat . . . il . . . da?' He split her name up and his voice held the last syllable as if it were a note before he added, 'I think you are a woman of mystery; you have a past, a past that Matthew does his best to hide. I have tried to probe but without avail; all I could gather from him was that your late husband was a gentleman, a mine owner by the name of Trotter. Well, it may surprise you that as far as can

228

be ascertained by my agent in England, and he, I understand from his letter, has gone into the matter thoroughly, there is no such coal owner under the name of Trotter in the North of England, or in any other part of it. . . . What was your husband, Matilda?'

She felt slightly faint; the anger was seeping from her and the fear was replacing it. If this man ever discovered the truth life would be unbearable; he was a Catholic, a narrow-minded Catholic. On Sundays he held some kind of a service in his study; where he spent an hour alone with lighted candles, a standing crucifix, and a Bible. He had at one time, Matthew had told her, held a service for the Mexicans.

Aiming to keep her voice steady, she said, 'My husband was a coal owner; he was a gentleman as were his forbears. Tro . . . Trotter was his middle name.'

'Oh! Then may I ask what his surname was?'

'You may, but I won't give you the satisfaction of telling you; you can enquire of Matthew when he returns. And finally, Mr Portes, I shall inform you that one of the reasons I was searching for Matthew was to take up the matter of our home, and this conversation has now made it imperative that we have our own establishment as soon as possible. And should you, Mr Portes, decide to put any spoke in this particular wheel I shall express my desire, and strongly, to leave this place, if not to return to England then to establish ourselves in another part of the state; and I, knowing my husband, know what course he will choose. If I were penniless then there would be a problem, but as it is there is nothing to stop me leaving, and I can assure you, Mr Portes, that your supposed nephew will accompany me. . . . Do we understand each other?' Again she knew a moment's fear of danger. 'Perfectly, Mrs Sopwith, perfectly,' he said, his words coming from between his teeth.

How her legs carried her from the room she did not know. When she got into the bedroom she dropped on to the bed and buried her face in the pillow, and Katie, coming from the other room holding the child by the hand, paused for a moment before relinquishing the boy and running towards her. Putting her arm around her shoulder, she said, 'What is it? What is it, Tilly?'

After a moment Tilly, raising her wet face from the pillow, gasped as she muttered, 'He . . . he knows.'

'No! Oh God, no!'

'Not everything. Not everything' — she shook her head — 'but he's written to England to find out if there was a mine owner called Trotter. I'll have to get hold of Matthew before he tackles him.'

'What's he done it for? What's his game?

'His game, Katie' — Tilly now wiped her eyes — 'his game is to separate Matthew and me. He wants him for himself, he's resented me from the minute I came here.'

'Aye, I guessed that much; but if the master's got to pick and choose I know which direction he'll throw his quoit.'

'Yes, I've told him as much, but how far it'll check him I don't know.' She now leaned forward and picked Willy up from the floor and held him in her arms, and she stroked his hair as he chatted at her. Then she said, 'You know, Katie, that man's bad, evil bad; there's something about him that's frightening. I can understand how Luisa feels. At one time, he must have done something to her that has created her hate of him. But her hate will be nothing compared with mine if he comes between Matthew and me. And he can you know, Katie, he can, even while we're together he can come between us.'

Katie stood staring at her shaking her head; and then she said, 'Pity the Indians don't get him.'

This pronouncement did not bring the retort, 'Oh, what an awful thing to say, Katie,' for she found herself endorsing it in her own mind.

It was almost two hours later when Matthew returned. He came riding towards the ranch with Doug Scott and Pete Ford.

She was standing at the gate, and the road from it led straight for some way until it forked off into two directions, one seemingly to the horizon, the other quickly lost in a jumble of foothills and low scrub. They came out of the foothills, the three of them galloping side by side, and they were still galloping when they passed her and brought their mounts up to a skidding stop in the middle of the yard.

Matthew was first to alight and he paused for a moment, stretched his body upwards, banged the sides of his tight hide trousers with his hands, then stamped one high-leather-booted foot on the ground as if to ease cramp, passed some laughing remark with Doug Scott, then turned and walked towards her.

Tilly hadn't moved from the gate, she wanted to be well out of earshot of anyone when she spoke to him; and she did not put her hands out to touch him as was usual after they'd been separated even for only a short while, but she held them tightly joined at her waist; and his first words told her that he sensed trouble. 'What is it?' he asked, and when she didn't answer immediately he closed his eyes and screwed up his lips before saying, 'Oh, don't tell me you and Uncle again?'

'He knows, Matthew.'

'Knows what?'

'Well, what is there to know?'

'How can he?'

'Because he's crafty and cute. He . . . he has sent to England to . . . to find out if there was a coal owner named Trotter.'

He actually took a step back from her before making a small movement with his head; then he said, 'No!' The word rumbled in his chest. 'You're mistaken.'

It was she who closed her eyes now and she sighed before she said, 'He told me he put his agent on to investigating.'

'The devil he did!' As he turned and looked towards the house, his dust-covered skin showed a tinge of red; then looking at her again, he said, 'You're not mistaken?'

'No!' She had shouted the word and now she put her hand tightly over her mouth and looked out away into the endless land beyond, and in this moment she longed to be gone from this place, back home, oh yes, in spite of everything, back home. And the intensity of her feeling almost made her give voice to the desire, but it was checked as he said, 'I'll put a stop to this.' He took her arm. 'Come on.' Yet he did not lead her towards the front of the house but round the side, saying as he went, 'I want to clean up before I see him, he's always so spruce he puts one at a disadvantage.'

It was the first time she had heard him say anything that could be taken as a condemnation, however slight, of the man.

On their way round to the back door she said, 'I'll get Diego to fill the bath.'

'No, that'll take too long,' he said; 'I'll go into the wash-house.'

'But the water's cold there.'

'Well' — he looked at her with a forced smile — 'it may clear my head and sharpen my wits, I feel they're going to need it. And send me some clean clothes over.' Stopping for a moment, he took her hand and pressed it tightly, saying, 'Don't worry. This will be the last time he'll interfere in our lives, I'll see to that. And I think you may be right about a place of our own.'

She returned the grip on her fingers, and he left her and went towards the wooden hut that had on its roof a tank with pipes leading from it that ran over the ground for almost half a mile until they reached the river. The tank was filled by a hand pump, an ingenious contraption, and a lever inside the hut released the water through a perforated tin plate and so formed a shower.

It took him no more than fifteen minutes to get undressed, have his wash, and get into his clean clothes; after which he did not immediately leave the wash-house but stood for a good five minutes more weighing up how he would approach the old man and tell him what he thought of his intrusion into Tilly's private life.

But as often happens things didn't work out as planned and it was Alvero Portes who took the initiative. He was sitting before the fire, a book on his lap, a glass of wine standing on a small table to his side, and he did not raise his head when the door opened and Matthew entered the room. He did not even raise it to look at him when Matthew took up a stand opposite him at the side of the fireplace, but he spoke to him, saying, 'I know exactly what you're going to say, Matthew: it was none of my business, why did I do it. To say the least, it was a most ungentlemanly action. You have heard your wife's side of the conversation we held and no doubt you are furious. Now you're going to hear mine. Sit down.'

'I prefer to stand, Uncle.'

Alvero now raised his head and smiled, saying, 'That's the attitude your wife took. Well, just as you please. To begin with. As you know, I have interests in London, shipping interests, and I have corresponded with my agent there for many years. We have never met but we have formed a sort of . . . what you would call distant friendship, we end our letters by asking after each other's family. He even hopes we're having no trouble with the Indians. He has a great respect for Mr Houston. Of course, his is only one man's opinion, but I am not so foolish as to tell him that his respect in my opinion is misplaced. Anyway, our correspondence does not deal solely with business and so it was most natural for me to say that my nephew had returned bringing with him a wife, a lady who had been widowed, that she was a very beautiful lady.' He inclined his head now to the side and his eyes slanted upwards towards Matthew. 'And I went on to say that she came from good stock, that her late husband was of the landed gentry and a mine owner into the bargain.' He paused here, before adding, 'As yet, can you find anything wrong in that, Matthew?'

Matthew said nothing, he merely waited, no muscle on his face moving, his eyes intent on the old man.

Alvero now went on, 'Well, it should happen in the last mail I received a letter from Mr Willis stating briefly that he was glad to know that you were happily married, but to his knowledge there was no gentleman by the name of Trotter who owned a mine.'

'Why should he go to the trouble to find out?' The question was slow and the tone of it cold.

'There is an explanation for that too, Matthew. He is not only my agent but he is an agent for a number of mine owners in the north of the country who have their coal transported by sea to London . . . Now does my explanation coincide with your wife's version?'

'No, because as you have told it to me it hasn't upset me, and I am sure it wouldn't have upset her stated in this way.'

'Well' — Alvero now rose slowly to his feet — 'I don't happen to be on trial, Matthew. I have told you how this incident came about; I can do no more. You must believe me or you must believe her.'

'Why did you speak of it at all?'

'Oh' — the old man shook his head — 'if I remember rightly it came up in the course of conversation. I am sorry if she has been troubled by it, but on the other hand if she has nothing to hide why should she be troubled? You said you have known her for many years?'

'Yes that is what I said.'

'And her husband was a coal owner?'

'Yes.' Matthew swallowed, jerked his chin upwards, then said, 'Yes, he was a coal owner.'

'Well then, that is all that can be said about it. My agent is wrong. I shall tell him so when next I write. In the meantime, let us forget about this trifling matter. What happened at Boonville?'

'Nothing much. The stock was mixed and Pete thought not worth bargaining over, they were in very rough shape, even the mustangs.'

'Oh. Well if Pete thought they were in bad shape, they were in bad shape. I'll go and have a word with him. I'll see you at dinner.' He now lifted up his glass, drained it, replaced the glass on the table then walked slowly down the room; but he did not go through the main door, he went towards the end of the room where the dining-table was set for the meal, and he paused and looked at it before reaching out his hand and moving a silver cruet further into the middle of the table; then slowly made his way out.

Matthew stood for a while looking towards the far door; then lifting his gaze, he looked about the room as if seeing it for the first time: the roughness of the wooden wall vying with the elegance of the china cabinet, the silver on the dining-table, and these in turn looking incongruous against the array of animal skins, the heads dangling over the back of the couch as if gasping for breath.

There was a pain in his chest. It was just such that could be created either by a broken friendship or by the knowledge that one's father was a liar. And there was the point. In a way he had come to look upon this old man not as an uncle but as a father, one to replace the man he had rejected in England, the man who had for a time created a hate in him because he had taken to himself a particular young girl. For a moment he thought as a woman might think: men were ruthless, all men were ruthless, and he now saw his uncle as Tilly saw him, and he shuddered. If the old man had failed in his attempt to divide them, then he was just as likely to try again. . . . And what if he should divulge the other business, his own personal private business? Immediately he shut off his thinking and hurried from the room, and his body, from being cool, became hot with the thought that instead of saying to Tilly, 'I believe you, he's up to something,' he must say, 'You must go careful with him. If we mean to live with him we must placate him.'

God! he felt sick.

4

It was June. The earth was like a volcano; so great was its heat Tilly would not have been surprised if it had erupted and burst into flames. There was no colour in the sky and no movement outside or inside the ranch. It was as if everyone else was asleep or dead. All that is except Luisa. Tilly was sitting beside her in the dog run. The open space did not create a breeze, nor could you say it was cool, it was only less hot than outside.

The constant motion of Luisa's rocking-chair was getting on Tilly's nerves, and her voice, rapid and moving from one subject to the other, told her that something was amiss; but it was no use asking for an explanation because Luisa rarely gave you a straightforward answer.

'Think this is hot! You should have been here in '49 when all that mad scum was rushing for gold, swarming across the country, all making for San Antonio; then from there across the Comanche Plains to the God-forsaken outpost of El Paso, and dying in their hundreds. They buried them where they dropped. It wasn't the Indians who killed them, you know. Oh no, it wasn't the Indians. Smallpox and the cholera got them; and it got the Indians too. Pity it didn't wipe the beggars off the map; had a good enough try at that, together with the measles and the goat's disease.'

'The goat's disease?' Tilly's voice was a limp enquiry.

'Yes, syphilis you know, syphilis. Men are no better than beasts. Beasts are better than men, any day. Funny but all the soldiery and the rangers and the Mexican troops, oh yes, the Mexican troops, they aimed to wipe the Indians off the face of the earth but 'twas the Spanish smallpox took over and nearly did it, nearly wiped them all off.'

'The smallpox did?'

'Aye, yes, the smallpox did; but that's some time ago. I ask myself why anyone wants to come and live here, I keep asking myself that, I've been doing it for years.'

'Couldn't you have gone away, I mean years ago?' Tilly's question was quiet.

'No, I couldn't.' Luisa turned on her as if she were answering a condemnation. 'I haven't a penny, I haven't any clothes but what I stand up in and my winter serge and skin coat.'

'But . . . but' Tilly now pulled herself upward in her chair and looked round at Luisa as she said, 'You mean you haven't got anything at all? Doesn't your father give . . .?'

'No, he doesn't; but he would if I asked for it. He's just waiting for me to ask, but I wouldn't let him provide me even with a shroud, I've got that set aside, a white night-gown, and embroidered. Yet every penny, everything he has should belong to me, because it belonged to my mother. He has only his looks and his tongue and his so-called ancestry, but as soon as he got her he fastened up every penny. Then he murdered her. Yes, he did, he murdered her.'

'*Oh no! No!*' Tilly was shaking her head, her face screwed up in protest.

'Oh yes, he did. If you pull someone in front of you to save your own skin, that's murder. Oh, I could tell you things. He stops at nothing to get what he wants. You know, he's as mad as an Indian on the warpath 'cos your house is going up. And it's just as well it is, you're going to need it. Oh yes, you're going to need it.'

Tilly pulled herself to her feet, then rubbed her sweating palms down the sides of her print dress as she said, 'What is it, Luisa, what's troubling you? There's something on your mind?'

Luisa bowed her head and muttered, 'Can't tell you. Can't tell you.'

'Is it to do with me?'

'Sort of, yes; sort of, in a way.'

'Matthew!'

237

'Yes, yes, Matthew.' Now Luisa rose from the chair and, standing close to Tilly, she looked into her face as she said, 'It'll be up to you.'

'What will be up to me? I must know, Luisa.'

'Can't say.' Luisa turned her head away now. ' 'Tisn't for me to say, but I just want to put you on your guard, he's up to something. The thing is, he's dangerous. He's lost me, and the thought that he's lost Matthew an' all must be unbearable to him. That's why he's done it.'

'Please, Luisa' — Tilly's voice was low, with a pleading note in it now — 'tell me what's facing us. Please.'

'You'll know soon enough, this time tomorrow when the wagon comes in.'

'Whose wagon? You don't mean something's going to happen to Matthew? Has he sent him and the others on a raid or something?' Her voice was rising high in her head now and Luisa was quick to answer.

'No, no; nothing like that, Matthew will be all right, he's with the others, and they'll all be back in the morning. But tonight I'd ask yourself how much your feeling for Matthew is worth.'

Tilly stood staring down at the shabby-looking little woman and she shook her head slowly but didn't ask any further questions because she knew that it would be useless. She had come to know Luisa's ways, and the more one probed the less likely one was to find out anything. She turned from her and took up a large straw hat from a hook on the wall and, putting it on, she went slowly out into the white light, and as slowly she walked past the cook-house and towards the back door and into her room.

The child and Katie were upstairs and she knew that both were asleep. It had become the pattern of the day now to sleep if possible through the high heat. She went into the adjoining room and sluiced her face with tepid water, then sat down in front of the little dressing-table in the corner of the room and stared at herself. Her face was tanned, yet looked ashen; her eyes were red-rimmed; her hair, wet at the front, was sticking to her brow. She slanted her eyes towards the mirror as if not recognising the reflection in it. She knew there was hardly any resemblance to the woman who had left England just eleven months previously. She had hardened in lots of ways, both physically and mentally: she could ride and she could shoot; she had withstood the cold nights and now she was coping with intense heat; these had brought about physical change in her. The mental change went deeper and had come about through Alvero Portes' attitude towards her and her consequent fear of him, her acknowledged fear of him because she recognised he was a man it would be foolish not to fear, and fear made one wary, even sly.

Since she was sixteen she had known fear, the fear of the villagers, the fear of McGrath and his family; but the fear of Matthew's uncle put the other fears in the shade, yet at the same time created in her the strength with which to face it. It seemed to her that both she and the old man were fighting for a prize, the prize of Matthew. Yet he was already hers, avowedly hers; hardly a night passed but he made fresh vows. Once they were in that bed together the world was forgotten, their love and loving was something that could not be defined in words; yet with morning and the breakfast table there was the man, the tall Spanish-looking man, who was like a sword waiting to cleave them apart.

But what was this new thing hanging over them? Luisa had said, 'Ask yourself how much your feeling for Matthew is worth. . . .' So it was something to do with Matthew, something he had done when he was out here before. But what? What could he have done that would make Luisa think it would have any effect on her feeling for him? She now bent her head deeply on to her chest and what she said was, 'Please God, don't let it be something that I couldn't countenance.'

5

The men returned around noon, dirty, sweaty, but, as usual, entering the ranch in a flurry, their faces and their shouting expressing their pleasure at being back.

For once Tilly was not in the compound waiting to meet Matthew but was up under the eaves looking out from the low window. She had sent Katie and the child over to the dog run; Luisa was always pleased to see them, in fact she seemed to unbend more with Katie than with herself.

She had been up here for the past two hours and now her chest was heaving with the heat from the roof.

An hour ago, from the side window, she had seen a small wagon train appear from out of the last hillocks and make its way towards Diego's and Emilio's house. The lead wagon was canvas-covered, barrel-shaped and fully flapped at the front; as for the man driving it, she could not tell from this distance if he were old or young, nor if the small woman by his side was old or young. The second wagon was covered too but more rudely; the third looked like the open carts used on the farms back home, with high wooden sides which were keeping in place a jumble of what looked like household furniture and utensils. She saw Emilio's children and Diego's boy come out and greet them. The children were jumping up and down by the side of the wagon. Mack McNeill had come into her view. He had stood in the open for a time, staring towards the wagons, before striding across to meet them.

She noticed what seemed to be an altercation going on between him and the man who had been driving the first wagon.

240

And now here were the men back, and Matthew was standing in the yard looking about him, looking for her. That he was perplexed, she had no doubt, for not only was she not in the yard but his uncle too was missing.

She watched Mack again coming into view. Because of his limp his tread was usually slow but now he was moving towards Matthew almost on the point of a hopping run. She watched him talking eagerly: and whatever he said made Matthew hunch his shoulders, then take off his soft felt hat and dash it against his legs before turning round and looking in the direction of the wagons now stationary in the distance; then slowly turning back towards Mack he put up his hand tightly against the side of his face and leant his head to one side. It seemed to be akin to the action of someone suffering severe earache. Almost immediately he swung round and looked towards the house, and as he seemed about to spring forward she saw Mack catch him by the arm and swing him about. It said something for the strength of those wiry arms that he could do this, for Matthew's body, always solid, had now toughened to a strength that could match that of any man on the ranch.

The cowhands had not moved from the compound and were joined now by Two, Three and Four, their black faces straight, their eyes wide.

Tilly now watched Mack gently guiding Matthew towards the ranch-house, and when they had disappeared inside, those in the yard, after a pause, resumed their normal business.

She rose stiffly from her cramped position on the floor and as she had been wont to do as a child, or even as a young girl, when upset or worried, she now pinned her hands under her oxters and rocked herself backward and forward, while asking herself, What was it? What had he done? But search as she might her mind gave her no answer; and she was afraid to know the answer, but she knew that once she met Matthew she would have the answer for he was bound to tell her what this all meant.

How long she walked up and down the room she didn't know, but she was brought to a stop by the muted sound of voices coming from below. Instantly she was out of the room and down the shallow stairs; but she came to a halt at the foot of them as she heard Matthew's voice saying, 'Why did you do this?'

'I tell you it is not of my making, my doing.'

'You're lying. Weeks ago you sent a message to Josè Cardenas through McCulloch's Indian scout.'

There was a pause before Alvero Portes's voice came to Tilly, saying now, 'Whoever informed you of that is possessed of a vivid imagination.'

'It is no imagination; how other are they here?'

'Apparently they decided on their own to return. Likely the longing of Leonilde to see you once more.'

'Don't say that. You know as well as I do it was by your order that they left never to return. What do you hope to gain by this? You're out to destroy my life, aren't you?'

'No, no, Matthew; never yours, never yours.' The words were uttered with deep feeling; and Matthew's voice, slow and bitter, now replied, 'If you spoil Matilda's you spoil mine; whatever hurts her hurts me doubly.'

'That you will be hurt more than she will be by this remains to be seen. The question is, will she be big enough to accept your little mistress and your child?'

The last words brought Tilly's mouth agape and her head drooping slowly; in fact, her whole body drooped with a sudden weakness, and she was about to slump on the stairs when she stiffened and remained poised for a moment. Then softly she made her way along the passage towards the back door.

There was no one in the back compound and she leant against the rough wood and plaster wall. So that was it, he'd had a mistress, a Mexican girl, and they'd had a child. Yet he had professed over and over again that he loved no one in his life but her, that she had been in him from when he could remember and would be there and be part of him until he died. . . . But he'd had a little, which she took to mean young, Mexican mistress and a child.

What about Mark and her? She had been his mistress for twelve years. Was it so different?

242

Yes, because Matthew had known about it, he had known everything about her, whereas she knew nothing of the life he had led until he returned to the Manor last year.

What was she going to do? His mistress and the child were on the doorstep so to speak, brought there by that old devil who was determined to wreck their marriage.

She brought herself from the wall and asked herself a question that had been prompted by Luisa: Would this make any difference to her feelings for Matthew?

The answer didn't come immediately, but when it came it was a definite no. But having said that she knew she was filled with jealousy of this other person, this girl who had been in his life before her. Yet again that wasn't true; she was the one who had always been in his life, and if she hadn't become his father's mistress he would likely have shown his hand much sooner; perhaps years ago she would have become Mrs Matthew Sopwith. Even if not his wife, then his mistress, for who could tell how she would have reacted under his pressing charm.

She turned her head to the side to see Luisa coming towards her, and it was with an effort she pulled herself from the support of the wall. Luisa didn't speak but, taking her hand, she hurried her past the cookhouse and into the dog run, and when the sitting-room door was closed on them she faced Tilly and said, 'Well now, I can see you know. They're still at it in there. What are you going to do?'

It was some seconds before Tilly answered, 'I don't know, I . . . I still can't believe it somehow.'

'What can't you believe?' Luisa's voice was harsh. 'You're a grown woman; you've been married twice. You show me the man who says he went to a woman as she to him and I'll tell him he's a confounded liar. Look.' She pushed Tilly towards a chair, then seating herself in front of her, she placed her hands on her knees and leant forward. It was a manly gesture and her voice had almost the roughness of a man's as she said, 'When Matthew first came out here over four years gone he was dour and unhappy. Something had soured him, I don't know what. Leonilde was seventeen years old. She was working in the house.' She jerked her head sideways. 'She was a little thing, and bonny; hardly spoke a word of English, just Spanish. She was nearly all Spanish, hardly a trace of Indian. The Indian shows in her father Josè, and her brother Miguel. Well, it was summer and Matthew saw Leonilde flitting about and, the nights being hot, he flitted after her. But let me tell you this, he wasn't the only one. There was Emilio. He and his wife rowed over her. Then there was Andy O'Brien. You know' — she again jerked her head but towards the bunkhouse this time — 'he isn't permanent, he comes and goes, hot feet. She was seen with him more than once and with a dirty Mexican who was here but a short time, but mainly her eyes were on Matthew. And, of course, her father, who had an eye to the pesos, he pushed her, he could even hear wedding bells and see a nice little set-up for himself and his no-good son. Well, the top and bottom of it was she had a child, Josefina. But once that appeared Father saw what Cardenas was up to, and so he packs them off, and undoubtedly paying them well. Now in the ordinary way their coming back wouldn't mean much because this kind of thing goes on all the time. Who bothers about Mexican Indians, they're there to be used, all women are there to be used. The Indians rape their captives, and that's the only merciful thing they do to them. The Mexicans rape their captives. And don't say the white man is any better. God no! The things I've seen. I tell you they're all alike where their wants are concerned, it is only their skins that are different. Language is no deterrent to that part of the business. Well—' She now straightened her back, joined her hands together on top of her white apron and asked, 'What do you mean to do?' But without giving Tilly time to answer, she was again bending forward, her finger wagging now as she said, 'Do you know what I would do if I were in your place? But then you don't hate my father as much as I do.'

'Don't be too sure of that.' The reply came so quickly that it silenced Luisa for a moment; and then she said slowly, 'Well, that being so we could be of like mind and beat him at his own game.'

'What would you do?' Tilly's question was flat.

'Well, I would go over to the little Cardenas and I'd introduce myself, and I'd be nice to Leonilde; then I would take the child by the hand and bring it over here, up the front steps and into his very presence. And something more, I would indicate that I had known they were coming.'

Tilly moved her head slowly. 'No, no; I . . . I don't think I'd be able to do that, Luisa. And what would Matthew say anyway?'

'Well, it would take the wind out of their sails, and it would show that old devil straightaway whose side you were on. And if I'm any judge of men it would make Matthew become a better slave than either One, Two, Three or Four.'

As they stared at each other Tilly's mind raced. It would be a wonderful retaliation if only she could do it. Was she strong enough to carry it out? No, not on her own she wasn't; perhaps with Luisa by her side. She said, 'You know I know no Spanish, do . . . do they speak English?'

'No, very little, just a word here and there. Spanish yes, but little English. But I tell you what, I'll come and interpret for you. What do you say?' There was a look of devilish glee in Luisa's eyes that was almost frightening and for a moment longer Tilly hesitated, for she sensed that Luisa was anticipating a personal triumph through the failure of her father's plan. But what did it matter as long as she herself beat the man.

Getting to her feet, she said, 'Right. Right, Luisa. Let's go. . . .'

The Mexicans had unloaded the cart and taken the household goods into the last empty cabin when Tilly and Luisa arrived at the door. The two men, the young woman and the child were all in the room. It was strange, Tilly thought immediately, that the father looked very like Alvero Portes, with the same shaped features, the same stance; but the son wasn't half the size and, unlike that of his father, his body was podgy. The father was a man in his late fifties and the son appeared to be in his early thirties; but the young woman . . . the girl, for she still looked a girl, was small and dark complexioned . . . and beautiful, yet her face was utterly without expression. Looking into the eyes was like looking into a void.

And the child by her side? It was nothing like her except in its smallness, for it was tiny, with straight black Indian hair; its skin was dark; the eyes deep-set; the upper lip was short, the mouth thin; the nose was like a brown button; and yet the whole combination of features presented a strange effect that went beyond beauty. Tilly found herself searching the face for some resemblance to Matthew, but there wasn't a feature she could recognise.

That they were all amazed to see Luisa and Tilly was clear, and it was Luisa who first spoke.

It seemed that her words were a greeting, for the two men bowed their heads towards her and answered briefly; and seconds later, the girl, too inclined her head.

Now Luisa was talking and what she was saying was certainly having an impression on the father for he kept looking from her to Tilly.

When Luisa paused the man began to speak, his words seeming to tumble out of his mouth. He pointed first to his daughter and then to the child, and then out through the open door.

Again Luisa was speaking, but this time she had preceded her words with the man's name 'Josè Cardenas,' and she wagged her finger towards his face and her speech now was rapid as she pointed to the child, then to Tilly again. When she stopped and there was silence in the room, Tilly, speaking softly, asked, 'What are you saying?' and in clipped English now but without taking her eyes from the old man Luisa said, 'I told them that the big boss had sent for them in order that you should see the child and take it into your family.'

'What!'

'Be quiet! It's the best thing you can do if you want rid of them; if not you'll have them on your doorstep for the rest of your life here. Do you want that?' Her eyes had not moved from Josè Cardenas. 'Do you?'

'No, no. But to take the child, that's an admission. And Matthew. . . .'

'Well, have it your own way. But as I said they'll be under your nose and Father'll make the most of it. Oh yes, mark my

246

words, he'll make the most of it. You won't be able to stand it.'

'But I can't just walk out with the child.'

'Yes, you can; all this old devil wants is money. I might as well tell you he's as surprised as you are at this minute. He didn't know Matthew was married. It puts a different complexion on things; they're Catholics. Well, what do you say?'

Tilly gulped in her throat, paused for a long moment, then said, 'Go ahead.'

Luisa went ahead, and Tilly could not make out one word of what was being said except that Luisa and the old man repeated 'pesos' again and again. There was some kind of bargaining going on. Then for the first time the son spoke, only to be practically jumped on by Luisa who, swinging round to him, wagged her whole hand in his face, then pointed towards the doorway and, using both hands now, made a sweeping movement as if she was sending them all back along the road. This seemed to have an effect, at least on the father, for he spoke to his son now, and the man said nothing more but stood looking sullenly down towards his feet.

During all this the young girl had neither moved nor taken her eyes off Tilly, but when her father spoke to her she looked down on the child and seemingly without any qualms pushed her forward towards Luisa, who, taking the child's hands, smiled at her and spoke to her gently.

Her eyes wide, her lips apart, the child looked from Luisa to Tilly; and then she smiled, and the smile seemed to transform all her small features into a central light that shone out of her eyes, and when she held her hand upwards Tilly took it.

There was a great restriction in her throat; she had the greatest desire to draw the child to her. She turned and looked at the mother of the child. The vacant look had gone but there was no sign of regret on her face; in fact, Tilly had a momentary impression that she was glad to let the child go.

Outside, Luisa turned and once more began to speak in rapid Spanish, this time gesticulating between the wagons and the pieces of furniture in the cabin; then, the child between them, they moved across the open ground towards the main gate of the ranch; and as they went Luisa said, 'Tell Matthew,

247

I want a hundred pesos. I'll take it to them; he mustn't see that at all. They'll be gone in the morning.'

'Oh! Luisa.'

'What?'

'I don't know what to say.'

'Well, don't bother; keep your spittle for the next few minutes, you're going to need it to loosen your tongue. Now I've gone as far as I can go, the rest is up to you. When you take her in there you'll be confronted by a very surprised man, if you ask me; but I know one thing, Father won't believe what he's seeing. Well you're on your own now. Shooting it out with the Indians is going to be nothing to it.'

As Luisa relinquished her hold on the child Tilly looked at her and she experienced a feeling of resentment for she knew that Luisa was enjoying this business, and that she had pushed her into something which in a way was going to alter their lives almost as much as a separation would have done. Yet no, no; a separation was unthinkable. But here she was saddled with a child, a half-caste child, and it had all happened within the space of minutes. Were the consequences ahead worth the triumph she would achieve over Alvero Portes?

She muttered, 'How . . . how old is she?'

'Oh, she . . . well, she'll be coming up for four, give a month or two.'

'What!' Tilly gazed down on the child. 'She looks no more than two, if that.'

'It's the way they're made. Some of them are like suet puddings, others like elves. It all depends which part they come from. Leonilde and her brother weren't from the same mother, that's for sure.' And on this Luisa walked away from her.

For a moment she stood looking at Luisa's back; and then she herself was walking towards the main gate.

The child caught her attention by saying 'Josefina'. Slowly she nodded down towards it and said, 'Yes, yes,' and the child started to skip by her side. And this action touched some chord in Tilly for she could see herself hitching and skipping whilst holding on to her grandmother's hand, and her grandmother chiding her, saying, 'Stop it! bairn; you'll wear your shoes out.' But this child was barefoot; its small brown feet were dust-covered, and its toes seemed to grip the ground with each step.

What had she done? What had she done? She would never be able to communicate with the little thing. Oh! Luisa. Luisa.

Once again all activity in the yard seemed to stop at the sight of the young boss's wife leading by the hand Leonilde's child and making straight for the ranch-house.

Mack stopped on his way to the corral. He was walking between two horses, his arms outstretched gripping their halters, and he stared at her open mouthed; as also did Doug Scott, and Numbers One and Three and Ma One who had come out to empty some slops. They all became still and she walked through them as if in a dream of the past with her old friends surrounding her, but they being without life.

When the child found difficulty in negotiating the steps to the verandah she bent down and whisked it up into her arms, and like this she entered the long room and came face to face with Alvero Portes and her husband.

Of the two, it was Matthew who showed the more astonishment. Alvero Portes was adept in hiding his true feelings, yet even he gaped at the woman before him, tall and slim, with the dark shabbily dressed bundle poised on her arm, and for a moment he might have been seeing an apparition, something that his mind told him could not possibly be there. But she was there and he could see in her eyes the light of battle, a battle indeed already won. His voice was unlike the suave tones he usually allowed to escape his lips as he said, 'What is the meaning of this? Why have you brought this child here?'

Tilly purposely raised her eyebrows and stretched her face questioningly before saying, 'Oh, am I mistaken? Was it not your intention that we should take the child?'

Alvero Portes forgot himself so far as to turn and look helplessly at Matthew; then he said, 'It was certainly not my intention, madam; and I would thank you to take her out of this room.'

'But she, I understand, is my husband's daughter.' She

249

turned and looked straight at Matthew and she felt an overwhelming feeling of pity for him because her words had
created a look on his face that she had never seen before. It was
as if in this instant she was bringing him low, humiliating him.
. . . But she was doing battle, and so she turned her attention
again to the old man, saying now, 'You claim Matthew as your
nephew, then this child is in some way related to you. Isn't that
so?'

'How dare you?'

'I dare.' Her voice now was as harsh as his and she repeated,
'I dare, Mr Portes, because I am aware of your intention in
bringing the child's mother back here.'

'I had nothing to do with their return.'

'You lie and you know you lie. I have known for some time of
your intention.' Now she was lying and lying so well she could
almost believe her own statements. 'In fact, I have been waiting for a small cavalcade to put in an appearance. Well
now' — she turned her attention to Matthew, who was looking
at her in the most odd way, but a recognisable odd way for
there was something about his expression that touched on that
of the children in the village when they had called her witch,
and she inhaled deeply before she said in a tone she attempted
to make airy, 'I shall need a hundred pesos to pay for the
child. Your uncle was quite willing to pay them for coming
and staying, so it is only right that we should pay them for
going.'

'Madam, you have gone too far.'

'Then, sir, I feel I am level with you and your tactics.'

They stared at each other, and for a moment Alvero Portes
seemed lost for words. Then pointing to the child, he said,
'That' — he did not even add the word child — 'cannot be
allowed to remain under my roof.'

'I have no intention of allowing the child to stay under your
roof, sir; nor are we staying under it. As from today we shall
take up our abode in the new house.'

'It is unfinished, you can't.'

He was looking from her to Matthew now.

'There is one room habitable and the cooking range is in, we

250

shall survive quite happily.' She now turned and looked at Matthew, and, her tone lowering, she said, 'Will you accompany me, Matthew, we have things to do?'

Not one word had he uttered during the whole scene, and even now he could say nothing. He glanced at Portes and for the first time he saw a break in the polished armour: the old man was shaking his head. It was a pleading gesture but he ignored it and, turning, he followed his wife out along the corridor and into their room.

Katie was there with Willy, and immediately Tilly put the child down on to the floor Willy went towards her; but when Josefina, in real fright at seeing this eager strange white face so close to hers, backed from him he grabbed at her. She struck out at him as she screamed, and when he joined his scream to hers pandemonium reigned for a moment until Katie, astonishment causing her mouth to gape, grabbed their hands and cried, 'Come on. Come on.' At the door she stopped and, looking from the child to Tilly, she said, 'It's all right to take her upstairs?'

'Yes, yes.'

The door closed on the cries of the children and she was left alone facing Matthew. . . .

Standing apart, they stared at each other, neither of them speaking or moving, and when his head drooped forward and he muttered her name she made no response, not until his hand came on to her arm, when as if she had been struck by a spark she jerked herself from him, saying, 'No, no; not yet.' And she backed from him before turning and going towards a chair that was placed near the window. Here she sat down and dropped her head on to her hand; and like this she stayed for a full minute fighting to dissolve the great lump of pain in her chest, the pain of jealousy. She was jealous of the fact that he had held the body of that slight dark beautiful girl in his arms, and that that holding had produced the child up above whilst here was she who had lain in his arms and experienced his loving night after night but as yet had shown no sign of producing visible evidence of it.

When the tears burst through her long-drawn-out moan he

was at her side on his knees before her, his arms around her waist, his head buried in her lap, his voice muttering her name over and over. 'I'm sorry, my love, I'm sorry. Oh, Tilly darling, I'm sorry.'

It was some time before she found her voice. Her hands were on his head now stroking him. He still had his face buried in her lap and he did not raise it until she said, 'Why didn't you tell me?'

'I couldn't. And . . . and then at the time of its happening it seemed nothing. She . . . she was with others.' He lifted his head fully now. 'I'm not making excuses but it is true. Cardenas uses her. Then she is with child and he comes and says I'm responsible. It all happened in the first year I was here. Uncle paid him off and he left. I never saw the child until . . . until today. Tilly' — he was now gripping her hands — 'do you know what you've done, what you are doing?'

'Yes; it was either that or having her hanging over my head for the rest of our time here.'

'Did you know about it beforehand, really, for you didn't seem. . .?'

'No, no, I knew nothing until yesterday. Luisa warned me something was coming and. . .'

He knelt back from her. 'You've made this decision just today?'

'It was made for me, Luisa did it.'

He nodded his head slowly now. 'Luisa would; she was making her ammunition for someone else to fire.'

'Don't blame her; I . . . I think this is the right thing we are doing.'

He was holding her again, their faces close. 'You still love me?'

She nodded, 'Yes, but I'm experiencing jealousy for the first time.'

'Oh my dear, my dearest, that's ridiculous. Jealous of Leonilde? Oh, I tell you, she was just a. . . .'

She put her fingers on his lips now as she said softly, 'Don't say it, there is the child.'

'But Tilly' — he was now on his feet looking down at her —

252

'I don't really know whether it's mine or not, in fact I have my doubts. I looked at her. There's no resemblance; she's . . . she's real Mexican Indian.'

'I thought that too. But anyway, she's supposed to be yours, and your uncle played on the fact that she was yours, and he would have gone on using both the mother and the child as a weapon to come between us, and like dripping water wearing away a stone who knows? Only his tactics don't drip water, they drip acid and acid eats away quicker.'

He turned from her as he said, 'I've tried not to believe it of the old fellow but now, my God! this last proves what lengths he'll go to just. . . .'

'You might as well say it, just to keep you.'

He turned to her again and, coming back, he dropped on to his knees once more and, holding her to him, he said, 'You've been connected with every action in the whole of my life. The first woman I went with I did it not because the urge was on me, but in some roundabout way to spite my father and you. Every time I took a woman I imagined it was you.'

When he dropped his head on to her shoulder she stared straight before her. It was like a revelation. Why had she been so simple? She had imagined that that dark Mexican had been the first and now he spoke casually of the women he had had before her. But then his father too, what about Lady Myton and the others he had had?

It was the way of men.

It was in this instant as if she suddenly awakened to life. All she had gone through in her thirty-three years had taken place in the girl, but with Matthew's casual confession she had been turned into a woman, a woman who must go on loving, who couldn't help herself loving, even with the knowledge that she was last in a succession of women, even perhaps not the last. Oh no! Her mind rejected that thought. She had him and he had her and she would see that there were no more escapades.

If only they hadn't to carry the result of his latest with them, for how were they going to explain a Mexican Indian in their family when they returned home? What was she thinking about? She would never go home now.

6

They made the move to the unfinished house at the top of the slope which lay to the right of Luisa's dog run the day after they had acquired a new daughter. But they were no sooner settled in when Matthew who had hardly spoken to Tilly for most of the day made a sudden statement. He was going to find a homestead for them, preferably one already made with a suitable acreage of ground. It didn't matter he said, if it was back towards the south and Galveston or over to the west near San Antonio. He had talked the matter over openly with Mack, and Mack had agreed with him not only about the situation of a new home but about making a move as soon as possible.

Towards evening Mack came up to the house and for the first time during their acquaintance he talked openly and it became apparent to Tilly that he didn't like his employer any more than she did, and she guessed the reason he stayed on here was Luisa.

One thing he advised: they should not venture north-west any further than Fort Worth. Although there were lots of homesteaders settling around Dallas, it was still too near the Indian territory to be safe for, as he said, those beggars couldn't be trusted. The moon and fire water together could make them forget any treaty. And then there were the Comanches. They were a different proposition altogether, the Comanches, for at times they didn't need fire water or the moon to get the blood lust up.

Then all thought of moving was shelved for a time when Alvero Portes became ill with a fever. At first it was thought he had caught cholera, and this caused slight pandemonium in

254

the compound because many men were more scared of the cholera than they were of the Indians. And so it seemed to be with Pete Ford and Andy O'Brien, for they shouldered packs and left.

But Alvero Portes didn't have the cholera, nor yet the plague, it was some kind of intestinal disturbance that weakened him so much that at one time Matthew really thought the old man was about to die. Emilio and Diego between them did most of the nursing, Luisa never went near him.

Matthew visited him every day, but there was little conversation between them; what there was would follow the lines of:

'How are you?'

'Better.'

The next day. 'How are you?'

'It has returned.' This was with reference to the diarrhoea.

Another day. 'How are you?'

'Does it matter? I want to die.'

Then one day he looked at Matthew and said, 'Will you ask Luisa to visit me, please?'

It was on that day that Matthew really thought the old man was on his last legs, but when he took the message to Luisa she looked him straight in the face and said simply 'No!'

'He's dying, Luisa.'

'He's not dying; he won't die, it'll take more than a dose of diarrhoea to kill him. . . .'

Alvero Portes remained in bed for two months and after he finally did get up his recovery was slow. He spent his days sitting in the long room reading or looking out on to the compound and watching his horses being exercised.

When Luisa remarked with a sneer on the slowness of the convalescence to Tilly, Tilly repeated her words to Matthew. 'Luisa says he's spreading it out purposely to hold you here.'

At this Matthew didn't shake his head denying any such strategy on the old man's part, but what he said was, 'Then he's wasting his time. And yet if he is feeling well enough I don't know how he can sit there and look at his latest acquisition of horse flesh and not want to jump on its back, because as you know he lives horses.'

So the weeks passed into months. The house was finished and it was comfortable and she would have looked upon it as home if out of the window she didn't see the ranch in the near distance.

The house consisted of a living-room, an eating-room with a kitchen next to it, and two bedrooms on the ground floor with an indoor closet adjoining, and, above, a run-through room in the roof. This latter held two cots, Katie's bed, and also served as a makeshift play-cum-schoolroom.

Strangely, after their first tempestuous meeting the children got on extremely well together; in fact, where one was you'd always find the other.

The first two weeks had been very trying for the little girl cried each night for her mother, but it seemed as if she had taken naturally to Tilly being her new mother; and stranger still, Tilly had taken to her and had given her the same attention as she had bestowed on Willy. But with Matthew it was different. Matthew never consciously touched the child. Whenever, following Willy's actions and words, she would run towards him, saying 'Poppa! Poppa!' he didn't if he could help it put his hand on her. When Tilly said this was unfair to the child he replied he couldn't help it, that he had no feeling whatever that she belonged to him.

But here they were in November again. They had been here over a year now and during that time had received only three lots of mail from home. But on this day they were sitting before the fire, Tilly in the corner of a wooden settle that was padded with skins, Matthew in his favourite position on a bear rug on the floor, his back against her knees, his legs stretched out towards a rough stone hearth that supported a huge blazing cradle of wood. They were both reading their letters, and when she bent over to him he turned his face up to hers and they spoke simultaneously on a laugh, saying, 'They're married.'

He swung round and leant his elbow on the seat beside her as he said, 'Oh, I wish I'd been there. And it's almost three months ago.' He looked at his letter again, saying, 'He sounds very happy, over the moon as it were.'

'And so he should be, Anna's a lovely girl. And she's very funny. Listen to this.' She read from her letter: 'The taffeta was so stiff with age it made an odd sound like moths beating their wings against the window-pane, and as I went down the aisle I thought, Wouldn't it be funny if all the moths suddenly became alive and I took flight. And I wanted to giggle, but I coughed instead and Lord Bentley looked at me with concern. Fancy being given away by a Lord!'

Tilly looked laughingly at Matthew now, saying, 'She put that last bit in brackets.' Glancing at the letter again, she hooted with laughter as she read, 'He must have thought he was bestowing enough on us by his gesture because his wedding present was very mean. Lady Bentley said it had been in the family for years, it was an heirloom. Whatever its use I have yet to find out. It is not a vase because it has holes in the bottom; it is not a colander as it is not big enough. John thinks it is something that was used for a head cold: you put it over a bowl of boiling water, put your head in it and sniff.'

Tilly now leaned forward and dropped her own head towards Matthew's and as she laughed he brought himself up on to the seat beside her and, putting his arm around her, he said, 'Oh, it's good to see you laugh.'

As she dried her eyes she answered, 'It's good to laugh, and with you. You don't laugh enough, Matthew.'

His face straight, he said, 'No, perhaps not, dear. But we will, we will soon. Once away from here we will laugh till we split our sides.' He had yelled the last words; and now their heads were again together and they were laughing hilariously.

When he kissed her it was a long blood-stirring moment, and so it was with an effort that she disengaged herself from his arms, saying, 'Look, there's another three letters. And what did John say?'

He wrinkled his face at her, 'Oh, he's full of life and sounds quite important. Believe it or not, the mine is going well, no more trouble with water. He speaks of the under-manager being a good fellow. A Mr Steve McGrath. You remember, Mrs Sopwith?' He now rubbed his nose against hers. 'The gentleman to whom you let your cottage, the man you were going to marry to escape me.'

'Nonsense!' She pushed him away.

'It wasn't nonsense. Come on, own up, you were, weren't you?'

'Yes, yes, I was, Mr Sopwith.'

He looked at her in silence for a moment; then pulling her into his arms again, he pressed her tightly to him, saying now, 'I want to tell you something, I was for murdering him.'

'Don't be silly, you weren't.'

'Oh, yes I was. By accident you know, pushing him into a pot hole down the pit, then holding him under.'

'Oh Matthew! The things you say.'

'It's true, I had such thoughts.'

Again she pushed at him, but this time she looked into his face and she knew that although he had spoken jokingly there was, nevertheless, a trace of truth in what he said, and she felt a tremor go through her as she realised that he would kill anyone who attempted to come between them, all that is except the man over there in the ranch-house.

Slowly now she opened the first of the three remaining letters, then said, 'This is Anna's handwriting but it's from Biddy,' and slowly she read the stilted paragraphs aloud: 'Dear Tilly, I hope this finds you well as it leaves me at present. Everything here is fine. Mistress Sopwith is a good mistress.'

She glanced up at Matthew, saying, 'Anna must have found it rather embarrassing to write that,' then went on, 'I miss you very much. I miss Katie an' all. There are two new helpers in the house but it isn't the same, pardon me saying so.' She turned to Matthew again. 'I wonder whom she was apologising to?' Then continued: 'Master John and his lady are well, thanks be to God. I hope this finds you as it leaves me at present. Ever your friend. Biddy Drew.'

There was a lump in Tilly's throat, and she bit on her lip before saying, 'Do you think we'll ever see them again?'

'Of course, of course. Why say such a thing? Of course we'll see them again. We'll go home for holidays and try to inveigle more of them to come out here.'

She had opened the next letter, and now she exclaimed on a

high, excited tone, 'It's from Mrs Ross; you remember, the parson's wife back when I was a girl? Oh well, you won't remember her, but she was the one who first taught me to read and write . . . and dance. Oh yes, and dance.' Her face lost its smile, and she read the letter. It was short and telling: 'Dear Tilly, I am sorry to give you the news that my dear husband died some six months ago and I have returned to my family. I have had no news of you for some time but I trust that all is well with you. The last I heard of you was through a relative, who understood you were working in the Manor as nurse to the master who had been hurt in an accident. I have heard since coming home that he has died. I hope you yourself are well and that you have progressed in your studies over the years. Perhaps we may meet one day. I think of you with fondest memories. Your sincere friend, Ellen Ross.'

She looked at Matthew as she said, 'It's like hearing of someone from the dead. Strange, I've hardly thought of her in years. Life is funny, isn't it?'

'Yes.' He nodded at her; then putting his arm gently around her, he added, 'And beautiful and exciting and filled with wonder.'

As their heads went together again, a knock came on the door and Matthew turned and called, 'Come in,' and Luisa entered.

It was very rarely she came over in the evening and Tilly got to her feet, saying, 'Something wrong, Luisa?'

'Well, I don't know. It could be if it comes this way. Doug's just come back. He met up with Peter Ingersoll, his Bert and Terry, and the Purdies. They'd been on a bear hunt. Got three, but a mother was wounded and she and her two cubs made off. It was bad light and they couldn't find her. She got into the foothills and the brush, so she might come this way. It's too far for her to make for the forest, I think, and her wounded, so I thought I'd tell you.'

'Thanks, Luisa. That's all we want, a wounded bear running loose, and with cubs into the bargain. If she gets into the stockade — God! give me an Indian any day, or a couple for that matter. What is she, do you know?'

'A black, and mighty big by what Peter Ingersoll said. And

she's likely very hungry and wants to fill up before she beds down for the winter with the young ones.'

'Funny time to have cubs, isn't it?'

'No, not really. And they mustn't be all that young. Anyway' — she grinned towards him — 'don't go outside and shake hands with her, she mightn't like it.'

'Come and sit down, you look cold.'

'I am. I tell you what.' She nodded towards Matthew. 'If she should come this way and you get her I want the skin; I'm badly in need of another bed hap.'

'Have a drink.'

'I won't say no.'

As Matthew was pouring out three glasses of brandy Luisa looked round the room, saying, 'My! you're cosy here. You know what I was thinking, if it's all the same to you I wouldn't mind taking it over when you're gone. The dog run gets a bit dreary at times.'

Tilly looked over the back of the settle towards Matthew. His eyes seemed to be waiting for her. He had forgotten during the last half hour or so that they weren't settled here, and a minute later when Matthew handed Luisa her glass she looked up at him and said, 'I'll miss you, I'll miss you both. God! how I'll miss you.' Then she added, 'If only the old bugger would peg out.'

Human reactions were strange, Tilly thought, as she again glanced at Matthew because she knew he was as shocked as she was at the vehemence, at the cold brutality in Luisa's words, yet at the same time she knew that they, too, wished Alvero Portes dead. Then Luisa laughed, her strange forced laugh, and they joined in with her.

Katie couldn't sleep, she had a lot on her mind, she had fallen in love and was finding it a different feeling altogether from that which she had felt for Steve McGrath all those years ago. Anyway, she had known there was no hope for her with Steve, the only one for him was Tilly. When he had gone away she had quickly forgotten about him, and when he returned, a different Steve altogether, there had been less likelihood of him looking the side she was on for he was going up in the world; not that he was an upstart; and what was more he had turned out to be a handsome man, there was none of the dour, shy boy left in him. And now, of course, being the silly fool that she was, she told herself, she would go and throw her cap at another big fellow, a red-headed one this time whose very glance from under that big hat of his made her go hot and cold.

What was troubling her now was the fact that she might again be throwing her quoit on to a stone wall. Yet Doug Scott was always going out of his way to have a word with her, and he joked with her an' all. He had once put his hand on her shoulder and laughed at her and said, 'You're a plump little dump, aren't you?' The words themselves hadn't conveyed a compliment but the way he had said them had.

She was cold. Why did it get so cold at night? She brought her knees up to towards her chin, and as she did so Willy muttered in his sleep and gave a little sob.

She raised herself on her elbow. She hoped he wasn't going to have a nightmare, not tonight, and wake up the other one for it was enough to freeze you. When the sound was repeated and louder this time, she flung the bedclothes back from the bottom of the bed, grabbed up a fur-lined coat which Tilly had given her at Christmas, and, dragging it on, she made her way across the room towards the cots. She had no need of a light for the winter moon was illuminating the land, except when it was obliterated by scudding clouds.

It was as she passed the window that she saw in the distance a huddled form coming across the open space towards the house. Her mouth dropped open, her eyes widened. The next instant she was kneeling by the window ignoring Willy's crying and gaping at the thing that had now become a shadow as the moon was momentarily obliterated. When it next came into her view it was only a hundred yards from the house and she saw what she took to be a huge man bent slightly forward and making stealthily towards the house.

Indians! Indians! The scream that erupted from her brought the two children immediately awake and Willy also screaming at the pitch of his lungs.

'*Indians! Indians!*' She was scrambling down the steep stairs yelling as she went, 'Indians! Indians! Tilly! Indians!' She was about to bang her fist on the bedroom door when it was wrenched open and she was confronted by Matthew in his nightshirt, and he was almost knocked on to his back as she flung herself on him, crying 'Indians! Indians!'

'Shut up! woman. Shut up!' He was growling at her now. 'Where? What did you see?'

She bounced her head a number of times and swallowed deeply before she managed to bring out, 'I saw one coming towards the house, a big, big fellow in . . . in war paint.'

'Quiet! Come on.' It wasn't to her he was speaking but to Tilly now, and at a run they all went into the living-room. There he snatched up his gun from the side of the fireplace, where it had been resting in a clip; then throwing open the lid of a box on a rough side table he took out first one Colt revolver and handed it to Tilly, then a second one to Katie. When her hand refused to grasp it he growled slowly, 'Take it, woman. You'll likely be glad of it before the night's over. And listen.' He gripped her shoulder. 'If they should get near you use it on yourself. Do you hear?'

Katie could utter no word, for every pore of her plump body was oozing trembling sweat.

All this time Tilly hadn't spoken. Twice she had glanced upwards to where the children were still crying, and when Matthew pushed Katie towards her she gripped her arm and led her to the window and, having pressed her down to one side of it, she took up her position at the other.

Matthew had gone down the room to the second window, that was to the left of the door, and, standing to the side of it, his gun cocked, he peered out into the compound and waited.

There was no sound but he knew from the various horrific stories he had listened to that that was how they came at first, soundlessly. They would let all the horses out of the stockade, leaving some of their warriors to herd them, and their own horses would be held at the ready. When they'd finished their work they would mount with their captives behind them and race back to their base, which could be two, three, even four hundred miles away; they had been known to ride a hundred miles in a day stopping only to change their mounts. If it wasn't that, like every other man, woman and child who had settled in this state, he feared them he would have admired them simply for the magnificence of their horsemanship. It was said that they had more concern for their animals than they had for their own women. He had never been in an Indian raid or seen the devastating effects left by one but he had heard enough to make his blood run cold and to know that if it came to the push he himself would kill Tilly and the children rather than let them fall into the hands of any Indian, especially a Comanche.

He had been given to understand when he first came here that should there be any sign of trouble three shots would be fired: this would alert the whole ranch. Well, he had heard no shots, so they mustn't have made themselves felt down below. Perhaps their intention was to take this place first.

Suddenly he thought of the back door. Was it locked? He had never locked it. He hissed now, 'Go and lock the back door, Katie.'

When there was no movement from the window, he sprang across the room, through the kitchen and to the door, and thrust the bar across it, then stood for a second breathing deeply before running back again to the window.

The moon was bright now, and he could see no movement outside, no sign of anyone. He wondered if he should set off the alarm. It would mean opening the window, and the slightest creak could put them on their guard or be a signal for them to begin their attack.

As he hesitated there came the sound of movement from the end of the house where the meat store was. They were likely raiding that first. It was often their way. If the buffalo and deer were scarce and the winter hard many of those in the small camps died of starvation, even being reduced to eating their horses, which only anticipated death, because without horses they couldn't hunt.

The noise became louder. They were dragging the meat out. They had likely overturned one of the barrels; he had helped salt down three hogs yesterday.

When the dark hump came into view, his body stiffened; then he dropped onto one knee and gently slid open the window, rested the muzzle of his rifle on the sill and waited. A shadow crossed the moon but he could pick out a figure moving towards him, slowly lumbering, nothing like the stealthiness of an Indian.

Of a sudden, the cloud left the moon and there, not ten yards from the house, stood an enormous bear and at its feet a shoulder of hog, and gnawing at the shoulder was a cub.

Matthew almost laughed with relief, but his laughter was short-lived when the bear took a limping step forward and he could see that its right shoulder was badly shattered. A healthy bear was dangerous but a wounded bear was something else.

'It's the bear, Matthew. It's the bear.'

'Yes, I know. Be quiet.'

A decision had to be made: to shoot or not to shoot. If he didn't kill the beast outright it could charge. The door might hold but not the window, and the beast was now almost opposite the window where Tilly and Katie were standing. Anyway, if he missed, as he could easily do from this angle, the sound would bring the others out.

The report of his gun seemed to shatter the room, and the children upstairs screamed louder; but the bullet had found its target for the bear reared on its hind legs and gave a cry that was almost human, and the cub, leaving its meal, ran in agitated circles around its mother.

But the animal was far from finished. It began to lumber now straight towards the window, attracted perhaps by the glint of the moonlight on the glass and the shadows of the figures behind it.

Knowing that he couldn't get it within his sights from where he was standing, it took but a split second to whip the bar from the door, and then he was in the open facing the animal which had now turned towards him. When Matthew fired again his aim must have been erratic; he had been aiming for the beast's heart, but the bear was still lumbering towards him.

Again he reloaded and pulled the trigger, but the lock stuck and the animal was now not more than eight feet from him. For the first time in his life he experienced panic: he was aware of shouts coming from the ranch and knew that the men would be here in minutes, but by then it would be seconds too late. He also knew that Tilly was by his side and he wanted to scream at her 'Get away! Get away!' But he had no voice. As he went to thrust his arm towards her he heard the shots, and when he glanced at her he saw that she was holding the Colt in both hands and he imagined she had her eyes closed.

As he and the animal fell to the ground together he felt a breath-tearing pain rip down his arm; then he was smothered in a weight of stinking fur. It was in his mouth, wet, sticky, sweet. He couldn't breathe, he was finished. Not until the hot blood-smeared weight was dragged off him did he realise he was almost naked and covered with blood.

'Tilly! Tilly!'

'She's all right, Matt, she's all right.'

'Where is she? Where is she?'

'It's all right, she's indoors. It didn't touch her, she fell clear, but it got you. Boy! it got you. Still, you're lucky. By God! I'll say you are, you're lucky. She's the biggest I've seen in years. She is the one that got away . . . but not quite, not quite.' Doug Scott talked all the while he was settling him in a chair in the room.

Luisa, her hair tucked underneath a white cap, her feet in top boots into which were thrust the sides of her nightgown, and this only partially covered by her old fur coat, was attending to Tilly. She too, like Doug Scott was talking all the time. 'There now. There now. Come on, say something. It's the shock. It isn't every day you kill a bear. Brave lass, you are that. And a good shot. I saw you, you held it steady. I would have smacked your chops for you if you hadn't after all the lessons I gave you. Here, drink this. And you Katie, stop your shaking.' She turned to where Katie was huddled up in the corner of the settle. 'You've got the house trembling. Anyway, what is it after all? Only a bear. But by God! I thought for a moment they had come. Somehow, been expecting them for years. I didn't stop to think they'd been pushed back too far this time to make it.' On and on she prattled, and not until her father appeared on the scene did she stop.

Alvero Portes didn't enquire what had happened, he could see for himself, and his concern was solely for Matthew. 'Bring him down,' he said to Mack McNeill; 'there are proper medical dressings down there.'

'I'm all right.' Matthew didn't look at him as he spoke.

'You're not all right. With that tear from those claws you could lose your arm, so don't be foolish, come down. Bring him down.' He again looked at Mack who, looking back at his boss, said nonchalantly, 'I can't carry him; and if he doesn't want to come, boss, he doesn't want to come.'

On this Alvero cast his glance from Mack to Doug Scott, then on to Matthew, and he said, 'Well, when you lose your arm you'll remember my words.' And on this he turned and went out.

Pressing Doug aside with his good hand, Matthew walked over to the settle, and there, dropping into a seat Luisa held out for him, he took hold of Tilly's hands, saying, 'It's all right, my dear, it's all right. You were wonderful . . . wonderful.'

As she looked into Matthew's face, Tilly wasn't thinking, I saved your life, but, I killed that poor creature. It looked at me and knew what I was going to do. I have killed a creature.

Other people could go out on bear hunts; the Indians could raid a homestead and massacre the inhabitants, the army and the rangers could retaliate and massacre the tribes; it was all hearsay, like listening to a story, nothing became true until you did it yourself. She had taken up a gun and killed a creature. That she had saved her husband's life didn't weigh against the fact that it was her hand that had killed. Was there something wrong with her that she should think this way?

She waited for the answer, and when it came it said, No; the only thing that's wrong is that you are a misfit in this country, and always will be.

7

Matthew's arm healed slowly. Although the rip had been but a surface one, one claw alone having done the damage, it caused him a great deal of pain. The rough stitching carried out by Mack with the help of a hefty measure of whisky had left a zig-zag weal from below his shoulder to the inside of his wrist; and each day he made a point of exercising the arm, stretching it, bending it, twisting it behind his back even while he had to grit his teeth in the process. The pain would be spasmodic, and he described it to Tilly as being like an attack of toothache.

And toothache was another thing. At times Katie was reduced to tears with the pain of a diseased molar but on no account would she let anyone extract it. Once Doug almost succeeded. He had got the pincers into her mouth but, before they had touched the tooth, she had clamped down on them and let out a yell as if the offending molar had left its socket. Katie's toothache had become a topic for joking down in the bunkhouse.

Tilly herself kept well in health, as did the children. Josefina had fallen into the pattern of the house as if she had been born to it. She spoke in a mixture of Spanish and English; and in turn Tilly, too, was learning a deal of Spanish.

Since the night of the bear, as that episode was referred to, Tilly had felt a change in herself. She couldn't actually put a name to the change, she only knew how it affected her; and even then the explanation she gave to herself was not the one that had come as an answer to her question on that particular night, for in her heart she knew that she would have to get used to this country because it had become Matthew's country, so what she told herself was, that she felt nearer the earth some-how. Yet when she tried to analyse this, the meaning behind it escaped her.

Now she had her own home she was kept more busy than usual, for she did her own cooking, with only one help. His name was Manuel Huerte. He was a full-blooded Mexican and from the beginning of his service he made it plain that he would have nothing to do with Diego or Emilio; to him they were Indian. In addition to his own tongue he spoke Spanish quite well, and it was through him that Tilly progressed in the latter and so was able to talk more with Josefina, and coach Willy too.

Katie came from the living-room where she had left the children playing on the rug before the fire and, sniffing loudly, said, 'Me nose tells me something.'

'And what's that?' Tilly turned from the table.

'You're making a peach pie.'

She came and bent over the table and sniffed at the dish of fruit, saying, 'Eeh! I never thought those wizened pieces of chopped leather, 'cos that's all they looked like, would ever turn into that. Why didn't they dry fruit like that back home?'

'Yes, why didn't they? Why didn't they make ice like they do here? And why don't they use animal hides like they do here? By, we'll make a difference over there when we go back.' Tilly grinned at Katie, and Katie, her face straight now, said, 'Think we ever will, Tilly?'

'Yes, yes, of course. Matthew's promised to take us over once we're settled away from here.'

'Is that still on?'

'Yes, definitely. When the spring comes he's going on the lookout for a homestead.'

'Oh, that'll be grand. But . . . but about hands?'

'Oh, we'll be able to hire hands.'

'Would any of them leave here?'

Tilly kept her head down as she replied, 'I should think so; all except Mack. I don't think he would leave.'

'No, I don't suppose he would.' Katie's voice had a bright

note to it now. 'But do you think Rod and Doug would move?'

Tilly still kept her head down. 'Oh yes. Yes, I think they would come with us; they're very fond of Matthew.'

'Aye. Aye, they are. . . . Well I'd better get back to the terrors.' She was making for the door when she turned and said, 'You know it's touchin', Tilly, to see how she' — she jerked her head back into the room — 'looks after Willy. She hates me to do anything for him. I had to slap her hands yesterday 'cos she pushed me. And I'm sure she was swearin' at me in that tongue of hers.' She laughed, and Tilly laughed with her as she said, 'The main thing is, they've taken to each other.'

'Aye. Aye, they have that.' As Katie went to turn away Tilly said, 'When I get this in the oven I'm going to slip down to see Luisa. She wasn't too good last night, she's got a heavy cold on her. If I'm not back within half an hour look to the oven, will you?'

'Aye. Aye, I'll do that.'

They nodded at each other.

A few minutes later Tilly, muffled to the eyes in a long skin coat and hood, hurried over the hard ridged ground. The sharp air caught at her throat and she tucked her chin into the collar of her coat; but she lifted her head before entering the open passageway and looked about her hoping she might catch a glimpse of Matthew for he'd be somewhere in the compound, if not there over in the corral. But the only one she saw was Rod Tyler struggling with a mettlesome horse as he aimed to get him into one of the sheds; horses that had been used to roaming the plains took badly to cover.

When she tapped on Luisa's sitting-room door and she heard her croaking voice say, 'Come in,' she wasn't all that surprised to see that she wasn't alone. Mack McNeill was standing to one side of the fireplace, and Lusia sat at the other side.

Tilly nodded to Mack, then to Luisa and said, 'How is it?'

'Doing nicely, I should say. It seems to have taken up its abode on my chest. Damn the thing!'

Tilly now looked at Mack and said, 'She should be in bed.'

'Aye; I told her that.' The remark was brief, after which Mack lapsed into his habitual silence. Except for the one time he had come to the house and talked of them moving, she hadn't heard him speak more than half a dozen words at a time. She had become used to the fact that this man could be in your company for two hours and not open his mouth. If he answered a question it was brief and to the point. However, one thing she was sure of, nothing ever escaped him. She had no doubt that even though he might already have been here half an hour or more yet when he answered her it was perhaps only the second time he had spoken.

She had seen him at times standing silently listening to Luisa's prattle, and when he left it would be without a word of good-bye, merely a lifting of his chin; yet she knew there was a strong affinity between them. She oftened wondered why Luisa hadn't married him. Perhaps the answer was he hadn't spared the words to ask her. She smiled to herself now as she wondered how he might pop the question were he ever to get round to it.

But this time he surprised her by speaking as he was about to make his departure. Looking towards Luisa, he jerked his head at her, then said, 'Aye well'; then nodded at Tilly before turning and going out.

The door had hardly closed on him when Luisa, also jerking her chin upwards, said, 'You get tired of his constant chatter.'

At this Tilly burst out laughing, saying, 'He doesn't get the chance, poor fellow. Anyway, it's as he said, you should be in bed, and not down here on your own either. Why don't you do as I ask and come up and let me look after you. It's warmer up there. That passageway of yours, as Katie says, would blow the hair off your legs.'

'Katie' — Luisa pursed her lips — 'do you know that Doug Scott's for courting her?'

'Well . . . I'm not quite blind, and I've got the idea she won't run from him.'

'You wouldn't mind then?'

'Why should I? I'd be delighted if she could get married.'

'You might have to find another helper.'

270

'I doubt it; she won't want to leave me, we've been friends for many years now.'

'You know, I think that's funny, you and her friends. You're like chalk and cheese.'

'Perhaps that's why we get on so well together. She's a good woman is Katie.'

'I'm not saying a word against her, but when the man bug gets you it can beat any friendship feelings.'

'I think Doug would come with us.'

'Aye, he might at that.'

At this point the door opened and Ma One came in, and hurriedly wobbled across the room to Luisa's side, saying, 'Better let on. Big boss slidin' along backway makin' for here while back. Then boss McNeill come, an' he did back off. But now he's on trail again. You see him? Or will I tell him no?'

Luisa had risen to her feet and she looked from Ma One to Tilly; then turning from them, she stared into the fire for a moment before swinging round again and looking at the old negress and saying, 'Let him come.'

'You know what you doin'?'

'I know what I'm doing, Ma.'

'Well, God d'rect you.'

On this she quickly wobbled out again, and Tilly, pulling her hood on to her head, said, 'I'll be off, Luisa. It's better if. . . .'

'No' — there was a plea in Luisa's voice — 'don't go. For two reasons, don't go. One, I don't want to be left alone with him; the other is, if he doesn't see you you might learn things that you'd never guess at and which I couldn't bring myself to tell you. Go in the bedroom there. He doesn't know you're here else he wouldn't have come.'

Tilly hesitated for a moment as she looked towards the outer door, then turning, she hurried into the bedroom.

The room was dead cold and she stood shivering as she glanced about it. It was the first time she had been in this room. It was as sparsely furnished as the rest of the house; the only feminine touch about it was a silver-backed brush and hand mirror on the rough wooden dressing-table, and a

271

wooden-framed picture of a man. She moved nearer and picked it up. It showed a young, pleasant-faced man in a slouch hat, the brim turned upwards from his face. He was wearing a neckerchief very much like the mufflers pitmen wore on a Sunday back home. His hair looked to be fair; his eyes round and merry; it was a nice face.

At the sound of Alvero Portes's voice coming from the next room she quickly replaced the picture on the dressing-table and, moving nearer the door, her head to the side, she listened. And as she did so she had to tell herself that it was Alvero Portes who was speaking, yet she could not associate the soft, whining tone or the buttered words with the man, the austere man who usually spoke in precise correct English, and Spanish too, for he would nearly always address Diego or Emilio in Spanish.

'You are not well, Luisa,' he was saying; 'I am worried about you, my dear. Please, please, can't you let bygones be bygones. I promise you things will be entirely different. . . . You look ill, child.'

'I am not a child.'

'You will always be a child to me, Luisa.'

'If that is so then why did you try to turn me into a woman?'

There was a pause; then Alvero Portes's voice muttered, 'Oh, Luisa! Luisa! I suffer nightly because of my sins. I pray to God nightly to forgive me.'

'If I remember, you've always prayed to God but it didn't stop you, did it?'

'Luisa! listen to me. Please listen to me. I promise you that if you will come and live with me again I shall not lay a hand on you, I shall not come nearer than an arm's length to you, and I'll swear on Christ's crucifix.'

'Huh! don't make me laugh; I have a cold on me and it hurts my throat. There was a crucifix, remember, hanging above my bed, put there by yourself before you first crept into it. It was winter, remember? like it is now. "I'm cold, Luisa, warm me," you whined. And my mother downstairs needing to be warmed. I was twelve years old, remember? *Twelve years . . .*

272

old, and no one to run to, for I daren't tell Mother; she had enough to carry without that. Yet she found out, didn't she? So, you took pleasure in killing her and killing the man who was about to take me away from your dirty claws.'

'Luisa, Luisa, why keep recalling the past. And I didn't, I didn't kill her, not your mother. I didn't kill her.'

'You didn't? You only held her in front of you and let Eddie's bullet go into her. Don't tell me to disbelieve the things my eyes saw. It was no wonder afterwards I lost my mind. And I'm telling you this, Father, whenever your hand touches me again it will be the end of you, and the same verdict you managed to wangle will be repeated, self defence. Self defence.'

Tilly was leaning against the wall next to the door; she had her hands beneath her collar holding her neck. She was feeling sick and her mind kept repeating, Poor Luisa. Poor Luisa.

Now Luisa's voice came to her again, saying, 'Well, you've had your answer and I'll thank you to go.'

There was no immediate movement. Then Alvero Portes's voice came again, saying, 'You have turned into a hard woman, Luisa. What if I were to tell you that I am a sick man and my days are numbered?'

'I would answer to that, that you've got the number of days under your own control. That business a little while back with the diarrhoea, you might have fooled others but you didn't fool me. You took enough horse jollop to make you ill but not enough to kill you. And all in vain, because you've now lost Matthew as well as me. You had him beguiled for those first three years but when he brought a wife back with him you couldn't bear it. You've done everything in your power to break them up, haven't you?'

'Only because she's not right for him.'

Tilly's head lifted sharply as Alvero's voice, now more recognisable as his usual one, said, 'There is something about her; she's not what she appears.'

'You'd like to think so, wouldn't you? Perhaps she keeps one step ahead of you.'

'I didn't come here to talk about her but about us. Luisa, if you'd only believe that I'm in earnest. You are my daughter, I love you, you're all I've got. What I did I did out of love for you.'

'*Get out!* If you stay a minute longer I'll swear to you I'll leave this place.'

'Don't talk foolishly. Where would you go?' His voice held a scornful note now.

'The Purdies; Tessie Curtis; or the Ingersolls. Any of them would gladly house me. The only reason I haven't gone to them before is because I didn't want to shame you. Nor did I want one or other of the men to come and beat the daylights out of you, which they would have done years ago if they had known the true set-up here. But there is one on this ranch who does know it, so in case I call for his help you'd better make yourself scarce.'

Luisa's voice ceased, and there was no response now from her father, nor did any movement come from the room, but it was a good minute later when Tilly heard the door close.

She didn't go immediately and join Luisa; in fact she didn't move until Luisa opened the bedroom door and without even glancing at her turned back into the sitting-room and seated herself once more in her chair by the fire.

Slowly Tilly walked into the room, but she didn't face Luisa. Somehow she couldn't look at her; nor apparently could Luisa look at her, for her attention was turned to the fire as she said, 'Well, what do you make of that?'

'It's unbelievable.'

'Ah well, you can believe it. He didn't deny a word I said, did he?'

'Why haven't you left before?'

'Where would I go?' Luisa now swung sharply around. 'Oh yes, I said I could go to the Curtises or the Ingersolls or the Purdies; but wherever I went what could I do? They would put me up for a few weeks, in fact tell me to stay as long as I like; but what use would I be to them? The mothers and the daughters do their own cooking and their men wouldn't tolerate a woman riding out with them. Of course' — she tossed her head now and her voice was scornful — 'I could have gone to one of the forts and been a laundry-woman and made a dollar on the side supplying the soldiery. They're always wanting laundry-women at the forts because there are not many wives there.'

'You could have married. I'm sure you could have married.' Tilly spoke quietly now with the thought of Mack in her mind, and her statement was answered on a laugh that had no mirth in it.

'Yes, if anybody had asked me.'

Tilly now took the seat opposite to Luisa and she brought her attention towards her as she said, 'You mean to say Mack hasn't?'

Luisa coughed, then rubbed her chest with the heel of her hand before nodding and repeating, 'Yes, that's what I mean to say, he hasn't.'

'He . . . he cares for you, Luisa; I'm sure he does.'

'Aye, some people are fond of dogs.'

'Oh, don't talk like that.' Tilly got to her feet abruptly and she walked completely around the table before coming to a stop again; and then she said, 'I've wanted to say this for some time, and I'm speaking for Matthew, too. We've both got money. I have interest from shares; I don't need it. If you won't take money from Matthew then take it from me. I can't bear to see you any longer going round like a. . . .'

'A squaw? Seventh wife of Big Chief Buffalo Horn?' Luisa laughed now, but it was a laugh without bitterness, and she put her hand out towards Tilly and, patting her arm, she said, 'Thanks. I'll think about it in a year or two's time when I've got to save me nakedness.'

'Oh, Luisa!' Tilly now dropped on to her hunkers in front of the small woman and, gripping her hands, she said, 'I thought I'd had a rough time of it in my young days, but looking back it was nothing compared to what you've been through.'

'How did you have a rough time if you married into the gentry?'

Tilly dropped her gaze away as she muttered, 'I didn't

always live with the gentry. Well, perhaps some day I'll tell you about it.'

'Ah yes, I'd like to hear because I agree with him about one thing, you're not all you seem. I've known that from the beginning, from the day Matthew brought you in. . . . I've always wanted to ask you, did you know Matthew's people? He didn't talk about them; I felt he hadn't much use for them.'

'Oh, I think he had, at least for his father.'

'He was all right then, his father?'

'Oh yes, yes; he was all right.' Tilly now got to her feet, saying, 'I'd better be getting back, I left a pie in the oven. I'll come down later. Is there anything you want, I mean in the food line?'

'No. No, thanks; Ma sees that I'm well stoked up. . . . And Tilly.'

'Yes Luisa?'

'Don't repeat to Matthew what you've heard this morning.'

Tilly didn't answer immediately, and so Luisa said, 'Please, because if he knew I don't think he'd go near him again or wish to speak to him. For the remainder of the short time you'll be here now, let things rest as they are.'

'What do you mean, the remainder of the short time?'

'Oh, I can smell change on the wind. I should say you'd be gone by spring. Matthew's been making discreet enquiries about homesteads.'

'It'll be for the best, Luisa; although I'll miss you.'

'And me you. Still' — she let out a long, slow breath — 'who knows what might happen before the spring. You know, it's always amused me the folks who have come in from the towns, the casuals. They get bored, they say, because nothing happens along the plains. Dear God!' She moved her head slowly now. 'There's more tragedy and comedy happening in one week than you'd get in a town in a month of Sundays. A few years back people could be hale and hearty one day and without their hair the next; and the lads who rode in yesterday say they're breaking out again, the Comanches. And after all, this isn't such a long ride away for them.'

'Oh don't talk like that, Luisa. I thought you laid great stock

276

on the rangers and the army, and Matthew says we're hundreds of miles away from them, especially the Comanches.'

'Yes, yes; but as I've said before what's a hundred miles to a horse Indian. The only time you're safe from Indians in this country is when you're dead. People around here are getting too complacent. They imagine that the politicians have them all nicely railed off in their tipis, but you can never rail an Indian off. Anyway, what am I talking about? If they come I'll scream for you like Katie did about the bear. And by the way, I still think it's a mistake to have kept the cub, 'cos cubs grow up, and then what? Far better to have shot it.'

Tilly said nothing to this but went out. She knew that Luisa's chatter about Indians was in the way of an attempt to erase from her mind the conversation she had heard from the bedroom. She liked Luisa, she was very fond of her, but she didn't profess to understand her. She had a strange turn of mind; yet could you wonder at it after what she had gone through with that man? that aping aristocrat, that hypocrite, that praying Christian who had aimed to seduce his daughter when she was but twelve!

Had he succeeded?

8

The ranch had become like a camp divided against itself. More and more Alvero Portes had excluded Matthew from the rides. In the beginning he had made Matthew's lacerated arm the excuse, but now when Matthew went down to the compound he would often find that Rod and Mack or Mack and Doug and the black boy Three, together with spare hands, had gone out on a round up.

One day last week Matthew had returned to the house furious because five of the men had been sent off almost at a moment's notice on a branding trip, which meant rounding up the already branded shorthorns and marking their calves by splitting their ears in a special way.

Stamping up and down the room, Matthew had exploded, crying, 'He's testing my temper! He's using breaking-in tactics, but he'll find out I'm no horse.' Then stopping abruptly in front of her, his voice sank deep into his chest as he said on a note that almost sounded like one of sorrow, 'I've had to keep telling myself he's the same man I knew before I returned home, but now there is no comparison, he's as sly and devious as an Indian, and he's vicious. Yes' — he had nodded at her — 'he's vicious. You know, you aren't aware of this and I didn't mean to tell you, but likely Luisa would when she gets prattling, but he flogged Four last night.'

'Flogged him? Oh no! But why? What had he done?'

'Supposed to have caught him ill-treating a horse. Can you imagine it? All Four ever wants to do is to get on to a horse's back. I've half expected him to steal one before now and go off. No, it's my opinion, and Doug's also, that he found the boy

278

with Eagle, and having reared the animal himself, he values it more than any other in the stable, and likely Four was just admiring it. It would be enough for Uncle to see him put his black hand on it: daring to touch his precious thoroughbred! But I'm sure that was merely an excuse for the thrashing; he happens to be Luisa's boy, so it was a way of getting at her.'

After a moment of resting her head against his arm, she said, 'Let's get away from here, Matthew, soon, please,' and he nodded slowly as he replied, 'Yes, you're right; we must get away from here, and as you say, soon, the sooner the better. . . .'

On this particular morning the sun was shining, the air was clear, the sky was high, the grass on the plains was rolling in green and yellow waves on a never ending sea.

The young horses in the stockade were kicking their heels and galloping here and there as if they had suddenly become aware of the power in their sinews. Willy and Josefina were playing in front of the house with the tethered bear cub now named Nippy; they also had a wooden horse with a real horse's tail nailed to its end and a similar mane on its roughly carved head.

For all her one year advantage over Willy, Josefina was not as big as he, nor as strong, as was proven when she tried to dislodge him from the saddle of the wooden horse, and so she attempted to straddle Nippy; which caused Katie to remark to Tilly who was passing through the kitchen, 'They're at it again, those two; fighting to see who's cock-o'-the-walk.'

Tilly turned her head on her shoulder and laughed as she said, 'Well, as long as it remains fifty-fifty we needn't worry.'

'Here's the boss comin'.' Katie pointed out of the window, and Tilly, hurrying through the room, went to the door and opened it and awaited Matthew's arrival with some trepidation, for he hadn't been left the house more than half an hour. However, she could see by his face that he wasn't troubled, but even pleased about something.

He came into the room with his hand outstretched, saying, 'It's a letter from the Curtises. They're having a barbecue at the weekend; they would like us to go and stay the night.'

'Oh, that would be nice. But why are they having a barbecue at this time?'

'The letter says' — he pulled it out of the envelope and handed it to her — 'two visiting dignitaries. It could be Houston, it doesn't say. Anyway . . . visiting dignitaries will have their entourage with them, and you know Tessie has three redheads to get rid of; although I wouldn't like to be the one who'd tackle either Bett or Ranny or Flo, unless they like dray horses.'

'Oh! Matthew.' Tilly flapped her hand at him. 'They're nice girls.'

'So are buffalo cows.'

'Matthew!' She pulled a long face and they both laughed. Then becoming serious, she asked, 'Has *he* got an invitation?'

'Oh likely; there was a letter for him.'

'Who brought them?'

'Oh, three cowboys on the trail; they've been working for Lob Curtis. I left them down in the yard. I think they're asking to be taken on for a day or so.'

'Do you think that Tessie didn't mention the name of the dignitaries in case one is Houston and they knew that your uncle wouldn't accept?'

'Could be.'

'Why doesn't he like Mr Houston? I can't just think it's the senator's policies.'

'I think it's because Mr Houston has never stopped here on his travels. He's travelled for years over the State, I understand, but has never given this ranch the honour of being his headquarters or Uncle his host. But one of the reasons Uncle says he can't stand the man is because of his sojourn with the Indians when he was a young fellow. At one time he lived with them for three years, so to my mind he should know them more than most. Anyway' — he waltzed her round the room now — 'we go to a real party and for the first time I'll have a chance to show you off.' He stopped abruptly and, pulling a grave face, said, 'You will wear your very best gown, Mrs Sopwith, and every piece of jewellery you own for I'm determined to be the envy of every American, rough or smooth neck, at that gathering.'

'Yes, master.'

They now pressed close to each other, laughing as Matthew said, 'I'm glad you know your place at last.'

Her voice serious now, Tilly asked, 'What kind of people will I be expected to meet really, because this won't be any little barn dance, will it, not with Tessie sending out formal invitations?'

'Oh, a political group likely, and between the eating and drinking and the jigging there'll be a lot of serious discussion; and decisions will be taken in quiet corners of the garden, mostly about the slavery question. Strange —' He turned from her and walked up the room and, standing with his back to the fire now, he said, 'At one time back home I thought of going into politics because I felt I understood the situation, but here' — he shook his head — 'a man seems to be for one thing today and changes his mind tomorrow, just as they're accusing Houston of doing; and on this point I think I am with him and against the extension of black slavery, yet because of his stand he's been branded as a traitor. And, of course, he's wholeheartedly for the Indians. It's odd, you know, but I find myself with him in this too. Of course, as Rod pointed out to me when we were talking along these lines a few weeks ago, I've never seen the result of an Indian raid else I wouldn't talk such codswallop. He wouldn't have it that most of the raids were in retaliation for the Government reneguing on their promises. And you know' — he nodded towards her — 'it's shamemaking the way they've done this. Two years ago just before I returned home I was talking to one of the Indian agents. By the way, these are not Indians, they're white Americans who are supposed to look after the welfare of the Indians who are living in reserves. He was a decent enough man but he told me of some of the practices that the agents used to rob the Indians of the very food supplied by the Government for them. Oh' — he beat the top of his head with the palm of his hand — 'it's all beyond me.' Then opening his arms out to her, he said, 'All I'm concerned about is you. Come here.'

When she was standing within the circle of his arms, he put his head on one side and said, 'I've got some news that I'm sure will please you, Mrs Sopwith.'

She waited, saying nothing until he said, 'Aren't you going to ask what it is?'

'Yes, master. What is it?'

He jerked her so tightly to him that she cried out; and then he said, 'Mack tells me of a place going over Cameron way.'

'Is that near the Red River?' Tilly put in quickly.

'No! No! it's miles from there, two hundred miles or so. No, this ranch lies about fifty miles west as the crow files, between Caldwell and Cameron, but we'll have to go Washington way and cross the Brazos there. And so we'll have to travel about a hundred miles. But you needn't worry, we'll be well outside the Comanche country. Anyway, there's enough soldier-manned forts dotted about to keep the peace; of that I'm sure. Mack says it's an excellent house and he thinks they must have marked out three or four thousand acres. It's good grassland too with wood in plenty quite near. It somehow seems the realisation of a dream because I've thought for a long time now I'd like to start a good beef breed, not just rangy Longhorns, but half and half, the Longhorns for the stamina and say a Scottish breed for their fat. This business of letting them range wild on the plains is all right when there's no alternative, but I can see an alternative. Things are moving fast; there's railroads beginning to extend all over the States and they'll come this way. It might be a few years but they'll come this way. We have the rivers but we want the rails. Just imagine if there was a railroad near at hand and the fellows hadn't to go on that death trail with the herds, because they lose at least a third of them in the dry season. But' — he spread his palm out wide — 'imagine an engine with countless wagons behind.'

She moved from him, saying primly now, 'Yes, yes, I do imagine it, and the poor cattle herded into them with no room to turn or squat. Yes, I imagine it.'

'Oh —' He caught her by the shoulders, saying softly, 'Tilly! Tilly! You're in a wild country; you've got to become hardened to these things else you're going to suffer. Cattle are bred for eating. You like your joint as well as anyone.'

She closed her eyes and drooped her head and said, 'Yes, yes, I know, don't stress the point, I know. Anyway, about the answer to Tessie's letter. I suppose it will have to be formal.'

'Yes, I suppose it will.'

'Well, I'll get down to it right away. Honestly it's funny when you come to think of it' — she was laughing now — 'anyone expecting you to be formal in this —' She wagged her fingers in front of her face and ended weakly, 'place. It seems as if we are back in the county.'

'They have their standards.' His face was straight as he answered her. 'And I think that if you were in the towns you'd find more snobbery and social awareness than ever you did back home. In England ancestors are taken for granted and you rarely speak of them, here they mention them on every possible occasion. If you can discuss your great-great-grandmother what's-her-name, then you can claim distinction. . . . Go on and write your prettiest acceptance, and I'll see it is sent off later today. . . .'

Tilly wrote the letter of acceptance; then she told Katie she was going down to Luisa's to see if she had received a similar invitation; or perhaps, if it had been included with her father's, she would as yet know nothing of it.

She paused on the slope before entering the compound and looked over the land away in the direction she thought the house would lie, and she knew a rising excitement within her and a feeling that she wanted in this instant to mount a horse and gallop across the land to see this place for herself. In her mind's eye she imagined she saw what it was like, a two-storey house with a white-pillared verandah and steps leading down to a green lawn. Matthew had said it was good grassland, but she told herself that his idea of grass and hers were two different things.

Such was her feeling at the moment that she only stopped herself from running the rest of the way down to the dog run and Luisa.

It was as she entered the compound through a rough log gate that two men, coming out of the bunkhouse, stopped and looked towards her. They were strangers and she surmised they were two of the three new hands about whom Matthew had spoken. She returned their glances and smiled, and as she turned away one of them spoke, saying, ' 'Tisn't, is it?'

283

Feeling the question was aimed at her, she turned her head and looked at the man coming towards her. She didn't know him. He had a long face which was bearded on both sides of his cheeks and met his hair underneath the big slouch hat; he was roughly dressed, not unlike the rangers, in long tight trousers and short jacket; he also wore a pocketed leather belt. He was about three yards from her when he stopped and said, 'Can't be two of you.' His voice was unlike those of the other hands and she had to recall where she had heard it last; and when it came into her mind she screwed up her eyes as she stared at the man. The inflexion was northern, English northern.

'Miss Trotter?'

'Yes, I . . . I was Miss Trotter.'

'Oh aye, I forgot. Sorry. Dad wrote 'n told me. Only had one letter from him since I came over. Aw, I've got you on the wrong foot. You don't know me? Well, you wouldn't remember me with all this, would you?' He stroked both sides of his face. 'And three years out here changes a man. I'm Bobby Pearson, you know.'

'Oh! Oh, Mr Pearson's son? Oh yes; he told me that you were bound for America. Well! Well!' For a moment her voice had been pleasant as if she were pleased to see him, but it had only been for a moment for the import of his presence rushed at her with sickening awareness.

'It's a small world, ain't it?'

'Yes, yes, indeed. What . . . what are you doing?'

'Oh, me an' me mate's trekkin' across country, makin' for the mines really . . . gold mines. But as I said, there'll be nowt left by the time we get there. That doesn't worry me though. Live for the day, that's me. We could've been there weeks gone but we dithered; laid up in the bad weather. Eeh! by, it is funny comin' across you here an' talkin' like this. Don't think I passed the time of day with you back home but I saw you many a time when you went out in the carriage. Aye.' He nodded his head as if recalling the scene. . . . 'Mr Sopwith, he here? But of course he will be.' He nodded, then looked around the compound, saying, 'Good set-up this, well stocked as far as I've seen. The big boss has set us on for the drive.'

284

'Oh! has he?' She brought her head forward and wet her lips, then said, 'Well, if that's the case we'll be seeing each other, Mr Pearson.'

'Aye, we likely will.' He backed a step from her, his head bobbing, his face wide with a smile. 'Can't help but bump into people here. Yet there's so much space outside, it's apt to scare the breeches off you at times. . . . Well, be seein' you.'

She inclined her head and turned swiftly away and went towards the dog run; but once in the open corridor she didn't knock on Luisa's living-room door, she paused for a moment, screwed up her eyes tight, then went straight through and out the back way. Here again she paused and put her hand out against the wooden wall for support. He would talk; that man was not like his father, he was a jabberer, he would talk, he would lay claim to knowing all about her. She could see him holding the floor as he described her life back in the Manor, and also the attitude of the villagers towards her. She must find Matthew and put him on his guard.

Where was he? As she turned about to go back through the run into the compound Emilio came out of Luisa's kitchen, and so she hurried toward him, saying, 'Young boss. Have you seen young boss?'

Grinning widely at her, Emilio thumbed over his shoulder, 'He in. . . .' he said.

'Oh, thank you.'

When she rushed into the kitchen, both Luisa and Matthew turned and looked at her. Luisa was preparing some food at the table and Matthew was standing munching a small cake. At the sight of her he gulped at the food in his mouth and swallowed deeply before placing the other half on the table, then putting out his hands, saying, 'Here. Here. What's the matter?'

She looked from him to Luisa for a moment; then as if suddenly making up her mind, she said, 'One of the men that came in this morning who brought the letter, I've just seen him.'

As she paused, he said, 'Yes, what about him?'

'He's . . . he's the son of Mr Pearson. You remember? Or perhaps you don't, but Mr Pearson, he was the odd-job man in the village. He . . . he was very kind to me, always took my part. The last time we met he told me that his son was going to America. Well' — she nodded over her shoulder now — 'he's here, one . . . one of the three men.' She cast her glance at Luisa now and, as if explaining her attitude, she said, 'He . . . he knows all about me, about us, and he's a loose-tongued man, I can tell you. He'll tell them everything, and your uncle —' She was looking at Matthew again, and now she paused and her head moved in one wide sweep as she ended, 'This will be all he needs.'

'Leave him to me. If he dares open his mouth he won't close it for a long time; I'll make that plain to him.' As he marched towards the door she ran to him and caught his arm and said, 'Go careful, Matthew, be tactful, I mean, don't . . . don't get his back up. Ask him, rather than tell him, not to mention my name.'

He looked at her hard for a moment before turning from her and going out; and when the door was closed she leant against it and looked towards Luisa.

'Is it as bad as all that?' asked Luisa.

'It . . . it isn't to me, it never was, it's how people will look at it.'

'Look at what?'

Tilly bowed her head, 'Me being . . . named a witch, and . . . and living with Matthew's father as his mistress for twelve years.'

She raised her eyes to see Luisa staring at her with her mouth agape. She had moved from the table and her back was almost against the wood-stoked oven. Then her remark surprised Tilly, for what she said was, 'A witch? Dear God! how strange.'

She hadn't shown any feminine horror over the knowledge that she had been Matthew's father's mistress, nor was she showing horror with regard to the witch question, rather her expression was one of amazement.

It was at this point that their attention was wrenched from each other and to the window and to the sound of the cries coming from the compound. Suddenly Tilly put her hand to her mouth and let out a high cry before rushing to the door, with Luisa after her; and there they stood together for a moment as they watched Matthew and Bobby Pearson come staggering out of the bunkhouse, their fists flailing.

When Tilly went to run towards them, Luisa, gripping her arm, hissed, 'Be still for a minute.' And so she remained still while at the same time her body seemed set for a spring. The yard was now full of people. Rod Tyler, Mack and Doug Scott were circling the combatants. The new men were in the bunkhouse doorway. One, Two, Three and Four, and Ma One were outside the stables, and Diego and Emilio were at the bottom of the house steps. But at the top, on the verandah, stood Alvero Portes, a look of amazement mixed with disdain on his face. And not until he saw Matthew borne to the ground by the new hand and the pair of them rolling in the dust did he hurry down the steps and shout, 'McNeill! Stop them! Stop them this instant!'

Mack moved away a little from the circle and, looking towards his boss, made a gesture with his hand which plainly said, 'No.' But when he saw that Matthew had the younger man pinned by the throat and was almost throttling him and that the man on the ground had ceased to thrash his legs, he sprang forward. Immediately Doug Scott was at his side and together they hauled Matthew upwards on to his feet; and it took them all their time to hold him. One of the men now ran from the bunkhouse doorway and, going to Bobby Pearson raised his head from the ground. Rod Tyler, too, went to his side, saying, 'You all right!'

Pearson jerked his head and felt his neck; then looking towards where Matthew was glaring at him, he gasped, 'Bloody maniac!'

'Get out!'

Both Mack and Doug felt Matthew stiffen like a ramrod when Alvero Portes's voice, rising above the murmured hubbub, said, 'I engaged this man, I'll tell him when to go. Now what is this all about?' He looked towards Pearson for an answer and he, his voice a growl, cried, 'All because I was speakin' about his bloody wife, so-called.'

'Steady! Steady!' Doug's voice came as a hissing whisper to

287

Matthew. 'You can't stop him talkin' now; he's spilled it already, anyway.'

And he was right, for Pearson, looking towards Alvero Portes, cried, 'I knew her from I was a bairn, lived in the same village. She was hounded 'cos she was a witch; she caused trouble wherever she stepped.' Again he felt his neck and with his other hand wiped the blood that was oozing from the top of his lip and soaking his beard. 'She was the means of two men being killed; then she goes whorin' up at the Manor and was his da's mistress for years. She had a bairn to him . . . aye, aye. . . .'

As Matthew's body heaved itself forward he almost dragged the struggling Mack and Doug to the ground; this brought Rod Tyler to their assistance, saying, 'Get him up to the house.'

As the men managed to turn Matthew about, Tilly, too, turned away. There was no need now for Luisa to restrain her, nor did she attempt to follow Matthew and the men, but she allowed Luisa to lead her along the dog run and into the living-room, and when Luisa pressed her gently into a chair she made no resistance, she just sat with her hands on her lap staring before her.

A moment later Luisa, handing her a good measure of brandy, said, 'Get that down you.' And she did as she was bid, she swallowed the brandy in two gulps.

When Luisa said quietly, 'Well, you've been through the mill and come out ground down, haven't you?' she bowed her head and the tears oozed from her lids, and Luisa put in quickly, 'Don't worry your head, I'm not censuring you, I'm only amazed at the witch bit.'

'I was never a witch, nor did any witch-like things.' Tilly's voice had a weary flat note to it; it was as if she had suddenly become very tired.

'I believe you. But what I'm amazed at is that you too have suffered through being a so-called witch; I'm like I am today, a frustrated spinster, through much the same thing.'

When Tilly blinked the tears from her eyes and they widened, Luisa said, 'Witchery is a dirty word in some areas.' Then turning, she pulled a chair up and sat down and, her knees almost touching Tilly's, she said, 'You know the photo back in my bedroom? Well, his name was Bailey and he lived in Massachusetts; at least he was born there, but then his father brought him here when he was about two years old. Well, it should so happen that my father lived in Massachusetts and his people had lived there too for some generations. They were as poor as slaves but as proud as Lucifer. Well, the Baileys were ordinary people and someone of that name had in the far, far past during a witchery time named a Portes as some kind of sorcerer. Anyway, one of Father's relatives was hanged. Now as far as I can gather there were dozens of people by the name of Bailey roundabout the countryside, not so many Portes. Anyway, we were here and I was eighteen before I heard a word about this. You see' — she bowed her head now — 'I was never allowed to talk to men, never allowed to be alone with a man for five minutes, even a ranch hand, and never, never was I allowed to ride out on my own, he was always with me.' She jerked her head towards the house. 'Well, during our rides we often passed a homestead this side of Wheelock. It was a poor place, and nearly always I saw a young man and a woman in the fields, and the young man would straighten his back and look in my direction, and I in his. Then one day Father was ill and I went riding on my own and in the direction of that homestead; and for the first time I met and talked with Eddie Bailey, and straightaway we both knew what had happened to us.

'During that week I escaped the house three times and rode towards Wheelock. At our third meeting he took me in his arms and kissed me. It was as quick as that. But Father soon got better and I became hard put to slip away; I don't think we met more than six times during the next twelve months. And Eddie knew better than to show his face here, for he had heard enough about Senor Portes' — her voice held a sneer on the Senor — 'to know that he'd be kicked off the place for no other reason but that he was a man who was interested in me.'

When she stopped and rose to her feet and went towards the fire, Tilly turned her head slowly and looked at her and she could hardly hear Luisa's voice as she went on, 'When I was eighteen something happened, it was inevitable, we loved each other, keen mad about each other, so I told my mother about Eddie and my mother told him. God above!' Her head drooped on to the back of her shoulders as if she were straining to say something; and she stayed like that for a moment before she went on, 'He acted like a madman, he became almost insane . . . not almost' — she now shook her head — 'he did go insane, and over the name Bailey. Then it all came out: Eddie could have been one of a thousand Baileys, but no, he was the Bailey, or a descendant of the Bailey who had been the instigation of that poor Portes ending with a rope round his neck.'

She turned now and looked at Tilly. 'It's funny,' she said, 'how little things stick in your mind. I remember, as I watched him raging up and down the room, dashing things off the table on to the floor, I remember thinking he could make those steps into a dance. Wasn't that silly?' She gave a small laugh, then went on, 'You don't know how silly it was because I stopped him dancing by saying, "I have got to marry Eddie Bailey because I am going to have his child."

'I thought he was about to kill me. I remember crouching on the floor and Mother leaning over me to protect me from him. I can see him now grabbing at her arm and flinging her aside. She was thin and small and she spun like a top across the room. And then he was bending over me; and I looked up at him and you know what I said, Tilly? I said, "You are a filthy, dirty bugger of a man!" It was the first time I'd sworn in my life, and I ended by yelling, "You lay a hand on me and I'll drive this knife into you!" and, you know, I had a knife in my hand. He had scattered the cutlery off the dining-table and the knife was there to my side, and I would have used it, I know before God I would have used it, because I knew he was going to grab me. But at that moment Mack came into the room. How long he had been there or what he had heard I don't know, but he saved me from killing him because I had the knife held like that' — she demonstrated — 'and pointing upwards at the bottom of his belly.

'I kept in my room for almost three days. Then Mother told me that Mack had got word to Eddie about the situation, and that he was prepared to come over and get me on the Friday.

That was two days ahead when Father had arranged to ride out with the hands for a round-up.

'Well, Friday came.' Luisa now paused and slowly seated herself again in front of Tilly. 'Mother and I watched them all ride out of the compound. We saw the dust settle. Then we waited for Eddie coming. It was almost half an hour later when he galloped into the yard leading another horse. I was all ready with my bundle, I'd thrown some things into a sheet, and there I stood in that room' — she jerked her head again — 'my heart beating fit to burst. Eddie came in through the doorway and we looked at each other across the space. It was the first time he had seen my mother, and it was was the first time she had seen him. He said, "Hello, ma'am," and she answered, "Hello, Mr Bailey". It was all so slow and easy-going, there was no need to hurry, we had four days to get away, so we thought. Eddie spoke a little to my mother and told her he'd always take good care of me, and she thanked him. The tears were running down her face. It was as he picked up my bundle from the floor that Father appeared in the archway leading to the corridor. There were no words to explain the feeling of terror I experienced even before he fired. The bullet caught Eddie in the chest just below his left shoulder. He staggered and fell on to his side. But he was no sooner on the ground than he drew his Colt, and as he did so Father went to fire again, and at this Mother rushed at him. He could have thrust her aside but he didn't, it all happened in a split second. She was pinned to his chest when the bullet from Eddie's gun hit her. Then father let blaze. He emptied the other five bullets into him.'

Tilly's mouth was open and it remained so for some time before she gasped, 'Oh, Luisa! Oh, Luisa dear!' When she put out her hand, Luisa said, 'It's all right, it's just a memory now, but I've told you because I don't want you to feel too bad about what that swine of an English fellow spilled.'

Tilly now asked gently, 'The baby? Your baby?'

'Oh, I lost it, and, you know, I don't remember losing it. I screamed for days, they told me, then I went quiet and hardly moved or spoke for two years. It was another four before I recovered, if I ever have.' She smiled a sad smile now. 'The awful thing about it is, I couldn't move away from this place when I did recover. Ma One became my mother in a way and Mack . . . what has Mack become?' She shrugged her shoulders now. 'A prop to keep hold of.' She became thoughtful for a moment before saying, 'I said it was all a memory, but what still fills me with bitterness is the fact that evil men can be honoured for their actions, because in some quarters Father was upheld for having killed the man who had left me with a child. Some of the sanctimonious hypocrites, and there are a number along this line, and the Curtises are among them, so are the Purdies, they upheld Father's action. It was, they said, just exactly what they would have done in the same circumstances should one of their daughters have been deflowered. That's the word they used, deflowered. Yet the things that go on in some homesteads! But they rarely creep out because the name must be kept clean, except when a brother might get drunk and attack the fellow who is making eyes at his sister, whom he himself has already had. And you hear them talking about the sacredness of womanhood! Oh my God! they would have you think that these things only happen in the forts. . . . Anyway, my dear —' She once more rose to her feet and, putting her hand on Tilly's shoulder, she said, 'This is the end of your sojourn at the Portes's ranch. Matthew was telling me that he's got a place in mind. You must ride out there and see it, and soon, because after this he'll make your life unbearable.'

Tilly, too, got slowly to her feet, saying, 'I don't know how I can face the men after what's happened.'

'Oh, they'll think what they think, you can't stop men thinking; and they being men, you'll lose their respect. But what do you care about that? You've got Matthew, and he's one in a thousand. And you're a lucky girl. Aye, you're lucky; for what he feels for you is something that doesn't happen to many women. He might become hard to live with as the years go on because in a way he's as possessive as my father and. . . .'

'Oh, don't say that.' Tilly's voice was loud now, and Luisa answered, 'Oh, don't get me wrong, I don't mean that he's like him in any other way, except that he'll never bear the thought of anyone else sharing you.'

Tilly moved her head slowly, saying now, 'Yes, yes, I know

that only too well, for even now I've got to be careful in the affection I show to the children, especially Josefina. Poor Josefina.'

'Oh, she's not so poor, she's got a home now that she'd never had with her mother, because Leonilde's a little whore if ever there was one. . . . But now, now you'd better go up for I'm thinking Matthew might be needing more attention than the fellows can give him. I'll be up later. And tomorrow get yourselves off if possible to look at that place. I'll keep an eye on Katie and the children; they'll come to no harm.'

They went out of the room together and into the dog run and as they neared the end of it they both stopped, for there, as if he had been waiting for her, stood Alvero Portes.

The man's face looked grey under his tan and his eyes appeared black round balls lying in their sockets but looking fiercer than Tilly had yet seen them. She watched his thin neck swell, his Adam's apple jerking up and down behind the tight high collar of his blue serge coat; then he spoke directly to her. He did not shout but his precise tone and the way he threw the words from his mouth seemed to spray them far and wide over the compound and halt the men there.

'You unclean thing!' he said. 'A witch indeed! for only one such could enslave a man like my nephew, after having entrapped his father. You will leave this place. . . .'

His words were cut off now by Tilly's voice which was indeed a scream. 'How dare you! Just how dare you put the name unclean to me, you filthy, horrible man! You who raped your own child. You . . . *you* dare to call me unclean! *You*!' The saliva was actually running from the corners of her mouth, she was consumed by a rage that was so fierce she had no control over it; and when it prompted her to spring on this hypocrite she obeyed it. Her fingers clawing at his face, he was for a moment utterly taken off his guard, so much so that he staggered back, bringing up his forearm to protect himself. But what he would have done next had not Luisa, Ma One and Emilio pulled her from him is doubtful; likely he would have felled her to the ground; but just as a short while previously the men had had their hands full restraining Matthew, now the same was happening with Tilly. The veneer of this pseudo-lady that Mr Burgess and Mark, between them, had created was stripped away, revealing almost a wild woman. And in this moment Tilly was wild, her whole being was retaliating against the injustice meted out to her by the villagers, the McGraths in particular. She was once again on the ground fighting as if for her life against the weight of Hal McGrath; she was in the stocks being pelted; she was in the courtroom being exposed as a witness; she was holding her Granny in her arms after the cottage had been burned down; she was in the kitchen of the Manor being subjected to the taunts and hate of the majority of the staff; she was suffering the humiliation of being turned out of the house; she was being brought low by Miss Jessie Ann's disdain and for the second time being forced to leave the Manor; she was in the Market Place avoiding Mrs McGrath's stick that then blinded her child; she was standing stiff-faced and straight-backed under the sneers and insults of the ladies of the county; and finally, here she had to suffer the hate of this dirty lecherous old beast who dared to say that she was unclean.

She ceased struggling, then shook off the hands that were clinging to her, and stood gasping for breath. She was speaking again as she looked at the man who was standing holding a white handkerchief to his face and whose features had seemed to assume those of the devil, and, her voice loud once more, she cried at him, 'Witch, you say I am. All right, as a witch I'll say this to you: One day you'll wish for death, you'll be so alone you'll wish for death.' And on this she turned and, pushing Luisa and Ma One roughly aside, she marched out of the compound and up the hill and almost burst into the room.

Rod Tyler, Mack and Doug turned as one to look at her. Matthew was the last to turn towards her for he had been sitting in a chair, his head bent forward, but he immediately got to his feet when he saw her.

She was gripping the side of the table and looking past the men towards him and she said, 'You'd better be prepared to get out of here as soon as possible because I've just left my signature on his face.'

'What!' Matthew came haltingly towards her. He was

gripping the arm that the bear had torn as if it were causing him intense pain. Standing in front of her, he said, 'What did you say?'

She had to take a tight hold on the table to steady herself but when she spoke each word was on a tremble. 'He . . . he told me to get out because I . . . I was unclean, and I don't know what came over me . . . oh, yes I do' — she now shook her head — 'I became inflamed with the injustice of it, one more piled on top of the others, and I . . . I told him what he was, a filthy old man.' She now turned her head and looked at the three men who were gazing at her, and when she caught the eye of Mack he bowed his head and she said to him, 'You know to what I am referring, don't you?' She didn't wait for an answer but, looking at Matthew again, she said, 'We . . . we must get away to . . . to that place, no matter what it is like.' Then glancing at Mack again, she asked, 'What's it really like, this place?'

'It's a fine place. You could make it as good as this any day; but it's fine as it stands, and they want out soon as possible.'

She nodded at him, then said, 'That settles it then,' and, releasing her hold on the table she went up the room and slumped into a chair.

Moving uneasily now, the men nodded towards Matthew, and it was Doug who said, 'You all right, Matt?' and Matthew answered, 'Yes, yes, I'm all right. Thanks.'

Without further words, one after the other filed out, and now Matthew, going to Tilly, looked down at her as he muttered, 'You actually hit him?' She lifted her head wearily and, her voice expressing her feelings, she said, 'No, I didn't hit him, I clawed at him. I drew blood and I hope he carries the marks for a long time.'

'Oh Tilly! Tilly!'

She gave a weary laugh. 'Very unladylike.'

'To hell with being ladylike! What I'm thinking is that I've caused you to suffer this, my dear.' He sat down near to her and, taking her hand, said, 'Nothing's gone right since we came here, but once we're on our own things will be different.'

She looked down at their joined hands. 'Rumours spread.

Fifty miles here is equal to a mile at home! I'll be known as a tainted woman, father and son.' She raised her eyes to him and the pain in them made him stretch out his arms to her, only for him to wince, and at the sight of his twisted face she said, 'Your arm . . . your arm, has it broken open?'

'No, no.' He shook his head. 'It's just that I haven't used it, not in that way for some time.' He smiled wryly now.

She looked anxiously at him as she said, 'You'll be able to ride?'

'Of course. Of course. And we'll go first thing in the morning, taking Manuel with us. He's an intelligent fellow and he knows the countryside well. There's not a chance of any of the others coming with us, not at the moment anyway. But when we're settled I think Doug will join us. He was saying as much just before you came in. Of course as I've said before, I think it's Katie that is the attraction, but what matter, he's a good fellow is Doug.'

'How long will it take?'

'To get there? Well, I don't suppose the way we travel we'll do more than forty to fifty miles a day; two days on the road there and we'll be able to settle matters in a day, and no matter what it's like we'll take it for the present, then two days back. Well, we could be settled in eight or nine days.'

'I can't believe it.' She leant her head against him now and her words were low, scarcely above a whisper, as she asked, 'You wouldn't want to return home, would you?' She waited for his answer without looking at him, and when it came his words, too, were low as he said, 'Never to live there, Tilly. Somehow this is my country. For good or bad it's where I want to be. I feel at home here as I've never felt in any place before. I can't explain it to you; I knew when I first set foot in it I wanted to live here and die here. But listen, my darling.' He lifted up her chin and looked deep into her sad eyes. 'Don't worry any more because once settled on our own, our life could become ideal.'

He bowed his head towards her, and when he placed his lips gently on hers she murmured to herself, Ideal. Ideal. But the picture the words presented brought no glow to her mind.

9

She was amazed at the beauty of the land. They had ridden for
the last half-hour through shoulder-high grass and had just
emerged on the high bank of a river. She was so impressed with
the sight that she could find no words with which to express
her feelings, but, like Matthew, she sat gazing down on the
slatey-blue water winding its way swiftly between golden
banks that looked from this distance like sand-strewn beaches;
and away in the near distance like a vivid painting lay a line of
purple hills. She had never seen such vivid colouring. On the
journey from Galveston to the ranch they had passed through
fine country but this was different, this had the appearance of a
mighty mural, in fact, she thought it looked too beautiful to be
real.

'Wonderful!'

She turned her head and looked at Matthew and repeated
'Wonderful! Yes, wonderful!' Then she asked, 'Will . . . Will
it be like this all the way?'

'No, I'm afraid not.' He shook his head. 'Over there' — he
pointed to the right — 'the land is like an endless pancake
except for a few cottonwood trees and grass.'

'It would be lovely to have a homestead here.'

'Not good for homestead, mistress.'

'No? Why?' She turned to Manuel.

'All hills, no pastures; hills no safe.'

'Oh.' She was about to ask, 'In what way not safe?' when
Matthew said, 'Well, we'd better be pushing on; the light will
soon be fading and we're some way from the trading post.'

For the next hour they rode by the river, and curiously the

hills seemed to remain the same distance away throughout the journey. Suddenly from twisting and turning through hillocks large and small, the land fell into a great flat expanse of nothingness again, and there, not a hundred yards from the river bank, stood a substantial timber-built trading post. In front of it were small groups of people, some standing, some leaning against what looked like a stout single pole fence that did not surround the post, merely ran along in front for a short distance. Others were squatting on the ground. And tethered to the fence were a number of small horses.

They were the first real Indians that Tilly had seen and it appeared that she was the first kind of white woman they had seen for those who were sitting rose from the ground and those who were leaning stood straight and with unblinking stares they watched her and the white man dismount. They watched the Mexican take their horses; then, their heads slowly turning, their eyes followed the progress of the tall thin woman whose walk was unsteady and who had to be aided by the sturdy young man up the steps and into the post; and slowly they drew together and gathered round the open doorway.

'Hello there. Pleased to see ya. How do you do, ma'am? Hello there, Manuel.' The man had inserted himself between Tilly and Matthew and was shouting through the doorway, 'Didn't know you were coming this way again. Thought you had settled with Portes. Hello, sir.' He had turned his attention to Matthew. 'What can I do for you?'

The tall, thin middle-aged, clean-shaven man who spoke with a strong Scottish accent and, unlike his countrymen, was anything but dour, now brought forward two wooden chairs, one swinging from each hand. The first he placed with a thud just behind Tilly's knees and she found herself sitting down without the effort. Then she looked to where Matthew was now seated and telling their host why they were here, where they were bound for, and that they would like to be put up for the night.

Tilly said nothing, she merely looked about her, all the while trying not to sneeze or to put her hands to her buttocks in an effort to ease the pain. She had been in a trading post before

298

but not one as well stocked as this. Against one wall was a rough wooden table and on it were stacked piles of skins which apparently had been graded into sets. Lying at right angles to it was a smaller bench on which was a jumble of pelts; on the other side of the room was a counter at the end of which was a pair of large brass scales and below them, on the floor, a weighing machine. In front of the counter was a row of sacks with their tops open, full, as far as she could guess, of grain or meal; and behind the counter were shelves holding an assortment of tins and bottles.

Against the other wall was set a line of tools: shovels, picks, hoes and ploughs. Behind this, high up on the wall, were a number of guns, large and small. The only two she could recognise were a Colt revolver and a German rifle. The latter type Matthew had already tried to get her to handle but she had found it difficult, cumbersome; the Colt he always said was for men, most useful when fighting on horseback. But what caught her eye and held it by its very incongruity in such a place was a glass case.

In this rough store it looked as much out of place as did the china cabinet in Alvero Portes's sitting-room. From this distance she could just make out that it held a number of trinkets, mostly strings of beads and cards studded with bright buttons.

'Well now, ma'am, have you viewed everything?'

Somewhat startled, her attention was brought to Mr Ian Mackintosh, for there could be only one such man to correspond with the name on the board at the door. 'You've had a good look round?'

'Yes; it's . . . it's fascinating.'

'That's the word, that's the word' — he wagged his hand at her — 'fascinating. Aye, Aye, that's the word. Everything about here is fascinating. But now I suppose you'd like to get the dust off you. Are you sleepin' in or out?' he said, turning to Matthew, and he, getting to his feet, asked, 'Have you accommodation?'

'That room there.'

He did not indicate the room by either a toss of his head or his thumb over his shoulder but with his heavy leather-booted foot which he scraped on the floor in a backward movement very like a horse pawing at the earth, then went on, 'Dollar a night, including bedding. Or you can use your own. Soap and towel provided.'

Tilly could see that Matthew was striving not to laugh outright and he spoke politely, saying, 'Thank you, Mr Mackintosh; we'll be pleased to take it.'

When Tilly was shown into the room she did not endorse Matthew's last remark, for it was quite bare except for three beds and a rough, a very rough hand-made wash-hand stand with a tin dish and jug on it, a piece of blue soap in a saucer, and a towel that would have been used for taking hot dripping tins from the oven back in the Manor.

But once the door was closed she smiled at Matthew and, pointing to the three beds, she said in a whisper, 'Is it likely we'll have company?'

'I shouldn't be surprised. . . .'

She had taken off her hat and coat, washed her face and hands, and was now sitting on the edge of the bed watching Matthew sluicing the water over his head when she said, 'Oh, I am stiff, all I want to do at this moment is lie on my face.'

'Tomorrow will be better.'

'So you say. Well, I hope so. By the way, those Indians out there, are they all right?'

'What's that?' He turned towards her now, blowing into the towel.

'I said those Indians out there, are they all right? They look . . . well. . . .'

'Oh yes; you needn't worry about them, they're from the reserves. A number of them will be scouts.'

'Scouts?'

'Yes; they scout for the army; all the forts have their Indian scouts. They can pick up a trail like a bloodhound, they know all the signs.'

'You mean they lead the soldiers on to their own people?'

'Aw, Tilly.' He now drew a comb through his thick stubbly hair as he said, 'It's no use, it's hardly any use explaining, I really don't understand it myself. There are so many tribes and

300

so many different camps inside a tribe and as far back as anybody can remember the tribes have been fighting each other, in places they've almost wiped each other out. I understand at one time there might be five thousand in one camp and that would be only one section of a tribe; and their rights and their laws would fill a hundred books. Someone some day will get down to it. I only hope it isn't a politician, because they will only hear one side of it. Anyway, let's go and see what our friend, Mr Ian Mackintosh, has to offer us in the way of supper.'

As she rose stiffly from the bed, she asked quietly, 'How is your arm?'

'Not as bad as I thought it would be; it's still strong enough to put round you.'

They stood close for a few moments looking at each other, until he said, 'I love you. Do you know that, woman? I love you. I love you more every day. I thought that when we married my feelings couldn't possibly grow stronger, they were so intense then, but now . . . well, it is strange but the intensity has taken on a kind of. . . .' He paused and turned his head away and she asked gently, 'Kind of what?'

'Fear.'

'*Fear?*'

'Yes, fear. I've never really known what it was to be afraid until now and I have this strange fear on me that I am . . . well, too happy where you are concerned; even with what happened back there and the irritations that he's forced upon me during the last few months, these should have been predominant in my mind, but no, they have been pressed down by this real kind of fear that —'again he bowed his head, but now she didn't speak she simply waited and when he looked at her again he ended, 'that I may lose you.'

'Aw, don't be silly, my dear.' She was now holding him tightly. 'You'll never lose me. Nothing or no one can separate us. If he didn't, and Josefina didn't, no one can, not now. The only thing that can separate us is death, and not even that because we're so joined, we're so one in every way that if I go first I'll wait for you. I know this inside myself.' She tapped her breast. 'Perhaps that really is the witch part of me . . . and you'll do the same. I feel that wherever we're meant to go after death we'll fight against it until we can go on together.'

'Oh, Tilly! Tilly, there's no one in the whole world like you, no one.' His voice had a catch in it; and now they hid their faces in each other's shoulder and remained still.

It was just after first light next morning when they left the trading post. Tilly was so stiff she didn't know how she rose from the bed, and when she stumbled and almost upset the single candle that was their only form of light Matthew caught her, and pressing her down on the bed again, he massaged her limbs, laughing at her as he did so. She had always been amazed at his good humour first thing in the morning, so different from his father's, for Mark's temper had been taciturn during the early part of the day.

They hoped to reach their destination in three hours' time, do what business had to be done and be back at the trading post this evening. In fact, Matthew had not only paid for their bed in advance but had paid for the entire room. They had been lucky last night to have the place to themselves, but as Mr Mackintosh had explained that was unusual.

The countryside had changed again. They were riding now among low hills, crossing streams, some small and some not so small. They were surprised, at least Tilly was when, passing through a narrow gully, to see stationed on one of its heights a man in uniform with a gun at his side. Matthew and Manuel had also seen the man. They drew rein for a moment; then Manuel, turning to Tilly, smiled as he said, 'He's the soldiery, one of the new cavalry.'

'What's that?' Matthew asked.

'There are bands of cavalry about now, sent to fight the Indians.'

As they rode out of the gully, they came upon a company breaking camp. The situation was in a depression bordered on two sides by hills and Manuel, looking about him, spoke now in rapid Spanish, then turning to Matthew, he said, 'Good bed to die in.'

Before Matthew had time to make any retort a young man marched smartly up to them. By his uniform he looked to be an officer and he spoke as one in command in a rather high-falutin manner, saying, 'Captain Dixon at your service, sir. And may I enquire your destination?'

Matthew stared down at the man for a moment; then with a wry smile, he said, with not a little mimicry in his tone, 'Matthew Sopwith at your service, sir, and our destination, as I understand it, is about five miles from Cameron.'

'Oh yes; Cameron. Well, that's all right.' He now turned and looked up at Tilly and, bowing slightly, he greeted her with one word, 'Ma'am,' and she in return merely inclined her head towards him.

The officer again turned to Matthew and said, 'I'd be obliged if I could have a word with you, sir.'

Matthew glanced first at Tilly and then at Manuel before dismounting and walking away with the captain towards where the men were now standing by their horses.

Tilly gazed at the soldiers. Most of them looked young. They were all staring towards her except for a sergeant who now began to shout unintelligible orders.

Within a few minutes Matthew returned, the officer with him. After mounting his horse again he looked down into the clean-shaven face and said, 'I wish you good-day.'

The officer said nothing, he merely stepped back and saluted, then waited for them to ride on.

As they passed the group of soldiers the sergeant was still barking his orders at them, but it didn't stop the men from casting their glances in Tilly's direction, and when she smiled at them she was answered instantly by wide grins.

But they were hardly out of earshot of the men when she rode abreast of Matthew and said, 'What did he want to say to you?'

'Oh, nothing. It strikes me he's very young to the game and he wouldn't have much chance of keeping that rabble in hand if it wasn't for the sergeant.'

'Matthew' — the tone of her voice brought his head round — 'don't keep anything from me, please.'

He blinked his eyes, then wet his lips before he said, 'Well, I'll tell you what he said. He suggested that we didn't go back to the trading post tonight, he thought we should make for the fort.'

'Because of danger?'

'Oh no!' He shook his head. 'I happened to mention that we stayed at the trading post and he didn't think it was any fit place for a lady such as you.'

She stared at him for a while before she said, 'Honest?'

'Honest; why should I lie?'

Yes, why should he lie.

'Come on,' he said; 'let's put a move on. I want to see this place.' And at that he galloped ahead while she urged her horse after him and Manuel came up in the rear. Manuel, she had noticed, like most Mexicans, became part of the animal he sat on. She had heard it said that it was from the Mexicans the Indians first learned how to ride and were now so famous in their handling of horses that they had become known as the horse Indians and, besides, so infamous that the very name of them chilled the blood.

They neared the homestead about eleven o'clock. They stopped on a rise, the three of them in a row, and looked down on it, and Tilly's eyes brightened and her face went into a broad smile before she turned to Matthew and said, 'Oh, isn't it nice?'

The house was long and low, with a verandah running along its front. This was supported by stout pillars. It had a wood shingle roof, and one end of it was covered with creeper. On three sides there was a white railing and on the fourth a large stockade, but dominating the whole scene was an outsize barn. It was higher and wider than the house and the other outbuildings all put together.

She felt Matthew letting out a deep sigh and when she looked at him his eyes were waiting for hers and he said simply, 'It was made for us; and if the outside's anything to go by, the inside should be all right too.'

'That won't matter, I'll make it all right.' She smiled at him, then turned her head to Manuel and said simply, 'It looks good.'

304

'Good. Yes, good. Hans Meyer good man. Work along here one time . . . good man but no more.'

When he shook his head she said, 'He has gone?'

He now pointed towards the earth and she put in quietly, 'Dead?'

'Dead.'

She turned to Matthew saying, 'Did you know this?'

'No; I know as little about them as you do. But come, we'll soon find out.'

It was as if Frau Meyer were waiting for their approach for she met them outside the white railings and, extending her hand first to Matthew and then Tilly, she spoke with a strong German accent. 'You velcome, very velcome. You kom sooner than I expect.'

'You expected us?'

The small woman nodded at Matthew, her round face one bright smile as she said, 'Oh yes, I knew early tis morning.'

Both Matthew and Tilly looked at each other, and it was Tilly who asked now, 'But how?'

'Oh, scout on his way to fort, he told me of your presence and vy.'

Matthew gave a brief laugh now as he said, 'Quicker than smoke signals.'

'Yes, yes, quicker 'n smoke signals, but do to kom in. You are very velcome, very velcome.'

Tilly found the inside of the house as pleasing as the outside. The furniture was all wooden and hand-made but with a difference, for there was a touch of artistry about every piece in the room from the dresser to the row of wooden mugs arranged on a shelf to the side of the fireplace, very much like the pieces of brass that used to bedeck the mantelpiece in her granny's cottage. The floor-boards had been sand-scrubbed and were covered here and there with bright hand-made rugs.

Tilly saw that the room was both living-room and kitchen. There were two doors going off it that spoke of other rooms, and at one end a steep wooden staircase that led to the floor above.

305

'I have meal ready for you, I am sure you hungry. . . . You vill eat?'

'Yes. Yes, thank you very much. It is so kind of you, but tell me.' Tilly now glanced at Matthew, who had seated himself in a rocking-chair and was looking silently about the room, evidently pleased with everything he saw. 'Are you really thinking of selling this place, your . . . your home?'

'Yes.' The answer was brief; and then she put in, 'Your name is?'

'Mrs Sopwith.'

'Me, I am Anna Meyer. And yes, I must sell, for my children I must sell. Big Hans, my husband, he die two years. Little Hans he is twelve years and not strong, never like big Hans and Berta. She is nine years. No life for small children. Be very strong to stand life here.'

'Have you no men, I mean hands around the place?' It was Matthew who asked the question now, and Frau Meyer turned to him and said, 'We had two, Johann Braun and Franz Klein. They very good ven big Hans was here but not so good ven he was gone. Then they leave like that' — she snapped her finger — 'to go to gold mine. Gold rush been on a long time and they don't go, but sudden they go like that.' Again she snapped her finger.

'They just walked out and left you?' Matthew's brows were puckered now, and she nodded at him and said, 'Yes, they valk out. Vanted double pay. I couldn't pay double pay. They say that ven they came back I'd be glad to pay double pay, place get in bad state, but I von't be bullied or frightened so I sell and take my children back to Germany. I have been here twenty year but it is not home. I long for home. I have sisters and brothers my children have not seen.'

'Did you build all this yourselves?'

'Yes, nothing here when ve came. Big Hans and me ve vork all time. Ve make small huts first, not this.' She smiled now as she waved her hand. 'Then ve buy cattle, and horses, one, two and three, four, and on and on. Then ve build barn. Many hands to build barn but many hands come by this way in those days 'fore gold rush, and lots of help from good friends. Then

last, 'fore my son is born twelve years since, ve build again.'
She waved her hand. 'This vas not finished ven he kom, and he
saw first light there.' She pointed to a space before the stove.
'But now' — she turned away and walked towards a table that
was fully set for a meal — 'all is finished. Life is split ven man
goes, power leaves your arm. But kom, you vill vant to refresh
yourself 'fore you eat, and I vill call my Hans and Berta to the
table.'

They ate a substantial meal, joined by Manuel and Frau
Meyer's two children. Young Hans touched Tilly's heart
immediately, for she had seen so many pale faces like his
back in England and heard the same sharp cough. Then there
was Berta. There was nothing wrong with Berta; she was a
bright replica of her mother, her eyes laughing, her tongue
chattering.

After the meal they made an inspection of the outbuildings
and both Matthew and Tilly expressed their amazement at the
size of the barn. It had looked big from outside but inside it
appeared enormous. It was filled mostly with dried hay but
there were also sacks of grain and animal feed, yet there was
still room enough left to drive a cart and horse into it. There
were four milking cows and three calves, and some chickens.
Following this, they mounted their horses and rode round the
extent of the land. In one corral there was a herd of crossed
mustangs, and Matthew noticed straightaway that, as horse-
flesh went, they were of little account; but that didn't matter,
the land was good and included in it there was a large stretch of
woodland to the east. Its presence explained the extensive outbuildings and the well-built house.

Altogether he was delighted with the place and showed it.
The only thing that remained now to be settled was the question of the price.

Back in the house, drinking strong black coffee, he looked at
Anna Meyer and said, 'Well now, Mrs Meyer, what are you
asking for your place?'

The little woman joined her hands together and rubbed one
over the other as if washing them and she moved her head in

small jerks before she said, 'Eight hundred dollars. No less, no less.'

He opened his mouth as he stared at her. Then he looked towards Tilly and shook his head, and Mrs Meyer, taking the action that her price was too high, began to talk rapidly, her words interspersed with German, as she went on to explain about all the work they had put in; there was the stock and the land they had cultivated, and then this house.

Matthew was smiling widely when he held up his hand and said, 'Please, I am not disagreeing with your price, I am only surprised at its moderation.'

'Oh!' Mrs Meyer now dropped on to a chair and her round face slid into a smile and it broadened as she listened to Matthew saying, 'I will add half to that and gladly.'

'Oh, tank you, tank you.' Mrs Meyer now rose to her feet and held out her hand towards Matthew; then looking at Tilly, she said, 'You satisfied?'

'Oh yes, yes.' Tilly nodded at her quickly. 'And I love the house.' She spread her arms wide. 'I haven't seen one I like better. Oh I noticed some more pretentious ones in Galveston but I am sure they weren't half as comfortable.'

Showing her pleasure in the brightness of her face, Anna Meyer now said, 'I have only seen Galveston once; but I have seen Mr Houston, that vas an honour ven he kom to Caldvell. All vent mad to see him.' She waved her hand in a circle, and at this Matthew asked, 'Who is your nearest neighbour? We passed a number of homesteads further along the trail.'

'That would be the Owens, and further on there are the McKnights. They are about five miles back. Oh, there are plenty of neighbours that vay back, scattered but plenty. Not so many that vay. Austin is over there.' She waved her hand to the side. 'And far beyond in that direction,' she swooped her arm round, 'to the Comanche country.'

'Do you . . . I mean have you had any Indian raids this far?'

Anna Meyer now put her head to one side and lifted her shoulders as she said, 'Not for some years. Too many forts and Rangers; they good as Indians in fighting. The ve first kom in the third year, yes; but Big Hans and the three Vaqueros fought them off. The only thing they did was to burn our prairie-schooner.'

'Prairie-schooner?' Tilly twisted up her face in enquiry and Anna Meyer laughed as she said, 'The vagon that ve kom in; Ve call it prairie-schooner.'

'Oh! prairie-schooner.' Tilly looked at Matthew, and he repeated, 'prairie-schooner'; and they both laughed as he said, 'Good name for it, because they had to sail some rough seas, those wagons.'

'Yes, yes, rough seas.'

It was after Matthew and Tilly had spent some time doing another round of the outbuildings when they heard the boy and the mother talking. They were passing the open back door of the house and the boy was saying, 'We are really going, Mama?' and the answer came with what sounded like a deep, deep note of relief, 'Really going, my son. Really going.'

It was then that Tilly looked at Matthew and said, 'Such a lovely place, why are they so anxious to leave do you think?'

'Well, you heard what she said. And I can understand it: men don't work for a woman like they do for a man, at least not a timid little creature like she is. She's too kind, she'd be taken advantage of.'

A moment or so later, standing near the white railing, Tilly leaned her back against it and spread her arms along the top and looked up towards the sky as she said, 'I never thought I'd ever settle here because somehow I felt I wasn't cut to the mould. I didn't seem to fit in like any of the women I've met. I could be as strong as them in body but not in the spirit it takes to pioneer. I would have stayed . . . oh yes, because of you.'

She turned her head and glanced at Matthew, then went on, 'But now, here in this place, I've got a feeling I've come to the end of something, or to the beginning of something. For the first time since I stepped on to this soil I've got a feeling of peace in me, as if I'm on the point of beginning a new life.'

Matthew came and stood in front of her. He said nothing, but, taking her arms from the railings, he brought her hands together and to his chest and he pressed them there; then bending his head, he kissed them.

When the little girl came running up to them they both turned and beamed down on her, and she said, 'Mama says will you stay tonight?' Then looking from one to the other she pleaded, 'Please do stay. It will be lovely. And Hans will play on his whistle for you and I will dance. I know how to dance.' She lifted up her long print skirt and exposed her tiny ankles, then to their merriment she executed a few hopping dance steps.

Tilly looked at Matthew. His face was unsmiling now, it was as if he were considering, gravely considering. Then he turned to her, saying brightly, 'Well, what about it? There's no hurry really.'

Tilly paused for a moment as she thought of the children. But the children were with Katie, and so she said, 'Why not? Why not?'

So it was arranged that they stay the night; and just as all decisions bear fruit, so this one altered the course of their lives.

10

The evening was sweet and calm. They sat on the verandah, Frau Meyer and her two children, Matthew, Tilly and Manuel.

Manuel was good company; he amused the children and them all with imitating the cries and calls of birds and animals, pulling his long, lean face into various shapes in the process.

Hans played his whistle while Berta danced to it on the smooth boards of the verandah. The evening seemed perfect.

When the moon came up and a chill spread over the land they went indoors; all except Manuel, who had arranged a warm place to sleep in the barn.

Indoors they did not immediately disperse to bed, there was so much to talk about, so much, Tilly considered, to learn from this little woman whom she wouldn't see again after tomorrow morning, that it was a full hour before they began to say their good-nights.

Both Matthew and Tilly had refused to take Frau Meyer's room whilst she slept on a palliasse in the living-room. His wife, Matthew lied loudly, was used to sleeping rough; not that sleeping on the floor of this comfortable room could be considered roughing it. . . .

It was all of half an hour later when they lay enfolded in each other's arms, talking in whispers about their plans for the future, that they heard the cry or rather the scream from outside. This was followed by the sound of a gun shot.

Almost as one they rolled out of the blankets and were on their feet. Matthew had been sleeping in his small clothes but Tilly had on a night-dress, and as she grabbed for a coat he rushed to the corner of the room where his pack and rifle lay, and he was already kneeing by the window when Frau Meyer scrambled down the ladder, the two children tumbling close behind her.

'Vat is it? Vat is it?' Then she added on a high cry, 'Oh no! Oh no!'

'Have you a gun?'

'Yes, yes.' She answered Matthew's words by running to a cupboard at the side of the mantelpiece and there she took out two guns and after thrusting one into her young son's hands, they both ran to the further window at the other side of the door.

'Is your back door barred?'

'Yes.'

'Your windows upstairs, are they open?'

'No, no.'

The questions and answers were thrown back and forward in whispers.

Tilly was kneeling on the floor at the other side of the window opposite to Matthew. She was holding the Colt revolver in her shaking hand, and Matthew didn't look at her as he said under his breath, 'It isn't a bear this time, so remember what I told you.'

Oh my God! My God! She did not say the words aloud but they kept revolving in her mind. The children and Katie, what would they do? Oh my God! don't let it be Indians. Please, please God, don't let it be Indians.

When the lighted brand flashed up past the window and on to the roof she knew it was Indians; and when another one flashed upwards Matthew said, 'They can't do any harm, there's no straw there.' Then again he added, 'Remember what I said.'

The next minute Tilly closed her eyes tightly against the unearthly scream. When she opened them again it was to see Indians, mad, excited, bloodlust Indians for the first time. She did not know how many, but the verandah seemed full of them; then they were battering at the door.

When she heard Matthew firing, she, too, pulled the trigger

312

of the Colt, and she was amazed to see a man fall backwards
below the end of the room as the whole window was burst in,
and almost at the same time there came through it three terrifying creatures. She did not see Frau Meyer fall, she only heard a
long high moan and the children screaming. Then Matthew
fired again and one of the Indians grasped at his neck. As
Matthew reloaded his gun, she too fired, then she knew a
moment of agony as she saw young Hans clutch his chest.
There was no time to think, Oh God! Oh God! what have I
done? for the two demons were almost on top of them. The
very sight of them was so terrifying that it paralysed her finger
on the trigger. They were like devils out of hell; their heads
were crowned with buffalo skulls, the horns giving them every
appearance of devils. Their faces and bare trunks were
painted, and round their necks hung strings of bones.

She saw the axe lifted and about to cleave Matthew's head in
two, but as he lifted the gun, which he had been unable to load,
to ward off the blow and fell the Indian, the axe cleaved
through his shoulders and he fell on to his side. It was then that
she fired again, but she didn't see the man fall for his companion had gripped her by the hair. He, too, had an axe in his
hand but he didn't use it on her. As he pulled her forward she
fell over Matthew and her face and night-dress were covered
with his blood. As her hands sought for something to grip to
check herself being dragged outside she found nothing to stay
her progress. Her screams were ringing in her ears. The roots
of her hair were being dragged from her head. She was on her
knees now, then on her belly, and her hands still flailing for a
hold found something. It was the stout leg of a cupboard and as
she hung on to it for a moment her other hand passed over a
known object. It was the Colt. How she brought her arms
upwards she never knew, she only knew that she was firing at
random, and after the third shot the hold on her hair was
released. And when this happened she didn't pause to rest but
jerked herself to her knees to see the fearful creature bending
over double and holding his guts while he stared down at her.
She watched his mouth open into one great gap. He now
turned his great twisted painted face from her and looked at his

two companions lying in contorted heaps on the floor among the rest; then he swung about and stumbled back to the window and fell through it on to the verandah.

Dragging herself to her feet, she walked backwards, the gun still in her hand. At the top of the room she almost fell over Matthew's bloody body and, like one sleep-walking she ignored it and looked out of the window and there she saw what appeared to her to be a strange sight, for standing clear in the moonlight were two other fearsome Indians and they were helping the wounded one down the steps. She watched them dragging him across to the railings where the horses were tethered.

The scene was as light as day for now the moon was assisted by the flames from the barn. She saw the two Indians now gesticulating towards the house again as if they were coming back, and she stood rigid for a moment until she saw them mount their horses and move off. And then there settled on the whole place a quiet, a peaceful quiet such as had enveloped it not more than half an hour ago.

Oh my God! Oh dear God! Oh my God! She must do something. But what? She was going to faint. In this moment she remembered telling herself many years ago that it was only ladies in church who fainted, but she was going to faint now. No! No! Matthew, Matthew. She found herself kneeling by him and she closed her eyes tightly for a moment and bowed her head over his arm that was almost cleaved from his body. Slowly she laid her ear to his chest, never expecting for a moment to hear a beat, but when she did, she became galvanised into life and, looking around wildly, she grabbed at the rough holland sheet in which they had lain such a short while ago and, tearing it into strips, she set about aiming to join the arm to the shoulder. When she saw this was hopeless she simply bound the strips tightly around his chest and the great bleeding gap. But when his life blood soaked the sheet immediately she quickly rolled a piece of the linen into a flattish ball and pressed it into the gap, then pushed the arm against it and bound it with the remainder of the sheeting. Then she straightened out his legs and put a pillow under his head; after which she bowed her body over his unconscious one and whispered, 'Don't go, Matthew. Don't go. Oh my love, don't go.'

Slowly now, she pulled herself to her feet and for the first time she looked about her. And again she felt she was going to faint, for now she was looking past the two dead Indians to the crumpled Frau Meyer, whose head looked like a bright red ball. Closing her eyes she muttered, 'Oh Christ Almighty! Why? Why?' When she opened them again she was looking at little Hans.

Well, perhaps he had died mercifully. She had heard that they took children as captives and of what happened to them. But to think that she had shot him. Where was Berta? And Manuel?

She heard herself screaming now, 'Berta! Manuel!' For the first time the door was opened. Throwing the bar aside, she rushed on to the verandah and down the steps; and there she stopped and now she knew that she was going to faint, she must faint to get away from this sight, and as she sank to the ground she kept crying, 'No! No! not to little Berta.' What kind of creature would knock the brains out of a child against a post?

As she came out of the black depths into consciousness she knew she was being carried and the first thing she did was to scream, until a voice said, 'There now, there now, you're all right.'

She tried to open her eyes but she couldn't, and the voice said, 'Lay her down here.'

Someone was holding her head now and someone was making her swallow a liquid which burnt her throat. She coughed, and gradually she looked upwards and she thought for a moment it was a dream, that she must have fallen asleep after looking at that captain this morning, because here he was again bending over her, calling her ma'am.

She hung on to the thought of it being a dream until she heard the voice say softly, 'We've got him out, sir, but he's almost burnt to a cinder.' And then she knew it was no dream, it was Manuel they were talking about; and once more she was screaming, but sitting up now screaming, 'Matthew! Matthew!'

'It's all right. It's all right, ma'am; they're seeing to him.'

She was staring into a rough looking face now and she recognised the voice. It was the sergeant who had kept bellowing, and now she spoke to him in a voice that was a croak: 'My husband?'

'They've strapped him up, ma'am. We'll get him to a doctor as soon as possible. Do you think you're fit to ride?'

'Yes, yes.' She tried to struggle to her feet but had to lean on the sergeant's arm, and now she asked dully, 'The others?' for she had forgotten for a moment what she had seen, and the sergeant turned his eyes away from her as he asked, 'How many were there?'

'The mother, and her two children, then Manuel, our guide, and my husband. . . .'

He still kept his head turned away as he shook it and muttered, 'Well, ma'am, I'm sorry to say 'tis only you and your husband who are left.'

'Oh my God! My God!'

'Indeed! Indeed, my God! ma'am. Indeed! Indeed! But we'll get the maniacs, we'll get 'em, never fear. They're on the warpath all along the line, but they'll suffer for it. Aye ma'am, they'll suffer for it, 'cos so are we, so are we, we're on the warpath an' all. Oh ay.'

'Other places too?'

'Yes, other places too, ma'am. It's been a night of blood all right.'

'I . . . I must go to my husband.'

The sergeant now supported her up the steps and into the room. She was surprised to see no bodies on the floor, only Matthew, and she saw immediately that he was conscious for he looked at her for a moment but he had no power to speak.

'He's all right, ma'am, but he's lost a great deal of blood. We'll get him to the fort as soon as possible.'

'Home.' The word was a whisper and both the sergeant and the captain, who had now come on the scene, bent over him, and it was the captain who spoke, saying, 'You must see a

316

doctor, we'll have to take you to the fort first.'

'Home.'

The captain now drew Tilly aside, saying, 'If his wound isn't stitched up ma'am, he'll bleed to death. We can have him in the fort within an hour and a half. Do you agree with me?'

'Yes.' She nodded wearily.

'We'll have to carry him by sling, but once there they'll be able to provide a cart.'

'Thank you.'

She looked around the room, then closed her eyes tightly as the tears rained down her face. And now she spluttered, 'It was so peaceful, so beautiful,' and the captain replied, 'I have no doubt, ma'am, I have no doubt. But they have a habit of breaking the peace, in all ways they have a habit of breaking the peace. But I warned your husband this morning for there's been unrest all along the line. There were a number of raids last week, and once they start they go on until their lust is dry, or until we manage to finish them first. . . . Come, there is nothing you can do here.'

When he put his arm out towards her she raised her head and looked down at her blood-smeared coat and night-gown, and now she said simply, 'I must dress,' and he answered, 'Yes, of course, ma'am. Yes, of course,' and both he and the sergeant turned briskly about and went out.

She got into her clothes, all the while looking down on Matthew's dead white face and inert body. And as she did so she silently asked, 'Why should this happen to us? We could have gone back. I could have insisted. I should have insisted. But no, I seem fated to bring people to their deaths. Little Hans. But the Indians would have got him anyway, if we hadn't stayed, or he would have soon died from the disease that was eating him up. But why should it fall to me to shoot him? Oh God, why don't you give me an answer? Why am I plagued like this?'

The moon was still high when they placed Matthew in a canvas sling and four of the soldiers carried him out. Then, supporting her, the sergeant led her down the steps and lifted her bodily on to a horse, and when he spoke to one of the soldiers the man mounted and rode close to her, putting his hand out now and again to steady her in the saddle.

There was a numbness on her now and she had a great desire to sleep. Automatically she would turn from time to time to look back towards the men carrying the sling.

The tiredness lifted from her somewhat when, it seemed eons later, she passed through two big gates and into a stockade and what appeared to her a confused bustle of soldiers and civilians . . . and Indians.

Her eyes, wide now, focused on the Indians. They alone weren't moving about, they were in one corner of the stockade, and when the soldier assisted her down from the horse she turned and stared open-mouthed towards them as if as much in surprise at seeing women and children among them. Some of them were lying on the ground and some were standing, but they were all motionless.

When dully she turned to go towards the men with the sling two women came and, standing one on either side of her, moved her away towards some steps and up them into a room. This room, too, seemed packed. At one end were cot beds with people lying in them, their heads and arms bandaged. There were also men lying on the floor.

The women sat her in a chair and one of them said, 'Where are you hurt, my dear?' and she shook her head at them, then pointed to where the soldiers were carrying the sling into the room, and she said, 'My husband.' The words came out on a rasping sound.

Her throat was dry as if she had been swallowing sand and when one of the women said, 'Drink this,' she gulped at the water, then pushing the women aside, she now stumbled up to where they had laid Matthew on the floor. It was near a table on which a man was working. She noted he was wearing a rubber apron and that every part of him seemed covered in blood, even his face, and when he looked down towards the sling his voice was a growl as he said, 'What's it here now?'

As she went to say this was her husband who was very ill, the captain came to the table and drew the man to one side.

318

A few minutes later they lifted a still form off the table and put Matthew on to it.

The women were at her side again. One had a very soft voice and she said, 'Come, my dear. Come.'

'No! No!' Her old strength was back in her arms and she thrust them forcibly from her, much to their surprise, and watched the sheeting being unwound from Matthew's body. And when the man pulled the pad away and unwound the last binding and she looked on the great, gaping hole she closed her eyes tightly for a moment; then they sprang open again as the man said, 'I can do nothing with this; let's have it off.'

When she saw him lift the chopper, an ordinary chopper, it was as if the Indians had come back to finish the job they had started, and when it came down through the remainder of the bone and Matthew's arm fell to the ground she let out a high, piercing scream and went to rush forward, but there were arms about her and she was literally carried down the room. When she screamed again someone poured something down her throat and the soothing voice said, 'There now. There now, my dear. He couldn't feel it, he was unconscious.'

She was gulping on the liquid that was still being poured into her mouth. She prayed to God to make her faint again but He didn't answer her prayer, instead He made her vomit. The good meal that she had eaten the night before, the main dish of which had been roast hog, came bursting up; but when her retching was over they again poured something down her throat.

After a while she became quiet inside, but she fought against it because this was no time to sleep, she must be with Matthew. Matthew! Matthew! Oh, my love. My love. His father had lost both feet and now he had lost his arm.

Why God? Why?

She was lying on a bed when she awoke. The sun was streaming through a small square of window. She lay looking about her; the quietness was still on her, yet she was aware of all that had happened.

A door opened and a woman entered. She was tall and thin,

almost as tall as herself she noted, and she recognised her voice when she spoke. 'There you are, my dear,' she said. 'Do you feel rested?'

Tilly stared up at her. There were questions in her mind, words in her mouth, but somehow she couldn't get them through her lips. When the hand came on her head and stroked her hair and the voice said, 'Your husband has regained consciousness,' she came up in the bed like a spring; but the woman held her by the shoulder, saying, 'Now, now, he's all right. He has lost a great deal of blood and he is very weak, but otherwise he's all right.'

'You are sure?'

'Yes, yes. I am sure. Now if you would like to refresh yourself you will find everything you need inside there.' She pointed to a door. 'When you're ready you might eat a little breakfast; and then you can go to him.'

'I . . . I couldn't eat, but . . . but I must see him.'

'You will see him, dear. Come.' She helped her from the bed, then again pointed to the door.

The room was a sort of closet, not unlike the one back in the nursery of the Manor. A bucket stood underneath a wooden framework on which was a round seat; there was a bench holding a basin and jug, also a table with a small mirror on it.

The table was opposite the lavatory seat and whilst she sat she looked at the face staring back at her. There was no recognition in the eyes. She seemed to be looking at an old woman, an eyeless old woman with great dark sockets where the pupils had been.

When she came out of the room the woman was waiting for her. She had put a tray on the foot of the bed and Tilly, looking at it, shook her head, then said, 'Thank you, but . . . but I couldn't eat anything.'

'Well, drink this coffee.'

She had merely sipped at the coffee when she said, 'Please, please, let me see him.'

The woman hesitated for a moment, then on a gentle sigh she said, 'Come along then.'

She remembered the room with the cot beds in it and the

table at the end of it and, too, the man in the rubber apron, but she didn't remember the smell; it was a mixture of blood and sweat and singed hair.

The man was still at the table, but he had a clean apron on and his face was no longer spattered with blood. He glanced towards her but said nothing, and the woman turned her gently and led her to a cot at the end of the room. Now she was looking down on a man who had changed as much as she had in the last twelve hours.

Matthew had his eyes open. The colour of them was the only recognisable thing about him. She leant forward and her face hung above his for what seemed an interminable time, then gently she laid her lips against his. But there was no pressure from them. When she raised her head his lips moved and he whispered, 'Tilly.'

'Oh, my love.' Her words weren't even audible to herself, her throat was dry, she felt she was about to choke.

'Tilly.'

'Yes, my dear?'

'Home.'

'Yes, my dear, we're going home. Lie quiet now, we're going home.'

She slowly raised herself upwards and was about to turn to the woman at her side when the voice of the doctor rasped through the room, saying, 'Let the filthy buggers wait. If I had my way I'd burn the lot this minute right in the compound, there, and slowly. Aye, slowly.'

There were a number of people attending to the wounded and they all stopped what they were doing and looked towards the table. A man in uniform was speaking to the doctor. His voice was low so that what he said did not reach the listeners; but the doctor's reply to him did, and what he cried now was, 'Sanctions, treaties, what do they know those sitting on their backsides down there? Tell them to come out here and they'll damn soon see what their sanctions and treaties are worth. . . . Sanctions and treaties!' He actually spat the last words.

Now the officer's voice was louder and stiff as he said, 'They need attention. Because they act like savages it doesn't mean we've got to retaliate in the same way. Shoot them, yes, but don't let them die in agony.'

'Oh, away with you! Don't talk such bloody claptrap to me! Die in agony, you said.' The doctor's hand holding an implement on which the sun glinted flashed in the air for a moment, then as he bent over the patient on the table he cried, 'Sometimes I wonder which side the bloody army's on. The Rangers don't ask questions, they act.'

'You'll hear more about this.' The words were low and muttered, and the officer now turned abruptly and marched towards the door where a soldier smartly opened it, and his last words were not inaudible but plain for all to hear as he said, 'Drunken fool!'

When Tilly looked at the woman at her side who had her head bent low she paused for a long moment before she asked her, 'Who . . . who am I to see for a conveyance?'

The woman slowly raised her head and for the first time Tilly saw that she, too, looked old. Yet she was younger than herself. 'I'm sorry' she said; 'he's . . . he's worn out, my husband's worn out. Two days and nights he's been working with hardly a rest.'

A doctor's wife in this place, in this shambles of a place. She glanced now towards the still form on the bed. Matthew's eyes were closed. She herself was here in this shambles because of love for a man, and this girl, for she was little more than a girl, was here too because of love for her man. Love. Love was a chain that dragged you through pity and compassion to places like this.

The young woman had hold of her arm again and was leading her out of the room. And now she was in the stockade and seeing it really for the first time. A large space surrounded by a stout high wall of timbers, just below the top of which ran a platform and on it dotted here and there were soldiers. The stockade itself was buzzing with life and the incongruity that struck her immediately was that of a small group of children playing at one side and the group of Indians huddled in a corner at the other side. There were few of them standing now and when her glance stayed on them she could see the reason

322

for the officer demanding the doctor's attention. Yet in this moment there was no pity in her for them because the sight of them was overshadowed by the picture of little Berta's hairless skull and spattered brains, and she saw them for a moment heaped on the bonfire that the doctor had envisaged.

The doctor's wife had taken her by the arm and she was now being shown into the colonel's office. The colonel was a short man with a beard and he rose from behind his desk and bowed towards her, then pointed to a seat and as if to waste no words, he came straight to the point, saying, 'It would be unwise for you to travel without an escort and I have no soldiers to spare at the moment. Moreover, your husband would be better resting for a few days, anyway until the countryside has settled down again.'

'How . . . how far have they got?' she asked.

He understood her question and answered it immediately by saying, 'I'm not sure. I have three patrols out. The one that brought you and your husband in yesterday reported four other homesteads ravished. You can consider yourself fortunate, for there were no other survivors, that is unless they took some prisoners.'

She said now, 'I . . . I have left my children with friends. I am very anxious to return.'

'You live, I understand, just beyond Boonville. Well, I don't think they will have got that far. But again, you never know, they are unpredictable. Years ago, they thought of them as being so far away on the plains that they could never reach San Antonio; but they reached it and passed it and made for Gonzales. And people in the border area were always prepared for them, and they weren't soft-footed new settlers, they were Americans born and bred. Both they and their forefathers had fought Mexicans and the Indians time and time again, yet what happened on that August day? Well, it's history and I suppose you've heard all about it so I've no need to go over it, but the point I'm making is we never underestimate the length an Indian, especially a horse Indian, a Comanche, can ride, and so you'll understand, Mrs Sopwith, that it would be very unwise for you to travel without a full escort until we're sure that it is safe for you to do so.'

'When . . . when will your men be riding that way?'

'None of my men patrol as far east as that but we could be having a company of Rangers dropping in at any time, they brought in some wounded last night. Yet again, the way things are at present I doubt if you'd be able to travel in their company; the best we can do for your husband on such a journey is to loan you a flat wagon, and in his condition that would have to be driven carefully. I'm afraid you'll have to have patience, Mrs Sopwith.'

She stared at him for a moment before rising to her feet, and as he rose stiffly from his chair the door opened and a sergeant saluted, then stood to attention.

'Yes, what is it, sergeant?' The colonel and the other officer in the room were looking towards the sergeant and he said in a voice that held a strong Irish accent, ' 'Tis Captain Collins's Rangers have come away in, sir. They have six wounded with them and there's a Ranger McNeill who asks for a word with you, sir.'

Before the colonel had a chance to answer him Tilly swung round, crying now, 'Ranger McNeill? Michael McNeill?'

The sergeant still standing stiffly turned his head towards her saying, ' 'Tis what he said his name was, ma'am.'

Tilly did not take leave of the colonel but turned and rushed to the door, and there she actually threw herself into the arms of Mack and he held her for a moment, embarrassment on his face as he looked over his shoulder at the three men standing within the open door. Then gently disengaging himself, he said, 'It's all right,' and looking at the colonel and saluting, he said, 'Ranger Michael McNeill, sir. I had leave of Captain Collins to speak with you, but now. . . .' he ended lamely. Then looking at Tilly again, he asked quietly, 'Matt, is he all right?'

She shook her head, but before she had time to answer him the colonel said, 'Tell Captain Collins I would like a word with him.'

'Yes, sir.' Mack saluted smartly and as he turned away Tilly hurried by his side, saying, 'Are they all right? You left them all right?'

'Yes, yes; but when Dan Collins called in soon after you left and told us of the trouble at this end I asked to join in.'

'Oh, Mack!' She clung to his arm now. 'I've never been so happy to see anyone in my life as I am you at this moment. Matt's in a bad way.' She shook her head, moving it wildly from side to side, saying, 'They came so quickly. It was a tomahawk. He . . . he brought it down on his shoulder, right through. They' — she gulped now on a mouthful of spittle before she could say — 'they took his arm off last night.'

Mack said nothing, he just continued to walk looking straight ahead. But then stopping, abruptly, he said, 'Wait there a minute, I must see the captain. I'll be back. I'll be back.'

She stood where he had left her and watched him go towards a group of dust-covered riders who were busily feeding their horses, and he spoke to a tall man in a slouch hat. This man's clothes were grey with dust but this did not cover the dark stains on his shirt front, nor those on his trousers. She had heard of Dan Collins, he was famed as a Ranger who rode as fast as any horse Indian and had followed the raiders into the very heart of the Comanche country up in the high plains where the Indians felt safe among the great herds of buffalo and mustang.

He now looked in her direction; then saying something to Mack, they turned together and came towards her.

'Ma'am' — he touched the front of the upturned brim of his hat — 'Mack tells me of your trouble. I'm sorry we can't escort you back to your home, ma'am; the best I can do for you is to release Mack and one other of my men to see you in safe passage.'

'I am very grateful.'

He inclined his head towards her, then said, 'It has been a bad night, we must soon be on our way. Excuse me, ma'am.' He now turned from her and in an undertone to Mack said, 'Take Len with you; he's had more than enough. I know he's got a flesh wound in his leg but he won't have it seen to. See what you can do for him when you get settled. . . . Good luck.'

They stared at each other for a moment until Mack said,

'You an' all. Thanks, Dan. Be seeing you soon. I'll join up with you near the Falls, or with Bill's lot.'

'You might be more use back in the ranch, Mack. This thing isn't over by a long chalk. Now they've started others could break out.'

'We'll see.'

They nodded at each other; then Mack turned towards Tilly again and asked, 'Where is he, Matt?'

She pointed, and they went towards the long hut where the wounded lay.

That Mack was shocked at the sight of Matthew was evident in his face but not in his voice, for it was rough and brusque as he exclaimed, 'What d'you think you've been up to eh? You went out house huntin', so I understand.'

'Hello, Mack.' Matthew's voice was low, scarcely audible, as he added, 'Going home.'

'Going home.' Mack nodded at him. 'We'll have you in your own bed 'fore you know where you are.' He took two steps backwards from the cot nodding as he went, and when they were again outside the hut he looked at Tilly, saying kindly, 'Doesn't look too good.'

'No; he's lost an awful lot of blood.'

'Well' — he gave a twisted smile — 'broth made with bullock's blood will soon put that right. The main thing is to get him home. I'll go and see about this wagon.'

'Thank you, Mack.' She put her hand on his arm. 'Oh, I am grateful to God you are here, Mack, you'll never know. . . .'

He grinned again, nodded, then marched off, his limp very much in evidence; through tiredness she guessed, for after doing a day's work he must have ridden through the night with few stops on the way, for his clothes, too, had dark stains on them.

Just an hour later Matthew was carried in a sling to the wagon and laid gently on a bed of sacks and blankets with a buffer of boxes at one side and Tilly seated with her back against the wooden rail at the other.

Len Wilson was driving the wagon and Mack was riding by

the side of it, two mustangs on leading reins behind him. As they passed through the gates the last face she looked at was that of the doctor's wife who seemed sorry to see her leave. She hadn't said good-bye to the doctor for she couldn't thank him for cutting off her husband's arm. Another doctor, she told herself, would have tried to stitch it together.

When the big gates were closed behind them and the wagon moved over the rough ground she pressed her side tightly against the sacks in an attempt to stop Matthew being jolted.

The sky was high and clear. The day was warm. For a time they passed through waving grass, then along a river bank where the wheels of the wagon almost touched the water to avoid the cottonwood trees that bordered the river to where it narrowed almost into a small stream.

When they had crossed the river Len Wilson and Mack lay on the bank and ducked their heads deeply into the flow. They then helped Tilly down from the cart, and she, too, lay on the river bank and ducked her head into the water. Afterwards she took a mugful of it back to the wagon and with a handkerchief she bathed Matthew's face, then wetted his lips with water from the water bottle.

As Mack was about to mount she said to him in an undertone, 'How long will it take us?'

'About another five hours. We'll cut quite a slice off the distance going this way; Len knows it like the back of his hand. It'll be rough in parts but it'll be better than the main trail, and we'll be less likely to meet anybody.'

They stared at each other for a moment; then he turned from her and mounted his horse, and once more they were moving on.

Matthew appeared to sleep most of the time; at least so Tilly thought, until he opened his eyes and said to her, 'How much further?'

She bent her head over him. 'Not much longer, dear. Not much longer. About an hour I should say. . . . How are you feeling?'

He didn't answer her question; instead he said, 'Tilly,' and to this she answered, 'Yes, dear?' She watched him moisten his dry lips and look away from her before he spoke again, and then his words were low and spaced as if attuned to each sway of the wagon. 'If . . . if anything . . . happens . . . to me . . . go straight . . . back . . . home.'

'Oh, my dear. My dear.' She placed her two fingers gently on his lips, and he made an impatient movement with his head as if aiming to push them aside and went on, 'Do as I ask. Take Willy and go, not Josefina. Don't take her.'

She made no answer to this but simply stared down at him. He had closed his eyes once more. . . . She did not expect him to love the child, but he did not even like her. Whatever happened, Josefina was going to become a problem. . . .

They had left the river and the twisting bone-shaking path, and now she recognised the country they were passing through. In a short time they'd be home. Her heart was heavy with dread, yet she told herself that once he was in bed and she was able to nurse him he would recover. Look at the different men she had seen walking about with one arm or those hobbling about on one leg and a crutch, many had lived for years and years. Once they were back she would get him well. She would have to put up with Alvero Portes until Matthew was able to be moved to a new home. Where that would be she didn't know. But there'd never be another house like Anna Meyer's. No, there'd never be a house like that again.

On the last thought new hope sprang in her, perhaps this terrible experience they had gone through would change Matthew's idea of living here for the rest of his days and he'd be only too glad to go back to England.

They were nearing the ranch; there in the distance was the first boundary fencing. As the wagon rumbled along the road she looked towards the corral and her eyes widened. There wasn't a horse in sight.

They had ridden for about another half mile when she saw Mack come to the back of the wagon and tie the two mustangs to the back-board, and then before she could ask him what was wrong he was riding off again. Now standing up and swaying she reached over to Len Wilson and, touching his arm, she shouted, 'What is it? Something wrong?'

It was some seconds before he turned to her and said simply, 'Smoke.'

She repeated his word, 'Smoke?'

'Aye. It might be nothing but Mack thought he'd better go and see.'

Of a sudden she slumped down on to the floor of the wagon, her hands now joined tightly between her knees, her head bent towards them, and again she was saying, 'Oh no! no! they couldn't have been this far. Oh no! Willy! Oh Willy! And Katie. And the child, and Luisa.' She found herself going through all the names, and then she was jerked forward as the wagon was drawn to a halt.

Again she was standing upright, staring ahead now towards a smoke haze in the distance, and her voice was a mere whimper as she muttered, 'They couldn't. They couldn't have got this far.'

'They can go to hell an' back, ma'am, that lot, hell an' back. But it may be nothing, just a barn fire. Stay still now.' He put out his hand as she attempted to climb down from the wagon, and again she whimpered, 'My children!'

He said nothing, just sat staring ahead; and the minutes passed and went into five, then ten, then fifteen.

They had reached thirty when she saw Mack come riding back towards them. Then he was facing them. Under the dirt, the tan, and his beard, his face looked as grey as the dust on his clothes. Len Wilson and he exchanged glances.

Now he was looking at Tilly and saying quietly, ' 'Twill be better if you don't go in. Drive round the west side. Your house is still standing, why I don't know, the. . . .' — his head drooped now — 'the rest is burned out.'

'The children?' She was gripping his shoulders, her hands like claws dug deep into his coat. 'The children!'

He kept his head down. 'There's no sign of 'em, ma'am, no sign of 'em.'

'Oh God! Oh God!' She rocked on her feet and Mack put his arm about her, saying now, 'They might've got away.'

She drew a long, long breath before she gasped, 'Katie! Luisa!'

'There's no sign of 'em either.' Again his head was drooped.

'They . . . they could have taken them? They do awful things. . . . Oh God Almighty! God Almighty!' Her hands were in her hair now as if attempting to pull it from the roots.

'Come on.' As he assisted her along the road he nodded to Len Wilson, and when Matthew's weak voice came from the wagon they all ignored it.

Near the main gate, as Mack was about to direct Len Wilson away from it and along a side path that would lead to the house, Tilly, pulling herself from Mack's arm, cried, 'No! No, I must find the children. They'll be in there somewhere, they'll be in there. . . .'

Mack gripped her arms and actually shook her as he said, 'They're not there. An' don't go in, I'm tellin' you, unless you want nightmares till the end of your days.'

They stared at each other, and then she whimpered, 'But my child and Josefina, they're . . . they're just babies, babies.' She shook her head wildly.

'I know ma'am, I know, but I tell you they're not there. If they've taken 'em there'll be a chance of them comin' back. They' — he gulped before continuing — 'they don't often harm children.' He didn't add, 'If they behave themselves and don't cry,' but tried to reassure her by saying, 'They've been known to be very kind to children. And I promise you, you'll get them back. Believe me. Wherever they've gone the Rangers'll follow, you'll get them back.'

She stared at him unbelieving. Then her body seemed to slump and, turning, she looked towards the gates and, noticing movement, she said, 'Somebody's there.'

'Yes, they're . . . they're clearin' up. The Curtises and Ingersolls were lucky; but the Purdies got it, and the Rankins.'

'Are they. . .?' She couldn't ask the question, but he answered it, saying, 'Yes, all but Mrs Purdie. She was under the floorboards. They found her afterwards. She's a bit burnt but she'll be all right.'

Huh! Ha-ha! Under the floorboards; a bit burnt; like taties in the ashes. Her granny used to split them open and put dripping in . . . split them open. Ha-ha! She put her hand over her

330

mouth tightly, she was going to laugh. She must be going mad.

Mack was supporting her as they went up the rise towards the house, Len driving the wagon behind them.

She stood in front of the verandah and looked at it. It was intact; even the bear was there straining at the end of his chain coming to greet them. Why had they left the bear? She now asked the question of Mack. 'Why did they leave the bear?'

'I don't think they got up this far, they were disturbed. Smith's Rangers group came along this way. That's likely what saved the house.'

'But . . . but not my children, not my children. Matthew! Matthew!'

She turned to the wagon where Len Wilson and Mack were now easing Matthew gently forward, and as they lifted the inert body into the house she walked sidewards in front of them and drew them through the room and into the bedroom; and when they laid Matthew gently down he looked at Mack and said simply, 'They've been here?'

'Yes, Matthew.'

'The children?'

'Don't worry.' It was Tilly hanging over him now. 'They'll be all right.' Her voice was high and squeaky as if she were going to burst into song. 'Mack says they're all right. Mack says he'll get them. Don't worry. Let me get the blankets off and wash you, and I'll see to your arm and I'll. . . .'

Matthew's hand came on her wrist and checked her hysterical flow of words, and he closed her eyes so tightly that her face became contorted. Her voice a little steadier now, she said, 'It's all right, it's all right.' But when she went to try to take the blankets from around him she looked up helplessly at Mack and said simply, 'Help me, please. . . .'

It was a full half-hour later when Matthew was settled comfortably in bed, and so she left him for a moment and went into the other room where she stood looking about her. She couldn't believe it, nothing had been disturbed. She looked towards the table. It was set for breakfast: there was Katie's place and the children's two fancy mugs; the bread-board with a knife lying across it; a pot of preserves; a round of butter with a pattern on the top which told her that one of the Ingersolls had called — Clara Ingersoll always brought something dainty.

Oh Willy! Willy! Oh, my dearest Willy, my baby. . . . Josefina. Dear little Josefina. She was a girl . . . they did things to girls. She had never discussed Indian raids openly but she kept her ears open. They gelded young boys and they used young girls. Mack had said they were kind to children, at least the men were, but the women were cruel to them, especially to girls. She'd heard of the things they did to girls. . . . Oh my God! she mustn't think. No, she musn't keep repeating the same thing, she must think of Matthew, he needed her.

She started to pace the room, her head bent forward, her brow in the palm of her hand. She hated this country, she'd always hated it since first putting her foot on it. She hated the people in it, not just the Indians. They were rough, coarse, some no better than animals. Alvero Portes . . . oh yes, there were men like Alvero Portes, men in the towns living in their grand houses, and ladies spending their time titivating themselves and entertaining the politicians, but in the main there were the people, just the people, and they were elemental, barbaric, and . . . and . . . oh, Mr Burgess would have been able to put names to them. There must be something odd about people who wanted to come and live on this terror-ridden plain.

She looked towards the fireplace where one rifle was still slung. She had the desire to take it up and clear this whole wide planet of people, people like Alvero Portes, people like . . . Bobby Pearson . . . and the Indians. Oh the Indians! Yes, she would do what the doctor said, burn them all on a great bonfire. . . .

Oh my God! what was the matter with her? Was she losing her reason? She must pull herself together; this was no time to go on talking like this, and she was talking, talking aloud. . . . She had to get Matthew well. What had she come out here for? Oh yes, to make him some gruel. Where did she keep the oatmeal? Her head was spinning. . . . What time was it?

She was about to look round to the clock when movement

through the window caught her eye. There outside were five dark figures. The great scream rose to her throat but she stilled it by stuffing her knuckles into her mouth. Two of the figures were tiny, two were women and dumpy, the third was a man, a tall man. She staggered to the door and pulled it open and gazed with her mouth agape and her eyes stretched wide at the five mud-covered creatures staring at her. Then a great cry was riven up from her bowels and she jumped the three steps down to the ground, crying, 'Willy! Katie, No! no! it can't be.' She was hugging the two wet mud-covered children to her while Katie and Luisa stood looking down at her. It was Doug Scott who spoke first, and what he said sounded so ordinary, 'You all right, ma'am?'

She looked up at him with tears making furrows down her mud-spattered face. She had no power to speak but she made a deep obeisance with her head until he said, 'And Matt?'

And now she struggled to her feet and looked back towards the house, and it was Luisa who stated, 'He's hurt.'

'Yes.'

'Badly?' Luisa's voice had still the crisp, terse note to it, nothing might have happened.

'He's lost an arm and . . . and a lot of blood.'

'Well, let's get inside.'

Luisa went first. The children were still clinging to Tilly, and Katie was still standing gaping at her. Katie hadn't yet spoken, but now she fell forward into Tilly's arms and the sobs shook her whole body as she kept repeating, 'Oh, Tilly! Oh, Tilly! Oh, Tilly!'

Her distress brought Tilly to herself for a moment and she said, 'Come on, come on, get cleaned up'; then looking over her shoulder at Doug, she asked quietly, 'Have you been down there?'

For answer he gave a small motion of his head and at this Katie's crying became louder and she spluttered now, ' 'Tis terrible, 'tis terrible. Oh Tilly! Tilly!'

'Go inside now, and stop your crying!' It was Doug Scott speaking with unusual authority, no laughter about him now. 'Get yourself cleaned up, I'll be back shortly.' He now exchanged a glance with Tilly and turned round and went down the slope towards what was left of the ranch.

They were cleaned up. They'd all had a hot drink but no one could touch food. Nor had anyone told Tilly how they had escaped, and it wasn't until Luisa walked out and down the slope to where once had stood her home that Katie's tongue became loosened. She stood staring through the open door at the sturdy figure who looked most odd now, dressed as she was in one of Tilly's dresses that was much too long and had been looped at the waist and so tight for her bust she'd had to resort to a shawl. 'She's brave, she is,' she said.

'How did you manage to escape?' Tilly asked.

At this Katie bowed her head and muttered, 'Likely 'cos I was about to misbehave meself.'

'What!'

Katie raised her head a little now and said, 'I was just on goin' to bed when Doug came up on the quiet an' tapped on the window.' Her head drooped again. 'We got talkin' like and —' her head drooped still further and her voice was scarcely audible as she muttered, 'I let him kiss me. 'Twas then we were both scared out of our wits, an' that was afore the Indians come, 'cos Luisa appeared on the scene and she went for Doug sayin' that he was sneakin' up here to do me harm an' take me good name an' that he wouldn't have done it if you and the master had been at home, and to get himself down there quick sharp an' —'now Katie gulped and seemed to find breathing difficult as she added, ' 'Twas just at that moment that we heard the screams. Oh my God! Tilly, they chilled you to the bone them screams. An' Doug stood frozen like for a minute. Then there were more screams and shootin' an' firebrands flying. An' then he yelled at us to get the bairns, and both Luisa and me flew up the stairs and grabbed them. Then he hustled us across the back way through that grass, and I had no shoes on and I wanted to scream myself. On and on he pushed us until we came to the river bank. An' then I couldn't believe it for he was stickin' us all into a muddy hole in the bank. He tried one first and it wasn't big enough; then he pulled us to another. We had to crawl in on our hands and knees and the river was flowing into it. It was almost up to our waist at one time; I thought I would die with cold. And then when Willy began to cry, Doug tied his hands behind his back and took off his neckchief and put it round his mouth. I thought the poor bairn would suffocate. Josefina never opened her mouth. It was as if, well, she had been in this kind of thing afore. 'Twas weird like, Tilly, 'cos she didn't open her mouth or make one squeak. Nor did Luisa, but me — well, I couldn't help it, I was groanin' like a stuck pig 'cos I was covered with mud and water an' I was so freezin'. An' then' — her head bowed again — ''cos I couldn't stop, he . . . well, he slapped me face —' she stared at Tilly now and her head bobbed as she said, 'he did, he slapped me face. Then he said something terrible to me that made me want to vomit. But it shut me up. You know what he said?'

Tilly didn't answer, and she gabbled on, 'I'll never forget it, not as long as I live, 'cos he hissed at me, "You'll have something to groan about if they get you, an' it'll shut your trap 'cos they'll cut off your breasts an' stuff 'em in your mouth." He did. I didn't believe it at the time, but it shut me up. But Tilly —' again she was looking up into Tilly's face and now she spluttered tearfully, 'I can believe it after what I saw down there, I can believe it all right. Ma One, Poor Ma One was split open, right open, Tilly, and there was this spear through her right into the ground, an' Diego an' Emilio an' all of them. Ee, but it was nothing to Mr Portes. They had him covered up on the ground when I saw him. He was covered up like the rest, what was left of him. One, Two and Four, an' poor Rod Tyler, too. But I heard Mack telling Doug what they'd done to Mr Portes. They had nailed him to the door and Mack said there wasn't a . . . some word like portrushun left on his body not from his nose to his toes. An' you know what? Luisa went to look at him, she did, she did. She pulled the sheet aside an' looked at him. And she never moved a muscle. She's brave but she's hard. . . . I wanna go home, Tilly. Oh, I wanna go home. I wanna go home, Tilly. I wanna. . . .'

'There now. There now. Don't cry. Don't cry.'

As she held Katie's face against her waist she thought: Not a protrusion left on his body. Dear God! Dear God! She hadn't liked the man, in fact she had hated him. And what had she said to him when she had last spoken to him? One day you'll wish for death, you'll be so alone you'll wish for death. And he hadn't died alone. She could only pray to God that he had died well before they started slicing him.

'Oh, I wanna go home.'

'There now. There now. If you want to go so badly we'll see about sending you off.'

Katie's head came up quickly, saying now, 'But not without you. You want to go an' all, don't you?'

'Yes . . . yes, I want to go. There's nothing I want more at this moment than to get on a boat and go home. But I've got a husband, Katie; and in spite of everything he loves this place. And I married him and so where he goes I go.'

Gently now, Tilly disengaged herself from Katie's hold and, turning, she went towards the bedroom and the man who was tying her to this barbaric country.

11

A month had passed, all sign of the Indian raid had been cleared away, in fact a rough homestead had already been erected, but Luisa had not yet gone to live in it. At night she slept on a shaky-down in the living-room but most of her days were spent down in the ranch planning and discussing things with Doug and Mack.

Two days ago she had come back from Houston where she had been to see a solicitor with regard to her father's will. Before going she had said to Tilly, 'It wouldn't surprise me if he has left the whole bang lot to some forty-second cousin just to spite me.' But when she returned she said simply, 'I bought meself a frock and a coat because I am a very rich woman.'

The change in her fortune hadn't seemed to alter her except that now whenever she rode out with either Mack or Doug she was always accompanied by Three, for he had escaped the massacre. It had been imagined that the Comanches had taken him prisoner but he had returned a week later, saying that he had gone, as he did often at night, to the corral and had ridden one of the horses. Apparently Mack and Rod Tyler knew of these escapades, but this one had certainly saved his life, for he had just returned the horse to the corral when the advance party of Indians rode in and herded the animals out and back along the trail to the high plains to add still further to their massive stocks.

There was great talk about the new measures being taken against the Comanches. The authorities in headquarters were issuing orders for a real drive this time, but all this talk, in fact all the commotion that went on about the place seemed to be floating over Tilly's head; all she was concerned about was Matthew, because Matthew wasn't improving.

The doctor had called twice during the last week because he wasn't satisfied with the condition of the arm, and only yesterday he had taken Tilly aside and said, 'I am afraid the matter has now become serious. Septicaemia has set in. There is little one can do now but pray.' It seemed to be a favourite saying of his, he usually ended any conversation he had with her with the words, 'There is little one can do now but pray.' But now, for the first time, it made her think kindly of the doctor back in the fort; he wouldn't just have relied on prayer, he would have done something.

Yesterday she had said, 'Isn't there any medicine?' and he answered, 'I have used everything possible. But he is of a strong constitution, we can but hope . . . and pray. . . .'

It was now one o'clock in the morning. The lamp was turned low. She had been sitting in a chair by Matthew's side for the past three hours and she must have dozed for she almost sprang to her feet with the touch of his hand on hers and she bent over him, saying, 'What is it, dear? Do you want a drink?'

'No, nothing, I . . . I just want to talk.'

'You'd far better rest, dear.'

'I've rested for a long time, Tilly. How many years have I been lying here?'

She gave a forced soft laugh, saying, 'Not a month, dear.'

'Every hour has been a year. Turn the lamp up so I can see your face.'

She turned up the lamp and sat facing him; then she took his hand again, and what he said now cut into her heart as if he had taken a knife and cleaved open her breast. 'I haven't much longer, dear,' he said.

'Please! Please! Matthew' — she closed her eyes tightly — 'I beg you, don't talk like that.'

'Look at me.'

She opened her eyes.

'We must face the inevitable, I know what is happening, nothing more can be done. This might be the last time we'll ever talk together.'

338

'Oh! Matthew. Matthew.'

'Please, darling, don't cry, just . . . listen to me. I'm not going to waste words telling you how much I love you, and how I have loved you since the first moment I set eyes on you, I've said it so many times before, you must be tired of hearing it. Nevertheless it is true. It is so true that you have become a sort of mania with me. I have been jealous of your very glance at another, even at the child. Oh yes' — he moved his head on the pillow — 'every soft glance you have bestowed on the child has been a dart in here.' He glanced wearily down towards his chest, then after a long pause, he went on, 'I know inside that I am not a good man because, had you ever said you would leave me, I know, and this is true, I would have killed you first; and if you were leaving me for anyone else I would have killed him too.'

When his chest heaved and he drew in a long breath she gripped his hand and said, 'Matthew, please, please, don't go on. You are tiring yourself.'

'No, no, Tilly darling; it's strange but I don't feel tired, I've got a sort of elation on me, a peaceful elation which really isn't me at all because I've never known peace. All my life I've been ravished with desire, desire for you. As I said, it became a mania, and although I have this feeling of quietude inside the mania still remains with me.' His fingers gripped hers now with an unusual strength and his eyes that were sunken in his head gleamed darkly as he gazed at her. And then he spoke again: 'I want you to promise me something. Will you promise me anything I ask, Tilly?'

It was some time before she could bring the words through her throat, and when she said, 'Yes, yes, darling, anything. But believe me, you are going to get well.' He shook her hand in a way that showed his irritation and, his voice changing, he said, 'You swear you'll promise me this?'

'Yes, yes, anything, darling; anything.'

'Then swear to me, swear to me that you will never marry again.'

Her head came forward, her eyes stretching wide. Her face dropped into pitying lines as she whispered, 'Oh, Matthew!'

'Promise me? I want to hear you say it.'

In this moment she could hear her granny's voice, saying, 'Peggy Richardson, poor Peggy Richardson, promising that mother of hers on her deathbed not to marry Billy Conway because he was a Catholic, and look at her now, a wizened nerve-tortured creature. Oh, the dying have a lot to answer for.' But here was her Matthew whom she loved with every fibre of her being asking for her to promise not to marry again. Well, would she ever? Never! Never! She brought his hand to her chest and, holding it tightly there, she said, 'I promise. Oh, I promise.'

'Say it. Say, Matthew I shall never marry again, I shall never put another man in your place.'

The words seemed hard in coming, she didn't know why because her heart was in the answer:

'Matthew, dearest, I shall never marry again, I shall never put another man in your place.'

His whole body seemed to sink further into the bed, he closed his eyes, the grip on her hand relaxed. Of a sudden she felt that she had just gone through some great travail, much worse than the first raid, or even the second, when she thought that the children were gone. Her body felt weak, her mind heavy with the pressure that was numbing thought. She looked at him. If he were to die, and yes, he would die, she knew that now, she had known it for days, well why not go with him?

And the children? Mark's child and Matthew's child. Whether he disowned it or not she thought of the child as his.

She lay back in the chair. She was so tired, so very, very tired. . . .

She slept and it was Katie who woke her up as the first light was breaking. She must have been in the room some time for she had done something, she had covered Matthew's face with a sheet.

Tilly sat staring at the sheet. It was a white sheet; then suddenly it changed colour to blue, then to black, and it turned into a wooden box, a black box, and she saw it being lowered into a black hole, and in it was all that had been worth living for. She had lost this man's father by death, now she had lost him; everything she touched turned to death. And there was young Hans Meyer, and Hal McGrath. She had killed as many people as the Indians. She now saw the Indian. He was walking over the bed towards her, his face was all paint, yet she could see the wrinkles in his brow and his great nose and the gap of his mouth. But what was coming right for her was the buffalo head — the horns were pointing straight at her — but just before he neared her he stopped and they looked at each other again as they had done a short while back. Then he lifted his tomahawk and cleaved her on the head, and as it struck her she knew her wish was coming true and that she was going to join Matthew.

12

The sun was shining. For days now, she had been looking at it through the window, but it was the first time she had really noticed it. It was causing a heat haze to cover the ranch like a low canopy. There were houses down there again, low rambling ones and high ones. Had it ever been a smouldering waste? At times she was confused in her mind about the ranch, believing that nothing had ever happened to it except that the shape of the buildings now was different. Yet the dog run had gone and the bunkhouse, and Alvero Portes's palace. Why did she still think about Alvero Portes with sarcasm? He had died a terrible death, a death that was far beyond any payment due for what ill he had done in his lifetime. Even Christ hadn't suffered that kind of death. But then Christ hadn't known Indians. Some day she would go down the slope and see the new house, Luisa's house with all its new furniture, not rough made, Katie had said, but real furniture, some pieces like those which had been in the Manor.

She had watched the wagons coming and going for weeks now, first bringing the wood and the men who hammered and hammered. At first, the nails had gone through her head, all knocked in by the tomahawk, and the blood had run all over her face, and Katie and Luisa had wiped it away.

How many times had she fought the Indians? After one terrible fight she had woken up in Doug Scott's arms. He was holding her tightly and for a moment she thought it was Matthew and laid her cheek against his until he had spoken to her, and his voice was not Matthew's voice.

Another time she had crawled out of bed and got the gun.

342

She had done it very quietly because she knew the Indians were all round watching her, and she had got it into her hands and was lying on the floor aiming it at the Indian who had jumped through the window. But this time it was Mack who foiled her aim. And after that they had tied her to the bed and let the Indians have their way with her. They were cruel, cruel; even the white people were cruel.

It had taken her a long time to recognise the faces about her. Even when she recognised them she still fought them when they kept pouring laudanum and aniseed into her.

She lay back against the pillow on the bed which was arranged so that she could see out of the window. She must have been a great trial to everybody during these past weeks . . . months. Had she been in this bed for nearly five months? She had been sick but once in her life before and now she felt she'd be sick for the rest of her life. She'd be tied to this bed for the rest of her life. There was nothing wrong with her limbs but she had no desire to move them; she had wished to die and she had died inside, for there was no feeling in her, not even for Willy, and this troubled her greatly. She could look at her son, into his beautiful eyes, one without sight and the other strain-ing to see, she could feel his arms around her neck and hear his voice, saying, 'Mama! Mama! Get up Mama. Take me for a walk,' and be quite untouched by his plea or by the look on his face.

Josefina had the strange habit of tracing her fingers lightly over her jaw bones as if she were feeling the texture of her skin, and she, too, would say, 'Mama! Mama!' but she'd make no request, she would just sit on the bed and look on her with those dark eyes filled with love. She knew they were filled with love, but she could not return the feeling in any way.

And then there was Katie. Katie, too, must have been ill. Although she hadn't taken to her bed she had lost her buoy-ancy; she did not chatter as she used to. The only one who appeared the same to her was Luisa. Luisa was brisk and stimulating; yet her stimulation could not probe the deadness within herself. If only she could feel again. Only yesterday she had heard Luisa say to Katie, 'I'd prefer her ravings to this dummy-like attitude. Something's got to be done, but what? It's gone past me. It'll likely take another raid to get her on her feet'; to which Katie's answer had been a groan: 'Oh, don't say that. Don't say that.'

And now here was Luisa coming into the room. She had some letters in her hand and she placed them on the bed, saying 'These should cheer you up, the mail's just come in.'

As Luisa pushed the letters under her fingers Tilly said, 'Read them to me.'

'I'll do no such thing; they're private letters, you read them yourself. Now come on. I'll open them for you and that's as far as I'll go. There you are!' She slit open the three letters and out of the first she lifted a sheet of paper which she pushed into Tilly's hand, saying, 'Get on with it. I'll come back later and listen to your news.'

Slowly Tilly raised the letter to her face and her eyes travelled down to the signature first. It was from John, and it began: 'Dearest Tilly, I don't know what to say, only that I am devastated, I cannot believe that Matthew has gone. I could never imagine Matthew dying; he seemed to be the epitome of life. Oh my dear Tilly, how sore your heart must be at this moment.

'I am sending this off immediately, and both Anna and I say, please come home, we want you, we need you. I cannot see to write any more, I feel heartbroken. We send our deepest love to you. Let me call myself your brother. John.'

John. John. Dear John. She wished she could see John. Oh, how she wished she could see John, to hear his voice, his stammer, his dear stammer. Come home, he said. Oh, she wanted to be home.

She saw herself rising from the bed, packing the cases, then taking the children by the hand and walking down the hill through the burning rubble of the ranch. . . . No, no; it was burning no longer. A new ranch had sprung up in its place and it was a better ranch. Under Luisa it would be a better place to live, but she would never live in it. No, she would pass through it, lift the children into the buggy and they would drive all the way to Galveston. . . . Oh, Galveston and the sea.

She dropped the letter on to the quilt and, putting her hands to each side of her hips, she pulled herself upwards; then looking down the bed where her toes made hills under the bedclothes she moved her feet.

If she could walk she could go home. Slowly she drew her knees upwards; then as slowly she twisted her body and let her feet drop to the floor, but when she made to stand she swayed and fell backwards on to the bed.

If you can walk you can go home.

She seemed to be reading the words in front of her eyes. Pulling herself upwards again she gripped the bedhead, then took in a long slow breath and looked about her. They had changed the room; naturally in placing the bed by the window they would have to. The little dressing-table was in the far corner. She looked towards it. Had she altered much? What little flesh she had seemed to have dropped from her bones and her skin felt dry, particularly her hair; her hair felt husky. She reached out and with the support of a chair, she made her way tentatively towards the dressing-table. Before it was a stool with an embroidered top. When she came within reach of it she leaned forward and placed her hands on it and rested for a moment before sitting down. Then she was looking into the mirror . . . staring into the mirror . . . gaping into the mirror.

Who was that woman in there? She even turned her eyes to the side to see if there was anyone behind her. But no; there was no one there but herself. Yet she could not recognise the face that was staring back at her. It was an old face, the skin drawn tight over the bones, no wrinkles, just taut skin. But what was that over her brow? It must be a trick of light. She glanced towards the window and looked back into the mirror again, and her hands went slowly up to her hair, her beautiful hair, the hair that Matthew loved. It was piled upwards on the top of her head. Katie dressed her hair every morning. She did it from behind the low bedhead, combing it off her brow. If she had thought at all about her hair it was to think that it wasn't so thick as usual. But then when one was sick your hair dropped out. But this wasn't her hair, her hair was a shining brown, in certain lights it shone with gold threads, but the hair that she was looking at was white, dead white.

As the door opened she turned her head from the mirror and Katie stood looking at her, her mouth wide open, her hands held up as if in horror. 'Oh, Tilly!' she said.

'My hair! Katie. My hair!'

'Yes, pet, yes.' Katie moved slowly towards her. 'It's . . . it's because of what you went through.'

'But . . . but it's white, Katie.'

'Yes, yes, Tilly, it's white. But . . . but it still looks good, lovely; in fact, I think it suits you better. . . .'

'O . . . h! Katie. Katie!' Something clicked inside her head, followed by a grating sound like that of a sluice gate, an unused sluice gate being lifted. The water gushed out on a high cry, it burst from her eyes, her nose, it spluttered out of her throat, even her kidneys were affected. She was swamped in water and so great was the noise she made as Katie held her that the children came running in from their play and stood at the bedroom door and joined their crying to hers.

Three, who was in the kitchen, taking in the situation, pelted down the hill as if competing in a race, and brought up Luisa. But when she entered the room she did not commiserate with Tilly; instead her face bright now, she said, 'Good! Good! At last.' And although she, too, put her arms about Tilly her words weren't soothing. She did not say, 'There now. There now. Give over,' what she said was, 'Let it come. This is the best thing I've seen in weeks, months. Go on, get it out of you. The past is finished, let it flow away, you'll start again now. Katie —' she looked at Katie whose face was close to hers and she said, 'Make a pot of strong tea and lace it with whisky.'

'Yes, ma'am, yes, ma'am.' Katie, too, was crying but now she was smiling as she cried and Luisa, left alone with Tilly, drew her to her feet and guided her into a chair, and not until Tilly's crying seemed that it would never stop did she take a towel and, drying her face with it, say, 'Stop it! Now stop it! Enough is enough, you're clear, it's all washed out. You'll pick up your life and go on from here, and it'll be up to you to decide where you're going to spend it.'

13

It seemed they had been packing for days on end, yet there were only two trunks and four cases, and the cases were mostly taken up with the children's clothes and toys.

Katie had a separate trunk. She took a long time to pack it. She would put something in it, then take it out again, saying, 'Well, I won't need that back there.'

After she had said this for the third time in an hour Tilly, making an effort, gave Katie her full attention. It was difficult, she was finding, to force her mind to dwell on any subject for any length of time, but she couldn't help but notice that Katie had been acting strangely of late. First of all she had put it down to the shock she had sustained; although she hadn't gone under like herself, nevertheless she had suffered from it.

'What's wrong with you, Katie?' she now demanded.

'Wrong with me?' Katie turned towards her. 'Nothing! Nothing! Nothing that two or three boat journeys and a long bout of seasickness and a ride in a train won't cure.'

'You really want to go home?'

Katie paused and bent over her trunk before saying, 'Well now, what do you think? And imagine you turning up at the Manor without me. Can you hear me ma?'

'You've been acting strangely of late, more so since Christmas.'

Katie straightened her back and looked up at Tilly as she said softly, 'We've all been actin' strangely of late. I don't think there'll be any of us who'll ever act naturally in our lives again.'

'No . . . no, perhaps you're right.'

'I know I am.' She turned away and stood looking out of the window, not speaking, quiet. Very unlike herself. . . .

It came to the night before they were due to leave. Luisa had been hovering about them all day. Only once had she referred to their going. When she said, 'Like emigrating birds there's everything pulling you back and nothing'll make you stay, but I'm going to miss you, Tilly.'

Tilly had answered, 'And me you, Luisa. Oh yes, I'll miss you. But I must go.'

'Yes, I know that, you must go.'

And then Luisa had added, 'Is Katie of the same mind?' Somewhat surprised, Tilly had answered, 'Yes, yes, of course, as far as I know.' And to this Luisa had answered, 'As far as you know,' and had then gone out.

It was towards evening when Doug Scott appeared in the doorway. Katie was upstairs with the children and Tilly pointed this out. 'Katie's upstairs, Doug; I'll call her.'

' 'Tisn't Katie I've come to see this time, ma'am, 'tis you.'

'Well, come in, Doug.'

Doug came in. He took off his slouch hat and held it in his two hands. His fingers didn't fidget but remained still on the brim and he came to the point, saying, 'Don't know whether you know it or not, ma'am, but I've taken to Katie, think highly of her, very highly of her, and . . . and as I've sounded her, she thinks the same of me, so that being the case I've done me best to persuade her to stay put an' wed me. Make it double-like, for as you may know, Miss Luisa, she's going to wed Mack.'

At this Tilly's face showed her surprise, and Doug, now flapping his hat against his side, said, 'Oh, I seem to have let the cat out of the bag, but she would likely have told you before you left. Anyway, she's offered me head man under Mack and me own house, this one in fact if you'll excuse me sayin' it, ma'am, if I can get settled with Katie.'

Tilly's face was now straight and her voice stiff as she said, 'Well, what does Katie say about this?'

'All she says, ma'am, is that you need her; she came with you and she'll go back with you, and as you had only one child when you came but you're taking two back, you can't manage on your own.'

Tilly turned her head to the side and looked down the room. Her own sorrow had made her blind to the things that were happening under her nose. Yes, Katie would go back with her, and this man here, this good man, because Doug Scott was a good man, would likely be the last chance she'd have of marrying, for she was no beauty was Katie and she was past the age when she could pick and choose, if ever she had been that age.

As if she conjured Katie up by her thoughts there was a movement in the doorway behind Doug, and Katie entered the room. She looked first from one to the other, then gave her attention to Doug Scott, and her voice was abrupt as she said, 'Now I told you. I told you.'

'I know what you told me, Katie, but I've got the last word in this.'

Katie now looked fully at Tilly and Tilly at her, and Tilly's voice was low as she asked the question: 'If it wasn't for me would you stay with Doug?'

'Oh' — Katie tossed her head from side to side — 'you might as well say to me if it wasn't for the moon there wouldn't be any tides, it's a daft question.'

'Don't talk silly, Katie, answer me.' Tilly's voice was harsh now. 'Tell me, yes or no.'

Katie now became still. Her head turned and she looked at Doug, the tall, knotty-muscled, good-looking man, a man she had dreamed about all her life, yet knowing that dreams never came true, not for people like her, plain-faced, dumpy women whose tongues were the only things about them. And this wasn't always an asset, far from it. But this man wanted her, he had told her that he loved her; he had held her tightly in his arms and kissed her and laughed as he did so for he had to stand her on a block. Never again in her life would she get such a chance of having a man like him; never again in her life would she get the chance of having any man. What was there for her back at the Manor in the way of men? A butler? a footman? They wouldn't look the side she was on. No, at best it would be some oldish man who had lost his wife and had a houseful of bairns. But here was this good-looking, gay, vibrant man wanting her; and what was more, Miss Luisa was going to give them this house. Imagine her ever having a house of her own, and such a one. But against all this there was the severing of the bond, the strong bond that tied her to Tilly, Tilly Trotter that was, Tilly Sopwith as she was now . . . and who'd be the sole lady of the manor back home. But that wouldn't do her much good. The only solace in going home would be she'd be rid of her fear of Indians.

The very thought of an Indian chilled her blood; but again, with Doug to protect her, well, she imagined he'd see to it that no Indian would get near her all the while she was alive.

'Answer me, Katie.'

'All right, I'll answer you. Yes, if I wasn't concerned about you an' the bairns I'd stay along of Doug.'

'That's settled then.' The reply came quick. Tilly was looking at Doug now as she said, 'There's no need to talk about it any more, Doug, she stays.'

'Aw, ma'am!' His hand came out to hers and after a moment she took it; then they both turned and looked at Katie. She was standing with her head bowed on her chest, the tears were running down her face, and it was Tilly who sounded like the old Tilly, saying now, 'Stop your bubbling, there's nothing to cry about. And if I can cross the ocean on my own with two children, then I'll take word to your mother that you and' — she nodded towards Doug — 'and Doug will come over next year or the year after to see her.'

'Oh.' Katie threw herself against Tilly now, and they clung together for a moment. Then Tilly pushed her away towards Doug, saying now, 'Take her outside, she'll wake the children.'

She stood for a moment and watched the tall spare man with his arm about Katie's shoulders leading her down the steps; then she closed the door and leant against it and put her hand over her mouth. What would she do without Katie? Apart from the actual help with the children Katie was the only one she could really talk to, the only one who knew all about her and about everything that had happened to her. Oh Katie!

Katie! Why had you to go and do this to me? I've had enough; I can't stand much more.

She pulled herself abruptly from the door, asking now as she generally did in self-criticism: Why had she to become Mark's mistress? Why had she to marry his son? Why? Why? Why?

She could give herself no answer except to acknowledge that Katie had to have the chance of loving too. . . .

Four days later at nine o'clock in the morning, she was standing on the deck of the ship. Willy was at one side of her, Josefina at the other. The deck was a-bustle with people, but it was as if she were entirely alone.

Through her misted gaze she could just make out the line of them on the dock: Luisa standing next to Mack; Doug Scott his hand laid firmly on Katie's shoulder; they were all waving. Even Three, the proud obstinate Three was waving. She kept her gaze on Katie. The children were shouting, 'Bye-bye! Bye-bye! Aunty Luisa. Bye-bye, Mr McNeill. Bye-bye, Mr Scott. Bye-bye, Three. Bye-bye, Katie.' The last they shouted a number of times, 'Bye-bye, Katie. Bye-bye, Katie.'

Tilly did not call out, she had no voice. Anyway, whoever she called to, no one would hear; she was alone as she had never been alone in her life before. She had known loneliness at all levels, but in this moment the loneliness had turned to isolation. Why was it everyone she loved left her? Her granda, her granny, the parson's wife, Mark, Matthew. Oh Matthew! Matthew! Matthew! . . . And now Katie.

She forgot for the moment she was going back to John and Anna, two people who did sincerely love her. She could only think of the villagers and those ladies of the county who had scorned her when she was Tilly Trotter, spinster. Yet she had never thought of herself as a spinster until the check weighman had written it down on that application paper the first day she went down the mine. Tilly Trotter, spinster. Then she had become Tilly Trotter, mistress, mistress of a man; following which she had become Mrs Tilly Sopwith, wife. Now she was Mrs Tilly Sopwith, widow, and was likely to remain so for the rest of her days, that is if she were to carry out Matthew's last request of her. And of course, she would carry it out. It would be easy to do so for she couldn't see herself ever having any desire to marry again. Oh no! never.

The figures on the quayside were merely dots now. The children had stopped waving, they were tugging at her hands. She looked down from one to the other; then turning them about, she led them towards their cabin. There she sat on the side of the bunk and as she prepared to take off the children's outdoor clothes they almost simultaneously climbed up one on each side of her and they put their arms about her neck and Willy said, 'Oh! Mama! Mama!' Whilst Josefina resorted to the gesture which she used when she wanted Tilly's full attention, she put her fingers on her jawbone and turned her face fully towards her; and now her round bright Indian eyes were looking into Tilly's and what she said was, 'I love you, Mama.'

Tilly stared back at the child and for the first time she actually remembered Matthew's words, 'Go straight back home, and take Willy, but not Josefina.' And now she asked herself how she was going to explain this small fragile piece of foreign humanity to those back home. Josefina had said, 'I love you, Mama.' The child would call her Mama, and what proof could she give that she wasn't the child's mama; Josefina was a year older than Willy but not half his size. There was no birth certificate, nothing in writing to say who she was. Could she yell back at the tongues that would surely wag, 'She is my husband's bastard'?

'Mama.' The fingers were moving on the jawbone again.

'Yes, my dear?'

'I love you, Mama.'

'I know you do, dear; and I love you too. Yes, I love you, too.' And at this she pressed her son and her husband's daughter to her and, looking over their heads, her gaze went across the ocean and to that stretch of land between Shields and Newcastle and she muttered aloud with all the fervour of a deep heartfelt prayer, 'God help me . . . and her.'

The End